W9-BCU-611

ALSO BY
JERRILYN FARMER

Mumbo Gumbo
Dim Sum Dead
Killer Wedding
Immaculate Reception
Sympathy for the Devil

PERFECT SAX

JERRILYN FARMER

PERFECT SAX

A Madeline Bean
Novel

FINKELSTEIN
MEMORIAL LIBRARY
SPRING VALLEY, N.Y.

MYSTERY

WILLIAM MORROW
An Imprint of HarperCollins*Publishers*

3 2191 00675 5002

This book is a work of fiction. References to real people, events, establishments, organizations, or locales are intended only to provide a sense of authenticity, and are used fictitiously. All other characters, and all incidents and dialogue, are drawn from the author's imagination and are not to be construed as real.

PERFECT SAX. Coppyright © 2004 by Jerrilyn Farmer. All rights reserved. Printed in the United States of America. No part of this book may be used or reproduced in any manner whatsoever without written permission except in the case of brief quotations embodied in critical articles and reviews. For information address HarperCollins Publishers Inc., 10 East 53rd Street, New York, NY 10022.

HarperCollins books may be purchased for educational, business, or sales promotional use. For information please write: Special Markets Department, HarperCollins Publishers Inc., 10 East 53rd Street, New York, NY 10022.

FIRST EDITION

Printed on acid-free paper

Library of Congress Cataloging-in-Publication Data

Farmer, Jerrilyn.
    Perfect sax: a Madeline Bean novel / Jerrilyn Farmer.—1st ed.
        p.   cm.
    ISBN 0-380-97890-3
1. Bean, Madeline (Fictitious character)—Fiction.   2. Caterers and catering—Fiction.   3. Los Angeles (Calif.)—Fiction.   4. Jazz musicians—Fiction.   5. Women cooks—Fiction.   6. Cookery—Fiction.   I. Title.

PS3556.A719P47   2004
813'.6—dc22   2003055846

04   05   06   07   08   JTC/RRD   10   9   8   7   6   5   4   3   2   1

For Rick and Julie Klein

who gave Madeline their home and more

Acknowledgments

Snaps for the jazziest people I am blessed to know:

SOLOISTS:
Smokin' Sam Farmer *on sax*
Cookin' Nick Farmer *on drums*
The Fabulous Chris "Daddy-O" Farmer *on lead guitar*

Lyssa "Manhattan Slim" Keusch, *editor*
Evan "The Living End" Marshall, *agent*
Mix-Master Michael Morrison, *publisher*
May "Chops" Chen, *invaluable assistant*
Big Gun Peggy Tataro, *firearms expert*
D. P. "The Doc" Lyle, M.D., *medical expert*
Hot Note Heather Haldeman, *Conrad's expert*
Boogie Woogie Barbara Voron, *first reader*

INSPIRATION BY:
Swingin' Susan Anderson
Jumpin' Jan Burke
Snap-Your-Cap Sally Fellows
Super-Murgitroid Margery Flax
Drivin' Doris Ann Norris
Cool Carol Tager
The Prince of Wails, Mark Tager
and
a great round of applause to all the Buds, baby

PERFECT SAX

"Mood Indigo"

I love big balls."

Wesley Westcott took his eyes off the road for a moment to glance over at the tall, thin blonde sitting beside him.

"Oh, stop!" Holly caught his look and laughed. "You know what I mean," she said, flushing. "Big *fund-raising* balls. Banquets. *Parties.*"

"Uh-huh." He turned back to the road, steering his new white Jaguar S-Type off the freeway and onto Sunset Boulevard as he doused a smirk.

Holly pointed at where the smirk had made its momentary appearance and demanded, "Stop it, Wesley."

"I *am* stopping it," he protested. "Go on, already. Tell me all about your love of balls."

She laughed. "Tonight, for instance. The music blew me away. And the dresses. And the caviar. It was all pretty freakin' faboo."

The Jazz Ball had been a stunning success. Six hundred Los Angelenos had gathered to celebrate the Woodburn School of Music and raise funds to support its prestigious Young Artists Program. The Woodburn, a private institute devoted to tutoring the West Coast's most gifted musical prodigies, liked to suggest it was even more selective than its better-known rival on the other coast, Juilliard.

Once a year, the fund-raising wing of the Woodburn put on a major social event to lure contributions from its well-heeled patrons. The Jazz Ball was famous for the star power of its guest list and the lavishness of the festivities. And this year, the event-planning firm that had won the plum prize of creating this *über*-party was none other than Mad Bean Events, Wes and Holly's own firm.

"I think Madeline outdid herself tonight," Holly said, referring to their friend and leader. "The black-and-white newspaper theme was awesome. She has the coolest ideas."

"That she does. It was a beautiful night." Wes turned the car south on Vine Street and said, "I wish she had come back with us to my house to celebrate."

"I think she's exhausted," Holly said, finger-combing her loose platinum wisps as she ran through the obligatory party postmortem with Wesley. "She doesn't usually leave a party so early."

"I know," Wes said. "But even Maddie needs a break."

Madeline Bean, the head of one of Hollywood's trendiest young event-producing companies, had managed to rise quickly in the world of spectacular parties. She might only be twenty-nine, but she had become a seasoned veteran of the ever rising and falling Hollywood social tide in a short time. And if the clients alone hadn't made her seasick, she'd managed to weather quite a few ups and downs of a dicey economy, too. Running a small business could be treacherous; one way she had found to succeed was simply to work harder than anyone else. A case in point had been the Jazz Ball. Madeline had been indefatigable for the past two weeks. The number of details involved in pulling off a grand party *this* grand was enormous. All the intense attention Maddie had paid to a zillion small concerns—the black linen napkins that arrived were, in actuality, puce; the white peppercorns she had ordered were, at the last minute, unavailable—must, by now, have finally taken its toll.

Wes stopped at a traffic light and looked over at Holly. "When Maddie and I decided to start the company, I don't think either of us realized how much real, honest-to-God work we'd be in for."

"Ah." Holly smiled broadly. "Now I finally understand why it was you so *quickly* hired an assistant."

"We were stunned by your talent." Wes was always a gentleman. And then he added, "You have no idea how hard it is to find a good schlepper."

Holly had begun as their assistant six years ago and worked her way up by mastering just about every party job she encountered. Holly filled in wherever she was needed, as an extra bartender, or the person to make the emergency run for more white asparagus, or the one in full-face clown greasepaint twisting a balloon giraffe for six-year-old birthday twins. Six feet tall, scrappy, and much more likely to wear a Day-Glo orange paisley polyester miniskirt than anyone else you might meet—ever— Holly Nichols was made for parties. And even though she was apt to gaze upon certain celebrity guests with more dogged affection than was entirely suitable for a staff member working a private party, she was in all ways a most valuable asset to the team.

Holly pushed her white-blond bangs off her forehead and six rhinestone-encrusted bangle bracelets clacked as they fell down her wrist.

Wes shot her another glance. "You sure you're up for coming to my place?"

"Absolutely. I'm wide-awake. And I'm starving."

"You're always hungry."

"True. And you always cook so divinely for me."

"True." Wes looked happy with the arrangement. He loved to cook and, together with Madeline, devised the menus and supervised the chefs at their events.

The traffic was thin at this late hour as they got south of Hollywood. Wes brushed his thick brown hair off of his forehead and eased his new car southwest toward his house in Hancock Park. His black leather jacket, he noticed with the habit of one who takes in every visual detail, looked not at all bad against the custom white leather seats of the Jag. It reminded him again of the Black & White Ball. They'd just pulled off another stunning event. He hummed a riff of "In the Mood."

"Is that jazz?" Holly asked, perking up. "I'm all about jazz now. The band that played at the ball was flat-out awesome. Who knew that kind of music could sound so groovy?"

"Jazz? You mean you don't listen to jazz, Holly?"

"Well, cha! I am major into Eminem. And Radiohead. And Vendetta Red. And, well, Mars Volta. And Clay Aiken. You know me. I dig rap. And rock. And show tunes."

Wes nodded, trying to follow her musical tastes.

"I always thought jazz was just too hard to understand. I mean, before. So I guess I'm evolving. Ya think?"

"I do."

"Tonight was amazing. The horn section! That trumpet drove me wild!"

"The instrument?" Wes knew Holly well. "Or the incredibly beautiful young man playing it?"

Holly had been pulling her light blond hair up on the top of her head and pinned it all there with a sparkly pink clip that she'd rummaged from the bottom of her enormous bag. "Yeah. He was adorable. True."

"Yeah, I thought so."

"Have a little respect here, Wes. That guy turned me on to jazz, you moron!"

"He turned you on, all right."

"Look," Holly said, her dignity clearly in need of defense, "I'm putting on the jazz station. See?" She punched a few of the preset buttons on the radio in Wesley's new car. The sound system boomed and sputtered as Holly rapidly punched in FM station after station, quickly discarding country music, an all-talk format, a string quartet, and an opera, to run out of steam at one that featured all news.

"Sweetie," Wes said, trying to get Holly's attention. "Try KJAZZ at 88.1 FM."

"You always know everything," she replied in a way that didn't sound entirely complimentary. But before Holly could change the frequency, the baritone voice of the news announcer had begun a new story.

"Tonight, organizers at the Woodburn School of Music were unavailable for comment on the apparent theft of a rare and valuable instrument that was the featured auction item at their annual fund-raising ball."

"Hey, it's about us," Holly said, cranking the volume dial.

The newsreader continued, "One of the school's instructors who was present at the gala event, famed jazzman Joe Bernadello, described the instrument as a one-of-a-kind silver tenor saxophone made in the 1950s by the Selmer Company, a top Parisian maker. Bernadello went on to say he was 'shocked and saddened' that the saxophone was stolen from the downtown Tager Auditorium, where the black-tie event was held earlier this evening. Police are looking for anyone who might have information to call the LAPD hot line." The station then began playing a commercial that was mildly persuasive if one had a deep need to buy the cheapest mattress in Los Angeles County.

"Bad news travels fast, huh?" Holly shook her head, her dangling earrings tinkling at the activity. "I was hoping that old sax would just turn up somewhere, misplaced or something." They had heard about the screwup with the missing sax before they left the Woodburn ball. Of course, the auction wasn't something Mad Bean Events was responsible for, so it hadn't been their nightmare.

Wesley frowned. "This is sad. After all our efforts, what will everyone in town be talking about tomorrow? That sax."

"That's the way life is. You plan and you plan. You work and you work. Then something always happens you weren't prepared for. That's Madeline's philosophy."

"She's right," Wes said.

"Something is always going to happen we can't predict and we can't control," Holly said. "But it's not usually something that makes the cops come running."

"Or makes the news," Wes agreed.

"How did they get this story so fast, Wes?" Holly looked at her wrist and shook several of the bangle bracelets until her tiny rhinestone watch was revealed. "It's only two A.M." They had begun breaking down the kitchen before midnight and then spent almost an hour standing around out in the parking structure with their crew overseeing the loading of their equipment and kidding around with the waiters and chefs as they left.

Wes eased the car into his Hancock Park driveway but just sat there, staring at the car radio, turning the sound level down as the commercials rolled on, while Holly pulled a tiny cell phone out of her giant bag and began to dial.

"You calling Maddie?" Wes asked. "Wait a sec, there, Hol."

"Shouldn't we let her know something is going on?"

"Not yet," Wes said, thinking it over. "What can any of us do about the missing sax? Look, Maddie left early. Chances are she doesn't even know about it. Let her sleep."

The newscaster's voice returned to the news after the commercial break and began another story. "With a disturbing report, we hear now from Ken Hernandez, who is out in the Hollywood Hills at the site of a criminal investigation. What is going on out there, Ken?"

"It looks like L.A. has been hit by another shocking crime, Jim. I'm standing in the quiet neighborhood of Whitley Heights, where police have just informed us there has been an apparent home invasion robbery that turned violent."

Sitting in the dark car, Wesley and Holly were once more riveted to the news. Whitley Heights was the tiny section of the Hollywood Hills where Mad Bean Events had its offices and professional kitchen. The company worked out of the lower floor of Madeline's home. Wesley's hand jabbed for the radio knob and turned up the sound.

"We have yet to get the whole story here, Jim, but the police tell us the body of a young woman, age approximately midtwenties, has been found in the house, which is the residence of one of the city's most successful party planners . . ."

"Oh my God. Oh my God." Holly's pale skin turned paler.

The original news anchor spoke up. "We understand it's the home of Madeline Bean. Are the police aware that Bean's catering company was responsible for producing the Jazz Ball at the Woodburn School earlier this evening—the scene, we have just learned, of yet another serious crime? Is there a connection here?"

"I don't know about that, Jim. I'll try to have more information for you in my next report."

Holly stared at Wes. "Oh my God. Oh my God. Oh—"

"Holly." Wes put his hand on her shoulder and she looked up at him, her face going blank with fear, the words dying on her lips.

Wesley Westcott had spent the past several years being the calmest man you'd ever want by your side in a kitchen crisis. His voice never rose. His cool never faltered. Whether it was because of shock, or habit, or sheer emotional fortitude, his calm voice betrayed almost no strain as he asked his assistant quietly, "Did the idiot on the radio just imply that Maddie's . . . *body* has just been discovered?"

"Nutty"

TWELVE HOURS EARLIER . . .
There are very few things as invigorating as trying to coordinate the efforts of a dozen wacked-out, overly sensitive, testosterone-driven gourmet chefs on the afternoon of a large dinner party. At the moment six of my prep chefs were ready to kill the other six. And I suspect those other six were ready to kill me. What would life be like without its little challenges?

"Philip," I chided, "the soup is supposed to be black and white, not brown and white." We were preparing two soups, a white cheddar cream soup and a black bean soup, which would be simultaneously ladled into the same shallow bowl until the two met in the middle, and then garnished with heirloom tomato salsa and sour cream just before it was served. It was to be the perfect start of our evening's meal, as it fit the black and white and "re(a)d" headline theme of the Jazz Ball.

"I know that," Philip Voron said, looking vexed.

"See what you can do to darken the black bean soup, will you?"

"I told you it was supposed to be blacker! Idiot!" Philip Voron spat out at his neighbor.

I moved on.

Across the room, Wes smiled at me and pointed to his watch. We had to keep moving. We were due at the Tager Auditorium, the site of the evening's party, in a few hours, but I took half a second to appreciate just where I was. On this party day, the day of our final prep for the Woodburn fund-raiser, our industrial-style kitchen could explode the senses of even the most seasoned caterer. The large white-tiled room, with its commercial-grade stainless appliances and high ceiling, was currently filled with the pounding sounds of chopping blocks punished by a dozen chefs' aggressive knives, the intoxicating perfume of freshly crushed garlic and just-picked basil, the heat of gas flames firing high under enormous bubbling stockpots. I love these sounds and scents and sights.

"Mad," called out Holly from near the sinks. She was helping two women who were rolling out our fresh angel-hair pasta. We planned to cook it later when we got to the Tager kitchen, quickly so it would remain al dente, right before serving it to our six hundred guests. The thing that made it interesting was adding the black ink we'd removed from the sacs of ten dozen cuttlefish, which we'd had flown in from the Mediterranean that morning. Cuttlefish are a sort of squid. Sautéed, they taste a lot like softshell crab. My partner, Wes, and I often lament the less than adventurous palates of most banquet planners, but this time, at least, we'd be out on the inky culinary edge. Our hostesses, the women of the Woodburn Guild, were taking the black-and-white theme seriously.

"I'll be right back," I called to Holly. I had to run out to my car, where I'd left a phone number for the ice sculptor who was carving jazz instruments out of black-tinted ice.

I ducked through the butler's pantry, both sides of which were made up of floor-to-ceiling glass-fronted cabinets. There, in the backlit cases, we displayed the hot-turquoise-and-lemon-yellow vintage pottery collection we often use, the serving platters and bowls we bring to our more informal events. The pantry led from the kitchen to the office that Wes and I share and then out to the front door by way of Holly's reception-area desk.

Outside, I started down the flight of stairs that takes you from my hillside home to the curb. It wasn't until I was halfway down that I noticed something was wrong. The street below, a quiet cul-de-sac where Whitley Avenue dead-ends right up against the retaining wall of the Hollywood Freeway, was covered in trash and papers and the like. What was up with that?

As I began to process the scene, I became angrier with the mess. Dozens of papers had been dumped in my driveway and beyond, like someone had maliciously emptied a wastepaper basket out their car window as they drove by. I had been out front only ten minutes before with Wesley and Holly, and the street had been quiet and neat and clean. Few people come all the way up this street, anyway, since there is no outlet. So whatever was this paper attack about?

I opened up the back of my old Jeep Grand Wagoneer and pulled out an empty carton marked LOUIS ROEDERER 1995 BRUT, removed the inner cardboard partitions that had cushioned and separated the champagne bottles a few months back when I first bought them for a wedding shower, and then, with distaste, began picking up trash off the asphalt. As I tossed handfuls of paperwork into the carton, I was thankful the stuff wasn't filthy. In fact, it was an odd assortment of officelike documents.

Hey, now. Wait a minute. Was that an actual U.S. passport tucked between the sheets of paper I just dumped? I pawed through the pages and fished out the navy blue booklet. Amazing. It looked real. I flipped it open and stared at the two-inch photo of a vital, lean man in his early sixties, judging by his iron-gray buzz cut and allowing for the standard ten years one must always add to the estimated age of anyone one meets in Hollywood. The name on the passport was Albert Grasso. His date of birth proved I could peg ages in this town with the best of them. He would be sixty-three next month. His address was on Iris Circle, the next street up the hill.

I leaned against my Jeep, resting the carton on the hood, and filtered through some of the other items I'd just gathered into the box. There was a handful of framable-size photos that had clearly fallen out of a manila folder marked PHOTOS. I quickly sorted them so they made a neat stack and all faced the same direction, but I could barely finish the task once I caught a glimpse of the glossy side of one of the pictures. It was an eight-by-ten color print, a glamorous studio shot of a seventies icon, autographed *To Albert—singing your praises! With love, Cher.* Cher. I mean, *really*! Whose trash *was* this?

Another photo was signed "Love, Michael," and showed a very young Michael Jackson. A third featured the cast of the Oscar-winning movie musical *Chicago*. Everyone in the cast had signed it to "Albert," offering an assortment of warm thanks and good wishes. Look at that. Richard Gere had mentioned their mutual interest in the Dalai Lama.

I became more enchanted with my trash find by the minute, shuffling through photos of David Bowie, Avril Lavigne, and Charo. The last of the photos proved more intriguing still. It was a shot of two people, one famous, one not. The young, dark-haired girl, maybe twenty or so, was smiling into the camera so hard you could see her back teeth. The older man with his arm around her had a face no one could help but recognize. It was President Clinton. They were standing close together in the Oval Office. The picture had a personal inscription, *To Teresa, with thanks*. And then the initials *B.C.*

Wesley's voice came from far away. I looked up and shaded my eyes against the glare of the sun. He was standing up at the top of the landing by the open front door. "Hey, Mad," he called down. "What's up? You need some help?"

"You've got to see what I found. All this stuff was littered all over the place. It seems to belong to a guy on Iris Circle."

"What is it?"

"Private papers and photos." I picked one item at random from the carton, a letter, and read it aloud.

Dear Mr. Grasso,

　　Enclosed please find my report on your psychiatric condition. You'll note the diagnosis code represents a diagnosis of anxiety-stress disorder, for which I've been treating you for the past seven years. If you have any questions, or if your insurance carrier requires any further information, please let me know.

　　　　　　　　　　　　　　Sincerely,

　　　　　　　　　　　　　　Dr. Stan Bradley, M.D.

"You have some guy's psychiatric files?"

"Apparently," I said, unable to resist paging quickly through a document that was clearly none of my business.

"And you're standing out in the street reading them?"

I looked back at Wes without a trace of guilt. "Hey, how am I supposed to know what all this stuff is? It was littered all over my property. Littering is a crime. I am simply investigating, aren't I?"

"Maybe you can put off your CSI inquiry until after we finish with the party tonight?"

I looked up from the thick psychiatrist's report on the many issues that had been vexing Mr. Grasso and nodded. Wes was right. I had to get my focus back. "Aye aye," I said, snapping to attention. "Do you think I should try to find this guy's phone number? He'd want his stuff back, I'd imagine."

"Can we do that tomorrow? We are under the gun here, timetable-wise."

"You're right. You're always right." I put the last of the papers back into the carton and hauled it up the stairs. "But, Wes, how do you think all these personal photos and documents ended up on my lawn?"

Wes relieved me of the box as I reached the top of the steps. "I'm sure you'll find out all about it. After the Jazz Ball."

"BETWEEN BLACK & WHITE"

Frankly, fund-raising is social warfare and the gentle ladies who volunteer to run the show are its generals. I had worked on several such events in the past, and I had the battle scars to prove it.

The committee in charge of this year's Jazz Ball was aiming to outdo all other elite L.A. fund-raisers in the cutthroat art of separating dollars from donors. To this end, each party decision was argued over by the Jazz Ball planning committee. Endlessly. Luckily, Wes and I have steady nerves. The theme had been changed up and back and up again a half-dozen times. But in the end, the newspaper design theme of black and white, with a touch of red, captured the final vote, and judging simply by the number of guests paying five hundred dollars a ticket, the gala appeared to be a hit. This was the largest turnout in the event's forty-two-year history.

No detail of the party was too small to delight one faction of volunteer women and cause an uproar of seething disapproval in another. Victory in such details took on way too much importance to be healthy, but this was not my call. For instance, one group heavily favored a traditional engraved invitation. Formal. Black on heavy cream stock. However, the chairs of this year's event were bored silly by the memories of too many staid and stuffy charity dinners. They wanted people to talk about this party. In a good way. And despite the disapproval of some of the older members of the committee, the distinctive invitations to the "Headliner's" Jazz Ball had gone out eight weeks ago.

The invitations had been written up in a parody of the style of newspaper articles, printed on authentic newsprint under the banner the *Woodburn Daily Jazz*, rolled up like the morning paper, tied with red grosgrain ribbon, and tossed onto the pool-table-perfect lawns of the city's most generous: those heads of private foundations and leaders of civic-minded corporations and individual donors who kept L.A.'s cultural wheels turning. Naturally, the families of the Woodburn's young musicians and the staff of the school were also invited.

In my role as creative consultant and caterer to the Jazz Ball, I had made many suggestions to Dilly Swinden and Zenya Knight, the cochairs of the fund-raising gala. I have found that timing suggestions is crucial. As an event draws closer, decisions must be made. I have learned to wait for just the right moment to bring up many items in order to prevent committee-itis from draining the energy out of every last creative impulse. It had gotten to the stage where we had to have some final decisions on the look of the event. We were discussing how much of their budget the ladies wished to spend on decorating the Tager Auditorium's grand foyer, where the dinner was to be served. Dilly and Zenya were both savvy to the bottom line. While they wanted to put on a spectacular party, they also wanted to raise the most money for the Woodburn. They asked what we could do that would cut down on costs but make the biggest splash.

We had been sitting in my office, sipping white wine and going over the numbers again. "Can you imagine," I wondered aloud, "if everyone at the ball were to dress up in our color scheme? Hundreds of gowns in black or white, with accents here and there of red?"

Dilly and Zenya glommed on to the idea like the purebred shoppers they were.

"I love it," Dilly said, turning to Zenya.

"Everyone wears black, anyway," Zenya responded. "The men are no problem. Black tie. White shirt. Tux. They're done."

"Who doesn't have a black gown?" Dilly added.

"Who doesn't have two or three?" Zenya asked. "Not to mention

something white. Or they could wear a black-and-white print. Or something red. I love this."

Dilly giggled and sipped her Chardonnay. "Oh, please. Who are we
kidding? We all buy something new for the ball, anyway. But I just love
telling everyone what they must go out and buy."

It was settled just like that. Dilly looked at her watch and shrieked.
"Sorry. I have to run."

Zenya, at least fifteen years younger than her cochair, but no less
busy, checked her own jeweled wrist and gasped. "Me, too. Let's meet on
Tuesday at ten. Will that be all right, Madeline?"

I nodded as the women rushed out. These ladies were always on the
go, their Palm Pilots filled with appointments. Dilly had a session with
her Pilates trainer across town, and Zenya was running late to meet the
manicurist, who was making a house call, so Zenya's second grader's nails
could be changed to a new shade of pink. I try very hard not to judge.
Very, very hard.

The ball's elegant black-and-white dress code had actually been one
of the easier decisions. Dilly had by that time managed to achieve a stran-
glehold on the rest of the committee. By pairing with a sweet-natured yes-
girl like Zenya, she was making all the power decisions. It was they who
had approved the gourmet black-and-white menu, daring to move beyond
traditional banquet bland. And I had to admire their resolve to make this
ball distinctive, both in food and in appearance. Sometimes, clients don't
really get it. But these two did.

As I stood in the grand foyer, two hours into their fabulous Jazz Ball,
I noticed Dilly Swinden a short distance away. She was standing with her
husband; he in a black Armani dinner jacket, with snow-white shirt and a
red bow tie; she in a simple, floor-length strapless dress covered in jet-
black beads. Her delicate neck was circled in the largest rubies I'd ever
seen. The presence of so many couples dressed all in black and white
made for a stunning effect, lending the party a more artistic ambience
than any amount of swag draping or flower arrangements alone might
have done.

Scattered in the crowd, twenty-five young Woodburn kids had volun-
teered to work at the event. These children left their instruments at home
for the evening and were dressed as turn-of-the-century paperboys, wearing black caps with a white sack over one shoulder filled with "newspa-

pers." Guests could purchase a "paper" for twenty-five dollars and take their chance at winning a great prize. The auction ladies had solicited donations from vendors all over the city and each of the "newspapers" in the sacks represented a donated item. One might find their newspaper raffle item was a certificate for a dinner for two at Patina Restaurant, a free eye exam by Dr. Stuart Milliken, or a seven-day Mexican cruise, the grand prize.

The party had been in full swing for more than two hours and I noted that most of our paperboys had done their jobs well. Their sacks were empty and they were ready to go home. They had done their greatest "business" while the guests were arriving and the hors d'oeuvres and cocktails had been served in the grand hall. Then, at seven-thirty, both paperboys and ticket-holding guests found their seats in the Tager Auditorium for the all-star jazz concert. The event featured twelve of the Woodburn School's very top jazz students, who got to play with some of the country's greatest contemporary jazz musicians. A tremendous silent auction and the black-and-white dinner followed. As my waitstaff moved efficiently among the sixty tables of ten, I kept an eye out for anyone gesturing for more coffee.

Holly joined me. "So far, so fabulous." She was dressed as all our female servers, in black pants and a white lace camisole with a red rosebud pinned to one strap.

"And we're on schedule." I looked at my watch. "In just a minute Dilly and Zenya will start the live auction."

"Are you going to bid on anything?"

I gave Holly an amused smile. "Like I could afford any of this stuff."

"Everyone at Table 23 is talking about the Selmer saxophone," Holly reported. "They say it's priceless."

"Oh, yes?"

"They say there hasn't been one of this type available for years. Something about the year it was made or the registration number. I'm not sure. But two of the guys were getting kind of steamed at each other."

I looked at Holly. She was grinning, adding, "Bidding war. Mark my words."

"That will be good for the Woodburn."

The auction committee had been ruthless in extracting donations to the cause. Every upscale business in town had been solicited and many had come through with splendid items for bid, most of which went into the silent auction. During the first hour of the ball, guests mingled among the overflowing tables and signed their names to bidding sheets, upping the bids on everything from a lavish basket filled with hand-embroidered baby clothes donated by a Brentwood children's boutique, to a certificate for six flying lessons, to a week's stay at Disney World, to four floor seats at a Lakers game along with a ball signed by the entire team.

The full fury of a silent auction is hard to describe. In the final few minutes before the bidding closes, the most competitive bidders hunker down beside the bid sheets of the items they covet most. Earlier this evening, with only sixty seconds to go, I'd seen two elegant women toe-to-toe. They were outbidding each other, back and forth, for a series of twelve facials donated by a hot Beverly Hills aesthetician so in demand, she was unlisted and unbookable. No sooner would one write down $3,600 than the other would fill in the next blank with $3,700 and so on until, battle-weary but determined, they finally called a truce. One suggested they simply split the prize up and each take six sessions. And all would have been settled if at the very last second a man hadn't come up to the bidding sheet and stolen it for $4,000.

I turned to Holly. "If the silent auction is any indication, I expect the live auction to be brutal."

The auction committee saved its most desirable and biggest-ticket items for live bidding. This evening, they had chosen a professional auctioneer from Sotheby's along with a celebrity auctioneer to handle the work. The celeb was Brianna Welk, a sunny-dispositioned news anchor on one of the local channels. I had noticed Brianna paying some serious attention to our martini bar throughout the evening and said a silent prayer for the best.

"I wonder how much money the luncheon we donated will raise?" Holly asked.

"Lunch for twenty women? Maybe five thousand?" I guessed, trying to factor in how much money those two women had been willing to pay for some facials.

"You think?" Holly looked excited. We had been asked if we would like to make a donation to the auction, and Wes had suggested we offer up a private party. He suggested we provide flowers and vases and he and

Holly could give a flower-arranging class for twenty followed by a Mad Bean Events catered lunch.

Wes appeared and we welcomed him to our huddle.

"Wes, how much do you think they'll get for our lunch?" Holly asked.

"Maybe six grand," he predicted, showing more confidence than I had. "Hey. You guys see the smoke? Think I should beef it up?"

We all looked over to the side of the grand foyer, past the sixty white-draped tables filled with black-and-white-dressed guests. Next to one of the entrances we had set up a smoking martini bar that Wes had designed, using enormous glass blocks with hidden wells that provided pools in which he had floated dry ice. Smoke swirled lightly around the bar and the bartender as he worked. I noticed Brianna Welk standing there, wearing a short, flaming red sequined dress, in line with some of the gala's most serious drinkers. They were getting refills of our special concoction, a new drink we discovered in Europe.

The "smoking martini" was a near-lethal mix of Ketel One vodka, dry vermouth, and a splash of Glenlivet. We couldn't help giving in to the drama of pouring bottles of vodka into a crystal tub and adding a large chunk of dry ice. That Ketel One really smoked. And it was quite safe, since the bartender ladled the spirits into long-stemmed martini glasses, carefully avoiding any dry ice. It definitely upped the party's pizzazz quotient.

"Well, for me," Holly said, "you can never have enough smoke."

"Say, did you see the seating chart?" Wes handed me a sheet. The party organizers had printed them up and placed one at each plate, thoughtfully encouraging guests to locate friends and/or enemies, the better to greet and/or avoid.

I love to see who's who. "The mayor is here," I noted, checking the names quickly. "And Tom Selleck? Table 30." I craned my neck. "Man, I never even saw him. I'll have to saunter by."

"And check out Table 10," Wes suggested.

I put my finger on the table and read the tiny print that offered the names.

"Wait." I reread the name and looked up at Wes. "Albert Grasso?"

Holly looked, too, but the name didn't register with her. "Who's Albert Grasso?"

"He's the guy . . ." Wes answered. "The guy who left all his private papers on Maddie's doorstep."

"That's amazing," I said, dazed to think the man would actually be at my gala. "But, Wesley. Now I feel so guilty. I should have called him. What if he's all worried about his missing paperwork."

"Madeline. We have hardly had a minute to breathe . . ." Wes started, but I didn't wait to hear the rest of his reassurances.

I headed for Table 10. Just then, a spotlight blinked on the small stage at the front of the hall. Dilly Swinden, in her jet-black beads, and her younger cochair, Zenya Knight, wearing a tight white silk gown, approached the microphone and smiled out at the crowd as the guests began to quiet down. The live auction was about to begin. Right on schedule. My eyes swept the room and I saw our crew prepare to serve dessert, black-and-white mini-cheesecakes, formed in the shape of musical notes, the black desert plates decorated with a touch of red—giant strawberries dipped in the darkest dark chocolate, each hand-monogrammed with a swirled white chocolate W.

"Ladies and gentlemen, let us welcome you all to . . ."

Squeezing between chairs that had been slipcovered in a black-and-white pinstripe satin, I made my way into the heart of the tight cluster of tables.

"Excuse me. Mr. Grasso?"

The face from the passport photo I'd examined earlier that afternoon looked up at me and smiled a perfect capped-teeth smile. Albert Grasso checked me out and appeared to like what he saw. He took in my slinky halter dress, his eyes lingering on my bare shoulders. I had to bend slightly to be heard over the auctioneers, who had just been introduced. Brianna, I noticed, was sloshed. When I turned my attention back to Table 10, I immediately regretted the deep V of my gown, as it now offered up my cleavage at exactly Albert's eye level. Albert's wife/girlfriend/whatever was on alert. She was a pale woman in her forties with a recently tucked chin and a short blond hairdo.

"I'm so sorry to bother you," I started again, unable to keep from putting my hand up over the deep neckline of my dress. "I wonder if I might have a word with you. It's important."

Albert's date had all she was going to take. She raised her voice and said, "Al doesn't make business appointments at social events, dear."

Another man sitting at the table smiled at me. Clearly a young woman bending over their table was more than most of these tuxedoed old codgers had hoped for when their wives had dragged them out for another fund-raising evening. "Are you a singer?" the second man inquired.

"A singer?" I was not following.

Albert Grasso said, "I might be able to fit you in my schedule. What's the problem? What's your label? Are you signed?"

"Mr. Grasso, I'm Madeline Bean. I'm an event planner. Actually, I'm surprised to see you here tonight—but you see, this evening's Jazz Ball is an event my company is producing."

"Very nice," Albert said. "Beautiful dinner." And then he leaned closer to my bosom and asked with a wink, "And you sing?"

What was it about singing? And then I remembered the pictures. Cher. David Bowie.

"Are you a singing coach?"

"A singing coach?" Albert's date/wife parroted.

"You don't know who I am?" he asked, a twinkle in his eye.

In the background, the auctioneer from Sotheby's was rattling off the first item and was already in high gear. The item up for bid was a week's stay at someone's private castle in Scotland, donated by one of the board members at the Woodburn. The last bid was $8,000, I heard as I turned back to Albert Grasso.

"I'm sorry to bother you here at the party tonight. I probably should have waited until a more appropriate time, but I was so surprised to see your name on the guest list."

"I work in the music business, Ms. Bean. I know many of the musicians who played in the concert tonight. I always try to give back to the community."

"I'm sure you do. I'm sure. It's just that I have a personal matter to discuss with you."

The woman seated beside Albert Grasso had been following the rapid bidding as the price on the Scottish castle week went up to $12,500. She raised a card displaying her bidding number and the auctioneer quickly called her bid of $13,000. Onstage, Brianna Welk put two fingers to her mouth and whistled.

"Yes?" Albert turned to me and waited for more.

"A private matter, Mr. Grasso."

Albert's companion pulled her bidding card down and snapped her head to hear our conversation.

"Private?" Albert again looked at my tight dress and stood up. "Excuse me, Caroline," he said, nodding to the woman and dismissing her as he turned to me. He put his hand on the small of my back as older men like to do, leading me out of the center of the tables and off to the side of the room.

"My girlfriend gets jealous," he muttered with a wink as we found a quieter spot to talk.

"I hope I'm not causing you any trouble."

"A beautiful young woman comes looking for Albert Grasso. That's the kind of trouble I dream of."

"Thank . . . you." I couldn't imagine if that was the correct response. "Mr. Grasso. I know this sounds like none of my business and it's a very unusual question, but are you missing a lot of your private papers?"

"I beg your pardon?"

Just then an eruption of applause drowned out my response. We both looked up at the stage, where the Sotheby's auctioneer was repeating the winning bid. The trip to Scotland with the castle that sleeps twenty-four had just gone for $28,500.

"I live in Whitley Heights," I started again.

"You're kidding! So do I." Albert smiled at me. He thought I was making a pass at him.

"I live on Whitley just below your house on Iris Circle. Somehow, a lot of paperwork and photos and files with your name on them were dumped on my property."

"Holy shit." The gleam went right out of Albert Grasso's eye. "Are you kidding me?"

"No. I can't explain how this mess got on my lawn, Mr. Grasso, but I found your passport and I was planning on calling—"

"My *passport*? What else do you have?"

"Photos of celebrities. Confidential reports. Insurance papers. Bible-study notes."

Albert Grasso stared at me, his face ashen. "Where are they now?"

"At my house. It's also my office. I would have tried to get in touch with you earlier, but of course I had this big job tonight."

"So," he said slowly. "Did you read my papers?"

"Not really. I mean, I was planning on tossing it all out. It was just litter. But then I noticed the passport."

He glowered at me. Didn't he realize I was trying to help him here? How do I get myself into these things?

"How much do you want?" he asked, his voice low.

"Do I want? I don't want anything."

"Yeah. Sure you don't. You better return every single sheet of paper. Every single file. I'll pay two thousand."

Over the loudspeaker, Brianna Welk's high voice came across with the slightest of slurs. She was the lead auctioneer on the next item and told the crowd that the bidding would start at $5,000.

"Mr. Grasso. I'm beginning to feel insulted here. I don't want any reward."

"Do I hear six thousand?" called out Brianna.

"I'll give you six thousand," Albert responded, raising his own bid. What was going on?

"Look, I have your address," I said sternly. "I'll have one of my staff return the box of papers to you tomorrow."

"I want it right now," Albert said, grabbing my wrist. "I don't know what game you're playing. You say you have my personal papers, but just how did you get them? Did you break into my house? Is that how you have my address?"

"No!"

"You must think you're clever. You knew I wouldn't call the police. I'm a big name in Los Angeles, dear. I'm the top vocal coach in town. I have the trust of every singer that gets paid a million just to open his mouth, you understand? I have to protect my privacy and that of my clients. This morning I went into my home office. I saw the file cabinet was open. Obviously, I should have checked more carefully. I looked around and the art was there. The cash was there. But I knew something wasn't right. I didn't get around to opening every drawer, checking every file. I have been distraught, young woman. You think I wanted to come here tonight? Caroline insisted I take her, since she's active on the board and I'd spent a thou on the tickets. Got it? So let's get down to business. I want my files back and you have them."

"You really don't understand."

"Calm down. You will get your payoff, young woman. Just tell me how much."

I pulled my wrist out of his tight grasp as the crowd applauded another winning bid. "Tomorrow," I said, through clenched teeth, "I will turn in all the papers that I found on my property to the police. If you want your things back, I suggest you report what is missing to them. That's what you should have done in the first place. They can sort all this out. I certainly want nothing more from you, Mr. Grasso."

"Ten thousand," he called loudly after me as I pushed through the crowd.

"I have a bid of ten thousand dollars for the private parking space at the Woodburn School," Brianna Welk said with excitement, suddenly pointing to the back of the room, directly at Grasso. "Do I hear anything higher?"

"All or Nothing at All"

Madeline," Dilly Swinden called out.

I pressed my lips together, quickly changing gears, readjusting my mood. The client deserves a cheerful event planner. "You look stunning, Dilly," I said, admiring her trim figure and the Prada gown covered in jet-black beads.

"No, you do. Look at your long neck. But just wait until next year. I'll look much better after my little trip," she said, winking. "Madeline, have you been watching? They are about to auction off your luncheon." Dilly gestured toward to stage, where Brianna was pulling the microphone out of the hand of the Sotheby's auctioneer.

Ah, yes. Our luncheon. "Thanks, Dilly. I hope we raise a bundle."

"We will," Dilly said, grabbing my hand in a girlfriendlike grasp, the largest stone in her ruby ring bruising my fingers in friendship. "Thanks to your smoking martinis."

Onstage, Brianna began reading the description of our offering, called a Flower and Gourmet Lover's Garden Party for Twenty Ladies, including the flower-arranging lesson (two arrangements would be made and taken home by each of twenty guests; all flowers, vases, and extras were included) and a gourmet luncheon (including a special lobster-and-avocado salad) catered by Mad Bean Events. Brianna's reading was surprisingly flawless, and it made me wonder if she was equally talented at reading her studio TelePrompTer under the influence. I would certainly be watching the local news with a new perspective.

Brianna asked the crowd to open the bidding at $5,000. I, alone, gasped.

Soon, a hand was raised, and although many of the diners were enjoying after-dinner refreshments and greeting their friends, enough guests were following the auction to keep the bidding lively.

Holly brought over a plate filled with chocolate-dipped strawberries about the size of billiard balls. "Schnitzel! It's up to thirteen thousand."

Brianna was getting dramatic, trying to keep the bidding going. "This money is going to the *children*," she pleaded. "Come on, people. Pay attention to me, here. Let's focus! I'm asking for fourteen goddamn thousand now. Do I have fourteen?" She got a bid of $14,000, but the cross-conversations among the happy dinner crowd did not subside.

"Did Brianna Welk just cuss out the guests?" Holly asked, with a whoop of shock.

"One smoking martini too many, I'd say."

"Holy moley."

There seemed to be three women who were still in the bidding for the garden party and gourmet luncheon and I was a little overwhelmed at the money folks were willing to pay. By the time the bids reached $18,000, I began thinking I'd better add caviar to the menu.

Brianna was wrestling to get the crowd to settle down so she could persuade the bidding upward. Just then, Albert Grasso's date, Caroline, approached from out of nowhere.

"You have some nerve," she said, right in my face.

"Hey, whoa!" Holly said, yelping as Caroline trod on her foot.

"Is there something I can do for you?" I asked. "Because right now they are auctioning off—"

"I don't care if they are auctioning off your ass, sweetie," she said, keeping her voice pleasant. "You and me are going to have a nice little talk."

I stared at her. What now?

"Albert wants his papers back and he said you weren't willing to cooperate. He's not going to pay your blackmail money. I'll have you know we have already called our lawyer and the police. Expect to find them at your doorstep with an arrest warrant."

"What?" Holly said, gasping again.

"It's a lucky thing, then," I replied, "that I have over a dozen witnesses to testify I was working in my kitchen on this party all day and an eyewitness to my finding the litter dumped on the lawn."

"You do?" Caroline hesitated for just a minute.

"Do I hear twenty thousand?" Brianna warbled over the PA. *"Please, people, settle down."*

"It is ludicrous for you and Mr. Grasso to come so unglued. But now that I think about it, I can't possibly know to whom all those files actually belong."

"What are you saying?" Caroline said, confused and angrier than ever. "Of course those papers are Al's!"

"Are they?" I asked calmly.

She looked furious, her tight little chin quivering.

The people near us were all laughing and joking loudly, unaware of our spat or the auction, which had reached $21,500.

"I have decided this really is a police matter," I finished. "I am a very close friend of a detective on the LAPD, and I think it's wise to let them handle it, Caroline. And my suggestion to Mr. Grasso is, please keep going to that therapist."

"Everyone . . ." Brianna called from the stage, her high-pitched voice projecting over the loudspeaker. *"Listen to me now. Everyone . . ."*

"Mad," Holly whispered as Caroline stood there, sputtering, "What the hell?"

"EVERYONE . . ." Brianna tried again, much closer to the mike.

"You are going to regret this!" Caroline shouted at me.

"WHAT?" Holly and I yelled at the same time.

"You leave my Albert alone!" she shouted back.

At which point, Ms. Brianna Welk, up on the stage, had simply had enough. She expected the crowd's respect. She assumed their devotion. And most of all, she demanded their goddamned attention. She screamed into the microphone, "SHUT UP!"

And at that, this assembled group of happily partying arts patrons, parents, and philanthropists, some soused, some flirting, some chatting loudly with friends not seen in weeks, along with Albert Grasso's over-wrought lady friend, simultaneously stopped speaking in sheer surprise and alarm.

"That's better," Brianna drawled over the mike, not noticing the stunned glares of disapproval. "I just wanted to say, the flower-thingie luncheon is going . . . going . . . *gone!* Sold to the lady at Table 4 for twenty-six thousand five hundred!"

"Gadzooks!" Holly said, shaking her head, as someone on the auction committee rushed onto the stage and managed to pry the microphone out of Brianna's hand. The Sotheby's auctioneer took over and the party guests went back to a slightly quieter form of chatter. "Say, what happened to that nasty woman?" We both looked around, but Caroline had disappeared. "And why was she so angry?"

"That's a good question. It has to do with the papers I found in front of my house this afternoon. There may be something private among those papers that our neighbors do not want anyone to see. Why else would they get so bent out of shape?"

"Just what you need, Maddie, more crazies."

I smiled.

"And what was that you were telling her about being 'a very close friend of a detective on the LAPD'? Are you speaking to Chuck Honnett again?" Holly asked.

"Well, no. I still hate him, of course. Nothing's changed there. But I was so sick of all her threats and intimidation. I thought it made me sound more substantial to say I have friends in high places."

Holly nodded. "It did."

I smiled back at her. "I know. I wish I still did have one, too."

Honnett and I. Now there was a story. He was this detective with whom I'd had a short, kind of passionate thing. It had started earlier in the year and had ended not that many months later. A pity the whole thing blew up, since we had some great chemistry. Really great. But he hadn't been honest with me. He hadn't told me everything.

"Being hot is not a crime," Holly reminded me, referring to Honnett's long, lean body and stong-jawed, edgy looks.

"We really had nothing in common," I said. I knew it was lame, but there was truth to it. My friends were chefs, artists, bohemians, writers, the unemployed. Honnett was a cop. His buddies were cops. He liked rules.

He liked guns. He liked being a macho man, not too many words. I was all talk. This thing would have ended sooner or later. I just hadn't seen the end coming quite as soon as it had.

"What are you talking about?" Holly asked, staring at me. "You and he were cool. So he was a little older than you—"

"Like about fifteen years," I drawled.

"Maybe a real man isn't such a bad thing to have around," she countered. "Maybe on him the years looked pretty good."

"It wasn't that. It was the fact that he hadn't gotten around to mentioning that he hadn't completely divorced his wife yet. That kind of got in the way, Hol."

"True. That wasn't good."

I smiled at her. Neither of us had had such good luck with men. Holly had an on-again, off-again relationship with an adorable young screenwriter. In fact, a few months ago they decided to run off to Vegas and elope. We all went out there on a moment's notice, Wes, me, Holly and her Donald, and a dreamy rebound guy I thought I should fall for, John.

Only, when we got to the Venetian Hotel, Holly started getting calls from her mother and her sisters. They wanted to be there when Holly got married. They couldn't believe she'd do it without them. Soon Donald's mother was calling them on their cell phone, too, pleading for them to set a date in a reasonable month and let the family come in from the Midwest for a real wedding. In the end, the impetuous couple gave in. Just goes to show what romantic havoc a cell phone can play. Holly swears if Romeo and Juliet had had a cell, they would never have been lying in bed together when the light from yonder window broke, what with Romeo's mother calling every five minutes looking for him.

Still, we did have a lovely time in Las Vegas. Wes won twelve hundred dollars playing Caribbean stud. Donald got his picture taken with an Elvis impersonator. My new date, John, was a doll and a real gentleman, despite the fact that I kept thinking about Honnett the entire weekend. And Holly was approached about trying out as a showgirl. Poor Holly. Poor me.

"Mad," Holly said, grabbing my arm to get my attention. "This is it. The final auction item."

"Thank God."

"No, it's the saxophone I was telling you about. The priceless one. I bet it goes for a fortune."

The auctioneer from Sotheby's was a dapper man in his later years. With Brianna Welk removed from the stage, he seemed much more at ease. "Ladies and gentlemen, this is the moment many of you have been waiting for. We present the ultimate musical instrument, as is only fitting in this illustrious group of fine music aficionados. May I present the rarest and some say nearly priceless Selmer Mark VI B♭ tenor saxophone in silver, with full engraving."

The folks in the room, table by table, dropped their conversations and stopped clinking their coffee cups. Soon the perfect quiet that Brianna had only dreamed about descended on the room. Two men came forward with a leather saxophone case and unclasped the lock. One opened the lid and they set the sax case on a tilt so the audience could get a look. The bright spotlight caught the highly polished silver of the bell and glinted.

"Ladies and gentlemen. You may never again see its like. This instrument was found in the storeroom of a shop in Milwaukee, Wisconsin. We must assume it has never before been played, since the original cork stops that were used to guard the valves during shipment from the maker in Paris are still in place.

"This exceptional horn really needs no introduction—it's the most famous horn on earth. If you are a professional player or you know a gifted young soul who was born to play the tenor . . ." He paused and looked out at the tables filled with proud parents, then continued, "If you've never played a Selmer Mark VI, you're missing out on the best saxophone ever made."

We all looked at the saxophone and began to dream of playing the best instrument on earth. Even those of us without any hint of musical ability.

"Ladies and gentlemen. Let me now tell you what has been said about the legendary Mark VI. It is accepted that those made in the 1960s are the best, and those made before 1965 are best of all because they have a better quality of brass and therefore better timbre. The instrument you see before you, and which will soon be going home with one of you, was built in 1961."

There was a palpable thrill running through the crowd. Holly pointed out the table she had waited on, the table with the parents eager to bid on this item. They were sitting quite still.

"Ladies and gentleman," the Sotheby's auctioneer continued, using his cultivated low-key patter to reel the thirsty buyers in even closer. "It is well known that the French-manufactured saxophones, like this beautiful Selmer, have more elaborate engraving, engraving you'll note that stretches to the bow, and it is argued that because of this extra engraving, they sound better and are worth more. For those who may not know such things, the head engraver at Selmer's Paris factory died in 1965, so this Selmer Mark VI before us is simply as impeccable as any instrument gets.

"But before we get to the bidding, ladies and gentlemen, let's talk about the fascinating history of this tenor saxophone. The Mark VI model was introduced by Selmer Paris in 1954 and produced for just the nineteen years. It has been said that no saxophone could equal it. But for those who scoff and suggest that not every Selmer lives up to its reputation, the proof is in the sound. We have come to offer you such proof tonight."

The crowd grew even more riveted.

"I have asked for the assistance of Mr. Sebastian Braniff. Would you come onstage, sir? Mr. Braniff, as most of you know, is the head of the woodwind department at the Woodburn School, and he is a noted saxophone expert in his own right."

There was a murmur in the crowd as the music teacher rose from a table in the middle of the room. I realized with a start that Mr. Braniff, a small man with a thick mop of dark hair, had been seated at Albert Grasso's table.

What a fiasco that whole Grasso discussion had turned into. Why should such a simple task as returning a man's missing papers cause an eruption of emotion and suspicion? Perhaps Albert and Caroline were simply reacting with shock at the idea that their privacy had been breached. But why would Albert immediately think someone would try to blackmail him for those items' return? What was there of such value? Maybe I should really look more carefully through the documents before I took them to the police in the morning. It might be wise. If I didn't fall dead asleep, perhaps I should just take a quick but thorough peek. After all, possession is nine-tenths of the law, whatever the heck that means.

Onstage, Mr. Braniff began assembling the coveted tenor saxophone. All eyes in the room were on Braniff as the auctioneer continued his refined pimping of the legendary instrument. By the time the sax was ready to play and the auctioneer had finished his spiel, we were all so impressed that I couldn't guarantee Holly wouldn't bid on the thing.

I looked up to see Wesley just making his way toward where we were standing.

"Need some help with the cleanup?" I asked, guilty I'd been standing around for so long.

"Don't worry. All taken care of. Our guys are loading the trucks. We should be ready to depart in an hour or so. The servers are making last rounds with coffee. Things look good. Relax."

"An hour?" I was tired.

"You don't have to wait around," Wes added quickly. "Just leave it to me and Holly."

"I'm wide-awake," Holly agreed.

"Well . . ." I figured if they were okay supervising the teardown, I might get home by midnight. I could take that carton of papers and just sort through it all so I had a rough inventory of what I'd found and what I would be turning over to the police. There was something about those photos that had me thinking. It's not that I wanted to invade Mr. Grasso's privacy . . . exactly. It was just that with all his accusations and threats, I was beginning to think I had better be prepared to defend myself.

Sebastian Braniff, the celebrated music teacher, was standing onstage with the shining silver saxophone now hanging from a strap around his neck. He slowly put the mouthpiece up to his lips. He stood in the spotlight, taking his time as the crowd waited.

"Ladies and gentlemen," the auctioneer whispered into his microphone, "I give you the Selmer Mark VI, serial number 91-023. Until tonight, never before played . . ."

First one long, low edgy note. The tone of the instrument was bright and hot. Nothing soft or mellow there. Then another dirty note ripped the air. "Harlem Nocturne" soared over the top of the hall. Not a word was spoken during the piece. We all listened, as perhaps many of us never had before, to the pure gutsy sounds cutting out from the silver horn.

When Mr. Braniff finished playing the piece, the crowd remained silent. Perhaps we were all in awe of the sheer guts and daring of the auction organizers. What if this fabled instrument had flopped? What if the pads had been dried out? Or worse. But despite the terrible risk the committee had taken, the instrument seemed to live up to its reputation. The crowd was 100 percent sold. Applause began on one side of the room, and soon all were on their feet, giving a deserved ovation to what might be the best saxophone ever made.

"Mr. Braniff would like our guests to know that he was using a mouthpiece-and-reed setup that would be appropriate for a theater pit band or a big band. These brighter mouthpieces will also usually produce the altissimo notes more easily than very dark-sounding mouthpieces."

I had no idea what he or Braniff was talking about, but still I felt let in on a sly musician's secret. Ah, I thought. A brighter mouthpiece.

The auctioneer, knowing he had us all in the palm of his hand, moved in for the kill. "This amazing Mark VI has been presented to the Woodburn School auction by an anonymous donor. Let's start the bidding at five thousand."

Several hands shot up and in less than ten amazing seconds we were at $25,000.

Holly turned to Wes and me and whispered, "Well, I guess that lets me out."

I laughed.

Wes said, seriously, "I am not sure this instrument is truly worth this kind of money. On eBay, Mark VIs sell in the five thousand–ten thousand range. I realize this one is a better year and in mint condition, but—"

"They sell the sizzle, not the steak," Holly said.

"Hell," I said, "if these people are willing to pay over twenty-six grand for our little lunch with flowers, I figure they aren't exactly hunting for a bargain."

"And they can write off any amount over the fair market value of the saxophone as a charitable contribution," Wes said.

The auctioneer was asking for $30,000 and getting it from a man near the front. Then, all of a sudden, something going on at one of the tables attracted the attention of the crowd. Two men, from that table where Holly had served food earlier, appeared to be sparring. We heard dishes crash to the floor, perhaps upended during a scuffle. At a table nearer to us, a woman turned and announced, "Two fathers. Both have boys in our jazz band."

"Do you know them?" I asked, addressing her directly. I could see nothing from where I was standing.

"I work in the Woodburn office," she said. "I know them. Ryan Hutson's dad and Kirby Knight's dad. Really."

"Please, gentlemen," the auctioneer said into the mike, trying to get things back on track. "Can I hear a bid, please?"

"Fifty thousand," said one of the fathers.

"Oh my God," Holly said. "Did he say *fifty*?"

"One hundred," said the other father.

Applause ripped through the crowded room. We had it all here, folks. A stellar musical performance. An object beyond price. A fistfight. Insanely competitive fathers with no budget constraints in a battle of testosterone and will. It just doesn't get better than this.

And that's when Ryan's father, or maybe it was Kirby's father, began strangling his rival.

"Party's Over"

Usually, I'm one of the last people to leave a party—I'm supervising, I'm carrying things, I'm working—but not this evening. Holly and Wes had it all well in hand, and I had this nagging urge to get back to my house in Whitley Heights and that carton of documents that Albert Grasso had been so excited about. As soon as the live auction ended, I went to the kitchen to grab my bag and headed out through the main entrance of the Tager Auditorium onto a tranquil, postmidnight, traffic-free Grand Avenue in downtown Los Angeles.

At the curb, a trio of uniformed valets (black pants, cool newsprint T-shirts—okay, we were obsessed with our theme) were running to get cars for departing guests. As they brought up the vehicles, the lineup at the curb displayed the latest in luxury SUVs. Silver was the color du jour, I noted. The lacquered finishes on car after car shone bright as a string of silver beads in the light of the streetlamp. Tired men in tuxes went through the ritual of finding their parking stubs, tipping the valets, and taking their princesses home from the ball. I noticed many couples had been successful in the silent auction, as quite a few were loading giant cellophane-wrapped baskets or other large items into the backs of their

SUVs. I handed my ticket to a young man with long sideburns and pulled my silk shawl more firmly around my shoulders.

"Madeline? Are you leaving?"

I looked up to see Connie Hutson, the Woodburn Ball's auction chairwoman. Tall, with a halo of auburn hair and the sort of prominent cheekbones that didn't need quite as much coral-colored blusher as Connie always wore, she was dramatic in white sequined pants. Her matching blazer dipped low, baring lots of tanned chest and a rather amazing diamond pendant.

"Hello, Connie. What a spectacular job you did with the auction!" In speaking to clients after a party, I often gush. Whether it's good PR or just exhaustion on my part, I have yet to determine.

"Ah, it was hell, my dear. Pure hell. But we did raise a staggering amount of money for the Woodburn." She gave me a look, half grimace, half smile.

"Do you have a total?"

"Liz Reed is doing a final tally, but I am simply dead on my feet. I've been here since nine this morning setting up the silent auction tables. Enough is enough."

Of course, I'd been at work even earlier, but it is a rare client who finds that fact compelling. Instead, I expressed my concern for Connie. "You must be so tired. I hope you plan to sleep for a week."

"I wish I could, Madeline. I've simply got too much to do. Ryan comes home from surf camp tomorrow and then he has his sax recital on Thursday, or we would have gone to our Cap Ferrat house and just unwound. Oh, look. Dave is waving at me." She waved back at a handsome man standing farther down the curb who was balancing a neon-yellow splashed, custom-made surfboard, which I remembered seeing on one of the silent auction tables, and turned back to me once more. "Our car isn't here yet, and Dave is not very patient. Well, I just wanted to tell you what a marvelous job you and your firm did for us tonight."

"Thank you."

"And listen, if you see that awful Patsy Stephenson, just whisper to the parking attendants to take their time retrieving her car."

"What? Tell me the scoop," I said, sensing a story.

"Ugh. Patsy. What can I say? She always volunteers to be on my committee and then does absolutely nothing. The rest of us are busting our tails tracking down leads and getting auction items, and she is always too busy or some other excuse. I swear, if her husband didn't give us a check for twenty grand to underwrite the bar, I'd just kick her butt right off the committee."

"Which one is Patsy?" I asked, turning to look at the well-dressed men and women who were continuing to make their way out of the party.

Connie's eyes followed mine and then she turned back. "I don't see her yet. Her daughter plays violin. Actually, the girl is not bad, but the *mother*!" Just then, one of the departing guests caught Connie's attention. "Good night, Mr. Braniff."

"Good night, Mrs. Hutson. Wonderful auction. And say hello to Ryan. Is he practicing?"

"More or less," the mother said, smiling, and then turned back to me. "Sebastian Braniff studied under Marcel Mule. He used to play with Skitch Henderson when he was only a kid in high school. He's my son's private lessons teacher. Wasn't he incredible tonight?"

"Listening to Mr. Braniff play the Selmer was the highlight of this evening."

"Anyway, Patsy," Connie said, easily slipping back to a favorite rant. "Avoid her like the plague."

I count on such insider tips about the private lives of the rich and famous, since I prefer to avoid doing parties and working for the truly beastly. "I'm trying to place her. What does Patsy look like?"

"Let's see. She's blond." Well, that could be almost every woman on the Woodburn Guild. "She's attractive." Ditto. "Her entire manner is off-putting, really. She never made it to even one of our meetings, so I doubt you have seen her. Oh, wait a sec." Connie pulled out the program book for the evening and flipped to one of the opening pages. "How silly of me. Naturally, she did make it to the photo shoot of the committee. There." She pointed to a thin woman in the program picture. "Wearing Gucci. She's so predictable it's galling."

"Oh, Connie. Speaking of off-putting, I had the strangest conversation with one of the Guild ladies. Is a woman named Caroline a good friend of yours? She dates Albert Grasso."

"Caroline Rochette with the terrible plastic surgeon?"

"That could be her. What is she like?"

"She's ghastly, Madeline. Why, what did she do?" Connie Hutson liked to dish the dirt. She enjoyed spit-roasting her friends over the judg-mental flames, but she was even more interested in lighting new fires.

"Well, she's threatening to sue me, actually. It's a long story, but I found some papers that may have belonged to Mr. Grasso. He and Caroline went crazy when I told them I want to return the stuff. I can't imagine why."

"Oh, Caroline doesn't need a reason to go crazy, she's already there, my pet." Connie Hutson chuckled.

"What's that story?"

"Albert's not in a hurry to get married for a fourth time, I suspect. He has a wandering eye. Hell, he has even put moves on me, and my dear, I'm too busy raising Ryan and raising money for good causes to raise any hell."

Connie turned to see Dave tipping the valet and she ran down the last two wide-paved steps and slid into their silver Escalade.

I took a minute to scan the incoming valets and the cars they were driving up to the loading zone, but there was no sign yet of my old black Wagoneer with the woody panels.

"Hello," I called to some new arrivals. Hilary and Mike Entemann were just coming down the wide steps. Mike moved on to take care of the valet while Hilary lingered with me.

"Wasn't the live auction spectacular?" Hilary asked. She was smiling. "Could you believe Brianna Welk yelling at everyone to shut up? We have certainly seen the real Brianna tonight, I'm afraid."

"Her judgment may have been . . . impaired," I suggested, smiling back.

"Exactly," Hilary agreed. She was another exceedingly well-groomed woman in her early forties or so. Her pale hair was swept up and held with a diamond clip. Her black gown clung to her athletic body, showing off her muscle tone to the best advantage. "But she kept the bidding rising on your item. Twenty-six five. That must have felt good."

"It's wild." I liked Hilary. The Entemanns' eleven-year-old twins were fine singers and members of the prestigious Woodburn Honor Chorus, a group that regularly won competitions in Europe and New York. "I'm so excited. Did you see who won my garden party? I'm afraid I was distracted at the time."

"It was Dilly Swinden!"

We both laughed. "Really? Dilly bought it?"

"She was absolutely determined. She's going to invite everyone on the committee to the luncheon."

"How generous," I said. It made a lot of sense, really. It would have been equally generous had Dilly and her husband written as large a check when they made their contribution to the Woodburn's annual fund, but in purchasing this party at the auction, she got more. In addition to making an impressive donation, she could provide a wonderful treat to the women who worked hard to support her in planning this event.

"I think Dil was feeling a little guilty," Hilary said in a low voice. "By June, she and Zenya were simply leaving their committee and the board out of everything. They were calling all the shots. I admit, they did a very nice job, but feathers do ruffle. You know how we are. This luncheon will go a long way to smoothing them down again."

"It sounds wonderful to me," I said.

"They'd like to schedule the party just as soon as possible. Next week, if that is okay with you and your partner. I think most of us are going to escape L.A. in August. So let's coordinate by e-mail and set the date."

The Entemanns' silver Mercedes SUV arrived at the curb and Hilary called out good-bye as she departed. I checked my watch. Where was my Jeep?

"Oh, Mad," Holly called, meeting me out on the steps. "I'm glad I caught you. Sara is in a bind. Sara Jackson, remember? The redhead? She's got to meet her boyfriend. It's urgent. And her car battery is dead. I don't have a car or I'd lend it to her. Wesley drove me here, and he's out now, driving one of the trucks back to the rental-company lot. What should we do?"

I looked at Holly. She was so compassionate. One of our servers, a graduate student at USC, I think, had a boyfriend problem and Holly was ever ready to help.

"Can't one of the other servers give her a lift?" I asked.

"That's the trouble. Mostly everyone has already split. She can wait around until Wes gets back, but that could take hours. I thought about calling him. I've got his spare keys and his car is still here. But I'm supposed to supervise the rest of the cleanup and I can't exactly ask him to lend out his brand-new Jag."

"No."

"Right." Holly fixed me with her bright blue eyes. "See, Sara said it was life or death, Maddie. She's got to see her boyfriend right this minute."

I watched as the valet finally pulled up in my old Grand Wagoneer.

I'm afraid I melt for any young woman with boyfriend problems so urgent. "Just ask her to please drive it back over to my house. Tonight."

"Mad, you're the best!" Holly yelled at me, turning to run and tell Sara.

"I mean it, Holly. And she needs to come in and put the keys on my kitchen table. Give her the combination to the kitchen door lock."

"Thanks, Mad. So how will you get home?"

"I'll catch a ride."

In less than a minute, Holly was leading Sara Jackson down to the valet and I met them so I could tip the guy. Sure, it had taken him twenty minutes to find my car, but even parking attendants have to pay their shrink bills in this town.

Sara climbed into the driver's seat and rolled down the window, giving me a sad smile. "Sorry to be such a burden," she said. "You are being so great. I can't thank you enough. Brett is just raging. His dissertation committee met and he's been told he won't get his degree." As she talked, she pulled out the band that was holding her hair up. As she rubbed her head, pulling the ponytail out, her fine red hair fell straight down her back. "I can't explain, but I don't think it was a good idea for me to leave Brett alone. I told him I couldn't bail on this gig tonight. We need the money. And I knew you were counting on me. I mean, Brett knew I couldn't blow off this job. I'd never be able to work your parties again."

I blushed. It was true. I would have been annoyed if any of tonight's crew hadn't shown. Being short-staffed puts an extra burden on all the other waiters. Hell, I hate being a boss sometimes.

"And then my VW stalled out. I mean, what next?" Sara asked, stress making a deep vertical line between her green eyes. "I'm scared. I know it's just a school thing, but you don't know Brett. He's sensitive. I just have to get home. Thank you so much, Madeline."

"No problem," I said. "So you think you can bring the Jeep back tonight?"

"I promise. You'll have it back in less than an hour."

I believe in helping out true love and all that. But I have heard more crisis stories from more temp workers than you can dream up. I'm all for kindness—but I needed my car, too.

"You sure you're gonna be okay?" Holly asked me, and I shooed her away, laughing. I watched her lean, long form trot back up the steps to the entrance, and when I turned back to the cars, I noticed Zenya Knight, one of the evening's cochairs, standing next to a huge, pristinely white Hummer H1, a tanklike, military-style wagon that goes for like $116,000, and that's without the options. The valet was holding the passenger door open, but Zenya was looking back toward the entrance of the Tager.

"Zenya, you leaving?" I asked, walking fast. Here might just be the wheels to get me home.

"Oh, hi, Maddie. How are you? Bill should be here any minute; he's getting the items we bought at the auction. Wasn't it the *best*? I thought you did a spectacular job on the party. We all owe you so much."

"You're welcome. Of course."

"Did you see Bill had the highest bid on the Selmer?" Zenya was enjoying an after-party high. She was younger than most of the Woodburn women, and filled with enthusiasm, even after such a long, draining day.

"Wow. Congratulations." So it was Zenya's table that was so hot to win the Mark VI tenor saxophone.

"Kirby is going to be out of this world with excitement. He's twelve and he's just going to go nuts. Hell, I think my husband, Bill, may even take sax lessons—and he's a guitar player!"

"Oh, Zenya. The bidding was ferocious, wasn't it?"

She shrugged slender shoulders and smiled. "That Dave Hutson. Honestly, we've known them for years, but Dave is just not a very nice guy, now, is he? Imagine him getting so upset over who was going home with that sax. Really."

"This was a wild auction," I said. "What a finish!"

Zenya tossed her long, thick wavy blond hair and grinned. "No one messes with Bill. Bill told me it would be a shame to see that fine instrument go to that Hutson boy. The boy actually writes out all his solos in advance! That's just not jazz." She looked sorry for the boy. "The dad really shouldn't push Ryan so much, you know? It's sad."

See, here is where I think parents really need to get their own life. But that was me. I steered the conversation back to the bidding. "It was such a generous winning bid, Zenya."

"Oh, Bill can afford it," she said, laughing. "My husband collects art, cars, vintage rock guitars. Over the years, I swear he's paid a fortune for his Stratocasters and whatnot. And he tells me the prices just keep climbing up. You know collectors. They want something and they have to have it now. You should have seen the way his eyes were gleaming when they were describing that saxophone. Anyway, the money goes to a good cause. We can't complain."

I shook my head, wondering what life must be like when one can spend a hundred grand on a whim. My personal reactions moved back and forth between discomfort at how these people seemed to take wealth for granted and gratitude that they supported worthy institutions. The Woodburn School people provide a number of full scholarships to some of the city's least-advantaged kids. And they also donate brand-new instruments to our city's beleaguered public schools. Without the fundraising work and generosity of supporters such as the Knights, these children would not have such wonderful musical opportunities.

"So you're leaving, Madeline?"

"By any chance, Zenya, are you driving near Hollywood on your way home?"

"We could. Do you need a ride?"

"Actually—"

Just then there was a commotion at the entrance. A man in a tuxedo, one of the guests, was standing at the main door to the Tager Auditorium, yelling.

"What's that?" I asked, interrupting myself.

"It's Bill," Zenya Knight said, her face perplexed. "What's he going on about?"

"Zenya!" Bill was calling to his wife and rushing down the steps toward us. "It's the goddamned sax. It's gone. It's disappeared. Can you believe that? I bet you that asshole Dave Hutson stole Kirby's priceless frigging Selmer!"

"DEAR LORD
(Breakdowns and Alternate Take)"

R ich guys. There are just not enough bucks out there to convince me to marry one. I get the part about the fabulous home, the fabulous shopping, the fabulous bling-bling. It's just I also see the huge hunk of her soul a girl has to pay in order to catch a rich guy and keep him. My mom used to tell me it's just as easy to fall in love with a rich guy as a poor guy . . . but it really isn't. Not for me. And judging by my father's modest teaching income, not for my mom either. So what the hell was she talking about?

"Saddle up!" yelled Bill Knight as he pulled open the trunk hatch, tossing in a heavy gift basket, and jumped onto the driver's seat of the incredibly large, incredibly white Hummer H1, ready to roll.

"Bill," called his wife breathlessly, "I told Madeline that we'd be happy to drive her—"

"Get in, y'all!" Bill commanded.

Both Zenya and I trotted around the white behemoth and jumped in.

"Are you sure—"

"*Come on!*"

I was not quite certain catching a ride home with the enraged Texan and his young wife was such a good idea.

Bill was still fuming. "Can you believe it, Zenya? I am just betting that Dave Hutson took our sax." His short, steely-gray hair seemed to bristle as he punched the gas pedal, jerking the gargantuan tank away from the curb with a burst of pent-up horsepower, nearly mowing down the parking attendant, and then slammed on his brakes at the last second. "Jeeesus!" he yelled. "Get that guy out of my frigging way!"

"Oh, dear." Zenya sighed, mostly to herself.

"If you want to let me off here . . . ?" I had *more* than second thoughts. I was trapped in a mammoth-size luxury vehicle with a madman who had just been robbed of his "precious." Holy cow.

"We'll get you home." Bill Knight's voice was tight and I could guess he didn't really want to hear much more from me in the backseat. I pulled on the seat belt and fastened it just as our tank cranked into a torque-frenzied sharp right turn.

Zenya sat quietly in front. "What did they tell you?" she asked, her voice holding just a hint of quiet concern. "Did they really say Dave took our saxophone?"

"No one knows *what* happened, Zenya," Bill said, frustration and anger making him mock her. "It was just *gone*."

"But the instrument case . . . ?" she asked.

"The case was there. Lucky I insisted they unlock it and show me the sax. And well, looky there, it was gone. Like they thought I'd hand over a hundred-thousand-dollar check and not even look at my sax? Right."

In the well-lit, almost vacant avenues of downtown, the extraordinary stainless-steel-clad Disney Concert Hall, with its massive silvery swoops and flips, loomed over us as Bill slowed before he took another turn.

"I'm sure it'll all get straightened out," Zenya said.

"Like hell it will. I was ticked off that they let Sebastian play the Selmer. That was bad enough. But now, who knows? Maybe that asshole Hutson is going to wake up his boy tonight and let him play it. I bought a sax in pristine, mint, *new* condition. Now that sure ain't what they are delivering, I can tell you."

"Oh, dear," Zenya said again.

I could see her face reflected in the side mirror. Despite her husband's aggressive driving, she remained serene. Zenya Knight was not like the other Woodburn committee women. She was probably only a few years older than me, maybe midthirties, tops. She seemed softer, more passive than some of the Woodburn women I'd dealt with. While the other women were undoubtedly attractive—their beauty was premeditated. These wealthy women had begun to take on an artificial sameness, hair all highlighted to perfection, acrylic nails polished, this body part reduced or that body part enlarged by gifted cosmetic surgeons. Dressed expensively in the same designer labels, they had become more perfect and less individual. In contrast, Zenya had genuinely lovely skin, a naturally youthful face, true beauty. Needless to say, Zenya was a second wife.

"Bill, we need to drop Madeline at her home. She's in the Hollywood Hills," Zenya said.

"I really appreciate this lift," I said, trying to get back to polite small talk.

"Zenya, I'll be damned!" Bill Knight was yelling again. "Who the hell is that in the silver Escalade up ahead."

We were just slowing down for a red light, all the more ridiculous as it was almost one in the morning and there were only two other cars on the entire eight lanes of First Street. These cars were slowing to a stop ahead of us, following traffic laws, despite the fact that there was no cross-traffic whatsoever. "Isn't that Dave Hutson up ahead of that Beemer? I'll be damned. Dave Hutson thinks he's making his getaway!"

"What are you going to do?" Zenya asked.

"Maybe I should just run him down. If that frigging BMW wasn't stopped right between our cars, I think I'd just give it a try. The Hummer could do it, too."

I gulped.

"Did I tell you, Madeline," Bill called back as we waited out the light, "that the Hutson boy, Ryan Hutson, can't play a lick?"

See, I realize Bill Knight is a successful businessman. I get that he's an old rich guy and used to getting his way. Sure, he's a little high-strung. I just wished like hell I wasn't strapped into his car, right about then, as the man envisioned pulling troop maneuvers over another man's Cadillac.

"You hear me okay back there, Madeline?" Bill called.

"Sure thing."

"I say, this Hutson kid isn't really much of a sax player. He got into the jazz band at the Woodburn, but it's pretty clear he doesn't belong there. The boy is a fair sight-reader, I'll give him that. He can read the sheet music a bit. But the thing is, he can't go off the page. He can't improvise. He's got no brain for it. And ear? Hell, that Hutson kid has no damn ear whatsoever, does he, Zenya?"

"Now, Bill. Ryan is a very nice boy," Zenya said, in her soft way. "He really is."

"I'm talking about an ear for jazz now, darling. Not whether we should invite the kid over to swim in our pool. But what I'm telling Madeline here is this Ryan is not like our Kirby. Kirby is a gifted individual and he can play the pants off of that Ryan Hutson."

Mercifully, the light changed. But that was when Bill Knight, fueled by smoking martinis, goaded by the pain of seeing his prize Selmer disappear, and empowered by the heft of a vehicle the likes of which Arnold Schwarzenegger drives, hit the gas.

"Hold on," Zenya called back to me, grabbing the side rail above the passenger door. I gripped the side of the table that is conveniently placed in the middle of the backseat, just in case anyone was in the mood for a picnic. And then to her husband she asked, "Bill, what are you doing?"

"Watch what you say, Zenya," he answered. "I've gotten rid of better wives than you, darling, for saying less."

See? Didn't I tell you the marrying-a-rich-guy thing was wildly overrated? How many vacations in Paris are worth withstanding such contempt? How many Rolexes? How many six-hundred-dollar pairs of heels?

Zenya just laughed a girlish laugh.

Well, perhaps I'm more sensitive than some.

"Here we go!" Bill had managed to shoot out and pass the BMW X5 and gun the Hummer right up behind the Escalade. "Looks like Dave is driving a new car. Let's say hello."

The large Hummer H1 closed in on the back of Dave Hutson's SUV. "They don't know we're here," Bill said, bugged at being ignored. "Can you believe this guy? He's not even worried about driving off with my saxophone. How do you like . . ." At that point, the front of the Hummer made contact with the back of the brand-new Cadillac Escalade. Holy shit. ". . . that?" Bill asked.

The horn blared from the car we'd just struck. Then it pulled into gear and barreled off, turning sharply up a nearly deserted Figueroa.

"Bill . . ." Zenya's voice was light, if slightly agitated.

"Drop me off anyplace here, folks."

"So Hutson believes his Caddy can outrun this cruiser? I don't think so," Bill said, and he gunned the engine, pulling across the double yellow lines and right up beside the Cadillac. We were now driving on the wrong side of the street, side by side, as both vehicles shot down the boulevard with their speeds, as near as I could tell, approaching fifty. Bill Knight pushed the button that rolled the power window down next to Zenya. "Pull over, Dave!"

The tinted window of the Cadillac SUV slid down and a round, red-faced man started yelling. "You're crazy, Knight. You're going to pay for the damage to my car." Connie Hutson, seated beside him, looked as pale as a piece of white bread despite her excess makeup.

"Right. Just subtract it from the hundred thousand dollars you owe me for stealing the goddamned saxophone, moron."

"Screw you!"

Just then, up about a block ahead, from out of nowhere, a lone Toyota Tercel carefully turned the corner. It found itself smack in our lane, aiming straight at us. Never mind that the small red car was in the proper lane and we weren't—we were doing nearly sixty miles per hour and we weighed just over seven thousand pounds. Let's say Mr. Tercel wasn't too proud to launch his car quickly up on the curb in order to avoid certain annihilation.

"Bill, this is getting dangerous."

"Not to us, darling. To that bastard Hutson. He could have pulled his car over anytime, but then he'd have to face arrest charges for stealing our property."

While we were avoiding getting ourselves tangled with the Tercel, Dave Hutson and his shocked wife had made another sharp turn, heading down Ninth Street. Bill cursed. We had already charged through the intersection, missing Ninth, but now Bill put his foot on the break and tried to pull a fast 180-degree turn. Not the H1's best move. Luckily, there was no traffic here, because the Hummer is a hugely wide, hugely tall, hugely heavy vehicle, one big enough and bad enough to strap a missile launcher to its hood, and I, for one, was thanking God Bill Knight hadn't ordered that option. But all that torque or G-force or whatever the hell was now pulling at us hard, swinging us out way too wide. A few seconds of painful tire screeching and we had overshot the street and blasted up on the sidewalk, picking up speed. In a few seconds more I realized we were about to barrel right back into the dazed Tercel, still hanging up on the curb. Hell.

"Excuse me, I hate to be a bother, but . . ." I was sure I could jump out if he would slow down for just a minute.

"Oh, don't worry," Zenya said, waving her hand like you'd dismiss a small indiscretion, like a lunch guest spilling her water glass, "it's just boys having fun with their toys."

"You think I'm having fun?" Bill hollered, and swung down onto the street just a few feet before he would have surely plowed into the stuck Tercel.

Zenya smothered a giggle. I smothered a scream. Bill maneuvered the turn onto Ninth.

"Where is he?" yelled Bill, searching the street.

"It seems he's escaped," Zenya said, also looking for the Cadillac that got away.

Bill began slowing down and turned to his wife. "You got the Woodburn directory?"

"I think so, but—"

"Give me their address. We'll surprise the Hutsons at home."

"Oh, Bill . . ."

"They live in Pasadena. What's the street?" Bill demanded.

"Looks like I have just about enough time to hop out," I said, not waiting for the car to come to a complete halt. I opened the door as Bill said, "Hey, wait. We'll get you home, sweetheart." He actually sounded, despite a touch of maniacal road rage, like a pretty sweet guy.

I was down on the sidewalk before Zenya could add her promise that they would take me home right after Bill "got this out of his system."

"I'll be fine," I assured them, and in a roar of exhaust they were off.

Only when I was standing there in my best high heels, in the still of the night on squalid South Broadway, as a breeze blew some litter into the gutter and swallowed the fading roar of the departing Hummer's engine, did I realize that I'd managed to leave my purse on the cute backseat table. Damn it all. I had no money. I had no cell phone. And I was standing in the middle of a deserted street, in a deserted section of a pretty freaking deserted downtown, way past midnight.

"I Guess I'll Have to
Change My Plan"

I considered my options.

I could walk all the way back to the Woodburn. I might still catch Wesley and Holly before they left for the night. But then . . . It could take me half an hour to toddle on over there in my wicked black satin sandals, probably longer. And what if I hiked all that way and they were gone, the lights were out, and the place was locked up for the night? I would be no better off than I was now. I considered the eerie ghost town of silent office towers, giant plazas, and public buildings all around me. Not that I was scared of being out alone at night. I could take care of myself. But I preferred to find the comfort of civilization, or what passes for it in Southern California.

L.A.'s downtown nightlife is spotty. Our party at the Tager Auditorium had been the liveliest thing going for blocks. And that was a couple of miles north and west. Now that the ball was over, there were few vehicles on the street. For instance, this section of Broadway was definitely not hopping. The once stately buildings here are old and decrepit. During the day, this street is jammed—a lively marketplace with a Hispanic flavor, crowded with shoppers—but now storefront upon storefront was locked down tight, metal security shutters covering all windows and doors for blocks.

I really half expected the Knights to return to their senses and come back for me. But as that was not panning out, I began walking as I continued considering my options. I wasn't entirely enthusiastic about the option of ducking into any hole-in-the-wall bar, either, should I happen to stumble across one, because (a) it was too near closing time for comfort, and (b) we were a mere vagrant's throw from the Nickel, the section of Fifth Street that has become L.A.'s skid row.

I could walk to one of the hotels downtown. I could explain my situation and ask to use a phone and call a friend and get saved. But I was more resourceful than that. This was my adopted city and I could take care of myself. And then the fog of possibilities began to clear. I actually said aloud, "The Red Line."

Los Angeles has a rather new if admittedly limited subway system. The best part was, the track ran right under downtown and there was a stop at Hollywood and Highland, easy walking distance to my house. I suppose it is shameful that I hadn't ridden public transportation since I'd moved to L.A., but just stop anyone here and ask if they even know what the Red Line *is*? Anyone except Wesley, I mean. Naturally, Wesley studied the plans, followed the morass of problems with its construction, and rode on the subway on its inaugural day. But that was Wes.

I was giving myself props because I knew all about it and I was just bursting with civic pride about the Red Line now. Simply bursting. And as I was practically on Seventh Street, I took a turn and began trotting toward Flower, where the Red Line station was waiting, saying a silent prayer of thanks to Wes for his long and at the time overly detailed reports. I had purpose in my step. I could take care of myself. I tried to keep my head-swiveling-to-check-if-I-was-being-followed-by-a-homicidal-stalker to a minimum.

Instead, I focused on not twisting an ankle in the enormous cracks in the sidewalk, on how resilient I was feeling about getting myself home in the big, bad city, and on just how I was going to come up with the dollar and change it would take to ride the Red Line train. I had hoped I'd find a few generous folks near the entrance to the metro station who might give a break to a young lady dressed in a thousand-dollar gown, even though I could hardly tell them I got it for 70 percent off. You know, depend on the kindness of strangers. But I began realizing it was pretty late for travelers. In fact, the entrance to the station, still about a block away, seemed fairly deserted.

Focused as I'd been on looking up ahead, scouting out late-night commuters from whom I might borrow the fare, I had not been paying close enough attention to my immediate surroundings. So I was startled—shocked, actually—by some nearby movement.

There, low in the shadows up against the building, something quite close to me had moved. My eyes readjusted to see into the recess of the building's entrance.

It was a man. He appeared to be sitting on the sidewalk. Well, lying was closer to the truth of it. He was semipropped against the building, with a jar on the ground and a rather sweet, if filthy, shepherd mix asleep beside him. The dog looked up as my heels click-clacked closer.

I had the best idea. What if this man might want to lend me the fare? The dog kept his eyes on me, but didn't move. I sort of hated the idea of waking the man, though. By his old clothes and the aroma of alcohol, I figured he could probably use all the sleep he could grab. And then I saw the quarters and dimes in the bottom of the jar.

It's not that I believe in fate exactly, but what are the odds that a desperate woman is walking alone down an empty street in the wee hours of the morning with only one need—and that would be exactly $1.35—and in almost the very next block she would come across a jar with change, just sitting there? Even I have to bow to a higher power, here.

I slowed and said, "Ahem." The man didn't budge. The dog raised his head and sort of smiled at me.

"Hi there, fella," I said, in my friendly-to-kids-and-dogs voice. "Are you a happy dog or an angry dog?"

I got no response. "Here's my problem," I told the dog just as his companion let out a soft snore. "I need a little money to get on the train that will take me home. It's called the Red Line, you know. We're pretty dang proud of it here in downtown Los Angeles."

The pooch stared at me.

"Well, anyway. I need a little money so I can buy a subway ticket, but the problem I was telling you about is, I lost my purse. Can you believe that? I know where it is, actually, but I can't get to it right now. So, here's my question."

Another soft snore came from the man. The dog was calm, but looking a little bored.

"My question is, do you think I can borrow a dollar thirty-five? I will return it with interest. In fact, I'll come back here tomorrow and give your master a ten-dollar reward for his help. What do you think?"

The dog didn't seem too stressed by the idea. He laid his head back down and I took that to mean, "Go ahead, help yourself."

It wasn't really stealing if you planned all along to give the money back, was it? Under better circumstances, I would certainly have left him my business card, but of course I keep my cards in my purse. And at this precise moment, my purse was in a hundred-thousand-dollar armored vehicle, which, for all I knew, was ramming into a mansion in Pasadena while its crazed driver screamed for his lost Selmer Mark VI.

I reached down for the jar, keeping my eye on the dog.

"This is just a loan. I promise," I promised the dog as I scooped out five quarters and a dime from the dirty glass jar that still had the Clausen's Dill Pickle label semiattached.

I put the jar back quietly and shot a glance at the sleeping man. He hadn't stirred. And, minding my manners, I said, "Thank you, doggy. I'll see you tomorrow, okay?"

I raced up the block to the Red Line station, feeling elated to be on my way home. This had been, admittedly, an odd evening. Not that there wasn't something a little odd about most of the events that our company organizes—parties bring out the oddest behavior imaginable—but tonight was getting to be some kind of record. Not only had the live auction turned ugly, but a priceless saxophone had apparently been stolen. Add to that the bizarre chase scene in the streets between two crazed dads and the fact that I'd just had to roll a drunk to get enough money to take the subway home, and I think even Holly and Wes would agree, this evening deserved a special monument in hell all to itself.

And that was even before the sign on the entrance to the Red Line station had time to sink in. THE LAST TRAIN LEAVES UNION STATION WEST-BOUND TO NORTH HOLLYWOOD AT 11:33 P.M. I looked at my watch: 1:38.

Well, no wonder, then, that the street outside the station had seemed so deserted. The last train had left over two hours ago. Damn the Red Line! Damn public transportation!

So okay, I may not know everything there is to know about train schedules, but there is something I do know about. I know every late-night restaurant there is in the 213 area code, and one of the oldest and coolest was just a block west and two blocks south of where I was standing.

It turns out our former Mayor Richard Riordan's legacy wasn't just the Democratic National Convention and the Walt Disney Concert Hall. It's also the landmark diner he owns, a twenty-four-hour T-bone-lover's haven in downtown Los Angeles, the Original Pantry Café. They say it opened in 1924 and it's never closed for an hour since, a legend in a town with less history to boast of than it likes.

I suddenly realized I was starving. It would be kind of nice to slip out of these shoes and order one of the Pantry's famous breakfasts, the #4, which gets you ham, bacon, or sausage, one egg, two pancakes, potatoes, and a cup of joe for only $5.95. I was already humming to myself, my Red Line woes behind me, as I turned down Figueroa, deciding I could use the money I had "borrowed" from the wino to phone Wesley. I liked to be self-reliant, of that there's no doubt. But I wasn't going to make a religion out of it. Maybe Wes and Holly would join me for at the Pantry for breakfast. And bring cash.

There was a whole different vibe on Fig. For one thing, there was some light traffic passing by, which made the scene instantly appear a lot less Twilight Zone surreal. For another, I could see the lit-up Pantry off another block. Dwarfed as it was by the skyscraper office towers around it, it still had the comforting aura of hot food and warm folks inside. In fact, there was actually a line of waiting-to-be-seated patrons coming out the door. At 1:30 A.M. on a Sunday morning. Hot dog! I hurried along, tying my shawl to keep it from flapping.

Just then, I noticed a sporty little car, a dark BMW something, slowing down, pacing me. I hurried some more and the car matched my pace. Good grief. I was so close to people and safety and food!

There was a lone guy inside and in that instant I got it. Look at me. I was wearing a low-cut black gown with a slit up to there and what used to be some pretty spectacular high heels. His window lowered and he said, "Hey, hello."

I probably shouldn't have looked over at him, but I was curious. And then surprised. He was a nice-looking guy. Quite nice-looking. I kept walking.

"Hi," he said, stopping his car a few feet from me..

I remembered the first time I watched *Pretty Woman* and smiled to myself. This guy wasn't Richard Gere, but he did have an aura of wealth, not to mention amazing great wavy hair, a lean, worked-out kind of body, and great, intelligent eyes. "Sorry," I said, still walking swiftly. I was close enough to the Pantry to yell for help if I had to. "I'm not the kind of girl you're looking for."

"Don't be so sure," the guy in the car said, again keeping pace with me, driving slow.

"Sorry," I said, noticing his hands on the steering wheel, strong hands, and the dimple in his cheek. "You're not my type."

"I can change," he offered. Again, the dimple. Now, what was this fairly cool guy with a laid-back sense of humor doing cruising around downtown at this hour? Didn't he know most of the hookers hung out in Hollywood?

Ever helpful to handsome tourists, I stopped right outside the Pantry and kept talking. "You know, you should try Santa Monica Boulevard, west of Highland."

"Can't do that," he said, smiling up at me. "I'm going to take you home."

The two guys at the tail end of the waiting customer line outside the Pantry turned to listen to our conversation. As I joined the line, my admirer kept his car idling next to the sidewalk.

"And what," I asked, with exaggerated force, perhaps inspired by the fact that I was defending my honor in front of a little audience, "makes you think I would ever put one foot in your car?"

"Well, I'm making the assumption here that you are Madeline Bean. And if you are, my sister Zenya sent me to take you home. I've been driving all over the upper-class-forsaken streets of this city for at least forty minutes just looking for you."

I stared at him. "What?"

"You must be tired. Want to get in and I'll drive you home?"

"You're Zenya's brother?"

"All my life."

"Prove it."

"She's a sweetheart. She's blond."

He had dark blond hair, cut kind of long. I kept looking at him.

"You want more? She's married to a jerk named Bill Knight. I've got a cool nephew named Kirby."

Ah, well. Look here. I was being minded by Zenya's brother.

On the downside, it appeared that my slit skirt hadn't attracted some adorable, random, night-cruising scum. On the bright side, it appeared I hadn't been abandoned after all. Zenya wasn't going to let me wander helplessly in the streets. While that husband of hers might have been out of his gourd with battle-tank fantasies of revenge, still, leave it to Zenya to call her brother and send him out to find me. "What instrument does Kirby play?" I asked.

"Kirby plays the sax," the man said, smiling. "Tenor sax. He's pretty good, too."

"Damn. I thought you were trying to buy my favors," I said.

The two guys who had been openly eavesdropping were told by the Pantry's host to move forward, and they went reluctantly in the door and to their table.

"Want to hop in?" the man asked, gesturing to his passenger seat.

"I don't even know your name. What if you are an extremely clever liar?"

"My name is Dexter Delano Wyatt." He looked out at me from the window of his neat little Z4. "You are something else, Madeline. I've come to rescue you and you won't let me."

Wasn't that about the story of my life? "Well, you look suspicious," I said coyly.

"You are even more paranoid and delusional than the girls I normally date. Which, if you only knew me better, you would find remarkable."

The Pantry's host opened the door once more and this time looked at me. "One?" he asked, brisk and efficient.

"Why don't you join me for breakfast," I suggested, turning to Dexter. "I can use your cell phone to check up on you. And don't try anything funny. I have friends at the LAPD, you know."

"Ah," said Dexter, "that makes you all the more desirable."

I laughed.

"I'll go park the car," he said.

I may have been dumped on the side of the road. And I may have misjudged the Red Line schedule. But my night was beginning to get just a little bit brighter.

"I Want to Talk About You"

And so, eventually, Dexter Wyatt drove me home. But first we'd had a fairly hilarious early-morning breakfast at the Pantry while Dex dialed his family and friends to give me instant character references. "To set Madeline's mind at ease," he explained to all on his cell phone. "she's still squirrelly." I talked to his sister Zenya who was bursting with apologies. She had managed to get Bill calmed down and they were already at home. I talked to Dex's college roommate from Penn, who said Dex was a decent-enough guy except for his habit of waking up East Coast friends at 5:30 A.M. Connecticut time on a Sunday morning. I talked to Dex's high school girlfriend, Mary Kate, who was now married to a Beverly Hills gastroenterologist, and seemed unworried by the call or the late hour, since she was up with her seven-month-old twins. They all agreed that Dexter was an easygoing guy who had a tendency to avoid conflicts, steady work, and marriage.

Over freshly scrambled eggs and refills of hot coffee, Dexter Wyatt and I had one of those weird, off-center, very personal conversations that can only happen between strangers at 2:30 A.M. Dexter admitted he was never going to fall in love completely.

"You may not have met the right person yet," I suggested.

"That's nice of you to say." Dex put his coffee cup down and gave me a slow smile. "But you know I probably have. I've met lots of right women. I've even been involved with a few. But they all figure out I'm not the right person to get involved with."

"Because . . . ?"

"Because," he said carefully, "I am a guy whose mother died when he was eleven. A guy who doesn't have a lot of faith that someone you love will make it until next week. A guy without much trust in life. In a nutshell."

"How did your mother die?"

"Cancer. I can almost remember when she was healthy. Mostly what I remember was that she was sick and then sicker and then she was gone. But things like that happen. Anyway, that was over twenty years ago. It's an old, old scar." Dex took in my concerned expression and began to laugh. "Hey, this is one romantic conversation, isn't it? So tell me why you believe in love."

"Who said I believe in love?"

"You don't?"

"Well, no. I do. But not just because I'm a 'girl' and we're programmed to want to fall in love or anything. I know that's what you think."

"You do?"

"Of course I do. You think there is a conspiracy among womankind to find husbands. To this end, you think we go out at night wearing sexy dresses and strappy sandals scouting out men with nice cars and good hair. And pretty soon everyone thinks they're in love. When they—or I should really say you—are most vulnerable, the woman will demand to be married and have babies and tie you down for the rest of your life, making you work like a dog to pay for private school and braces."

He looked at me across the table, a smile still on his lips. "Pretty impressive."

"Now here is the truly sad part. You need to believe women are out there trying to trap you into serious relationships."

"I do?"

I nodded. "So you avoid finding a steady career. You travel. You knock around. You won't take life or commitments or relationships seriously. But I'm just suggesting here that after you spend like ten years in therapy, you'll see it's all about protecting your heart from another horrible blow, like when your mother left you. In the meantime, these defenses of yours are costing you a real life. They're killing your chance to find a love that could really, truly heal your soul."

"More coffee?" asked Porter, our waiter, with perfect timing.

"So how much do you charge for that wisdom?" Dex asked, meeting my eyes.

"You don't want to know," I said, laughing.

"And what about you?" Dex asked, teasing. "Have you found love to be all that comforting and healing?"

"Me?" I pulled a handful of my reddish curls off my shoulder and smiled up at him. "Of course not. I was only speaking *theoretically*."

"Naturally," Dex said, pouring just the right amount of cream into my cup, stirring in just the right half packet of Sweet 'n Low. Clever boy. He had a gift for observation.

"In my own life, Dexter, I haven't managed the love thing at all well. I was seeing a cop. Honnett. He's married, apparently, and hadn't bothered to tell me the finer points. I guess he was separated, but then she wants to start seeing a shrink. You hear about this kind of thing all the time. So all along I thought we were building up some trust and some caring. I had hoped he and I might be right for each other. I had hoped he would see I made a difference in his life. But I can't ignore his past. The past is a powerful thing."

"That it is."

By the time Dexter Wyatt and I had left the Pantry, our conversation had lightened the heck back up. We were both amused at finding someone who shared a wry sense of humor, underlined as it was by the odd way we'd met. As Dexter transitioned his BMW onto the Hollywood Freeway, I appreciated, as only one who has drunk a few too many cups of coffee can, our strange first encounter, one that only a very jaded and playful fate could concoct.

"I'm glad," Dex said, as if reading my thoughts, "that if my jerk brother-in-law had to kick some chick out of his Hummer, and if I had to be the one called away from a poker game to fix things, that you were the chick that needed help and I found you."

"Thank you."

"Even though I was holding a winning hand at the time."

"Sainted sacrifice."

Dex watched the traffic and changed lanes, heading off at Cahuenga, the freeway exit nearest my house.

"And I'm glad that if I had to lend my car to a waitress in order to be abandoned downtown in order to make my way to the Pantry, in order to be sort of picked up by a virtual stranger, that you were the stranger, and that it could be said I tipped my hat to providence."

"You don't wear a hat."

"Figuratively."

"You are a trouper," Dex said heartily as he slowed and turned up Whitley.

"I hope it could be said of me," I added, filled with a hearty breakfast and comfy on Dexter's leather upholstered seats, "that Madeline enjoyed the journey, no matter how bumpy."

"You know, of course, that you have begun speaking about yourself in the third person."

"Has she?" I smiled at him. "She apologizes."

And then I noticed the police cars. There were three out in front of my house. There were mobile news vans parked in the street, and yellow tape across the gate to my house that read, POLICE LINE—DO NOT CROSS.

"DARKNESS"

This can't be good," Dex commented, his eyes shifting up, following a flight of picturesque steps on the hillside. We had been chatting all the way home, but now were struck silent. He found a spot to park as we both studied the strange activity surrounding the small Mediterranean-style house at the end of Whitley Avenue. My house.

The property, featuring beautiful old palm trees and great pots filled with exotic plants, perches snugly on the upslope at the end of the block. There it dead-ends right smack into the side of the Hollywood Freeway. I might like to think of my neighborhood as quaint and "Old Hollywood-y" but in the fifties this lovely area was cut right through by the construction of the 101. My palm-frondy side of Whitley forms a cul-de-sac now, where above us eight lanes of cars, zooming northbound and southbound, are hidden from view by the thirty-foot retaining wall. As for the late-night traffic beyond the wall, what we couldn't see we definitely could hear. It's funny what you can get used to when you don't have a lot of money and you are facing the insanely high prices of Los Angeles real estate.

All this was the usual thing. What wasn't usual were all the police types and media types who were presently milling about in the cul-de-sac and up the steps to my house.

"I don't know what's going on," I said, slamming the car door and walking fast, taking in the entire scene, including a familiar black Mustang convertible parked near the curb, "but I think you're about to meet my cop friend, Honnett."

"You lead an interesting postmidnight life, Madeline."

I nodded.

"Think he brought his wife along?" asked Dex.

"Shut up," I said politely, and pushed past a reporter I recognized from the local news. He didn't seem to know me, but then why should he? On the other hand, and more important, what was he doing out in the street in front of my house at three-thirty in the morning?

There was a uniformed police officer standing at the bottom of the flight of steps that leads up to my front door. When he noticed Dexter and me approaching, he glanced at us sharply, but quickly covered it with expressionless cop cool. "And you are . . . ?" he asked.

"Madeline Bean and a friend. This is my house. What's going on? Have I been robbed?"

"You live here?" he asked slowly.

"Brilliant guess," Dex said.

Oh, terrific. Dex was going to start something, for goodness sake.

"What's your name?" the officer asked Dex, his voice still even. "Let's see some ID on both of you."

Oh, brother.

"Look. This is a friend of mine who is dropping me off." This morning was definitely not going well. "I don't have my driver's license handy right now. In fact, I don't have my purse. I've had a really crappy last few hours and now there is police tape all over my house. What," I asked, my voice getting more heated, "the hell is going on in there? Why are you here? Can you please, please, *please* just tell me so we can get on with this?"

"I'm not letting—"

But before the officer could finish, I shot past him and ran up the stairs. Dexter, right behind me, tried the same move, but with a half second more to react, the cop grabbed him and slammed his body against the stucco retaining wall.

While my neighborhood is filled with lovely older homes built in Hollywood's early heyday, and the palm trees and yucca plants are lush, it is a fact of life that there is crime in these hills. Living on this cul-de-sac could fool anyone into thinking they were safe, but the creeps from Ivar Street and Selma were rather too close for comfort. Druggies looking for valuables to hock were a big problem. And for any felon looking for a quiet block or two of nice homes with a quick escape route only an easy freeway exit away, this area was sometimes a little too attractive.

I was wired on caffeine and weary from a long night and it looked like I had something very wrong going on at the house. I swore out loud as I topped the outside landing and again realized I didn't have my cell phone on me. I couldn't call Wesley yet. I had to get in the house.

The front door was ajar and all the lights were on inside. As I stepped into the entry hall that held Holly's reception desk, I heard the rumble of low voices coming from upstairs, the part of the house where I live, and there were other sounds coming from farther back on the main floor.

I walked quickly through my office and back into the kitchen. Three men and a woman stood around the room working. They were using small brushes to dust black powder over several spots on the white-tiled countertop, and on the wall near my back door, and on the door itself. They had a collection of things in plastic bags. This was too much. I had no time to deal with a break-in. I was too tired.

Near them stood a tall man with his back to me. I could tell from the way his white shirt stretched across his shoulders and then tucked into the narrow waistband of his faded jeans that it was Honnett, even before I noticed that his dark hair looked a little longer and had more gray mixed in than I remembered.

"Chuck, what the hell is going on?" I asked. Okay, I asked it sharply. Maybe I even yelled it.

Honnett turned and looked at me. His face wore an expression I'd never seen on it before.

"Maddie?"

"No one will tell me what happened. The guy downstairs wouldn't even let—"

In three fast strides Honnett was over to me and smothering my mouth with kisses. I put my hands on his chest to push him away, to get my bearings, to adjust to this new angle. "What the hell . . . ?" I said, sputtering.

"Maddie. We thought you were . . . I thought you were dead."

His words had no meaning to me.

"There's a body upstairs."

"A body?" I pulled back from his arms. I simply couldn't understand what language he was speaking. I had no reaction at all as he kept on explaining.

"In your bedroom. Upstairs. In your bed. I thought it was you."

My hand flew up to my mouth and muffled my words. "Oh my God."

"I didn't go into your room," Honnett said, still explaining. "I just thought . . . Can you believe that? I should have gone in, but I couldn't do it yet. The call came in over two hours ago. Gunshots reported. There was a break-in. A woman was shot. She's dead. I thought it was—"

"They found a dead woman in my bedroom? How can this be happening?" I turned away, but couldn't move. I couldn't sort out my thoughts, so fast did they rush one upon another. I was numb to the idea there had been a death in my house. It just couldn't be true. And what was with Honnett? His first reaction was to hold me and kiss me? Hadn't he just a few months back decided to leave me? What was with men, anyhow?

In my confusion and shock, I found myself more worried about what was going on between Honnett and me now than about the awful crime that had gone on in my house. It was easier to grasp, this anger at a man who had hurt me. This shame at realizing I wanted to pause, just push all this other business aside, so I could recall Honnett's exact expression, moments before, when he looked up and saw me, and how warm and safe and fierce it felt when he was kissing me. I shuddered.

It was the murder. In my life, there had been some deaths that had hit me extra hard. It seemed I had another one to deal with. I pushed my heavy hair back and took stock. Here I was, wearing my sexiest black dress with a slit up to my thigh, standing in my kitchen in the early-morning hours, while a woman I'd never set eyes on before, a criminalist, picked up what could have been a single strand of hair from my kitchen drain with a long pair of tweezers, and a man I'd never seen before blew black powder on my huge center island, and a guy I had been hung up on—a man who had walked out on me, but who was back now, big as life— apparently wanted just to hold me. And for all of that, I simply couldn't get myself to concentrate on the big thing. I had yet to experience any reaction to a mystery woman who might be dead in my bed. I mean, it couldn't have seemed less real to me.

"Oh, Maddie," Honnett said, putting his arms around me again, unable to resist touching me. I wanted to relax into him. Why not? I could be angry at him tomorrow. Or I could forgive him tomorrow. Or he could go back to his wife tomorrow. I just wanted to feel better right now. But something in his manner had changed. His voice was tight. "Don't tell me Holly was staying here tonight."

Holly.

I stiffened in his arms and he felt it. All of a sudden the problem about a woman's body upstairs got terribly real. I pushed my way out of the kitchen, heading for the stairs, and began running.

Holly. Oh, that just couldn't be. She had stayed on at the Woodburn and worked on closing the party with Wes. I realized that had to have been hours ago, but she wouldn't be here. She couldn't be. She would have gone off to Wesley's house. Or gone home to Donald. But Donald was out of town for a couple of weeks. I got to the landing and was met by two detectives, both casually dressed with sport jackets thrown over jeans. This was not Honnett's case, apparently.

"And who are *you?*" asked one of the men, the shorter one with the least hair but the best cheekbones. He was soft-spoken and polite and more easygoing than I would have expected.

"I'm Madeline Bean. This is my house."

For a minute, all I received were silent stares.

"Madeline Bean?" the soft-spoken one repeated, looking at the other fellow. They were taking a second or two to digest the news. If *I* was Madeline Bean, who the hell was the body in the bedroom? It's not hard to figure out what detectives are thinking.

"So you came home to a real nightmare, Miss Bean. Sorry about that," said the detective, his eyes watching me thoughtfully. "This is my partner, Detective Hilts. I'm Detective Ed Baronowski."

I nodded. By then, Honnett had joined us on the landing and shook his head. "Ed, I should have looked at the body. I—"

"Don't worry about it," said Hilts, the taller, muscle-bound guy with the tight, curly brown hair, cut short.

Baronowski kept his eyes on me. "So who's gonna answer the million-dollar question? Who is it in the bed?"

My house is not large. The short hallway upstairs holds just three small bedrooms and a decent-size bathroom. The largest bedroom is actually decorated as a living room, with a sofa in front of the fireplace. The middle room is used as a library/dining room. And the smallest bedroom contains my bed.

They all stared at me, waiting.

"I have no idea. No one is staying with me."

"You married, Madeline?" Baronowski asked softly.

"No."

"What about a boyfriend? You know, maybe he might have brought a friend to the house when you were out?"

I flushed as I realized Honnett was waiting to hear if I had a new boyfriend. "Nothing like that," I said.

The men looked at me.

"How long have you been away from the house? And where have you been?"

"I left about three-thirty this afternoon. My company organizes parties. We were doing a big charity benefit for the Woodburn School last night."

"And you are telling us that you haven't been home in the last twelve hours?"

I shook my head no. But it was a confusing way to phrase a question. Should I have answered yes?

"As you probably noticed, Madeline, there was no sign of forced entry downstairs and the place looks pretty undisturbed. Any girlfriend, then, who might have your key—"

"Look. This body. It's *not* my friend Holly." I was completely firm on this point. Adamant. Why were these cops always thinking the absolute worst thing? "Look, I'm sure it isn't. It can't be. I'm sure—" And that's when I was struck by a totally new and horrible thought.

"Oh no," I said, my voice coming out much lower now, so low I didn't think I'd said it out loud.

"What?" Honnett and Baronowski asked almost in unison.

I walked the five steps to the bedroom door and noticed more black powder on the doorknob, on the wall. "May I . . . ?"

"You ever see a gunshot wound before?" Baronowski asked, in his low-key way.

I turned back to him. "No."

"You gonna faint or something?" he asked, studying me.

I couldn't stand to be coddled and insulted in my own damn house. I opened the door and stepped into my bedroom. My electricity bill was not a concern to the police employees of the City of Angels. The lights were all on in there as well.

At first, I didn't even see the woman's body. I was dazzled by the sight of all the blood. The red-soaked sheets. The red-stained quilts. The red-blotched rug. The red-splattered walls. The smell of fresh blood, that slightly ironlike smell of a butcher shop, was everywhere. But then I saw her. And it was just as I'd feared.

The young woman who was lying in all that blood was half on her side, half on her stomach, one arm stretched up over her head, like she had been swimming and was caught midstroke. She was wearing slim black slacks and what had once been a pure-white lace camisole. The red of the rosebud pinned to one strap was drowned in the red of three open wounds.

I could see the side of her face clearly. Sara Jackson's green eyes were half open. Her skin seemed sickly white beneath the disheveled strands of her long red hair. Her freckles stood out in relief.

"You know her?" Baronowski was at the doorway, looking at my face, gauging my reaction. His voice was still soft. Maybe he was trying to be sensitive. My house. A huge blood-soaked mess. Maybe he was trying to soothe me into confessing something. He suspected me of being involved in this. He was watching to see if I was faking, lying, deceiving.

"She worked for me." For some reason, I was startled to hear my own voice. It sounded almost normal. How could anything about me be normal after seeing this? I knew the police were wondering why I was pausing. Every one of my actions and reactions was being measured. If I hesitated, would they think I was reacting to the traumatic sight of my bedroom awash in blood and murder, or would they suppose I was taking some time to come up with a plausible lie? I rushed on. "Her name is Sara Jackson. She sometimes works as a server at the parties we cater. She was working on the Woodburn School dinner downtown. I just saw her. I mean, the last time I saw her it was around midnight. She asked to borrow my car, which I lent her. She said she'd bring it back here before morning."

When I mentioned the Woodburn, Baronowski and his partner, Hilts, exchanged looks.

"Can you account for your time between midnight and now, Ms. Bean?" asked Baronowski, flipping open a small spiral-topped notepad.

"I . . ." I looked at the room, the dead woman, my trembling hands. "I had a little trouble getting home from the Woodburn, actually. It's a long story. I was sort of stranded downtown, but I ended up having break-fast at the Pantry on Figueroa with a friend. His name is Wyatt. Dexter Wyatt. He may still be downstairs. Anyway, he brought me home."

Honnett had been standing close to me as I took in the scene. Now he put his arm around my shoulders, a move that was far from lost on the other police detectives. But I needed space. I shrugged it off. There was a dead woman in my bed. The police thought I was connected to her death. I didn't need to melt into anyone's arms. I needed to think.

"THE CHILL OF DEATH"

We stood in the little bedroom, which was really getting claustrophobic, what with three men and myself and Sara Jackson's lifeless body. The morgue guys were running behind, I had been told. It was barely 4 A.M. The phone on the bedside table rang loudly.

"You expecting anyone to call?" Detective Baronowski asked, making me suddenly feel guilty about the phone.

"No," I replied. It rang a second time, and I felt I was somehow being viewed with even more suspicion. "But then I wasn't expecting any of this." I didn't have to gesture at the body in the bed. "Should I answer it?" I asked, confused, as it rang out again. "Or I could leave it. My machine picks up after four rings."

"Why not take it?" asked Baronowski quietly. "We're done fingerprinting in here."

I reached out for the phone, disturbed that I had to walk a step closer to the bed to reach it, a step closer to Sara Jackson's corpse. I was keenly aware of being observed.

"Hello."

"Madeline?" It was Holly's voice, very screechy and breathless. And before I could reply, I heard her continue to shout, but she wasn't talking to me anymore. "Oh my God, Wes! She's okay. I got her. She's home!" And then back to me: "Maddie! We heard on the news you were dead. And then we both kind of fell apart. But then we just heard on the news you were *not* dead."

"They already have that I'm not dead on the news?" I asked, realizing the news reporters down in the street must have talked to Dex or something.

"Maddie. Did you hear me? Wes and I thought you had been shot. We heard about it on the radio when we got home to Wes's house. And we have been just *falling apart*."

"Not that we believed it," I heard Wes say in the background, trying to manage Holly's end of the phone conversation.

"And hell, Mad," Holly said, "at first, Wes just kept calling the police, but all they would do was take messages. No one would call us back. They said it was too soon. And then, when we heard you were *not* dead, *you didn't answer your cell phone.* I've been calling your cell every five minutes until I thought I'd go insane. And we just can't believe you're, well, like, *okay.* I mean, really okay and not dead!" She was melting down. I could hear the tears. It might be the first time, too. Holly believed in the song "Big Girls Don't Cry."

I looked up and saw that Honnett, Baronowski, and the other detective were actively listening. And waiting.

"It's my friends. Wesley and Holly. They thought I was dead. And . . . and you can imagine their reaction now. I love them so much. They are just so . . ."

Honnett gave me a look. Yes, I knew he had felt it, too. He had panicked and I knew it. And that was something I would surely have to think over when I had the time. Even now, I could tell he was beginning to feel a twinge of jealousy over my relationship with Hol and Wes. Like he was a little left out. Like maybe now my real friends would show up and I'd turn him out.

"Well, that's pretty fucked up," said Hilts, who as a rule hadn't said much all night.

I had to know what the cops were thinking. "What's that?" I asked.

"The damn TV reporters."

Baronowski looked at Honnett for a second and spoke directly to him. "You gonna look after her? Maybe it's not a good idea for her to stay alone tonight, you know."

"What's this all about?" I insisted. "Lieutenant Honnett is not a close friend of mine anymore. So this is not his problem, okay?"

Baronowski turned back to me, assessing me anew. "I guess I didn't realize how the situation stood. My apologies. See, the thing is, Madeline, we do not know squat about what happened here, do we? Some girl was killed. Now it is possible that she was followed here. Maybe she was killed by someone that knew her. That's one scenario, and believe me, we will look into that carefully. But it is also possible the gunman was some random bad guy looking to break into this house that maybe startled her as she was returning your car. She might have been a witness to a lousy break-in who got into the wrong guy's way. Right?"

I nodded.

"Or maybe you yourself, Madeline, have an enemy. After all, this is your house and your bed."

I looked down at the bed reflexively. I had to get out of this room. Why were we all standing there? The harder I puzzled and demanded rational thought, the dizzier and more detached I felt. Enemies? I hadn't any enemies. It was ridiculous. But then so was the entire night. So was this awful, awful death. I began shaking a little. If I couldn't begin to figure any of it out, all I could think to do was to force myself to stay conscious. I tried again to focus on Detective Baronowski's soft voice and to concentrate on what he was saying.

"You and the victim both have red hair. You're both young and attractive. This whole thing could have been a case of mistaken identity, and your life may very well have been saved by a mistake, have you thought of that?"

I shook my head, passive. This was too much now. I looked very little like Sara Jackson. True, we were of a similar build and size. But the way we were put together was different. She had a thinner, athletic look. I have a lot of curves. My hair was more strawberry blond, and thick and super curly, while Sara had that lovely fine, straight hair, and it was much more red than blond. No one who knew me could confuse the two of us. But I was shaken by the thought just the same.

"And if that is the right scenario," he continued, sounding even kinder, "it might have been better if those newspeople could have just shut the hell up so the world hadn't learned you are officially 'not dead' so soon."

"Oh," I said.

"Oh," I could hear Holly's voice faintly say from the receiver of the phone, which was still gripped in my dangling hand.

"Now I'm not saying that's the case. I don't want to spook you any more than you are already spooked."

I nodded my head, probably looking like the poster child for "spooked." At that, Baronowski's partner, Hilts, laughed out loud. I noticed Honnett, standing back in the corner, looking like he'd like to punch the guy. He'd clearly been agitated all night and needed an outlet. Let a guy laugh at me, even, and Honnett was ready to knock him down. Baronowski noticed it, too.

"Look," he said, "I apologize if I misinterpreted your friendship with Detective Honnett. He's not officially on this case, as I think you know. He asked to come in on the basis of having worked with you in the past, so we may have assumed too much."

I looked at Baronowski steadily, not having the heart to meet Honnett's eyes. Here Honnett had rushed over to my house, presuming like all get-out that I had been murdered in my bed, telling his associates on the force that he and I had been close. Hell, he'd been so stricken he hadn't even been able to bring himself to identify my dead body. And these cops had respected him for it. And now here I was, acting like we were barely acquaintances. I could almost believe that I was, indeed, a horrible, ungrateful bitch if I didn't also remember that Chuck Honnett had been my lover for several months before he ever bothered to tell me he hadn't actually gotten all the way divorced from his last wife.

"Mad!" It was Holly, yelling at me through the receiver. I put the phone back up to my ear.

"Sorry, Hol. I'm here with Honnett and a few detectives."

"Wes says we'll come right over to get you. You're staying with him, he says."

"Thanks," I told her, and I almost burst into tears as the pent-up tension of the night seemed to explode at just the thought of escape and comfort and friends. "But I have my car here." I hadn't seen it parked down in the cul-de-sac when I had arrived with Dexter Wyatt, but Sara must have left it down the street.

"Oh. Okay, you sure?" Holly asked.

"I'll drive you over to Wes's," Honnett said, his deep voice sounding awfully warm and protective.

"Or maybe Honnett will drive me," I told Holly.

"O-kay," she drawled, with significance.

"Yo!" We turned and the cop who had been manning the outside stairs came to the door of the room. "This joker downstairs, Wyatt, won't leave until he finds out if the lady here needs a ride anywhere. He is a huge pain in the ass, and I'd like to tell him to take a hike, but he insists he's driving her around."

"Dex?" I asked, having lost track of the guy who was detained outside for so long.

"Right," the young uniformed cop said, his eyes now fastened on the body of the dead woman in the bed. "And the coroner's van is out front. They're here for the body."

Just the way fate does things, I guess. Only four hours earlier, I couldn't get a ride if my life depended on it. Just now, I had four offers of transportation, not to mention a chance to hitch a lift with the coroner's wagon.

"You stay put," I told Holly firmly. "I'll get to Wes's by five."

"Sure thing," she said, sounding more and more like the bubbly Holly and less and less like the shrieking fiend who might have just lost her best friend. "Wes said to tell you he's baking you something special and he doesn't even want to *hear* about you saying you have no appetite. He just doesn't care."

I smiled and said good-bye. And then it hit me.

Four rides. Had there been such a surfeit of transportation around midnight and had I come directly home, as I had originally planned, what might have actually occurred this evening? Would all be calm? Would all be well? Would Sara Jackson still be alive?

Would I?

"LITTLE THINGS
YOU USED TO DO"

Before I left the house, I made photocopies of the personnel file we had on Sara Jackson and handed it to Detective Baronowski, as he had requested. And following his instructions, I made a quick survey of the house. I did not find anything obvious missing. Honnett had stayed in the background. He had offered to wait for me outside, and by his tone, I knew I'd have to spend some time talking it out with the guy before I could leave. I owed him that, I supposed. And I had to admit I was still amazed he had gotten emotional over me. Of course, it had taken me getting murdered for him to do so.

The police let me pack a bag and take all my essentials from the bathroom since they had finished examining the upstairs section of my house long before I had arrived. I caught sight of myself in the bathroom's full-length mirror as I scooped up my makeup and stopped to take stock: Clear skin. Fairly straight nose. Full lips. Overdressed. I had to change out of this gown. I pulled it off in one quick movement and dropped it in a wicker basket.

Nice enough body, I thought, looking in the mirror critically. Well, first let me qualify that. No one is allowed to like his or her body in

L.A.—it's like a secret sick law that keeps us going to gyms and shunning carbohydrates—but I'm not an actress or model and I guess my standards are a little more realistic. I figured until gravity did its dirty work, I couldn't complain. Having a real bosom was a novelty in this town. I remembered, suddenly, a time I'd spent in this very room with Honnett. The steam from the shower had fogged this full-length mirror, but not so foggy that I couldn't still see us together as we explored a new use for the old claw-foot bathtub.

I knew this was a dangerous way to be thinking since I had to face the man in just a few minutes. I kicked off my high-heeled sandals. I was longing for a shower, but simply didn't have the time or the stomach for it right there, right then. As I heard the men from the coroner's office bump down the narrow staircase, carrying Sara Jackson out of the house, I stood in the center of the bathroom and shivered. I dressed quickly in a pair of old jeans with a black top and flats. Since it had gotten chilly overnight, I tied a gray cashmere sweater around my shoulders for warmth and went down to see Honnett.

He was waiting outside by the front door, where I found him eyeing Dexter Wyatt. Again, I had forgotten Dex was still around and I felt pretty guilty for letting him hang out all this time.

I put my suitcase down. "Dexter, did you meet Lieutenant Chuck Honnett?" It wasn't the timeliest introduction, since the two men had been standing around together for some time. But that's me, Miss Manners. I had these party habits so firmly embedded I would probably still be introducing folks when I got to heaven. Or wherever.

"Sort of," Dex said. "What the hell happened in there? The coroner came out with a body bag. Who the hell was it?"

"A college girl who worked for me," I said. "She borrowed my car tonight and—"

"Can we stop reporting the news for a minute," Honnett interrupted, "and just tell your friend here to shove off now. He's on the verge of getting arrested for interfering with an investigation." Honnett never used to get hostile. I think this whole scene was getting to him, too.

Dex, for his part, didn't seem too exercised by Honnett's attitude. He just kept his laid-back charm going, no matter how many bodies might have to be loaded and taken off to the morgue before we could have a moment to chat.

"Maddie, can you ditch the cops now?" Dex asked, meaning not just the detectives still upstairs in the house, but also the one hulking around my front door. Not exactly diplomatic, but to the point.

"They said I could leave," I answered. "I gave them the number where I could be reached. I'm going to stay at my friend Wesley's house for a while. Maybe for a long while."

Honnett just leaned against the wall, waiting for me to finish with Dex, but clearly not enjoying that I had a guy hanging around, interested.

"Good," Dex said, and smiled. "I'll take you over there. It's like my job, you know?"

I smiled back at him.

"Not that I mind," Dex said, "but you don't seem an easy girl to get home. You're a challenge. I like that."

"I aim to drive men crazy," I said, not bothering to check Honnett's reaction. "But the thing is, I'll have to take a rain check on that. I need to have my car with me at Wes's. You understand."

"Okay." Dex kept his voice kind of gravelly low. It must have been driving Honnett nuts trying to hear. "So you won't let me rescue you again?"

"Once a night is certainly enough," I said. "But I do appreciate it. Oh, and could you do me a favor? Could you tell Zenya I think I left my purse in her car?"

Dexter agreed, and then left, taking the number at Wesley's house and saying he would call me, maybe bring my bag by tomorrow. I thanked him again, he glowered at Honnett, and he was out of there.

Honnett and I were finally alone. "We really need to talk, Maddie. We've needed to talk for a long time, but you weren't that interested in hearing from me."

"I found the key to my Jeep that Sara left on the kitchen counter. It's probably parked up the street."

He sighed. "I'll walk with you."

Just as we turned toward the stairs, Detective Hilts stuck his head out the front door and stopped us. "Hey," he said, calling to me. "Wait up. We're going to need to impound that vehicle of yours. The one the vic was driving."

"Can you please refer to Sara by her name?" I asked, weary almost beyond words.

"Sure. Anyway, no one touches that truck until we get our lab boys to take it in and give it the works. So I'm going to need the key."

I walked back up the steps and handed Hilts the damned key, giving him the plate number and where he might find it parked.

"Thanks."

"But what am I supposed to drive?" I asked, suddenly worried that the entire tide of transportation was turning against me once more.

"Beats me. I can ask Baronowski if we can give you a lift, but we're not going to be leaving anytime soon."

"That's okay, Hilts," Honnett said. "My car is right here."

"Good, then," he said, and ducked back into my house.

Honnett grabbed my suitcase and waited for me to lead him down the front steps to the street.

That was when it hit me. What I had intended to do before all the bizarre activities of the past few hours began to twist and turn.

"Wait here," I said, and turned back to the house. I walked quickly through the entry and into the office I share with Wes. Below my side of the partner's desk, where the chair was pushed neatly into the kneehole, I bent to retrieve a cardboard box. Inside were the papers and assorted pictures and files I'd cleaned up much earlier in the day—Albert Grasso's paperwork.

I grabbed my backup diskettes from my computer and a few other necessary office folders and scooted out the door into the cool air. It was almost five and I realized Wes and Holly might start to worry again if I didn't show up at Wesley's place soon.

"You ready?" Honnett asked quietly.

"Let's go."

We got down to the street and I noticed that the cop guarding the house and the news vans were gone. Once the body had been taken away, they must have figured they were out of luck for any more dirt. It was late, they had deadlines. Thank goodness for that. The last thing I could handle at the moment was an array of microphones shoved in my face.

We got to Honnett's Mustang and he unlocked the trunk for me, placing my suitcase inside and holding out his hand to store the cardboard carton there as well. I gave it to him and settled myself on the passenger side of the car.

"You want me to drive or you want to sit here and talk?" he asked, when he was in the driver's seat.

"Drive and talk," I answered.

"Fine." He got the car in gear and did a neat 180-degree turn, heading back up Whitley. "Where does Wes live these days?"

My partner, Wesley Westcott, is constantly on the move. He's had eight addresses in the past five years. He has a side business of fixing up historic old houses and selling them. Each time he buys a new house, he moves into the wreck-in-progress and lives among the carpenters and the dust and the electricians. Every time he finishes one of his masterpieces, he moves in all his fine furniture and puts the house on the market. These past ten years, L.A. has been in a nonstop real estate boom and these top-of-the-line properties, fixed up to the hilt, sell very well. As it turns out, Wes spends about 90 percent of his time living in a gutted mess or a construction site, 5 percent of his time in a great mansion, and the other 5 percent boxing or unboxing all of his belongings and moving.

"He's in Hancock Park," I directed. "On Hudson. On the Wilshire Country Club side."

"Near Beverly?"

"Near Third."

Honnett nodded and steered his car out of the Hollywood foothills and into the flats, heading first south and then west.

"Look," he said finally. "You going to be okay? This is pretty tough, finding that young woman in your house."

"I can't believe it." It had yet to really sink in. Hadn't I just been talking to Sara? Hadn't we just put our heads together, Holly and I, to see if we could get her out of a jam? That boyfriend of hers. I just remembered him.

"Chuck," I said quickly. "I forgot to tell Baronowski and Hilts about Sara's boyfriend."

"You know him?" he asked, interested.

"No. See, Sara was just a temporary employee. She worked parties when it fit into her school schedule, that kind of thing. But tonight, the reason I loaned her my old car was because she was worried about her boyfriend. He goes to 'SC, I think. Grad student. Anyway, he was having a rough time with his Ph.D. Sara was sorry she left him alone tonight."

"Why?"

"Who knows?" I was frustrated. When you manage a constantly changing staff of young servers and bartenders, you don't always listen to every little detail of their lives. If you did, you would be more into soap opera and less into event planning. "I didn't pay the closest attention, but she was really worried. She thought he might be suicidal . . ."

Honnett shot me a look.

". . . but I'm sure she was just getting dramatic. Anyway, she was supposed to go home and then come right over and drop off my Jeep. I specifically made her promise to return the car to me tonight. I . . ."

Honnett stopped at a red light on Santa Monica and looked at me. He could see me thinking it over. He could see it sinking in.

"Maybe if I hadn't been such a hard case, she would still be alive," I said softly. "If I hadn't forced Sara Jackson to drive out to my place so late at night, maybe she wouldn't have been killed."

"We don't know what happened," Honnett reminded me. But kindly. "Until we do, this could have happened anywhere. Don't beat yourself up, Maddie."

"Right." Like I could ever let anything like this go.

"Tell me, why didn't Sara just drive her own car home from that party tonight?"

"Some mechanical thing," I said absently, thinking about the role I might have played in that young woman's death.

"So blame that. Blame her bad luck with her car. Don't blame yourself, Maddie. You were trying to help the poor kid."

"I know," I said. "Some help."

The light changed and Honnett accelerated through the intersection.

"Did you really think I had been killed?" I asked Honnett.

He didn't answer right away. And then he didn't answer directly. He said, "I know you don't trust me. I get that. But you should believe me when I tell you this. I never meant to hurt you, Maddie. I never intended to make you miserable. You are the last person in the world I would want to be unhappy."

That sounded okay, but I was leery of Honnett. I waited to hear it all.

The fact is, a few months ago Honnett dropped the bomb on me that he was going back to his wife. His *wife*. The wife, I should point out, he *never* told me he still had hanging around. He delivered this news flash at a big party I was putting on at one of the studios and I just about flipped out. There we had been, getting closer and closer, and I had thought we were actually making a sort of good start. Then he tells me there's a wife still in the picture. It was so classic. I couldn't stand that I had been tricked or deceived or played. The guy I was falling for had a wife, damn it! I don't know. I suppose there might have been a reasonable, rational way to continue such a conversation that night. For my part, I just told him to get the hell out of my life and ran off for a weekend in Vegas with a new male friend. Call me communicationally challenged. Whatever.

"You are so young," Honnett said, with affection in his voice. I loved that voice, so masculine and deep. When it held any softness at all, it made me melt.

"I am not," I argued. I knew Honnett had qualms about our age difference from the start. I'm twenty-nine. He's forty-four. Big deal. He had a thing about it, though. And here he was bringing it up again, like that was the problem. Like the fact that he was hiding a wife in the wings had nothing to do with it.

"I am not putting you down," he said. "Don't get so defensive. I just mean that you haven't had as many years to screw up your life as I have. You don't have as many ghosts from the past, I'm betting."

"I've got my share," I said huffily.

"Yeah, sure you do," he said, chuckling. "And so do I. Since you are such an experienced old woman, I know you'll understand how a person's history can sometimes catch up with him."

"You mean past relationships?"

"Well, in my case I think I told you I had been married before."

"Right. What a convenient way for you to have put it. Not too specific, were you? And I thought you meant it was all over. You were divorced. You were free to start something new with me."

"You want clear? Here it is. I've been married twice," he said. "Once to a gal I met in college. In Texas."

"Were you some big football hero?"

"I believe I was," he said, laughing at me. "We Texas boys love to play ball. Anyway, she was a sorority girl. A pretty sorority girl from a nice Dallas family. She liked having a good time. She liked to buy nice clothes. You can picture the type. She wasn't too wild about me joining the PD. Things had never been too good between us. We were too young. You hear that a lot, right? But I was working all the time anyway, so I didn't get how unhappy we really were. After about seven years, she left me for a guy who owned a plane."

"A plane guy?"

"Yep. His daddy owned a furniture warehouse in San Antonio, I believe. Anyway, we hadn't had any kids. She didn't want any, she told me. I tried to change her mind about the plane guy, but . . ." He smiled and shook his head. "I was young then. Maybe about your age."

"Shut up."

"Some time went by and I moved to Los Angeles, and a couple years later I met Sherrie. She worked for the LAPD, too."

I looked up, surprised. "She's a cop?"

He nodded. "She's a cop. Anyway, she had just gone through a rough divorce herself. We hooked up and just sort of fell together. I figured she was more my kind of person, you know? She loved being a cop and she was proud of how well I was doing, moving up, that sort of thing. We got married and thought we'd have a family."

"You have kids?"

"We weren't successful. Sherrie wanted to do the fertility things. We spent a lot of money and she really suffered, taking hormones and whatnot, trying to get pregnant."

"Well, now you've done it," I said. "Now you've managed to get me feeling sorry for this wife of yours. Thanks."

"Anyway, we were not successful in other ways. We had grown apart. She and I had never had that much magic. I began to realize how it really was with Sherrie. She was more interested in having a kid and being someone's mom than in being my wife."

"Oh."

"So we separated. This was maybe two years back. We should have gotten the whole divorce thing settled, but I couldn't afford it and she knew it. I'd used up all of my savings on fertility clinics and things like that. We'd even signed up for private adoption and that cost money, too."

"So why did you go back to her?" I asked. "Why did you leave me?"

"I am still tied to this woman, Maddie. I still care for her. I still feel guilty I wasn't committed enough to our marriage to make it work."

"Guilt!" I was tired of the concept, tired of its grasp. I knew it well. Hadn't I just insisted that some poor, overworked girl rearrange her evening so she could drive my filthy old car home? Hadn't that led to her death? I buried my head in my hands.

"Sherrie called me out of the blue. I honestly hadn't heard a word from her in several months, Maddie. She called me to say she had just been diagnosed with breast cancer." I stared at him as he drove in the dark night. "She was scared to go through it alone."

"But your marriage was over . . ."

"She made promises that we could go to see a counselor together. She wanted me to move back into our old house and . . . and to take care of her while she went through the chemo."

I shook my head. No words would come.

He drove on, waiting for me to catch up.

"Do you still love her?"

He took a while to answer. "Maddie, it's complicated."

What had I expected? An unequivocal no? He was still attached to his ailing wife. And really, in the light of this other woman's anguish, how could I think he wouldn't be? I was ashamed of myself. "Of course you should help her, Chuck. Of course."

"This isn't the way I wanted to tell you," he said, sounded frustrated.

"Honnett," I said, "I can't think anymore about you and me. Not tonight. I'm just not—"

"Shh. That's okay," he said. "You have every right to hate me, Maddie. I know it."

We turned onto Hudson and traveled silently to Wesley's block. I showed Honnett where to pull over. He helped me carry my luggage and carton up the drive. Wesley's new project was a large two-story English stone manor house, currently deep in the demolition stage. There was a Porta Potti out at the curb for the construction crew, and a large Dumpster next to the driveway, filled with debris.

"How are you going to stay here?" Honnett asked, looking at the state of the place.

"Wesley is living out back in the guest house. He's leaving it alone until he finishes up restoring the front house. I'll stay with him back there." I led Honnett along a path that wound around and behind the three-car garage.

"Is his guest house going to be big enough?"

We crossed the patio behind the garage and then the lawn that led up to the pool. The sky seemed to be lightening from black to navy blue.

"That's where you're staying?" Honnett asked, taking in the perfect miniature mansion beyond the pool. "It's larger than my condo."

"It's got two bedrooms. Wes has been using the second bedroom for storage, but I guess we'll figure it all out. I just don't want to think about any of this right now."

"Don't worry," he said, putting down my things and putting his hands on my head, brushing back my hair. "I know you are completely wasted. I won't try to kiss you again or anything."

"Oh, really?" It must just the perverseness of my nature that I couldn't let him leave like that. At the door of the guest house, I leaned into Honnett's arms and lifted my face.

As he bent down and gave me a tentative kiss, the door opened and Holly and Wesley started screaming with relief.

For better or worse, I was home.

"Living Space"

staggered to the love seat in the living room of Wesley's charming guest house and just sighed. "I am too tired to talk, too tired to stand, too tired to . . . itch," I said, collapsing onto the down-filled cushions. The white linen slipcover made an almost noiseless whoosh.

"Of course you are!" Holly took my heavy suitcase and the rest of my things and disappeared into the second bedroom. I closed my eyelids and felt my tired eyes burn, and then gently the tension began to ease. When I opened them again, Holly popped out of the bedroom on tiptoe.

"She's still awake," Wes whispered to Holly, ever alert to the flicker of my lids.

"We cleaned out the extra room," Holly whispered to me.

"I moved in that old Philadelphia spindle bed, the one you love," Wes whispered to me.

"Thanks," I said, trying to smile through my grogginess.

"Want to go to bed?" Holly asked, still talking low.

"I do," I said, but didn't budge. They waited. A few moments more and I had to ask, "Something smells wonderful. What did you bake?"

"Mandelbrot," Wes said. "I know you don't want to eat. I just needed to get it out of my system."

"Did you use my auntie Evelyn's recipe?" I closed my eyes again, breathing in the warm scent of bitter orange and walnuts and sugar. I knew he had. Wes loves authentic ethnic cuisine and had miraculously seduced several well-kept family secrets out of my eighty-year-old great-aunt. Mandelbrot is a dry, semisweet cookie, sort of like Jewish biscotti. My mother was Polish Jewish, my dad was Italian English. It makes for a schizoid culinary heritage.

"Yes, I did, but don't feel like you are obliged to taste them right now. You know they will keep. Do you want to go to bed?"

"I don't know," I announced, and then opened my eyes once more. "I seem to be stuck." There sat my two best friends, so concerned about me that they were willing to leave all questions and curiosity and worries about the events of the past evening for later.

"Just say the first thing that comes into your mind," Holly advised. "Maybe you don't know what you want, but something will pop out."

"Shower."

"See, there!" Holly chirped. "I should have my own cable show. It works."

Wesley's guest house has only one bathroom, but it was huge. Built in the thirties as a sort of folly, the guest house has ridiculously grand twelve-foot ceilings, which not only add a slightly surreal touch to the dimensions of the cottage, but also permit the extensive use of large crystal chandeliers—even in the loo. The vintage bathroom was tiled in the style of its Art Deco period, all sea-foam green six-inch squares on the floor and about eight feet up the walls. Border tiles were of forest green and here and there were Art Deco accent tiles featuring geometrical pink lilies with dark leaves on a sea-foam ground. All the porcelain fixtures, the toilet, sink, and tub, were a matching shade of pale green.

It was like stepping back in time as I stepped into the green tub, turned the hot and cold faucets until I got the right mix, and pulled the lever to switch on the shower. Under sharp spikes of hot water, I just drifted away to a time where none of the present evening's troubles could intrude. Steam filled the room as I stood there, thinking of nothing more disturbing than which of the five trendy shampoos Wes had neatly lined up on the built-in tile shelf might work for my tangle of wet curls.

When I emerged from the bathroom, clean and warm, with a pale green towel wrapped around my head, I was wearing a freshly pressed pair of Wesley's pajamas, soft white cotton, which he had kindly left out for me on the small chair in the bathroom. I had rolled up the waistband, and was doing the same with the long sleeves, but I felt so much better I almost couldn't believe it.

It is funny how tired you can be one minute, and then somehow you get that extra energy, that second wind. I know I missed an entire night of sleep, but I can do that sometimes, and just keep going.

"You look pretty good," Holly said, checking me out.

"I brewed you some tea," Wes said, also checking me out. "Darjeeling."

"I put it in the bedroom," Holly said, "on a tray with some mandelbrot."

"Well, what are you waiting for?" I asked, leading the way. "Wesley, bring that cardboard box. We have a lot to talk over."

Holly went to fetch extra teacups and then we all settled on the high bed Wes had made up for me in the guest room, each finding a comfortable perch. I started combing through my long hair, gently detangling it, and began to talk it out.

"Look, you guys. You are being so patient with me. But this evening — last night — is hard for me to deal with. So much has happened . . . And I have this feeling I'm missing some important connections. Like some of the answers are right here in front of me, but I haven't put it all together yet." I rubbed my head where my comb had pulled too hard. "Only I don't know which parts go together. It's like sorting through a pile of jigsaw-puzzle pieces and suspecting you may have a few pieces from another puzzle mixed into the wrong box. But you can't tell which belongs to which. And the whole pile is overwhelming." I looked up at my friends.

"Just start wherever you want," Wes said calmly. "We can help you sort."

"It's hard to start," I said, "because every time I think it over, I feel like I'm getting it wrong. Like it really must have started earlier. And then when I go back, it seems like it started even earlier."

"Then don't start at what happened at your house," Holly suggested gently. "Start earlier. Like right after the party tonight?"

I shook my head. "Earlier. Remember the rubbish I found outside my house yesterday? I thought it was just a case of teenage vandalism or lit-tering. Then, when I glanced at the stuff, I began to see the papers made sense—they belonged to a man and it didn't seem like he would want to lose all that stuff."

"Right," Wes agreed.

"But then I discovered that the man, Albert Grasso, was at the party last night. And he and his woman friend were livid. Remember, Holly? They were angry at me because they thought I'd stolen those papers. So what really happened? Maybe there was a crime up on Iris Circle yester-day and maybe those papers were taken from Grasso's office. Not by me, of course. But maybe they were stolen. As to why they were then dumped on our doorstep, I have no idea."

"I'm going to take notes," Holly said, and then left to find her note-book. She returned a few minutes later as Wes and I tried to make sense out of it all, and frankly couldn't.

"That's the first crime," I said to Holly, and she marked it down in her notebook.

"Saturday morning or early afternoon. Private papers taken from Grasso office on Iris Circle. Saturday afternoon. Private papers dumped one block below on Whitley. Saturday night. Albert Grasso learns his pa-pers have been found and goes ballistic," she read. "That right?"

"Yes. So then there is that tenor saxophone from the Woodburn. You guys may not have heard, but—"

"We know!" said Holly. "We were there when they called 911. One of the auction chairladies nearly fainted."

"The cops showed up and searched the hall," Wes added. "Whoever took it left the sax case. They were fingerprinting and such."

"I hoped maybe it had just been misplaced or something," I said, re-membering Bill Knight's rage. "You know Zenya Knight's husband won the sax in the auction and he was convinced that another Woodburn dad took it out of spite. But I thought he was just venting. He didn't have any proof. What do the cops think really happened?"

They filled me in. The Selmer saxophone case, along with all the other items, had been left in an unsecured storeroom right off the stage, where items were kept both before and after the auction. Lots of people had been milling about near the storeroom, and certainly several fund-raising volunteers had nipped in and out during the closing minutes of the auction, but with all that activity and so many people hustling here and there, no one saw anything out of the ordinary.

"I have to say, this maybe fits in with what Bill Knight was suggesting. I mean, how could this have been a premeditated crime?" I asked. "I realize a lot of people had knowledge that the Selmer had been donated to the Woodburn auction, so I get how it might have been the target of a theft, but who could have anticipated having any privacy in that storage area? Not even somebody with insider knowledge—"

"Like someone who worked on the auction committee!" Holly suggested.

"Right, someone on the committee might know there were no plans for armed guards, or locks or anything, but they *still* couldn't predict in a crowd of hundreds of people that they could get to the sax and not be observed."

"That's true," Wes said. "And if it *was* someone working as a volunteer, it would have been easier to steal the sax sometime before the ball. Fewer witnesses."

"So you're saying," Holly said, picking up Wes's line of thought, "it must have been done on impulse. Someone must have seen a few seconds of opportunity and pounced."

We all thought it over. I couldn't buy that some wealthy dad would risk his reputation in order to get his hands on that sax. It wasn't as if his son could ever play it in public, after this. What would be the point? Whoever stole the sax didn't give a damn that the Woodburn would end up losing a hundred-thousand-dollar donation, and Dave Hutson's wife was the chairwoman of the whole freaking auction committee. It made no sense.

"What sort of person would be likely to do it?" I asked.

"A crime like that. It takes real balls." Holly Nichols, criminal profiler.

Wes said, "Holly has been into a whole 'balls' theme this evening. Don't ask."

"But it's true," Holly said, defending her point. "They had to unlock the case when no one was looking, grab the horn, and just waltz out—who could have managed that?"

Wes picked up the heavy pot of tea and began to pour. "It's like one of those old locked-room mysteries where you'd swear it couldn't have happened. There were dozens of helpers milling about. Even if a disgruntled bidder suddenly went insane and was seized with an overpowering urge to snatch his rival's prize, how the heck could he get it out? Believe me, no one left the storeroom with a bulky, heavy, shiny, curvy, three-foot-long, fully engraved, sterling-silver tenor saxophone under his dinner jacket. *That* would have been noticed."

"Maybe you're right," Holly said thoughtfully. "But maybe no one realized what was going on. Just wait. Someone will remember something. Or no! I bet somebody saw something and just isn't talking."

We both eyed Holly, considering this.

I nibbled on the crunchy, crispy mandelbrot and tasted the fine tea, which was incredibly mellow and flavorful. Wesley had become a student of the subtle art of tea brewing and was a connoisseur of estate-grown Indian teas. Of course.

Holly took a piece of mandelbrot and considered motivations. "These Woodburn dads can get nuts."

"It's like they are secretly insane," I agreed, taking my second piece of mandelbrot.

"It's like Darwin," Wes suggested. "In more primitive times, these two dads would be clubbing each other to get dominance over their tribe. Today, they use their checkbooks to clobber their sons' musical competition."

Holly finished scribbling notes and then read: "Saturday night. Ten-thirty, tenor sax sold at auction for one hundred thousand dollars. Midnight, B. Knight goes to pay and finds the case is empty. Lots of witnesses report they saw nothing suspicious near the storeroom. Stolen sax may have been taken by D. Hutson out of primitive urge."

We shared a what-a-world, what-a-world look as we each sipped our tea. "This is fantastic," I said, breathing in the steam.

"Darjeeling, of course," Wes explained, our font of all things arcane. "Grown in the foothills of the Himalayan Mountains in northeastern India between Nepal and Bhutan."

"I knew that," Holly said.

We looked at her.

"Sort of."

Wes smiled. "You can tell, Hol, by its characteristic dryness and muscat overtones." He gazed into the rich golden amber liquid in his cup. "The Champagne of Teas, it's called."

"First flush?" I inquired nonchalantly.

Wes looked at me.

I took another small sip. I like to keep Wesley on his toes by throwing out the odd esoteric fact.

"Naturally." He raised an eyebrow in deference to my knowledge.

"What's *first flush* mean?" Holly asked, playing right into my hands.

"Tea plants hibernate during the winter months, Hol," I explained. "As March approaches, the warm sun stimulates the growth of the leaves, but the cool temperatures keep the growth rate slow. This first new growth of leaves is full of flavor and it's referred to as the *first flush*. It's considered the ideal time to pluck the classic 'two leaves and a bud.' "

"Wow." Holly looked into her cup.

I smiled. I had read all about it when I was working temporarily as a writer on a culinary game show. Who says TV rots one's mind?

"Chamling Estate?" I asked Wes. I knew I was pushing my luck, but whenever else would this sort of trivia come up in conversation?

"It's Thurbo Estate, actually."

"Go on," I urged.

"The Thurbo Tea Estate is located in the Mirik Valley of Darjeeling at an altitude ranging from 980 meters to 2,440 meters. It has a planted area of 485.11 hectares and produces 263,600 kilograms of tea per year."

"You are good," I said. You had to hand it to Wesley. He knew his stuff. "Too bad I'm not still working on *Food Freak*. I could have used all that."

Somehow, the camaraderie of my pals and this tea break had brought me back to myself. After all, with Holly taking notes, and Wes to puzzle it through, we had already gotten somewhere. I was fortified to deliver the rest of my story.

I approached the next part gingerly. I explained to Wes and Holly how I had been practically hijacked in Bill Knight's Hummer and raced around the streets and abandoned downtown and the hour it took me to finally find civilization. Naturally, I expected a reaction from my best friends. I got it.

"That's the funniest thing I ever heard," Holly said, cracking up.

"Well, not at the time it wasn't," I said.

"But you've got to love the part where it ends up with Maddie thinking she attracted a 'john,' " Wes said, grinning at Holly.

"Yeah, real funny," I chimed in with less enthusiasm.

"Well, at least you liked this guy Dexter Wyatt who came to rescue you. Is he cute?"

"Yeah. Too cute. It's just that I don't have the bandwidth to deal with cute at the moment," I said, feeling my energy ebb.

"So do you want me to write it all down in my notes about the Knights hijacking you and the guy picking you up?" Holly asked, with belated sensitivity. She held up her pen, a fuzzy-topped purple glitter Gelly Roll, showing me she was taking my pain seriously. Now.

"Not necessary," I said. "I can't blame anyone but myself for getting into trouble downtown. Remind me never again to ride home with one of our party guests."

"So what happened when you finally got to your house?" Wes asked, staring at me. He had been patient, holding on to this question as long as anyone could. But Wes and Holly had been up all night, too, worrying about me. They needed to be told.

"It was a total disaster," I said, suddenly sober.

Holly bit her lip. She also seemed to be coming down from her Darjeeling high.

"Was there a break-in at the house like they originally reported?" Wes asked. "And why did they think you were . . . dead?"

"They found someone else. It was a woman's body, " I said. And the light mood we had just enjoyed vanished in an instant.

"We didn't know that . . ." Holly looked at both of us. "We were hoping it couldn't be true. That it was a mistake, too."

"We heard about the break-in, but when they announced that you were really alive . . ." Wes quickly picked up my nervous reaction. "I guess we didn't pay close enough attention."

"But how could there have been a body?" Holly asked, truly perplexed. "Was someone killed in your house?"

I nodded, tears springing up out of nowhere. Apparently the news reports had been sketchy. And Wes and Holly had been frantic. And I suddenly realized they really had no idea what I had just gone through.

"It's someone we all know. It was Sara Jackson."

"I'm Beginning

to See the Light"

've been thinking," I said, walking back into the living room of the guest house. All the wooden blinds had been shut and the room, even in midday, was dim. Holly was trying to sleep on an inflatable mattress that Wes had put out for her. Her lean frame was much too long to fit comfortably on the love seat, even curled up. I noticed she was also wearing a pair of Wesley's white cotton pajamas. Even on her, the sleeves had to be rolled up.

"Aren't you sleeping?" Holly asked, pushing up on one elbow.

"No. Can't. Sorry, did I wake you up?"

"Not really. I didn't want to go home because I would just be alone and I don't want to be alone after hearing about what happened to Sara."

"I know." I sat down next to her and put an arm around her. "You must be missing Donald."

She nodded. "I wish we really had eloped. If we make it to our wedding day, I'll be an old lady."

"When's he coming home from visiting his sister?"

"Nine more days."

"At least you can dream about your wedding."

"I guess I could, if I could get to sleep. What have you been thinking?" she asked.

"I've been so overwhelmed, I forgot about Albert Grasso."

"What a geek! He and his friend Caroline went psycho last night. I hate it when people get so bent out of shape."

"That's what I mean. Look, he doesn't have to love me, but I am a young businesswoman. I have a reputation. Why would he jump to the hysterical conclusion I had stolen his papers?"

Holly sat up and wrapped her long, slender arms around her knees. "Look at how everyone runs around ranting and venting! All these people need a good massage therapist and some meditation."

She did have a point there. It seems like all the people we know keep themselves going on some secret recipe of adrenaline, deadline pressure, and Starbucks. A little too much of any one of those ingredients and they could explode from all the stress.

"Well . . ." Holly rubbed her white-blond topknot, a little droopy now after a few hours against a pillow. "How the heck did this guy Grasso's junk get dumped out on your lawn, anyway?"

"I don't know," I admitted. "But what if he had some very private things in his office, papers or photos that he thought no one would ever see?"

Holly nodded.

"And then I came waltzing up to him at the party, right there out in public, and started telling him I had a whole pile of his most secret, private papers."

Holly nodded. "That would screw up his night."

"He got incredibly defensive, you know? And then went on the attack. Like he assumed I would be blackmailing him. I didn't get it at first, because I was so blown away by his hostility. But maybe he was scared out of his head."

"O-kay . . ."

"This just feels right to me," I said, warming up to this new idea. "I would bet you a doughnut that there is something among those papers that Albert Grasso would hate to have discovered by anyone."

"Well, that's pretty scary," Holly said. "Do you remember seeing anything really suspicious when you looked through the junk yesterday?"

"Not really. Maybe that photograph of the president with a young babe, but—"

"Like there aren't a million Clinton pics floating around." Holly dismissed that idea and went on. "Perhaps something is buried in among all the bills and invoices? There might be something incriminating there—like showing he overbilled some celebrity or something."

"Or worse," I said, thinking it through.

I suddenly noticed Wes standing at the door to the master bedroom, fully awake, wearing the same white cotton pajamas as Holly and I.

"Very interesting," he said, joining the conversation. "Presuming Grasso had some secret papers, he would naturally be looking for your motivation, Maddie, for telling him you found them. You must have caught him completely off guard. But then you didn't act smug or menacing. You didn't appear to know anything worth blackmailing him over. You didn't act like you wanted his money and he must have been shocked."

We all nodded. As Wes, Holly, and I picked up this new thread, we carefully avoided the promise we'd made to one another that we would get some sleep and put all thoughts of theft and murder and littering out of our heads.

Wes continued, "What if he realized he and his lady friend had overreacted, and in doing so, they must have gotten you nervous. He would have to be afraid that you would run back home and look through the papers more thoroughly when you had some time."

"That makes sense," I agreed. "That is exactly what I intended to do. You think he might have gone over to my house last night to get the papers and photos back?" I was getting creeped out.

"Oh my God," Holly said, her hands flying to her mouth.

Wes picked up the story. "What if he found Sara there, coming over to return your car? And she saw him and what he was doing. He was afraid she would get him arrested for breaking and entering, not to mention the cops would have to look at the papers and might discover what terrible secret Grasso was trying to hide."

"So the singing teacher might have shot Sara. Just to cover up what he was doing?" Holly seemed to be getting paler. "That's horrible."

I spoke up. "What sort of paper could be worth killing an innocent girl?"

"Maddie, where is the carton with all of Grasso's trash now?" Holly asked.

"Was it gone? Did Grasso get to it?" Wesley's voice was alert. "It would look very suspicious if that box of papers is gone now. The police could make something of that."

"No, no, no," I quickly replied. "The box was still under my desk. I had such a difficult time getting home last night, I wasn't going to leave that box behind."

Wes and Holly just stared at me.

"You mean it's here?" Wes asked.

"Yes!" Holly yelled, suddenly remembering. "I brought it into Mad's room when I took in her suitcase."

"I've been weeding through the documents for the past few hours, reading every paper, checking out every receipt. But for the life of me, I couldn't find anything there that is truly shocking or juicy. Just a lot of private junk."

"Wait now," Wes said, his posture perfect, as always. "That would make Grasso even more clever, wouldn't it? What if he did break in, but he was careful to just pick out the one folder or photo that was the most sensitive and then left the rest? It would be much less suspicious. See? You would notice if the box was missing. Of course you would mention it to the police. But how would you ever notice if one slip of trash was gone?"

"To be honest, Wes, it didn't look like anyone had been in our office. And the box was exactly where I left it." I bit my lip, trying to remember.

"Maybe we should all go through the papers, Maddie," Holly suggested, her voice still subdued. Holly had taken the news about Sara Jackson terribly hard. Naturally. Like me, she felt responsible for Sara ending up at my house. After all, if not for Holly and me, that young woman would not have been at that very wrong place at that very wrong time.

"I think we need to turn it over to the police," I said. "I wouldn't mind having a copy of everything in case Grasso claims I stole anything. But otherwise—"

"Why don't I run over to Kinko's?" Holly offered, jumping up from her mattress on the floor. "There's one near the Grove.

"I'll just copy every damn thing in the box and we can go over them more thoroughly, later."

"Well . . ." It didn't sound like a bad idea to me at all. "And I guess I could call Honnett and tell him about our theory."

Wesley gave me a look, like he had heard this sort of thing from me before, and more important, he remembered, even if I didn't, the "high" regard Honnett held for my impressions of his cases. It was true. In the past, Honnett and I had had our share of encounters over his work. He was usually kind, but pretty unimpressed with my little notions of crime and punishment in the City of Angels.

"I'll get him to listen," I said, sounding defensive even to my own ears. "And this isn't even his case. I would just feel a little safer if a cop was hearing this and taking over the evidence."

"Fine," Wesley said. "But you might get further if you called the detective you told us about. The one who is in charge."

Holly returned from the bathroom, changed back into her black pants and white camisole, the outfit she'd been wearing the previous night. It reminded me of Sara Jackson and I suddenly felt queasy.

Luckily, Holly hadn't seen what I had seen. I went and retrieved the carton of papers from the guest bedroom and Holly left, taking the keys to Wesley's new Jaguar.

"What's wrong?" Wes asked.

"Nothing. Just . . . Wesley, the last girl wearing that exact outfit who borrowed a car, she ended up . . ." I shook away the memory. He came over and joined me on the love seat.

Wes was nothing short of six-foot-three, and he was thin and sinewy, with not an ounce of extra fat as far as I could tell. Still, when he held me in his arms, I found a spot on his shoulder that wasn't entirely bony. And I let a tear dampen the collar of his snowy pajama top.

"We look like twins," he said, changing the subject.

"Where on earth did you get so many identical pairs of pajamas?" I asked, my voice not sounding entirely natural.

"Oh, Lord! My mother sends me a new pair each Christmas," he said. "And they're all still practically brand-new. I never wear them."

"Do you sleep in the—"

"Maddie! No. I wear a pair of knit boxers or something."

I giggled, letting another tear escape. "I can't believe we are sitting here talking about your underwear."

Wes stood up and said, "All the better to get those other scary images out of your head, my dear."

"Why don't you just tell your mom not to send them anymore?"

"It would break her heart. She somehow got this notion that I love them."

"Somehow," I chided. I knew Wes was a big softie and I could imagine he thanked his mother profusely that first Christmas. This was typical Wesley.

There was a knock at the door.

"Holly? Back so soon?" I walked over and opened the door.

But it wasn't Holly at all. It was a tiny blonde with a tight face-lift. Caroline Rochette, Albert Grasso's lady friend, stood in the glare of the sun, smiling. "May I come in?" she asked.

I looked back at Wes, who was just finishing folding up the deflated inflatable mattress.

"Sure," I said, so surprised I automatically went into my default "gracious" mode when I had every right to be flat-out pissed off at this absurd woman.

"Thank God," said Caroline. "I just simply have to talk to you. I'm in terrible trouble."

"Hello, Goodbye, Forget It"

Caroline Rochette suggested we take a walk around the grounds of Wesley's fixer estate so we could have a little privacy for girl talk. I was stunned she had found me there. Who could have told her where I'd be?

But then, I was dying to question her about Albert Grasso. To see if my theories might be substantiated. How could it hurt to walk around Wesley's backyard, in broad daylight, as long as he kept an eye out the bay window of his guest cottage? I quickly changed into my old faded jeans and a black T-shirt from my little suitcase and met her in the garden.

It didn't seem an enormous risk, after all. We were not exactly in some abandoned alley, and we were hardly alone. Noisily performing demolition work on the main house were two Hispanic men I'd gotten to know on some of Wes's other projects. They were now pulling rotting shingles off the roof.

"Hi, Cesar!" I waved.

Caroline shaded her eyes with one hand and looked up. I think she got the point. I had men all over this property who were keeping their eyes open. Not that I was frightened of her. Aside from a nasty tendency to wear false eyelashes in the daytime, Caroline Rochette didn't scare me. Much. But naturally, I was a little jumpy with all the horrible things that had happened.

"I'm so sorry for all the . . . fuss last night," Caroline said, jumping right into the end of the conversational pool in which I most wanted to paddle around with her.

"Fuss?" I almost spit the word out. "You and Mr. Grasso behaved horribly." I looked her right in the eye. She was balanced upon four-inch heels, and still I had to look down a little. "You both made terrible accusations. None of it was true. And all I had wanted to do was to be helpful."

"It was an odd . . . thing," Caroline said, with a friendly chirp to her voice. She had a distinctive speech pattern, where she picked and chose odd words and gave each a separate inflection. Sort of like someone who is not terribly talented at conversation. Or lying.

"Odd. Yes. What sort of trouble have you come here to discuss?"

"It's as you . . . guessed. About the papers."

We had stopped walking in front of a stone garden bench at the far end of the yard, well away from the large formal pool. Beyond the far fence stretched an incredibly green fairway and one of the holes of the Wilshire Country Club golf course. The day had been warm and the shade of a jacaranda tree, just bursting with pale blue flowers, gave us a bit of a break.

I waited for the story and she went on.

"About Albert's . . . files." She batted ultrablack eyelashes against sharp little cheekbones. "Well . . . I know who took them."

"It wasn't me!" I said, staring her down.

"No, no. I know that. It was actually me."

"You?"

"Oh, damn." In an outburst of fluttering lashes Caroline sat down hard on the bench.

Now this was pretty interesting stuff.

"Look," she said, "you *have* to give me all of Al's papers. Please." She searched her tiny designer bag for a cigarette. Then a lighter.

"Well, excuse me for pointing this out, Caroline, but those papers don't belong to you."

"But . . . that's . . . just . . . I mean, you can't . . ." Eyelashes went ballistic. Cigarette waved in one hand, remaining unlit.

I stood there, waiting for her mouth to coordinate with the quick-excuse centers of her brain, but she was clearly not up to the fast retort, so I swooped in with a question of my own. "Why on earth did you take Mr. Grasso's personal papers, Caroline?"

Perhaps the shock of my flat-out accusation got her going. In any event, she began speaking rapidly. "It was nothing like you must think. It was simply . . . innocent. I was planning a surprise for Albert's birthday." As she explained, she lit her cigarette and took a sharp drag. "He is a hard man to shop for. Someone gave me this terrific idea. I was going to get him a new . . . briefcase to replace the horrible old one he's been lugging around for years. He likes a certain kind of leather case and I didn't want to get it . . . wrong. I was told I could simply bring in the old one and let the luggage store order one just like it."

"You wanted to buy him a briefcase," I repeated. I stood there on the flagstone path, looking down on her. She was dressed in a tiny St. John knit suit. Pink, white, and baby blue. Size 0.

"So yesterday morning, Saturday, I borrowed the briefcase and walked on down to my car, which I had left parked . . . on Whitley. Your street."

Parking could be very problematic in my neighborhood. She'd had to park down the hill.

She took another quick puff on her cigarette, leaving a cotton-candy-colored lipstick print around the filter end, and went on. "I got to the luggage store and thought I would . . . die. I wanted to die. I couldn't find Al's briefcase. I searched through my Mercedes and it just . . . wasn't . . . there."

"Imagine that," I said.

"I drove back. I swore at myself. Really, over and over. I retraced my route. I finally got back to Whitley Avenue. You can't imagine how I was . . . cursing. Yes, cursing. And then I got to Whitley, and half a block from where I had parked my car earlier I saw Albert's briefcase." She tossed her cigarette to the stone walk and crushed it with a jab of her pointy-toed shoe. "It was lying against the curb, almost under a parked car, cracked open. And then I remembered. I had rested the briefcase . . . on the top of the car. I placed it there while I was opening my car door. I must have left the damn thing there, right on the roof, and driven off. And then . . . it must have fallen off into the gutter and cracked open. I can only imagine that the papers inside were scattered about. That must have been near your house."

"You mean you took Mr. Grasso's briefcase without his knowledge and then accidentally drove off, causing the case to crash open in the street?"

"Basically . . ." she said, looking terribly upset. "Yes."

"Then—forgive me for speaking bluntly, Caroline, but what was all the bullshit last night at the Woodburn gala about calling the police and accusing me of theft?"

"Oh, I would never have called the police," she said, putting her gold lighter up to the tip of a second slender cigarette. She inhaled deeply and continued: "You're a woman, Madeline. You know men! I couldn't tell Albert what had happened to his papers. Believe me, I was reeling from shock to discover they had been . . . found, after all." She took another puff of nicotine. "Albert told me all about the little talk the two of you had, when he got back to our table. He was much more upset about all the missing papers than I had even imagined. So you see, I just couldn't go into the whole ghastly story right then. Of course I plan to . . . tell him. Someday. When the timing is right. But he was really amazingly angry." She exhaled a tight, white stream of smoke.

I was willing to put aside how easily Ms. Rochette had served me to the lions, the night before, to save her own surgically enhanced neck, if I could get her to reveal a little information about the contents of that briefcase. "That's the part of your story that concerns me the most. Why do you think Mr. Grasso was so very *unhinged*? Did he say anything to you about what exactly he thought might be missing among those papers?"

"No, dear. Not a word. But he was so angry and worried he insisted we leave the gala almost at once."

I hadn't noticed them leaving. "Did you go directly back to Mr. Grasso's house on Iris Circle?"

"I had left my . . . car parked there, yes. I wanted to make him a drink, put on some music. Albert loves to listen to his stars, as he calls them. He has coached the world's best voices, you know. He has CDs by everyone you can imagine and he deserves much more credit than he ever gets."

"I'm sure. But he didn't relax last night?"

"I've seen him upset before, but never like this. He refused to let me console him. Can you imagine? I was willing to do anything to make him feel better, but no."

"He told you to leave?"

Caroline's short blond bob was sprayed so stiffly that not a hair moved as she nodded her head. "Al said he planned to go over his office with a fine-tooth comb. He needed to figure out exactly what was missing. He said if the computer had been taken, he could live with that. He had a system to back up his hard drive or something and he kept the backed-up discs off-site. But he said if the briefcase was gone he was as good as *dead*."

That got my attention. I was certain I was on the right track. Albert Grasso must have suspected some very important, very incriminating document was missing. That was the only explanation for his extraordinary overreaction.

Caroline noticed my interest. "See what I mean? I just couldn't tell my sweetie I had done such a dizzy thing. Anyway, I'm sure he'll calm down when he gets his papers back. But in the meantime, last night at the ball I was in a pinch. I had to play along with him, you know? I had to pretend *you* were the . . . scoundrel. But I just knew you would understand it all when I told you what happened. We chicks have to hang on to our men, don't we?"

"I don't have a man," I admitted, meeting her eye. "And I don't think I would value one who required lying to."

Caroline laughed a pretty laugh and tossed her spent cigarette down on the flagstones next to its mate, crushing it with the pointed toe of her pink pump. "That is simply because you are so young and so pretty. You think you will remain this way forever. I know. I thought that, too. Just wait." She winked at me with one extra-thick artificial lash. "But I want to make up for last night. I think you do deserve a reward, dear. And I've brought . . ." She looked in the tiny pink bag she had hanging from her shoulder and brought out a stack of green. "Here. A thousand-dollar reward. For the return of Albert's papers and files. That should make up for the unpleasantness last night, right?" Caroline held up the crisply folded bills, which I ignored.

"I would like some information."

"Like what?" She looked at me shrewdly, her sweet-thing mask slipping.

"Does your friend Albert have a gun?"

"A what?"

I waited.

"Where is this coming from?" she asked. "Are you afraid he might come after you? Oh, no, no. That's absurd."

"He has a gun, then."

"There is one in the house, if that's what you mean. For protection. Everyone has a gun, don't they?"

"I don't."

Caroline Rochette squinted at me as I stood there with the sun behind me. "You don't? You should. This is Los Angeles, for heaven's sake. You never know when you're safe or when you're in danger here."

"I don't think I'm a gun sort of person," I replied.

"No? Well, you must be the only one in this town who isn't. How do you feel safe at night? No man. No gun. Do you have a dog?"

I gave my head a defiant shake.

"Foolish things happen to foolish girls," she said.

Was she threatening me? And why had I just admitted to this infuriating woman that I didn't have a prayer of a chance to defend myself? I just had to show off how self-reliant I was. Damn. I made a mental note to get a boyfriend, a dog, and a gun. Soon. I covered up my annoyance at myself by asking another question: "Do you know if Mr. Grasso went out again last night, after you left him?"

"Well, how would I know that? I didn't speak to him later, if that's what you're asking. What's this all about?"

"Perhaps I'm trying to judge how sincere you are. You admit to lying last night, so why should I trust you now?"

"Okay. But no more questions about Albert."

"I'm curious to know how you found me here," I said.

"Oh, that was just so easy. I went to your home on Whitley first. But there were policemen on the street and they wouldn't let me drive up. I figured you called the cops about Albert's missing paperwork. Naturally, I didn't want to have to explain anything to any nosy cops. But I saw Nelson Piffer, one of your neighbors. He was out walking his weimaraner."

"You know *Nelson*?" He was a dear man who lived two doors down from me. Nelson was a retired studio art director and I had heard he resented William Wegman deeply for getting the idea of photographing weimaraners posed in human clothes first.

"Oh, yes. Nelson walks Teuksbury up on Iris Circle. Albert and I like to take walks around the neighborhood, too, and we always comment on the fact that Nelson has taken to dressing up the dog in short-sleeve sweatshirts. He loves that dog. And he's worried she gets cold now that she's getting older."

I hadn't known that. I made a mental note to get Teuksbury a sweater next Christmas. "Okay, so you know Nelson Piffer."

"Yes. And Nelson didn't know what was going on at your house, but he said if you weren't home I should try calling your partner. Well, I made a few calls among the Woodburn women and got Wesley's name and it was very familiar. I'm a realtor, you know."

"No, I didn't."

"Oh yes. And I . . . recognized . . . the name Wesley Westcott. He has a favorite agent at my office on Sunset who keeps her eye out for special properties for him. I knew your Wesley bought and sold, of course." Caroline Rochette batted her thick lashes. After staring at her for the past half hour, I was startled to find I was beginning to like the look on her. "It was a quick search of my multiple-listing recent-home-sales database and . . . I found the address of this house."

Just like that. If I had any illusion that I was hidden or safe, I had just lost it.

"Now I'm through playing twenty questions," she said, standing. She swayed slightly, her narrow high heels finding the flagstone path uneven. "Give me Albert's papers and I'll return them to him with all my apologies. Then we can be done with it."

"I can't do that," I said.

"You what?"

"I don't have them here, for one thing."

"Then let's go back to your house."

"No."

Caroline dropped the girlfriend act fast. "Bitch. You think you can shake Al down for more than the thousand, you are just dreaming."

"This isn't about money, Caroline." I turned and began walking back toward the guest house. Our conversation was at an end.

"Oh, come on! Everyone can use some extra cash. Be real." She followed me on the trot. "Who pays for your nails? Your shoes? Your hair?"

"We're finished talking. Get out."

"Don't walk away from me!" she screeched, frustration making her small voice climb to the upper registers. She lunged for me, and, by some instinct, I quickly stepped to the side.

A small splash accompanied her yelp.

"Oh my God!" I couldn't believe my eyes as Caroline Rochette, dainty knit suit, taffy blond hair, face-lift, and all, sank to the bottom of the pool. Before I could react, Cesar and Rolando came on the run. Cesar threw off his hard hat and Rolando pulled off his shoes.

Caroline was not bobbing to the surface. Perhaps the shock of hitting the cold water had temporarily struck her senseless. Perhaps she couldn't swim.

One two three, we all jumped into the pool to rescue her. The last thing I saw before I hit the cold water was Wesley running toward us.

I got to her first, and with the faint memory of some Red Cross certification training from a long, long distant summer camp in Wisconsin, I hooked an arm under Caroline's chest and dragged the small, sopping woman to the surface, kicking and sputtering. She swore at us all as she was pulled to the shallow end, but adrenaline was working its magic and I wouldn't let go of her until I had her up on the steps and out of the pool. Frankly, I doubted I could remember CPR, and after watching her smoke all those cigarettes, I was determined to avoid experiments in mouth-to-mouth resuscitation.

"Don't squirm," I told her. "You might have drowned." Holding on to her, I got a close look at her tight little face and its expression of shock and fear.

"I must get," she panted out, "insurance."

Cesar had recovered Caroline's tiny handbag and Rolando fished around and captured one of her pale pink leather pumps. They handed the dripping accessories to her as she continued to curse at us all.

My soaking jeans weighed a ton as I slogged out of the pool. Wesley came over to me and put his arm around my shoulder. "Are you okay? I saw the entire thing. That woman just ran into the pool. I think she meant to push you in."

With what little dignity she could muster, Caroline stood up straight and stepped into the shoe Rolando had rescued. "This has been an absolutely horrific couple of days," she said. "I don't know what has gotten into me. I just don't know. No man is worth this, honey," she said, giving me a disgusted look. "No man. You can quote me."

I don't know if the dunk in the pool had cooled off her temper, or if she was going on pure realtor instincts. In the presence of a great client like Wes, a man who bought and sold a lot of expensive properties, she was probably trying to undo any professional damage she could. In any event, she seemed to revert to the "polite" social manners that were the mainstay of her trade. She opened her bag with a snap, sending off a small cascade of droplets, and pulled out the cash. I noticed the bills were fairly dry. She handed a hundred each to Cesar and Rolando, who both said, "No, no, señora." Eventually, they were persuaded to take their tips and went on back to the roofing job.

"Everyone in L.A. needs a little extra. Call me," Caroline said, with a wink. She was trying to pull off good-natured and jaunty, but there was definitely something uneasy about that wink. Then she turned and, dripping wet, left the property.

"Can you believe that woman? I mean, can you *believe* her?" I was staring after the spot where she had disappeared around the main house, noticing the wet footprints she had left on the path.

Wesley just shook his head. That's when Holly came through the back gate, holding the carton full of Albert Grasso's papers that she had just taken to be copied, missing running into Caroline Rochette by seconds.

Holly checked out my wet face, my wet hair, my wet clothes. "What's going on? Why is Madeline soaking wet?" she asked, looking from Wes to me.

"It's a long story," Wes said, "which Mad is about to tell us."

"Ew," Holly said, pointing into the pool.

But when examined more closely, the big, black bug that had grabbed Holly's attention turned out to be nothing more menacing than one of Caroline Rochette's eyelashes, gone dismally astray.

And while we found it easy to laugh at the bizarre woman and her bizarre visit, I began to wonder if she wasn't really more of a threat than I gave her credit for. Had any of the things she told me this afternoon been true? The birthday-gift plans? The briefcase accident? Her real reason for coming to see me, even? Was it to get Grasso's papers or to find out what I knew and how well guarded I was here? Damn.

The breeze blew against my wet jeans and shirt. I began to shiver. I am not one to make enemies if I can help it. But for the first time in my life, and over a discarded pile of junk, I realized I had just made a few serious ones.

I looked at Holly holding the cardboard box of paperwork that seemed to be at the center of my troubles. I would turn it all over to the police. We would look through the copies and see what we could see. But what then? My home was a crime scene and it appeared anyone who knew a real estate agent could track me down at Wesley's place in a matter of minutes. Plus Caroline Rochette had actually been here, scoping out the lay of the land. I began to wonder again why Sara Jackson had been killed at my house. Had she seen something that put her in danger?

Holly said, "You should get out of those clothes, Mad. It's getting cooler out."

"You're right," I said, trying to return her smile.

But as I followed her back to the guest house, I remembered Caroline's warnings and couldn't stop shaking. What should I do? I was away from home too often to keep a dog. I seemed unable to keep a boyfriend. But a gun . . .

"Who's Sorry Now?"

es and Holly and I had spent hours in Wesley's guest-house living room examining Grasso's private papers. We pored over the copies Holly had made of what had once been, if we were to believe the scheming Caroline Rochette, the contents of Albert Grasso's briefcase, but understood no more than before. As for the originals, I had left a message for Honnett. I wanted his advice on what to do with Grasso's junk. The police, it turned out, didn't want to take custody of it. When I called my local station, they politely suggested I toss it all out.

The pathetic fact was: Nothing new leaped to our attention. If there was something in the papers that warranted the sort of apoplectic reaction that Grasso had displayed, we were missing it. There were no notes of dirty deeds, no confessions of criminal activity, no admissions of illicit love. Nada.

"Okay, here are the pictures," Holly said, having neatly reorganized the Xerox copies of the fifty-some documents and photos once again.

Wesley was typing a master list into his laptop. He swiftly keyed in the names and inscriptions he found scrawled across a dozen autographed eight-by-tens, all from grateful Albert Grasso celebrity clients. Among others, the five-member boy band that made ten-year-olds swoon. The aging Vegas diva, a woman who was certainly due a free liposuction if her plastic surgeon gave an incentive gift for every dozen nips or tucks. The airbrushed faces of several young hopefuls who had become recent celebrities on *American Idol*. The legendary screen star from the fifties, Catherine Hill. Her face brought a smile to my lips. This glamorous old MGM superstar had become a "close personal friend" of mine, as Wes and I liked to joke. Catherine Hill and I had actually met several times. And in Hollywood, Wes and I had learned, any slight acquaintance (Phil Collins's plumber? Charlize Theron's optometrist?) seemed to be all it took to claim intimate relationships with the stars. And then there was the photo of the former president with the smiling young woman.

"I'm guessing that's Albert's niece or daughter," I said, rechecking the image. "Damn, I should have thought to ask Caroline if Albert had a daughter while I had her here, answering questions."

Wes pushed a few keys and was soon deep into a Web search on Albert Grasso. Duh. I mean, why hadn't I thought of that?

"Here he is," Wes said, his eyes scanning the screen. "I've pulled up his biography."

"What's it say?" Holly asked.

"Usual sort of things. He was born in Oklahoma City. He studied voice at the University of Oklahoma on scholarship. Opera. Broadway. Yadda yadda."

We waited. "Says he arranged music and did vocal work with Sonny and Cher way back when. And worked on their show."

"All these people," I said, "who surround the stars. They all manage to make a living, don't they?"

"As do we," Wes pointed out. That got all of us thinking for a minute. Then he said, "Here's all it says about his personal life. 'Albert Grasso lives in the Hollywood Hills. His daughter, Gracie, is a recent graduate of Georgetown University and attends Harvard Law School.' "

"Bingo!" I said, feeling rather pleased with myself. "She must be the intern in the picture with Clinton."

"Ew," said Holly. I was surprised at her reaction. Frankly, Holly still had a crush on the former president. I looked at her and raised a brow. She asked, "How can you name a kid Gracie Grasso?"

That was something to think about another day. "Can we look through the documents one more time?" I asked.

"I have just about finished logging them," Wes said. "There are seven letters of thanks or recommendation from various celebs and academies. There are four requests for donations to charities or thank-you notes from foundations. There are six receipts for various items."

"Can we go over those again?" I asked.

"Sure. One from CreateTech for an item called Digital Performer—"

"That's recording software," Holly commented. "You know, so you can turn your Mac into a recording studio sort of thing."

"One for clothing, specifically two Armani Collezioni suits and various shirts from Boutique Giorgio Armani Beverly Hills; one five-page itemized account from the Four Seasons in Las Vegas for a ten-day trip last October; one from a place called Art-4-Less for an oil painting entitled *Dog Living in Luxury with Cigar*; one sales slip for Grasso's Audi A6; and the deed to a luxury condo on Prince Edward Island."

"So what does that tell us?" I asked. "Nothing."

"Maybe Grasso has a love nest in Canada," Holly tried.

"Holly, don't blame our neighbors to the north," Wes said.

"He's dressing up in the new Armani," Holly continued, "driving his Audi out to Vegas, setting up private recording sessions—"

I finished, "And hooking up with the cigar-smoking dog?"

Wes laughed. "If Albert Grasso was sticking up a gas station one day, and one of these receipts proves he was in the area and busts his alibi—we're never going to know that."

"Maybe Albert had to buy those suits to replace two identical models that he ruined by spilling someone's blood all over them."

Context. Any little thing could be innocent or much more dangerous if one knew the context.

"So we agree," Holly concluded, stacking the papers up again, "we definitely don't know what we know."

"Comforting," Wes said, looking over at me, concerned.

"I left a message for Detective Baronowski. Since this carton of Grasso's things had been stored at my house at the time of the break-in, maybe he'll take a look."

"Good," Wes agreed.

I picked up the phone and dialed the number to get the messages off of my home voice mail. I was ready to handle the accumulation of work and backlog of messages that had piled up since yesterday. We often get called on the weekend. Party anxiety can hit our clients at the oddest times.

There were several events-related items: a couple who were picking dates for a September engagement party, a public relations agent who wanted to make sure we had allowed extra space for the paparazzi at her beach barbeque soiree, and already a call about the Woodburn flower-arrangement class/luncheon we'd been asked to schedule so soon. A flurry of short, sweet messages came in from Zenya Knight, Connie Hutson, Dilly Swinden, and four other Woodburn ladies, with praise for the Black & White Ball and thanks for putting on such a fabulous party. These women may have suffered a drunken celebrity auctioneer, a major robbery, and a hundred-thousand-dollar loss to their auction revenues, but you couldn't tell it by their warm thank-you calls. Had their mothers beaten these manners into them as small children, or was such graciousness genetic?

Surprisingly, there was only one message about the police activity at our house. My neighbor Nelson Piffer was wondering what all the fuss on the street was about. He'd heard a terrible rumor from another neighbor—a woman he detests with a yippy dachshund—who said the coroner's van had been spied on Whitley Avenue around 4 A.M. It sounded like Nelson was angling for some details, although he was much too well mannered to ask directly. He signed off by reminding me the Whitley Heights Homeowners Association meeting had been canceled for the month, and that, as always, Teuksbury sent her love.

The most intriguing message came last. "Hello, Miss Bean. It is Albert Grasso calling with deep and very sincere apologies. I seem to have made a royal ass out of myself last night. I was extremely upset, as I don't need to remind you. But, clearly, I was taking out my anger on the messenger, and what a charming and beautiful messenger you were, too.

"As for the terrible misunderstanding, all has been explained to me by Caroline. She came over this afternoon and told me everything. What the hell can I say? She begged for my forgiveness and she begs your forgiveness, too, of course, and whatever Caroline did, she meant well. I am so sorry our foolish little drama has impacted you in such a nasty way. Look, the point of this call. I'd like to apologize in person. You've been a trouper through this whole fiasco. If it is at all possible, I would love to get my papers back. Please drop them off at your earliest convenience."

I played that one back twice and then hung up.

"Million messages?" Holly inquired.

"Always," I answered. "The Woodburn ladies loved the party, despite the several glitches in their fund-raising efforts. Not our responsibility, of course."

"Thank goodness," Wes said.

"And a few other calls. Zenya Knight wants to talk to me. It's sure to be about her weird husband. I wouldn't be surprised if he was in jail after the way he was driving last night. And there was a call from their auction-bidding rivals, the Hutsons."

Wes looked up. "What did they want?"

"They'd like to plan a birthday party for their twelve-year-old sax genius. They suggest holding a 'battle of the jazz players' kind of competition."

"Oy," Holly said, and giggled.

"And then I got a call from Mr. Albert Grasso, very sorry and all that."

"Really?" Holly looked shocked.

"So maybe he's just a blowhard kind of guy. Big blowup last night, and apologies today."

"Men are weird," Holly said.

"Hey," Wes said.

"I think I better give him back his junk."

"Really?" Wes was surprised.

"Well, I realize Grasso was rude as hell to me last night. Unfortunately, that crime is not yet recognized in the state of California."

"Your problem is you are too forgiving," Holly said.

"If Grasso and Caroline are apologizing for their craziness, that's more than you usually get from the assorted loonies we work with."

"But—"

"And look at this stuff." I tapped the box that was piled with the man's items. "We have his passport and his therapist's report and his detailed Bible-study notes and his book proposal for *How to Sing Like a Bird*. There are three handwritten letters from his mother from like thirty-five years ago. Those have to be precious to him."

"True," Holly agreed reluctantly.

"And we've got all that other stuff he'll need, like the copies of his divorce papers. And the detailed inventory of his coin collection and those papers from Mid-Pacific Insurance and North American Home Insurance and every other legal document he's going to need in his life."

We all sat and thought about it.

"But, Maddie, what about Sara . . . ?" Holly said, shaking her head.

"We don't know what happened to Sara, Holly. Maybe it was just a junkie looking for something to steal, something he could hock for drug money. And then Sara showed up and she . . . If someone was breaking into the house and got scared, they might have followed her up to my room. Maybe she ran . . ."

Holly's eyes were beginning to tear up and I knew if I let myself go there, in a minute or two, mine would, too. It was funny how emotion could suddenly wash over you, like waves. And if a swell caught you unprepared, it could knock you down. I steadied myself and went on: "Look. This Grasso business needs to be cleaned up."

"I know," Holly said, tears running down her cheeks. Wes kindly handed her a box of tissues.

"I wanted to believe I could figure everything out," I said, sitting down next to Holly. "I thought I could make sense of Sara's murder and Grasso's anger. I was looking for one neat solution. But they just don't seem connected."

Holly wiped her eyes and nodded.

"We checked it out as best as we could," Wes said. "Holding on to Grasso's papers isn't going to help Sara."

"No." Holly blew her nose. "Maddie is right. I think we're all freaked out and twitchy. I know I am."

"That's right, Holly." I gave her a little hug. "And we just have to get past it. I've got to get back to normal. And I'm going to start by returning Albert Grasso's papers."

Okay. I wasn't 100 percent sure that Grasso was an innocent, if rage-challenged, jerk. I just had no real proof to the contrary.

"And just in case," I said, "I'll let Grasso know that I've already shown the papers to lots of people."

"Good idea." Holly sniffled.

"And tell him copies of everything in his files are going to the police," Wes added.

"Fine," I agreed. "Look, I've got to get out of here already. I'm going a little stir-crazy. I'll drop off the copies at Baronowski's office and give Grasso back his precious junk. And I've been thinking I should pay a condolence call on Sara Jackson's boyfriend. Sara said he was depressed. I can't imagine how he's getting through all this."

"I forgot about him," Holly said, in a hushed voice. "So do you think maybe he's a suspect?"

"I'm sure that's how the police view him. But he could just be a grieving grad student who needs some help. So, can you get me Sara's address?"

"That's okay, Hol," Wes said. "I've got it in my PC. And I am going to go along with Madeline."

"What?" I swung around and faced him. "Like I can't walk around without an escort?"

"Honey, we thought we lost you."

I quieted down. Of course they had. Why was I so defensive?

"Look, you've been dumped in the middle of downtown, dunked in an unheated swimming pool, and there's been a murder in your bedroom. At this point, I'd think you might appreciate a little company."

Wesley Westcott was a great guy.

"Big Nick"

After the heat of the day, the early-evening air was refreshingly cool. I brushed off my white jeans and smoothed the tan silk sleeveless shirt as I waited on the front walk outside Wesley's house, right next to a mammoth-size demolition Dumpster, in leafy old Hancock Park. From around back, I could hear Wes as he opened the garage door. But before he could pull his new Jag down the driveway, another car pulled up the street and turned into it.

Dexter Wyatt. Ah.

I was seriously annoyed to notice how raggedy my breath got as vast quantities of adrenaline, or something like it, began pumping up my senses.

Dex stepped out of the car in one languid movement and smiled at me. His hair tumbled over his forehead. His shorts showed off tanned legs, great calf muscles. His boyishness was extremely sexy.

"Impressive," he said as he walked behind his car and over to me at the curb. "You been standing out here next to a Dumpster all day hoping to catch a glimpse of me?"

"Maybe." Eye contact made me intensely aware of how warm the evening was, after all.

Dexter handed me a large sequin-dusted Hawaiian-print shoulder bag, the one I usually bring to our events because it can hold everything and it's hard to miss. "Yours, I take it. Properly returned, with apologies from my sister."

"Thanks." I took the bag and opened it to find my cell phone. I wasn't too surprised to discover the battery was dead.

"Nothing disturbed, I hope. No loose change missing. Never can trust that brother-in-law of mine."

I giggled. "It's fine, I'm sure."

"So you want to go somewhere?" Dex asked, gesturing a playful finger toward himself, and then me, and then hitching his thumb over to his cute sports car, laying on the charm. "Grab a bite, maybe? Seeing as you are looking so hot."

"Thanks. Now don't get me wrong. Normally, I would love to be picked up on the street by a passing guy. Really."

"I know." Dex had a great smile and he used it. "I remember last night with fondness."

"But things are just a little messed up right now . . ."

The red taillights of Wesley's Jaguar came suddenly into view, backing down the long driveway, until it stopped, blocked by Dex's car.

Dexter reassessed the situation. "Boyfriend?" He actually sounded crestfallen. My solar plexus did a little flip.

"Not exactly. Best friend. Partner."

"Gay?"

I mock-scowled at Dexter. "Look, I have a few errands to run and I better get going. Thanks so much for driving this by." I gestured to my purse. "You didn't have to go to all that trouble."

"Trouble? I wanted to see you again, Madeline. I have been thinking about you all day. Did you ever get to sleep?"

"No."

"Me neither. I kept thinking about you."

"Oh, man." I giggled. "What a line."

"Women," Dex said philosophically. "They never believe you when you are telling the truth."

"Maybe, but that puts us in an excellent position to *not* believe you when you are telling us big lies, you see." I leaned a little closer to him, catching his scent. He smelled yummy. I stepped back.

"You lack trust," he said, shaking his head sadly.

"I've got to go."

"How about later?"

"Why?"

"You seem like a complicated woman," he said. "Moth to the flame."

"I am so going to cure you of that," I said, laughing.

"Good." Dexter took a few seconds to look me over. "I take even the slightest scolding as encouragement. So when will you be free? Nine?"

"Make it ten o'clock. I'll meet you somewhere. I'll have Wesley drop me off."

"Where?"

"How about Fabiolus on Melrose?" I suggested a charming little Italian place in an odd part of Hollywood, right behind Paramount Studios. It seemed to fit us, as we had already set a precedent of eating off the beaten path.

"I'll be there." He walked me over to Wesley's car. "So it's a date, then." As he bent down to open the door, his lips almost brushed against my hair.

"Fine." I sat. "Wesley, this is Dexter Wyatt. Dex, Wes."

"Hi there," Wes said amiably.

"Good to meet you. And, Madeline, I'll see you later." Dexter Wyatt shut the car door, hopped into his own vehicle, and drove smoothly off, heading south. Wes pulled out of the driveway and turned north.

As we glided up the street, he cast a look over at me. "So I leave you for three minutes and you pick up a guy?"

"That was Zenya's brother, the guy I told you about. He was returning my bag."

"And what does he do?" Wes asked.

"I don't think he does much. Trust funds, I assume."

"Oh ho."

On our rounds, we dropped by the police station, where I left the copies of Grasso's paperwork for Detective Baronowski. He wasn't in. Next, I asked Wes to drive me downtown, where we scouted around the quiet Sunday streets looking for my loan officer. He wasn't in front of the building near Flower, but about two blocks over I spotted his dog. When I approached the dog, sitting alone on the sidewalk in front of a closed office tower, the owner came out from the shadow.

"I borrowed some money from your dog last night," I told the man, trying to remember if he was the same guy. It was the same dog, all right. His tail beat the sidewalk in happy recognition.

"Big Nick shouldn't be giving nobody no money," the man muttered, eyeing me. "What you want?"

"I owe Big Nick a dollar thirty-five, plus a bonus of ten dollars." I had the money in my hand and held it out.

"So give it to 'im," the man said, watching me like I must be a cop and he wasn't about to get pinched.

I could see no sign of the man's collection jar, so I just bent down and put a ten and a one and a quarter and a dime on the pavement.

Big Nick stood up and sniffed the money then sat back down, tail thumping.

"Big Nick don't like most people. So if he bite you, don't be blaming me. Big Nick is a mean mother."

"Thanks for the tip." Big Nick looked at me with love in his eyes.

"Don't I get nothing?" the man asked.

"Sure. Sorry. You have a jar?"

He kept staring at me.

So I opened my bag and took out another ten-dollar bill. I handed it to the man and he snatched it before I let go, almost ripping it.

There was no thank you involved, but I didn't mind. I had repaid a debt and gotten to see Big Nick again. Sometimes, low expectations help in life.

Wes had pulled his white S-Type into a no-parking zone on Seventh, just around the corner. When I got back, he was smiling.

"You always amaze me, Mad. The people you know, the friends you meet."

"I own this town," I said, and then asked nicely to be driven over to Iris Circle. As it turned out, no one was home at Albert Grasso's house. I decided to leave the cardboard carton of papers at the front door, and then I second-guessed that decision. After all the commotion, I hated to leave the stuff there unattended. But I hated even worse the idea I would still be stuck with them. I tucked the box behind a shrub to one side of the door and hopped back into Wesley's Jaguar. I must say I could get used to such service.

After that, I felt a lot better. I needed to pick up some vitamins and

Wes was uncomplaining as we ran a few other errands. Even though he was a dear, I longed for my own wheels. I needed some independence to get back to normal.

We stopped back at my house on Whitley to pick up a few items I'd forgotten to pack. I was pleased to see the crime-scene tape had been removed. Wes and I discussed what to do about the house and where I should stay. We agreed that it was best for me to hang at his place for a while. We'd open the office tomorrow, as usual, and work out of the downstairs rooms. Wesley had already called a cleaning service, which would arrive in the morning, and he insisted he'd deal with the upstairs rooms. He suggested we take this opportunity to remodel a bit, maybe push out a wall and expand the bedrooms. I was unfocused, unwilling to think about my bedroom the last time I stood in it. Unable to avoid it. And the awful memory of Sara Jackson.

Before we left the neighborhood, I asked Wes to swing around to Iris Circle again. I hoped the cardboard carton I had left by the door earlier had been taken in. But when we drove up to Albert Grasso's house, I could plainly see the box sitting half hidden by the shrub where I had left it.

"Wes, hang on half a second while I go up and ring the doorbell again. Maybe Grasso was doing laundry or giving a late singing lesson when we stopped by before. Maybe he didn't hear me knock. I'd feel better if I didn't have to worry about that box all night."

"Sure."

But again, no one answered.

"Enough. Let's get out of here," I suggested when I was back in the Jag. "I have a date for dinner."

Fifteen minutes later, Wes dropped me off at the Fabiolus Café. Dexter Wyatt was already seated at a table and I joined him.

"Am I late?" I asked.

"I was early," he said. "Hope you don't mind, but I already ordered for us."

That caught my attention.

I should explain. In most of my recent relationships, I'd had the upper hand in the foodie arts. It isn't surprising. I am, after all, a graduate of the Culinary Institute. A professional. I'd worked as a chef in Northern California and down in L.A. before Wes and I started our catering/event-planning firm. I love exotic cuisines and complex, demanding recipes.

The men I had dated tended to be less food involved. In fact, my longest-lasting boyfriend of record, Arlo Zar, was a certified food wimp. He was a Big Mac kind of guy. Among other oddities, Arlo eschewed vegetables outright. He refused to eat anything green, on principle, except for iceberg lettuce. And only iceberg when it was cut into a wedge and served with Thousand Island. Arlo was a comedy writer and sitcom producer and considered his food quirks charming. I had been amused, as I always was, by Arlo and his ways. At least, for the first couple of years.

Honnett and I only lasted a few months, and even then our romance had been on the erratic side. After Arlo, Honnett was amazingly open to trying new foods. But he was at heart a steak-and-potatoes kind of guy. I can always tell what people like to eat best, what flavors comfort them most. Holly says I have EFP—Extra-Foodery Perception. I claim no alien gifts, but I will admit this sensitivity to others' tastes and desires has served me well in my business, planning menus for so many clients. And I have relied on it, knowing I have an edge in evaluating new people.

I looked across the linen-draped table at Dex and smiled. What a guy ordered from a menu was a most revealing right of passage in a new relationship. I prolonged the delicious suspense a moment longer as I sipped my glass of cool white wine. The bottle of Valpolicella Classico Superiore "Villa Novare" 1997 sat on the table. Dex had good taste in wine. Very good taste. Extra points.

"Great wine." I looked up at him and found everything I saw appealing. This was dangerous. "What did you order?"

"For you," he said, "the goat-cheese-and-blackened-chicken salad to start. Balsamic dressing on the side."

I smiled.

"Okay so far? Followed by penne ai calamari—penne pasta made with sautéed calamari and a fresh sauce of cherry tomatoes, garlic, basil, and white wine."

"And for you?"

"I'm having polenta e poccio—cornmeal and prosciutto covered with a Gorgonzola sauce, and also the lonza di maiale al provolone e asparagi, which is the—"

"Pork loin in white wine and asparagus sauce," I interrupted, "covered with provolone cheese and served with sautéed spinach."

"Exactly," he said. "And I figured we could share if you found anything more appealing on my plate."

I eyed the menu quickly and discovered I couldn't have ordered any better myself. What a pleasure.

Another memory surfaced. Xavier Jones had been a true culinary genius. He was a boy I met in culinary school, the top of our class. He and I planned to open our own auberge in the wine country of Northern California together someday. That was all just a dream, of course. We never did anything like that. We didn't even get married. But it had only been with Xavier and, later, with my friend Wesley that I had found such extreme-sport cuisine compatibility.

"You judging me?" Dex asked, amused.

"A-plus. But don't let it go to your head."

"So," Dex asked me, refilling my wineglass, "how come you don't look tired? I look like shit and you look beautiful."

"Thanks." I remembered flirting. I liked flirting. I tried to remember how. "I can go without sleep. One of my few true talents."

"Too modest," he said. "If we're going to be friends, and I insist we are going to be, then you have to tell me the three best things about yourself. No, five."

"Oh, come on! I am much too demure. Too shy. Too—"

"Full of it. Come on. You must. And I'll tell you the five best things about me. You go first."

Our first course was delivered, which gave me a moment to think. It's not that I'm really demure and shy. It's just that I don't think about myself very often. I realized, too, that not many men had seemed all that interested in my view of myself. Which was interesting, really.

"You've had enough wine and you've missed enough sleep, so be totally frank," Dex said, looking at me over his wineglass.

"I'm a pretty good speller."

Dexter laughed loudly. A deep, handsome, masculine laugh. "More personal stuff, Madeline, or I'll have to raise your number to ten."

"No, no! Okay . . . I'm honest. Not everyone agrees that's a good trait, however. But I am really truthful. And I'm curious about everything, so I read a lot and tend to ask a lot of questions."

"Again, all your good traits seem to have two edges."

"Ain't that the truth? Let me think. How many is that?"

"You have given me two—you're honest and curious. I'm throwing out the good-spelling confession."

"Okay, but you must count how good I am without much sleep. I have great energy. That's three. And I'm a great cook. I love to cook," I added. "And I like sex."

Well, there. That got Dexter's attention. I couldn't believe I said it, but it was true.

Dexter said, "Well, well, well. We have a good trait in common, then. Count that as my first. Then as to the other four: I am loyal. I love my sister. I don't do drugs. Anymore. And I'm pretty talented at starting fires in fireplaces."

"That must come in handy," I said with admiration.

"It does. I also played tennis sort of professionally."

"So that's six things you are good at," I said, adding them up.

"Well, if I'd been *really* good at tennis, I might have done a little better on the circuit, but I can hit the ball around."

My salad was wonderful, and Dexter insisted we taste each other's dish. His polenta was very good, but not, I thought secretly to myself, as good as my own. I would have to cook it for him someday.

"Now your worst traits," Dex said, unable to hold back a grin.

"No way."

"You must. You said you're honest. Prove it. I want your three worst qualities."

I tried not to blush as he made a great show of refilling my wineglass yet again, the better to loosen my tongue, I gathered.

The waiter removed our plates and brought on the main courses. The aroma of garlic and basil and white wine rose from my steamy plate of pasta. It looked wonderful and I suddenly realized how hungry I had been. Dexter declared his pork loin to be perfectly cooked and the waiter retreated.

"Okay," Dex said, getting back on topic. "I'll show you what a good sport I am. I'll go first. My three worst traits."

I paused with a forkful of short, hollow penne noodles almost to my lips.

"First, I don't have a job." Dex spoke lightly, but I suspected not much escaped his notice as he confessed his sins. "Second, despite my extremely prestigious education, I don't have any skills with which to acquire a job."

"Where did you go to school?"

"Yale. Philosophy major. Played tennis and skied."

"Minored in girls?"

"You apparently know me much too well," he said, putting down his fork and meeting my eyes. "Alas, no great job market there."

"No. And what else?"

"And third, and worst of all, my trust fund is almost completely obliterated. I could blame the market, which as you know has been terrible, but against all the good advice in the world, I've been leaning rather hard on the principle. Eventually, it will run out. My family had money at one time, or so they tell me, but at present, they are pretty much broke. All except Zenya, thanks to her jerk husband, Bill. He's got bucks. But not me. In other words, Maddie, I don't have any money, or ambition, or goals."

"That's sad," I said, filled with wine and sympathy. "Isn't there anything in life that appeals to you?"

"I don't know," he said. "I like sports. I like photography. I like you." He smiled.

"Have you ever done anything with your photographs?"

"What do you mean?"

"Have you ever tried to sell them?"

"No. I used to take lots of pictures when I was playing tennis. I haven't done much recently."

"Okay. If I was in charge of your life, I'd suggest you call a few of your friends who are still playing professional sports and get passes to their events. You take some pictures, and if you like how they turn out, you sell them. Simple, huh?"

He gazed at me across the table. "So I guess your three worst traits are, you have no problem with meddling in sensitive areas, you can get a little bossy, and you have the extremely annoying habit of being right."

"That pretty much sums me up," I said, wondering if I had offended him.

"No wonder my sister was so keen on my meeting you," Dexter said. "Say, not to be nosy . . ."

"Nosy? You?" I laughed. "After demanding to know my best and worst traits. That's ridiculous."

"Well, thanks. I have been kind of curious about what was going on at your house last night. The cops. The body in the bedroom. Can you fill me in?"

"It's a long story," I said. "Long. And I don't understand most of it. Just a sad event. Remember, when you rescued me last night I told you I had lent my car to a young woman who worked for me? She came to my house to return my car. We don't know exactly what happened, but while she was there she got shot. The police are thinking she may have interrupted a burglar. It's all just horrible."

"That is tough," he said, putting his large hand over my hand.

"I want to help in some way, but I can't figure out what to do. I'm thinking, maybe her boyfriend could use a little help. I've never met him. I was going to see him this evening, but that was before I ran into you." I put my hand to my temple. I was getting a headache.

"This wasn't something I should have brought up. I'm sorry, Madeline," Dex said quietly.

"No, no. It's okay. I am suddenly feeling exhausted," I said. "I need to get some sleep, if you don't mind driving me back to Wesley's."

Dexter Wyatt didn't even ask for the bill. He just casually threw two hundred dollars onto the table and stood up. "Let's go."

"Sorry to spoil your night," I said as we walked to his car, parked out front.

"No, I understand," he said. "You have a lot on your mind."

"I do. I have to go see this dead girl's boyfriend tomorrow. And then, I am still hung up on old boyfriend."

"The cop?"

"Yeah.

"And I have a bad feeling about some papers I dropped off today. No one was home, so I decided to leave them at the door. Now I'm thinking that wasn't the best idea."

Dex touched a button on his key chain that unlocked the doors to his car. But before he reached down to open the passenger door for me, he turned and put his hands on my shoulders. "You need some sleep. In the morning, everything will look a lot better."

"I hope so."

"You'll see. The problem with the girl and her boyfriend. The papers. Me."

"You have been great. I mean it. You've been fun."

"I get that a lot," he said, with a sly smile. And then, standing out on Melrose Avenue with very little traffic, he pulled me gently toward him and kissed me. His lips were soft and light. I was tense but his body felt good, holding me close. By the second kiss, I had sort of given up much resistance. Why struggle to understand things that were beyond me? If I could just stay in the moment, I was fine. More than fine. I was hoping for a third kiss, but Dex pulled back and kissed me on the forehead instead.

"So when you get this cop out of your system," he said, "can I see you again?"

I had the strangest thought. I suddenly wondered if Big Nick would approve of this new guy in my life. More, I figured, than he'd approve of a married cop.

"The Shoes of the Fisherman's Wife Are Some Jive-Ass Slippers"

looked at the small clock on the bedside table. Seven-thirty. Eight hours of sleep, I calculated. Quite decent.

After a quick shower, I decided to let my hair dry naturally to save time. I'd deal with the wild, electric-socket ringlets later. I pulled on some khaki capris and a clean, white T-shirt, and found my way out to the tiny kitchen. Wes was preparing French toast.

"One or two?" he asked me as he began dipping thin slices of his home-baked bread into the egg mixture.

"Just one, thanks." I picked up the kettle of boiling water from the range and poured it into a mug over a humble tea bag. Wesley had already brewed himself a cup of estate-grown English Breakfast tea, but he kept a stash of Lipton's just for me, knowing I often preferred my morning cup of tea plain and simple and familiar. "I had a big dinner."

"How'd that go?" Wes asked, raising his voice slightly to be heard above the sizzle as he put rich, egg-soaked slices of bread onto the hot griddle.

"Fine," I said. "Okay. Pretty good."

Wes adjusted the gas burners, using just one-hundredth of his conscious brainpower, keeping the other ninety-nine hundredths focused on me, an expectant look on his even features, waiting for more.

"He's terribly cute. But I'm not sure I can take another mistake in the boyfriend department."

"Mistake? What's wrong with him? You know, Mad, my mother used to tell us, you can just as easily fall in love with a rich man as a poor man."

"My mother said the same thing!" We smiled at each other. "Only problem—the horrible sledgehammer of power I observe some rich men wielding over their women."

"Oh. Good point."

"Some of these women, Wes. It's like they are always worried they aren't cute enough, or thin enough, or young enough, or whatever. And I think the money does that to them. They realize their rich old husbands can always go out and get younger, cuter women."

"Well, then. Down with rich men," Wes said, amused.

"But on the other hand, it turns out that Dexter isn't rich."

"Really? Score one for him, then. So what's the problem?"

"I may still be in love with Honnett. I don't know."

"It will all sort itself out," Wes said, serving me a perfectly cooked slice of French toast. I sprinkled a quarter of a teaspoon of powdered sugar over it and joined him at the tiny table for two in the corner.

"Glad you aren't trying to stay thin to please some rich guy." Wes eyed my meager plate and smiled.

I got his point. "I think this is different. I'm single. I may not know what the hell I'm doing in the ocean of romance, but I still need to keep the bait fresh." I forked another small bite of French toast. "Mark my words. Someday, when I'm happily married to my soul mate, who loves me for all the right reasons, I may just let this whole body of mine go straight to hell."

"I'll rejoice in your happy fatness."

"But until then . . ." I pushed the plate away.

Over our breakfast, Wes informed me that while I had been out, Detective Baronowski had returned my many calls. He'd thanked us for dropping off the copies we'd made of Grasso's paperwork but didn't act like it was some great big lead. Wes sensed the detective didn't think there was much to go on there. We'd done our duty, at least. And while Baronowski had remained tight-lipped about his investigation into Sara

Jackson's death, he had asked Wes for more information on Sara's boyfriend. Unfortunately, we knew very little about most of our temporary waitstaff, so Wes couldn't be much help. Baronowski did confirm that we could get back into my house on Whitley, as their investigation there was complete. That was a good thing, since we'd already been back there last night. On the disappointing side, the cops would need to keep my car for a few more days. Their forensics people were pretty backed up.

When we'd cleaned up the dishes, Wes agreed to drive me to the Enterprise rent-a-car office up on Sunset. Now that my purse had been returned, I had my driver's license and my credit cards and I could finally get myself a rental. After driving my very old Jeep Grand Wagoneer for years, I discovered I was in for a treat. Renting a new car is fun. I decided to try a Chevy Trailblazer. I selected a red one and was thrilled to realize I now temporarily possessed more cup holders than had ever been featured in my wildest dreams. I couldn't wait to zip into the nearest In-N-Out Burger and try out every size cup of Diet Coke.

Out on the street, I felt a sudden uplift in my spirits. As I rode Sunset east, I heard a familiar beeping. My cell phone, all charged up overnight, was once again in working shape. One by one, the pieces of my world were coming back to order. I smiled.

"Hello."

"It's me." Honnett's voice sounded calm. He'd experienced his one evening of strong, barely controlled emotion the other night. I doubted I'd see that side of him again. Something to consider.

"I'm on my way to my office," I said. "You know, back to my house. I have got to face it, don't I?"

"It's still pretty soon, isn't it, Maddie? You can't rush things if you are feeling overwhelmed."

"Overwhelmed, get out of town. But it's sad. I'll never feel good about that house again." I was glad to be saying it out loud. I didn't want to let Wesley down, but I was nervous. Post-traumatic stress. "I don't feel safe there, Chuck. But it's where I work. I need to get back to work."

"You'll get through it. You're tough. Can I meet you there?"

I hesitated.

"Something wrong, Maddie?"

"Actually, I have a few loose ends," I said. "I need to visit a couple of people. Maybe I should do that first. What's this about, Honnett? Official business or—"

"No. I just need to see you. Things were said the other night. We haven't talked in months. We still haven't cleared the air, have we?"

"You mean," I suggested into my small cell phone, stopped at the red light at Laurel Canyon, "I still haven't forgiven you for being married."

"Now that you put it so clearly, yes." Honnett sounded amused. He could handle sarcasm. I liked that in a man. "Will you see me?"

"Why don't you stop by the house around lunchtime?"

"Great."

Great, I said to myself when he had clicked off. I looked over at the note I'd written with Sara Jackson's address. She had lived in the Promenade Towers on South Figueroa, in downtown L.A., just a mile from the Woodburn. If I'd realized she lived so close to the party, I'd have offered to drive her home the other night. If I'd bothered to ask her. I thought about how I had managed to know so little about my employees.

I turned onto the Hollywood Freeway and drove south, enjoying the horsepower and unfamiliar ride of the rental, then transitioned slowly to the 110, and finally pulled off on Third Street. I spotted the high-rise complex of the Promenade Towers located in the Bunker Hill section of downtown, and turned the Trailblazer into its underground parking lot.

The elevator took me to the large lobby, an impressive, two-story, marble-floored space. Beyond the lobby, through glass doors, I could see a water wonderland. Fountains and pools filled a courtyard that was sheltered by the many residential towers of the complex. There was a sign posted on the glass announcing that good apartments were still available for rent. A sign nearby boasted about the excellence of the building's swimming pool. Another claimed THE BEST FITNESS CENTER IN DOWNTOWN! ASK US ABOUT OUR STUDENT SPECIALS! FURNISHED STUDIOS—$775! PETS! LAUNDRY FACILITY!

I wondered what exactly I would say to him, to Sara's boyfriend. I knew Sara was carrying him financially. Maybe I could offer him a small gift. He might need a helping hand with the rent.

In the lobby, I went over to the courtesy desk and spoke to the guard.

"Apartment 4-2029," I said.

"You're here to see . . . ?"

"I'm here to see . . ." It was damned awkward. I stood there for a sec-

ond or two, and the guard, a tall, heavy African-American guy in his forties, began to look at me suspiciously.

"Yeah?"

"Sara Jackson in Apartment 4-2029, please." It was fairly creepy. I had
just asked for a dead woman.

"And you are . . . ?"

"Madeline Bean."

"You asking for Ms. Jackson?" He stared at me.

"Yes. Or her roommate. Sara's fiancé. I don't have his name."

"No one going to be home there," the man said. "You family or something?"

"No. I'm Sara's employer. She worked for me."

"So, you're her boss?"

"Yes."

"Hold on," he said. He didn't pick up the courtesy phone. Instead, he
lumbered away, down the hall marked EMPLOYEES ONLY.

I took the opportunity to peek over the high counter. There was a
well-worn three-inch black binder. The label on the cover was peeling. It
said MASTER. I figured it was the current listing of tenants and grabbed it
while the lobby was still deserted.

The listings were alphabetical. I had been hoping I could just look up
the apartment number and get the name of Sara's boyfriend quickly. Instead, I might have to page through hundreds of listings. I started at the
beginning. Amber Alviera, Daniel Anderson, Diego Arroya . . . As I
zipped through the index, I noticed several tenants shared the same apartment numbers. I tried to imagine three grad students sharing a studio
apartment and shuddered. Maybe I was looking too quickly, nerves getting the best of me, but I couldn't find another name that listed apartment
4-2029 aside from the listing for Sara Jackson herself.

A group of young tenants entered the lobby from the elevator that
comes from the parking garage. One young woman called to her friends
that she was just going to check her mailbox as she disappeared into a room
off the main lobby. The rest of them used their key cards to access the large
glass door that led to the courtyard with the pool and fitness room.

At about the same time, a young man came in from the street entrance, with a small beagle-ish dog on a leash. I walked over to the glass
door to the courtyard, absentmindedly rooting around in my purse.

"Cool dog," I said, still rooting in my bag.

"Yeah. His name is Waldo."

I smiled. "Where's Waldo?"

"He's right here," the guy-without-an-ounce-of-humor said, looking blank.

I giggled. "No, it's a joke . . ." I began to explain.

He stared at me, the pain of hearing a thousand "Where's Waldo?" comments coming to the surface.

"Oh, I'm so sorry. I'm so brilliant this morning. Duh."

Waldo's owner had long, unruly brown hair and troubled skin. He smiled at me, though, and found his own key card in his pocket "first."

"Here," he said, holding the heavy glass door open for me. "What building do you live in?"

"Four." I took a guess. Sara's apartment number was 4-2029.

"Yeah? Me, too. I wonder why I haven't seen you around here. I check out all the cute chicks."

"Aw, that's sweet," I said, walking with my escort across the landscaped courtyard. A large waterfall tumbled into a pool behind a forest of ferns. The ferns looked a little brown at the tips.

"What floor are you on?" he asked.

"What floor are *you* on?" I countered, flirting just a little.

"Nineteen," he said. "I get a great view, but it costs extra. I am on a waiting list to get a lower floor. You?"

"I'm staying in a friend's apartment," I said. "On twenty."

"So that's probably why I don't know you," he said. We had reached building four and he pushed the button to call the elevator. "Who's your friend?"

"Sara Jackson."

"Oh, Sara."

I couldn't read his expression. "You know her?"

"Pretty redhead about this tall?" He held his hand up. "I know her."

"Didn't you two get along?"

"Oh, I like Sara just fine. She's just out of my price range, if you know what I mean."

"No, I don't." We traveled up the elevator together as I thought how best to handle Waldo's buddy. "Look, my name is Madeline. Sara and I used to work together."

"That figures," he said. "That makes you out of my league, too."

"Huh?"

The elevator stopped at nineteen, but I got out and followed my new friend and his dog down the hall. He seemed embarrassed by something.

I persisted. "Aren't you going to tell me your name?"

"Arnie Creski. But what are you wasting your time talking to me for?"

"Arnie, I have a confession to make. I am really here to see Sara's roommate—her boyfriend, in fact. Do you know him?"

"Her boyfriend? I don't know who you mean. Sara had a lot of boyfriends, didn't she? Don't you?"

"What?"

We had gotten down to Arnie's apartment door, and he seemed to be on the retreat. I had only a few questions more and I was pretty sure he would disappear behind his door with his little dog.

"What are you saying, Arnie? Sara was a hooker?"

"Duh."

"Really? I can't believe that. She worked with me as a waitress."

Arnie gave me a look like the young man had seen all that the world had to offer, and if Sara Jackson was a waitress, then he was the queen of France. "She works at celebrity-type parties. With rich men. Right?"

"Wasn't she a student at USC?" I asked, feeling the rug had been tugged a little too hard and I was in peril of slipping.

"I guess," he said, trying to end our conversation. "I saw her with books. Now, could you just let it go? I don't want to get the girl in trouble. I like her."

"Arnie, you must not have heard the news. Sara Jackson died the other night. She was shot."

Arnie's little beagle mix, Waldo, had had enough of standing out in the hall. He wanted inside and whimpered in front of the door.

"I've gotta go," Arnie said apologetically. "I didn't know about Sara. I'm sorry to hear it. But that girl didn't have any time for me, I can tell you that. I didn't have any money and she just wasn't interested."

"And you're sure she didn't live with another grad student? A young man?"

"No. She lived alone. I know that for sure. But I saw her bring a lot of guys around, let me tell you. Suits, I would call them. Johns, probably." And then Arnie let Waldo into his apartment and quietly shut the door.

"Sing Sing Sing"

'm parked in front of Albert Grasso's house," I told Wes. I was calling in from my cell phone. I had meant to simply drive by on Iris Circle to assure that the blasted box of papers had been safely found and brought inside. "The box is still sitting there."

"That's not a bad thing," Wes suggested. "No one has stolen them."

"Yes. I suppose."

"And if you were concerned that Grasso was going nuts trying to get his hands on them again, this should reassure you that they are just, simply, a box of old papers. Nothing very pressing about them."

"Yes."

"But?"

"I found a good parking spot," I said to Wes, getting out of the red rental SUV. "So I'm just going to look around the property."

"MAD!"

"Wesley, I'm right up the street. The sun is shining. This will take ten minutes, tops. If you want, just walk up here and join me." I pressed the end button on my cell phone before hearing his reply.

There was a short brick path to the front door of Albert Grasso's large stucco house. As on so many of the upscale residential streets in the Hollywood Hills, space was at a premium. The tightly packed homes on Iris Circle were set right on the street, all hugging the curb. While these homes lacked much in the way of front yards, there was a trade-off. Sloping hillside lots, such as these, provided wonderful rearward-facing views of the local canyons. Neighbors looked down upon scattered red-tile rooftops and aquamarine swimming pools, partially hidden by the feathery greens and grays of bushy palms and yucca trees and thick, spiky century plants.

Albert Grasso's home was a large, English affair in the Tudor Revival style so popular in Southern California in the twenties and thirties. Wes had educated me on all the charming "faux" architectural details of that period, since older L.A. homes are his passion. The fanciful, storybook style of Grasso's house, with its steep, complex roofline and small-paned windows, was a version of Tudor Revival called the Cotswold cottage. His was quite a terrific specimen, although it looked in need of a serious rehab.

I approached the front entrance and rang the bell, hearing its muffled ring echo in the quiet interior. No one came to the door. I put my hands up to shield the sun from reflecting off the leaded-glass pane in the door. The old glass caused the image to blur, but I could see only the dark entry hall.

The floor plan of these Cotswold cottages tends to include numerous small, irregularly shaped rooms, and the upper rooms have sloping walls with dormers. I looked up but all was quiet. I checked more closely around the front of the house, walking to the side. There, I found the low gate had no lock. I unlatched it easily and followed the path around the corner to the backyard. I admired the home's cedar-shingle roof, even though I knew it wasn't considered fire-safe anymore for hillside homes to have them. Fires could spread too easily, cinders flying from roof to roof. But Wes had told me those who owned these older houses were exempt from the new ordinances, at least until it was time to reroof. I guessed that Albert Grasso had been in this house a long time.

I was soon standing on the back patio, checking out Albert's dusty potted garden, admiring the huge hot-pink-flowered bougainvillea bush growing all over the back of his garage, noting his pavers could use some sweeping, taking in his fabulous canyon view. All was quiet, save the swishing sound of a neighbor's sprinklers. All was perfectly peaceful. As long as I was there, I thought I might as well knock on the back door. Perhaps Albert was working in a quieter part of the house and hadn't yet heard me.

On the back door was a note in fine printing. It read: ENTER — STUDIO DOWN THE HALL.

I knocked. No response. And then I tried the door handle. The doorknob turned easily in my hand. Without thinking, I entered Albert Grasso's dark kitchen.

Grasso must expect his students to let themselves in. I had an idea. Perhaps I should just go get that carton of papers and photos and leave them here, inside the kitchen door. Much safer.

I strode outside and rounded the corner, around front where the massive stucco chimney dominated the right side of the house. I grabbed the cardboard box that had once held champagne bottles and trotted back to the kitchen door. Once inside, I felt better. Surely Grasso would appreciate that I'd done my best to protect his bloody files. I could detect faint sounds now, coming from deeper in the house. Music. Singing. He'd find it all when his session was over.

But after I'd put up with Grasso's extreme drama at the Black & White Ball, not to mention suffering a visit from Caroline on Albert Grasso's behalf, to let this incident go without giving the man a chance to apologize in person felt, well, unfinished. As the music continued in the background, I stood there, considering.

Grasso was down the hall in some almost-soundproof studio, working on his music, no doubt. Why shouldn't I let him know I was here? I called out, "Mr. Grasso!"

There was no reply, so I stepped a little farther into the kitchen. A thin shaft of sun shone through the curtains and lit up a slice of the fairly nice-size room, although it was one that had not been remodeled since the fifties, if I was to guess. This was the sort of fixer house that would get Wesley's creative juices flowing. Perhaps when all this business was settled and behind us, Albert Grasso would give Wes a tour.

I stepped into the back hall, calling more loudly: "Excuse me! Mr. Grasso! It's Madeline Bean. Are you here?"

The music I heard was coming from this rear hallway. One of the rooms at the far end had its door closed. That must be the room Grasso used as his recording studio. Here, I could more clearly hear the music. It was the sound of a young woman's voice going over the same musical phrase. The song was familiar. "Dancing Queen." I had seen the musical version of *Mamma Mia!* in Las Vegas with Holly and Wesley. We'd loved it. Maybe Grasso was coaching a performer from one of the road companies.

I was just outside the door now, and it was fascinating how Grasso would give an instruction and the singer would repeat the phrase. In fact, now that I was just outside the door, I realized she was singing the word *li-i-i-fe*, over and over. She had a rich clear voice. And then I saw that the door wasn't completely shut. I knocked, gently so as not to startle them, but the door swung open.

It was then that I realized my mistake. There was no vocal student in Albert Grasso's recording studio. It was only a voice on his Mac, playing and replaying a digital file. Her voice sang out again, "Li-i-i-fe." And yet the room was not entirely empty.

Albert Grasso was sitting in an easy chair, his headphones askew. His eyes were open. His posture was slumped. A dark red stain ran down his forehead. A bullet had gone straight through his head.

"Something to Remember You By"

The rest of the day went by in a blur.

Wesley had arrived almost immediately. He had already been on his way to Grasso's house to see what was keeping me. Together, we called Honnett and then he took care of the rest.

I spoke to the homicide detectives, Baronowski and Hilts, again, as they had been assigned to investigate the new Grasso murder. The police department couldn't ignore the possible connection between two deaths within two blocks in the same quiet neighborhood. The media were making a big stink. Our homeowners association was on the warpath, asking men in Whitley Heights to patrol the streets.

I tried to read between the lines as the investigators told Wes and me we could leave Grasso's house, but we were not to leave the city. As we walked down to my house, I worried to Wesley about how the cops had reacted. There I was, somehow connected to two deaths of people I barely knew. I had felt their eyes on me, reassessing. Wesley told me I was imagining things, but he is not to be counted on for the harsh truth when there is the least temptation to sugarcoat something.

Wes had made a few good points. It helped some that I had been up

front with the cops all along, telling Detective Baronowski what I was up
to. I had left several messages about my theories, about my visit from Caroline Rochette and her plunge into the pool, and I had dropped off copies
of Grasso's papers. I had frankly told the cops everything. Everything, that
is, except my penchant for spur-of-the-moment breaking and entering.

I smiled feebly at Wesley. "I haven't been arrested yet."

"Mad," he said, facing me seriously, giving my problems his full attention. "Don't worry."

"Don't worry," I repeated.

"Be happy."

"Don't worry. Be happy. I'm working on those."

Wes and Holly and I spent what was left of the day in the office, returning phone calls and paying bills. We were not our usual joking selves.
Honnett came by to check up on me after spending most of the day on
the periphery of the new investigation on Iris Circle. He couldn't or
wouldn't tell us much about what was going on there. Wes took the cue
to grab Holly and run out to do some errands, leaving me alone with
Honnett on the back patio.

"You hate me," I said to Honnett. "I keep getting mixed up with dead
people. This has got to hurt you with your coworkers, you knowing a girl
like me."

When he sat down next to me on a teak bench, he sat closer than I
would have expected, what with our relationship in suspended anima-
tion.

"How could I hate you?" he asked, watching me, checking me out
closely. "You look like hell."

"Ah." I laughed. Not the complimentary sort, my guy Honnett. But
observant. "The pity vote. And the sad thing is, I am grateful for it."

He laughed at that.

"But now, Honnett, I have to ask a big favor. As you know, two people
have ended up dead. Shot. And as hard as I've tried, I can't figure out
what's happening."

"It will get itself sorted out," he said.

"Someday. Maybe." I chewed my lip and then caught myself acting
anxious and stopped it. "Maybe it's this house. Maybe it's some instinct.
But I don't feel safe anymore."

"You're not staying here, are you?"

"No, but anyone who is looking for me can find me at Wesley's house." I shivered, even though the late afternoon was still warm. "Why are all these people dying? I feel like some shadow is following me, something I should see, and I'm just too dense to figure it out. I'm . . . nervous about staying at Wesley's house," I admitted. "What if I bring this trouble to him?"

We sat there quietly, Honnett and me. He looked deeply into my eyes and took a breath. "Move in with me."

"What?"

"I am not staying with Sherrie anymore."

"Since when?"

"I moved out the other night. We are not going to make it. She understands."

I nodded, but was more confused than before. He had left his wife again, he was telling me. But I wasn't happy. He left his sick wife. That made me feel like dancing all right.

"Maddie, I think you should stay with me."

"I can't."

He stared at me. "Why not?"

"Where can I start here?"

We looked at each other, both a little wounded. I found it hard to stay focused, sitting there beside him. The physical closeness reminded me of our short time together as a couple. It had only been a few months, but we had gotten to that point of comfort with our bodies, comfort in knowing each other's points of pleasure, and the electricity between us was even now still hot. It was dangerous sitting so close to a former boyfriend. So many doors, previously opened, seemed to beckon. One step, one easy step. Back in his life, back in his arms, back in his bed.

"Why not?" he persisted, putting his arm around my shoulder. "I'd take care of you."

I shook my head.

"Why not?"

"It's not right. I wouldn't be comfortable. You are married. I'm dating someone new. Pick one."

Honnett pulled away and put his hand in the pocket of his jacket. Then he lifted his head and met my eyes. "So you want me to back off?"

"I don't know what I want to do with you," I said.

His eyes stayed on mine.

"You had your reasons for doing what you did. You were worried about your wife's health. That's honorable, Honnett."

He smiled a sad smile. "Honorable."

Our situation had become irreparably complicated and he seemed to be asking me for simple answers. I tried again. "Look, it's nice of you to offer to share your apartment. It's nice you want to look out for me. But don't you know me better than that? Don't you know how important it is for me to be strong on my own?"

He shook his head. "You *are* strong, Maddie. But do you have to think so damned much all the time? Can't you go with your gut, here?"

"My gut?"

He nodded.

"My gut tells me stay away from you."

He exhaled. I thought he had run out of things to say, but then he finally asked, "Why?"

I looked at his intelligent blue eyes, his long legs tucked under the bench, and exhaled. "I've already been hurt enough, Honnett. It's enough. You say you've left your wife again. You've moved out for good. But what does that really mean? We can't just start up again like before. You're not really free. These entanglements have a nasty habit of hanging on to us. They take time to resolve. And your wife, she's been sick, right? And she probably hasn't been working. So whose medical insurance is she on?"

He looked at me, but didn't answer.

Health insurance ruled the universe. No one asks a woman in chemo to give up her husband *and* her medical coverage. That's inhuman. And then, there was the real state of Honnett's feelings to consider. Right now he wanted to protect me, but he had also wanted to take care of her. The time had come to call him on it.

"You may have moved out, but I know you still have feelings for her," I said slowly. "You do. So stop pretending you are here for me. You aren't. That's the truth."

He nodded and we sat there for a while, the sun moving far to the west and behind the house next door, leaving us in that perfect late-afternoon light.

"You look sad, Maddie," he said, brushing my hair off my face.

"I've been sad about us for a long time," I said softly. "First, I was pretty angry. Did some foolish things. That passed." He didn't comment and I went on. "So in a lot of ways, you are the last person I want to turn to for help right now, but the truth is, I do need you."

"Anything."

"I have given this a lot of thought. I want you to believe me, Chuck."

"Okay." He waited.

"Two people died. I don't know why. And now I don't believe I am safe."

He didn't challenge me or try to talk me out of my fears. He simply asked, "What can I do?"

I stood up and walked to the edge of my patio, grabbing a couple of bottles of water from a cooler, before I turned back to him. "I need a gun."

"What?"

"A gun. You know." I handed him one of the bottles of water. "A gun."

"Do you know how to shoot one?"

"No."

"Maddie, you aren't making any sense. First, you can never get a concealed carry permit. You will probably end up getting yourself into trouble. If you aren't going—"

"Hey. Stop. Time out."

He stopped, but gave me a very concerned look.

"I need to be able to protect myself. Just in case. Look, I'm staying out at Wesley's guest house. What if someone tries to get in? I mean, look what happened to Sara Jackson and Albert Grasso. They were inside houses and they were both shot to death."

He didn't answer. He didn't want to believe I was in danger.

"You told me to listen to my gut earlier; well, this is what my gut is telling me to do. I can't get through this night and the next night and the next. I won't be able to stand it. I need protection."

"You want me to come over to Wesley's every night and guard you? Because I will."

"I need to protect myself, Honnett."

"You want a gun? You?" Honnett looked upset.

"Why not me? I can go to the shooting range and practice. It can't be that hard."

"No, it's not hard. It's just so not you."

"Don't bet on it. I need a gun, Honnett."

"You can buy one, I guess," he said, not convinced.

"That takes weeks, doesn't it?"

"You go in and pick out your gun and do the paperwork. The state just passed a bill that requires you to take a safety course and pass an exam. And then California has a two-week waiting period."

I looked at him, frustrated. "That's what I'm saying. Maybe I don't have two weeks. Maybe someone will be knocking down my bedroom door tomorrow night, Honnett. I want a gun now."

He looked down to see my hands clenched around the seat of the bench. I loosened them immediately, trying to appear less worked up and insane.

"Look," I said, "can't you lend me a gun? Until I can get my own. Maybe I'll like what you give me and I can buy one just like it."

He looked at me.

"See, I don't know who else to turn to. I don't know that many people who might have a gun. We're kind of a peaceful crowd. And I figured you would understand about weapons."

"In case you haven't noticed, I'm not a real 'gunnie,' Madeline. I don't have dozens of firearms stored in my basement bunker, whatever you may think of me."

"Can you lend me a gun or not?" I asked, staring at him, waiting. He had let me down before, so I was just thinking about what I would do if he refused to help me now.

"All right. I'll bring you a gun. But only on the condition that you let me show you how to clean it and store it and that you really do take that safety course and go out to a pistol range and get some serious, professional instruction."

"Thank you, Chuck," I said, burying my face into his shoulder, hugging him hard. "I'll be fine. I'll practice. I'll just have it for an emergency, you know?"

"Okay," he said, hugging me back, but I could feel he wasn't as happy about the gun as I was.

"Can we go get it now?" I asked.

He looked at me, uneasy. "I'll bring it to you at Wesley's."

"When?"

"How about an hour, an hour and a half?"

"No later, okay?"

He kept looking at me. "And you promise you won't take risks. You won't take it out with you. You won't—"

"Honnett! I won't get you in trouble. I'll be good."

We stood up. Honnett looked apprehensive. Me, I practiced looking like an angel. An angel who would soon have a gun.

"I Get a Kick
Out of You"

got down to the Brea Indoor Shooting Range by 7 P.M. The box that held my first pistol, my loaner from Honnett, was beside me on the passenger seat of the rental Trailblazer. I had looked at it at Wes's guest house. It was pretty darn cool.

There were many reasons why I had never thought of owning a pistol before. I don't come from gun people. My parents didn't hunt or shoot. No one in my extended family did. My friends and I were not into guns and ammo. Before this, my weapon of choice had been my Cuisinart. But I had never doubted for a second that pulling a trigger and trying to hit a target might be fun. I have played my share of Tomb Raider. I enjoy games of precision, of cat-and-mouse intrigue, and to be truthful, a certain amount of animated destruction. I'm the first one to suggest we rent *Terminator* again. And in my present situation, I was certainly not immune to the lure of the power of a handgun. Hell, it was the very urgency of my situation, my powerlessness, that had propelled me to this northern section of Orange County in search of a shooting range and my appointment with Andy Abfel, my as-yet-unmet shooting instructor.

As he had promised, Honnett had brought the gun to Wesley's house by six o'clock. I had already been on the phone with the Brea Indoor Shooting Range to book a private lesson. The range closed at ten, but I offered a bonus if my instructor could stay even later and show me everything I needed to know. This would present no problem at all, I was told. And I'd end up with a certificate that would satisfy the state of California. Excellent.

I eventually pulled off the 57 Freeway at Lambert Road, as I'd been advised, and headed west a mile and then turned right on Berry. The indoor shooting range was located among the complex of commercial buildings on the east side of Berry Avenue.

In the reception area, I got my first surprise. Andy turned out to be Andi. Her black hair was pulled into a ponytail that reached almost to her waist. She was about my height, but about ten years older than I am, if I had to guess. Her dark brows were full and expressive and her dark brown eyes gave me a kind look. She wasn't as annoyed as I would have been to have her gender misguessed by a name. Just when you think there is no one on the planet more liberal-minded than you are, you get a wake-up call. Thanks, universe.

Andi asked to look at my handgun. I put the box on the counter and she opened it. Inside was a very clean, very shiny revolver. It was a .38-caliber Smith & Wesson Lady Smith with special custom engraving.

"This yours?" She couldn't have sounded more skeptical.

I became nervous they wouldn't teach me if I didn't own the gun. "A friend gave it to me." Which was, you know, technically true. "Why?"

"Must be a pretty good friend," she said, checking me out. "You know how much a gun like this is worth?"

"No."

She eyed me carefully.

"It must be a lot," I said. "So why would I come here with an expensive custom gun and not know the first thing about shooting it? you're wondering."

"Well, that's not a bad question," Andi encouraged me. "Go on."

"My friend is a cop. Lieutenant Chuck Honnett of the LAPD. He thinks I need to have something at home for protection. He just brought it over. I had no idea he would bring something valuable. Tell me about it."

Andi relaxed at the mention of a friend in the department, and I relaxed when she relaxed. I might know nothing about guns, but I do know people. I run parties, I plan major events. I deal with people all day long. I know what buttons need to be pushed to smooth away resistance.

Andi lifted the gun out of the satin-lined case. "It's beautiful," she said. "This is the 65LS, a thirty-eight-caliber revolver. You know about guns at all?"

"No."

"I didn't think you did. Well, a revolver is a good choice for a beginner. They're the simplest to clean and take care of. That what your cop uses?"

I had no idea what kind of gun Honnett carried. I was ashamed to realize I had never taken enough of an interest to find out. "I'm not sure."

"Well, standard issue for LAPD are the Beretta 92 nine-millimeter, Kimber 1911-style forty-five, or Smith & Wesson in either forty caliber or nine-millimeter."

"Oh." I wondered if she could tell I hadn't understood a word she had said.

"Let's take it slowly," she suggested kindly. "The caliber of the ammunition—like a police-issue forty-five?—describes the size of the bullet. The larger the caliber, say a forty-five versus a twenty-two, the more stopping power. Got it?"

I nodded. "So bigger is better."

"Well, some folks think so. But then the bigger guns are heavier and bulkier to carry, right? And they have serious recoil." She laughed. "They kick like hell. So there are always trade-offs. Everyone has a theory on what is best. But your cop friend's duty gun is going to be a pretty large piece of equipment in a serious caliber."

"So this isn't like that," I said, knowing I was a fool.

"Well, this is a *Lady* Smith. It's marketed for us women." She smirked. "But if that doesn't offend your feminist sensibilities, it's a fine gun."

"And thirty-eight caliber is . . . enough?"

"I'd say so. It's a pretty popular size. You find a lot of folks take to them. Not as hard to handle as a forty-five, although I love my forty-five."

I nodded, just like I knew what she was talking about.

Andi continued: "You should be very happy with it. This model is really an evolution of the famous Smith & Wesson Chief's Special, a revolver that cops have carried for years. No wonder your friend bought it for you. And then, she's a beauty. Look at that scrollwork. He must like you very much." Andi touched the fanciful etching on the stainless-steel barrel. And I had to admit, none of my girlfriends had ever before gauged the depth of my boyfriend's affection by the coolness of the gun he'd given me. The life lessons I had yet to learn were staggering.

"It's a revolver," I said. "Is that good?"

"Revolvers are easy to use. The mechanics of this type of gun are simpler and it has fewer parts than a semiautomatic, making maintenance — even very minimal maintenance — easier. It is also less likely to have firing problems — you know, jams — because of its design. And, assuming a clean gun using the correct ammunition, most such problems can be fairly easily cleared by the owner. For this reason alone, revolvers are often recommended to new shooters."

"Okay. That sounds fine."

"Revolvers are also easier to load," she continued, opening a box of ammunition as she instructed me on the gun. "The cartridges go into the cylinder, which is part of the gun. See? Like this. You put the rest in."

I did as she had done. The weapon felt good in my hands, I had to admit. Weighty and smooth and cool.

"Very good," she said, watching me. "Now unload the chambers. Like this." I did. Pretty simple, really. I began to believe I could get all this down and relaxed a little.

Andi nodded approval. "Okay, with the ammo back in the box, the gun is now safe, got it?" She made eye contact to check that I was staying with her.

"You a former cop?" I asked.

"Ex-army," she said softly. "My husband and I both."

"I was expecting I'd get one of those modern-looking guns," I told her, looking at a chart on the wall that showed a line of sleek black handguns. I read a bit of the ad copy. "A semiautomatic. Are they better?"

"Different," she said. "Some folks like them better, but a semiautomatic has a separate magazine and they can be a little more finicky mechanically. If you don't know about guns, you may not want to take on that learning curve right away."

I was only the lowest-rank novice, and already I was having gun envy.

Andi smiled at me. "Frankly, lots of folks like their looks. High tech and all. More *Matrix* than Bat Masterson."

I nodded. "But a revolver works. Right?"

"Yep. You've got a terrific handgun here. See, she's large enough to give stability and that means much less recoil. You'll get a chance to feel what I'm talking about in a few minutes."

I smiled, reassured.

"Really, the main drawback to a revolver for home defense is capacity."

"I beg your pardon?"

"Capacity. Most revolvers hold only six rounds. In many situations—one or even two attackers—this is plenty. In some situations, however, the gun owner might find herself in a fight that requires more than six shots."

I swallowed. "More?"

"A home invasion that ranges over a wide area, with no one immediately incapacitated, for example. Or if a second or third attacker was revealed after the first few shots were fired . . ." Andi turned her hands up, showing just how lame that would make one feel with one's revolver plum out of bullets.

Nice. Real nice. As if my nightmares hadn't been graphic enough before.

"But you'll be just fine," she said, and went back to instructing. "She's short-barreled, see? She comes with a pinned black-ramp front sight and fixed rear sight." As she talked, she pointed out the features. "Well balanced with the help of a full-lug three-inch barrel, and this rosewood grip feels great in your hand. And I have to say, the engraving here is as fine as it gets. Look at the scrollwork on the cylinder and all over the side plates?"

"Yes. It's pretty." Did people say that about guns? I was so lost.

"Have you ever shot a gun before?"

I shook my head no.

"We'll get you out in the range in just a few minutes. You'll have some fun then." Andi smiled.

————

Seven hours later I arrived back in Hancock Park, with enough training on handgun safety and cleaning and loading and aiming and squeezing the trigger to give me a little confidence. For one thing, I wasn't too bad out on the range. Not bad at all. Give Nintendo credit. For another, Andi told me that most defensive home handgun situations do not require you to hit a tiny circle on a target twenty yards away. Closer and larger targets are easier to hit. I found that comforting. Somewhat. Considering I was limited to six shots.

When I got to my room in the guest house, I found Wes and Holly were still out. They'd been working a small dinner party in Calabasas. I undressed, and then brought my gun case with me to the bathroom as I took a quick, hot shower. I pinned up my hair, put some cream on my face, and put on a fresh tank top and boxers, then, carting my gun case with me, I turned down my covers. I thought it over and then knelt down and put my new gun, case and all, under my bed. I turned out all the lights and then slid between the cool white sheets.

The house was quiet and very, very dark. I was exhausted. And yet I heard the ticking of Wesley's grandfather clock coming from the living room. *Tick-tock-tick-tock.* It was extraordinarily loud. And then I heard the creaking of footsteps, or maybe that was just wind in the floorboards?

I flicked on the light, climbed out of bed, and pulled the case with the revolver—my revolver—my Lady Smith .38—out from under the bed and opened it up.

I knelt at the bed and prepared to load the gun just the way Andi taught me to. The filigreed, engraved satin finish gleamed. I checked out the patterns, which covered the barrel and other metal parts. It was then, for the first time, I saw a variation in one of the scrolls. What I had taken for a flourish on one of the curlicues on one of the side plates was actually a fanciful letter. It was an *L* or possibly an *S*. I stared. It quite possibly could have been a *Q*. How intriguing. I opened the box of bullets and began placing them in the six chambers.

Andi had warned me that revolvers don't have safeties. She had advised me to be extremely careful with a loaded weapon. But there were no children in this household. And a gun was no good to me if it wasn't close and convenient and loaded.

I fought the strong urge to put the gun under my pillow. Instead, I placed it on top of the nightstand and again turned out the bedside lamp.

I tossed a bit under the covers. The night was still warm enough to require only a sheet. I kept imagining outrageous calamities. Wesley's maid comes in early and tiptoes into my room and inadvertently jostles the nightstand and . . . Impossible. Or, an early A.M. earthquake, one strong enough to knock the gun off the nightstand, then it hits the floor and discharges. In which direction would the bullet go?

I reached for the lamp switch. I climbed out of bed. I opened the drawer of the nightstand and moved my tangle of little thong underwear to one side. I carefully rested the Lady Smith in the drawer. Worst-case scenario, I'd grab the gun and have a pair of panties hanging from my fist.

That done, lights out, sheet perfectly arranged, I found I was finally able to get a good night's sleep.

"I Got It Bad
(and That Ain't Good)"

It's funny how a good night's sleep can change everything. I got up early and, first thing, unloaded my gun and stored it in its case, which, like a responsible adult, I then tucked into the nightstand drawer. The forceful wave of the previous evening's paranoia was now spent and gone. I pulled on a fresh pair of yoga shorts and a white sleeveless top, thinking the usual, normal things—like wondering when I might find time to do my laundry, rather than worrisome things—like why my life had become enmeshed in so many crimes.

I left Wesley a note. He had been out late the previous night, so instead of cooking myself breakfast in the smart little guest-house kitchen and maybe waking him, I decided to walk up to the old Farmers Market, only three miles away.

The early-morning air was fresh, cool. I pushed myself, moving fast, getting my heart pumping. I strode down Hudson until I came to the first major thoroughfare and then jogged west along Third, admiring the stately old mansions in the neighborhood: the gray mock French Normandy; the lilac Gothic Revival; the ubiquitous Mediterraneans in white or pink or tan, each with exquisite landscaping and perfectly trimmed trees. The majestic corner homes shared an edge of their upscale property with modern, car-clogged Third Street. City life. Say hello to the honking reality of L.A. real estate.

I stepped up my pace. In a little while, I was going to meet with Dilly Swinden and Zenya Knight to firm up our plans for the flower-arranging luncheon Dilly had bought at the Woodburn auction. I'd ask them about the menu and their choice of wine. We'd discuss decor and I'd offer a selection of invitations. They had settled on next Monday for their party, and since the event was to be held in just six days, we would construct the invitations ourselves; then a few of our regular staff would hand-deliver the them later this afternoon. I was to receive the final guest list at our meeting.

Maybe I might find out more about Zenya's brother as well. Maybe she and I would discover a quiet moment to chat. A sister could be a wonderful resource. Wait. What was I thinking? What was with me? I wished I would stop all this adolescent mooning. Somehow, Dex had wormed himself into my brain. I was, like, Dexified. Disgusting. Even as I drove home from the shooting range last night, it was Dexter Wyatt who filled my thoughts. Last night, just before I drifted off to sleep, it was Dexter Wyatt. Man!

It wasn't just his great laugh, or that he so completely got my sense of humor, or his unflappability among late-night escapades and odd restaurants. It wasn't simply the rush of his obvious interest in me either. He just seemed so free and unencumbered. Not only did Dex not have a *wife*, he hardly seemed to have had a serious girlfriend in his past. And yet, beneath his charm, I suspected he was serious about me. My stomach fluttered at the thought. And let's face facts, he did have a perfectly sexy smile with perfectly straight, very white teeth. And he had this disarming quality that was both sophisticated and antiestablishment funky. And his hair . . .

Snap! I told myself. Snap out of it!

I crossed a street, continuing west, nervous I was beginning to daydream about this new guy in my life like some thirteen-year-old staring at her Chris Martin poster. I swear, I didn't recognize myself. But as soon as I told myself, No more fantasies, I felt awash with a sudden sadness, a loneliness. Arlo had been the wrong guy for me, I was sure of that. And then Honnett . . . Honnett had seemed right, but he was still entangled with . . . I simply refused to think about his wife one more time.

I shook my head, crossing another small side street, and then looked back again. I was not only obsessed with a cute guy, I still couldn't shake the feeling that someone was watching me. But I stopped and checked again, thoroughly, and there was no one paying me the least attention at 8 A.M. on that busy street as rush-hour traffic honked by.

In just a few blocks, the older quality of the neighborhood had begun to brighten, freshen, become more fabulous. Everywhere I looked, I saw new buildings where old ones used to be. On my left were amazing, glamorous new apartments. On my right was the Grove, a brand-new shopping mall along with its huge new parking structure. I sighed.

All these new buildings make me sad. I love L.A.'s history, short and tacky and tasteless though it often is. I love to learn about the movie studios and neighborhoods. I collect stories of old-time residents. L.A. was never very "real" to start with. And each twentieth-century building that is leveled to make way for some brand-new "twentieth-century-*style*" building just messes with my head. How can they destroy all that authentic fakeness for this newer and more glam fakeness?

Anyway, I walked more quickly, happier pondering architectural philosophy than where I stood with my boyfriends, and headed for an actual relic of the old Los Angeles I admire.

To get a feel for L.A.'s history, one doesn't need to go back very far in time. In 1870, a guy named A. F. Gilmore drew straws with a partner and ended up owning a 256-acre dairy farm. It was just his luck that by the turn of the century, while drilling for water for his herd of dairy cows, Gilmore hit oil. By 1905, the dairy was gone and the Gilmore Oil Company was on its way to becoming the largest independent oil company in the West. Isn't L.A. grand?

By 1934, farmers were doing what they could to fight the Depression. They pulled their trucks onto empty land at the corner of Third and Fairfax, and displayed their produce on the tailgates of their vehicles. It was suggested that Gilmore could make some money by charging the farmers fifty cents a day to sell their produce out of wooden stalls. The original farmers' market was born. I read all about it in a book Holly gave me for my birthday.

Today, this ancient relic of a tourist site was almost overshadowed by its glamorous neighbor, the Grove, an upscale, open-air mall modeled after some grand old fantasy downtown with architectural facades inspired by L.A.'s Art Deco era. But why, I ask, would anyone prefer to wander through yet another Gap when she could, instead, explore old-time Farmers Market establishments with names like the Gift Nook? And the Gift and Gadget Nook! And the Gadget Nook Gourmet? This is incredibly authentic tourist-trap chic, people. To get into early-twentieth-century L.A., one can't be allergic to kitsch.

I turned into the old wooden complex, feeling perkier than I had in a week, as I observed the stands of fresh produce, where avocados were the size of grapefruits, and grapefruits the size of small planets. I would pick up a couple of gargantuan cantaloupes to bring back to Wesley—a little gift for his breakfast. And maybe I'd find a few special things and cook a dinner for Dex.

L.A.'s old Farmers Market is made up of a series of fifteen large, white wooden buildings with green roofs and brown shutters. They encircle an open-air quad, which is filled with at least thirty smaller, freestanding stalls, creating a maze of narrow, sunny walkways. I had entered at Gate 12—no grand entrance covered in limestone in sight—happily walking in through this modest side door between two sections of Mr. Marcel Gourmet Grocery. A small sign by their register announced they do local deliveries. How cool. I'd have to tell Wes.

Food. It was the central idea of Farmers Market, its core, perhaps the greatest reason I love this indoor/outdoor bazaar so much. Everywhere you turn, your eye is offered dazzling displays. In addition to dozens of shops and grocery vendors, there were all sorts of delicious things on display. There were three produce stands, two meat markets, a homemade-candy shop, two nut shops, two poultry marts, two bakeries, a flower shop, and two ice-cream parlors. I loved to smell fresh peanut butter being churned at Magee's Kitchen. Or to taste fresh horseradish ground from giant, gnarled roots. Everything edible is here. You can watch apples being dunked in caramel at Little John's, and over at Du-Par's restaurant a plate-glass window lets you observe their bakers rolling dough for their pies.

And there were dozens of cafés and open-air food stands. Cajun gumbo, Japanese sushi, Belgian waffles, Italian pasta, and on and on. Sometimes, Wes and I select a different item at three different stands,

often finishing up by sharing a magnificent crepe. But today I was looking for a place to think.

I turned left and walked halfway down the lane until I reached
Kokomo Café, a truly great breakfast place tucked among the Farmers
Market's fruits and nuts. Think modern California cuisine in a diner setting. Salads, soups, sandwiches, shakes, and the best thick-sliced bacon in
town. In a serve-yourself kind of environment, I found the funky sit-down
atmosphere and the quirky waiters at Kokomo's a bit of self-indulgence I
could afford.

My waiter, a dreamboat actually, came for my drink order.

"A large iced tea, please."

"Coolio." He made eye contact.

"Say, I can't help it, but you look so damn much like James Dean."

He smiled. "I get that all the time." And then he told me a story I
hadn't heard before, about how James Dean ate his last breakfast here at
Farmers Market just before embarking on his final, fatal auto trip. "Not at
Kokomo," he quickly added.

"Wow."

"But if you're in the mood for a current celebrity sighting," he said,
leaning his head to the right. "Drew Barrymore. Be cool now." And he
went off to fetch my tea.

I took a brief, California-cool peek. It's not polite to disturb the stars.
But a peek? No problem.

I checked the menu briefly. I know it pretty well. I considered their
famous red flannel turkey hash, and then their special huevos rancheros—
eggs prepared with smoked-tomato salsa—but life had been freaking
me out. I needed the carbs of comfort offered by Kokomo's fluffy pancakes.

"What can I get you?" asked the James Dean guy.

"Pancakes." I sighed, giving in.

"With a side of bacon?"

"Naturally."

The star spotting and breakfast ordering accomplished, I knew I
needed to get my head together. I pulled a notepad out of my bag and un-
capped a pen. I enjoyed the sounds of big-band music piped over their
stereo system. Benny Goodman. By the time my pancakes arrived, steamy
and hot, I had covered three pages in notes. Most were regarding the up-

coming Woodburn-ladies luncheon, but the last page veered off, of its own accord, in the direction of the missing saxophone. I guess it was all the big-band music in the background, but I began to wonder if anyone at the Woodburn had ever found out what happened.

———————

By nine-thirty that morning, I had made it back to Wesley's place. I showered and changed into my meet-the-clients clothes. In the ranking of my casual wardrobe, this higher level of formality required a snappier top and a pair of designer khakis. I chose a black rayon blouse worn open over a white tank tee, and high-heeled sandals to complete the ensemble. My hair was pulled into a high ponytail, as the day was getting hot.

I had been ignoring the pile of messages Wes had left for me, the topmost announcing I could pick up my Jeep from the police lot, and walked out to my waiting SUV. I liked the new-car smell and the extra cup holders in the Trailblazer. My old Grand Wagoneer could wait another day. At eleven o'clock, I climbed the steps to Zenya Knight's house in Beverly Hills, down the street from her neighbor and benefit cochair, Dilly.

In Zenya's living room, I found Dilly had already arrived and was sipping from a bottle of Arrowhead water. The three of us moved to the magnificently furnished dining room and put our heads together. In short order we nailed down all the details that needed to be nailed regarding the upcoming Monday luncheon, all of us very conscious of how rushed the event planning would need to be. It was fun to see Dilly and Zenya again, as we had spent a lot of time together over the past months working on the Woodburn affair. This time, we had no committee approval to get past or benefit to run. The flower party would be a relaxed and happy occasion.

"Are you traveling in August?" I asked them both, making polite conversation.

Dilly was a gorgeous dark-haired former model with long graceful legs and dancing eyes. Although probably around fifty, she dressed in an aggressive young fashion. Like a twenty-year-old with a $200,000 clothes budget. She gave Zenya a knowing look and asked, "Should I tell her?"

"Oh, Dilly!" Zenya giggled, flipping her long hair back, and opened a bottle of Chardonnay.

"What?" I asked.

"I'm telling everyone I'm going to Tahiti, but I'm not."

"Where are you going?"

"To the Desert Palms Clinic." She waited breathlessly, but I had no idea what she meant. "To get a lift."

"Really?"

"Just a partial. Not the eyes. I'm so excited. I shouldn't tell anyone, but I can't wait."

"You're getting a face-lift?" I thought Dilly Swinden was one of the most beautiful women I'd seen. She was tall and fine-boned and had barely any signs of age to notice, besides which I like people who look like they have had a life. "You look so young."

"No, I don't." She put the tips of her index fingers on her two cheekbones and tugged ever so slightly up. Then she let it go slack for a moment and again pulled upward. She repeated the demonstration a third time. "See?"

"Really, Dilly. It barely makes a difference."

"I can see it," she said.

Zenya, only thirty-five or so, looked down at her hands.

It was rarely talked about openly in these circles, but successful older men, the ones who could afford such fantastic homes as these and attracted such beautiful wives, did occasionally trade them in for younger models, a fact of which both Dilly Swinden and Zenya Knight were intimately aware. After all, they were both second wives themselves. Dilly had married her husband, Gerard, when he was in his midforties and she was just twenty-five. She must realize that at the time of his hurried divorce years back, Gerard's old discarded first wife had been younger than Dilly was today.

Gerard Swinden was the chairman of the board of a savings and loan and was also on the board of the Woodburn. He and Dilly had no children, but he had a family by his first marriage, and his oldest daughter had been an excellent cellist, I'd heard. At the time of his divorce, all those years ago, his first wife was literally shut out of her old life. She'd had to leave her friends at the Woodburn Guild since she couldn't stand to watch Dilly, the new Mrs. Swinden, take her seat on the board. Dilly found those early committee meetings chilly. It was hard to be accepted into this crowd of do-gooding women, each one eyeing the next young wife who made her entrance with the sick expectation that her own place could be taken . . . in time.

So here was Dilly today, agitated enough about her looks that she was obsessing in the mirror over almost nonexistent wrinkles.

These men. They come to believe they should always have the best. Always have something perfect. What pressure their wives were under. It wasn't for me. If I ever found the right guy, he wouldn't be the kind who was looking for the best he could buy, always on alert for the latest upgrade. While I thought my thoughts, Dilly and Zenya caught up on the latest gossip, discussing who in their crowd was having what "done." Plastic surgery. It was more of a lifestyle than I had realized. Then they turned back to me.

"Wasn't the Black and White Ball fabulous?" Dilly asked, unable to resist reliving the past glory. "We couldn't have done any better."

"It was gorgeous," Zenya agreed. It was an interesting dynamic between these two women. Dilly seemed to be the natural leader and Zenya always deferred to her opinion.

"Darius really came through for us," I said, referring to the most outrageous florist on the west side.

"Incredible. Those big arrangements with the masses of white roses! And I had never before seen *black* hollyhocks." Zenya smoothed her long blond hair off her shoulder with a swish.

"*Alcea rosea nigra*," I murmured, pleased.

"Oh, and then the dozens and dozens of Queen of the Night black tulips," Zenya continued. "Gorgeous. Didn't you think so, Dilly?"

Dilly nodded and picked up her wineglass. "There is nothing as sophisticated and simple as black and white. Like that etching, Zenya. Who's that by?" She referred to the artwork on the wall of the Knight dining room, a naked Madonna held aloft by putti. As we finished a lunch of cold artichoke salad, the two fund-raising cochairs nursed large glasses of Chardonnay and I sipped my Diet Coke.

"Oh, that one is called *Magdelena and Her Travel in Heaven* by Raffaello Schiaminossi. Sixteen-twelve. Bill has a thing for old etchings. His collection was borrowed by LACMA, remember, Dilly?"

Dilly shot her friend a quick glance, clearly remembering something she didn't want to mention while I was around. I wondered what that was.

The picture on the wall was large and impressive. sixteen-twelve. Wow. The little boy angels looked like they were tasked by a heavy load, however. Seems this Schiaminossi fellow liked his female models in the Raphaelesque tradition—hefty.

"The L.A. County Museum of Art borrowed this piece?" I was impressed.

"This and a dozen others," Zenya said. "We had a bit of bad luck with three of the best works, though. Dilly knows."

Dilly looked like this was the very thing she had been avoiding mentioning. "Zenya was so distraught," she said. "I didn't want to bring up something that would upset her."

"No, I'm fine," Zenya said quietly. "I know we can never truly possess anything. I'm making my peace with the theft."

Theft? I looked up from my artichoke, alarmed.

"What happened? If you don't feel terrible talking about it."

"I'm okay now," Zenya said, refilling her tall wineglass with the last of the Chardonnay and opening another bottle. "We had just lent the best pieces Bill had in his collection. Most of them were Renaissance-period etchings. This one here is by a relatively unknown artist, although he is rare and therefore more valuable each year. Bill collects with a passion. The thieves knew exactly what they were doing. Only his prize pieces were taken."

"They had a very nice 1502 etching of Adam and Eve by the German genius Albrecht Dürer," Dilly said sadly. "There is one like it in the Rijksmuseum in Amsterdam."

"Oh no." I was troubled. Was theft just a part of the rich person's life? "How horrible. Were they stolen from the County Art Museum while they were on loan?"

"No," Zenya said. "It was several months after they were returned. They were hanging in the living room again, but we were out of town. Bill and I had taken Kirby to our condo on Maui for a few weeks. We got a call one night. There had been a break-in here at the house. Three of our best pieces were gone. That was three years ago, and to this day they have never been recovered."

"Did your alarm go off?" Dilly asked her.

Zenya shook her head.

"Oh, that's right," Dilly said, remembering. "Your brother was staying here at the time, wasn't he? House-sitting?"

I looked up, alarmed. *Dexter?* Wait, now. Had Dilly just said Dexter had been here, watching his sister's house, while millions of dollars' worth of artwork up and walked out the door?

"Money Jungle"

I t was the season for last-minute parties. In addition to rushing to bring off the Woodburn flower luncheon on Monday, we had been asked if we could possibly do a teen's birthday brunch on the Saturday two days earlier. Connie Hutson, the tireless organizer who had helmed the Woodburn auction committee, was determined to throw a battle-of-the-bands-style affair for her son Ryan's thirteenth. Our business was enjoying a summer boom, and coming as it did after a particularly slow winter, we hated to say no to anything. Feast or famine—our business as well as our finances.

I pulled into the driveway of the Hutson house after briefly stopping by the office to give the invitation specs to Wesley and Holly. They were now busy producing the invites, glue-gunning dried, pressed flowers to vellum, while I took this last-minute client call. The Hutsons lived in Pasadena, a twenty-minute drive out of Hollywood.

"Come on in, Madeline," Connie called from the sunroom of her genuine Arts-and-Crafts-period home. She was seated on a dark settee, a Mission oak beauty that I would swear was an authentic Stickley. Connie's bright summer dress, a turquoise silk jungle print, perfectly set off her thick auburn curls, which she wore, as always, neat and short. Her makeup appeared pronounced in the natural light of the bright sunroom. Her full lips were painted dark coral, her cheeks set ablaze with blusher. And a funny thing: I began surreptitiously checking for any signs of plastic surgery. See how suggestible I am? I remembered Dilly and Zenya mentioning Connie's name and I couldn't help but check her out, up and down. Her boobs may or may not have been real, but they were awesome.

Before we could begin our discussion of the birthday party she wished to host, a quiet young Hispanic woman brought in a large pitcher of lemonade and left.

"Thank you, Graciela," Connie said before she called out for her son to join us.

Ryan appeared at the sunroom door, looking awkward and skinny and just about thirteen. Surf camp had bleached his long stringy hair blond. Adolescence had left his skin in a muddle. "My birthday is not until August twentieth," Ryan said in a sort of a whine.

"But we're going to France in August," Connie said to him.

"That's what you keep saying," Ryan replied. "I don't want to go to stinking France."

"You'll love it," she answered patiently.

"So my mom wants me to have my party now." Ryan Hutson's hands found the pockets in his long, baggy shorts and settled there.

"You're inviting all your musician friends?" I asked him, opening my notebook.

"Sure. The kids who are still in town. I told my mom we should wait until school starts and more of my friends are here," he began again, addressing his mother.

"I need to get this *over with*," she said, in a measured way.

Ryan's eyes darted down and I bit my lip. I'm sure Connie didn't hear how it sounded. And I had learned never to jump to judgment with parents of teenagers. Never.

"We want you to have something nice," Connie coaxed. "And this is our last open weekend in three months, sweetheart."

"Right," Ryan said under his breath.

His mother gave him a penetrating look and he sulked back to her. Oh, lovely. Another happy family.

"I'd love to help plan Ryan's party," I said. "But you do realize we are limited in what we can provide with such little time to prep. What sort of food did you want?"

"Nothing dorky, Mom."

"How about In-N-Out?" I suggested to him. He smiled at me, suddenly a kid again, and happy. "We can get a truck to come to your house."

"Awesome."

"That sounds fine," Connie said, easily agreeing to the fast-food burgers the kids all loved. The popular restaurant chain had a few mobile lunch trucks in which their cooks grilled up fresh fries and cheeseburgers to order.

"I just have to see what strings I need to pull to get a truck here this Saturday. They book up at least six months in advance. We may be asked to pay a fairly steep premium, if it's available at all."

"Mom?" Ryan was now on board. "Please."

"Oh, fine," she said, happy to see her son get into the party spirit. "Don't worry about the money."

"I can't promise," I said to Ryan, "but I usually get what I'm after."

"Cool."

"Entertainment?" I asked.

"Wynton Marsalis is coming," Connie informed me. I was stunned to hear her casually drop the name of one of the world's most famous jazz greats. "Dave invited him and he had a day free. That's why Saturday is the date we must have, you see."

"Wynton Marsalis is going to play for Ryan's party?"

"And his jazz ensemble. Oh, yes. Dave took care of it."

"So you'll need a sound system and chairs set up for . . . how many?"

"Just a hundred," Connie said firmly. "We're calling friends and doing it all very impromptu and fun. Don't worry about invitations."

"Can I get a contact number for Mr. Marsalis's people?" I asked, scribbling notes quickly. "We'll want to arrange to have everything he needs."

"Oh, wonderful," Connie said.

"And for the adults," I asked, "would you like us to do a small buffet? A few salads, some fresh fruit, desserts, coffee?"

"Yes, whatever you think would be appropriate is fine with me," Connie said, looking pleased.

"Or we could bring in sushi?" I said, thinking aloud.

"That's perfect," she said. "Absolutely perfect. My husband, Dave, loves sushi."

I wrote more notes. In-N-Out burgers and sushi. Ah, yes. Another eclectic kids party. However, this was all doable. We'd get my favorite sushi restaurant to deliver on Saturday. I'd pull in a big favor with the burger people and get the truck to cook up fresh Double-Doubles right in the driveway out front. The biggest challenge would be getting the staging and audience section set up. I needed to get a plan of their backyard. I asked and Connie Hutson agreed to have it faxed to my office.

"What about the cake?" I asked Ryan.

His mother answered. "We'd like a large cake, Madeline. One that will serve all the teens, so make it for a hundred and fifty, just to be on the safe side."

"Chocolate," Ryan said. "With whipped cream."

"Sounds great," I said, writing.

"And how about in the shape of a saxophone, Ry?"

He wrinkled his nose. "A tenor?"

"Sure," his mom said. "Ryan has been begging to move up to a tenor sax. He currently plays alto. We're trying to get the Woodburn to let him change instruments, but his instructor there, Mr. Braniff, has been reluctant."

That was interesting. I thought again about all the fuss that had been made over the great Selmer Mark VI saxophone that had disappeared from the Woodburn after the live auction on Saturday night. I couldn't help but wonder if the wealthy dad who had arranged for Wynton Marsalis to play at his boy's party hadn't also thought a spectacular instrument like the Selmer might make the perfect birthday gift.

We talked over a few more essential details, and although I knew Mad Bean Events was cutting things close on too many events, I said we'd do it.

Ryan quickly slipped out of the room, relieved to escape the grownups, to get back to his waiting Xbox.

Connie walked me to the door.

"Thanks, Madeline. This is going to be fun."

"I'll fax the budget to you later," I said. "We need approval and a deposit before we can start renting chairs and ordering food. I'll begin lining up vendors and contact the Marsalis people, but we have to move quickly."

"No problem. I'll have Dave run a check over to you tonight, if that's okay."

"Fine." I looked at Connie, who was taller than me, even standing in her flats. "By the way, I've been curious about the Woodburn auction. Did it do well?"

"Well! We did *fabulously* well," she said, her face all smiles. "We out-earned every damn benefit ever thrown for the school in forty-two years of fund-raising. We surpassed our goal of four hundred and fifty thousand dollars."

"Wow." That was an incredible amount of money.

She nodded happily.

"Even after losing the money for the sax?"

"We didn't lose any money," Connie said.

"Bill Knight still paid you the money?" Stranger and stranger!

"Uh, *no*." We both chuckled at the idea. "It was insured, sweetie. We wouldn't have risked bringing such a priceless instrument to the event without insurance."

"That's so lucky."

She winked at me. "It's smart. One of our members took care of it for us." And in an instant, Connie's face changed from sunny to cloudy. "Oh, dear. It was Al Grasso who took care of it. You know about what happened to him?"

I stared at her. Grasso was connected to the stolen saxophone. He'd arranged for the insurance. How did this add up?

"Connie, I have to ask you a question. Was your husband terribly disappointed to have lost out on the bidding for the sax?"

"Of course not," she said, her face completely composed. "He didn't really want it at all."

I looked at her. She had to be the best liar I'd ever met. Or perhaps what she was saying was true. "Really? I thought he was bidding it up against Bill Knight."

"Yes, well . . ." She winked at me.

"What?"

"We were doing it for a good cause, you understand. That made it all right."

"What made what all right?"

"Before the auction, Bill Knight asked Dave to keep the bidding going on the sax."

"No way!" I looked at her, but she was grinning. Not a sign of guilt on her.

"We wanted to raise the pot, you see? Bill said he was going to buy it, but he wanted to get the price high, make a big donation, and get a big write-off. He thought it would make for good drama, and we wanted to inspire other bidders on other objects to be really generous. We thought it was a sweet idea. So Dave played the game."

"Played the game?"

"Well, okay. It got way out of hand. Bill was hamming it up, scuffling with Dave at the table during the bidding. That was outrageous, but that's Bill Knight. He's larger than life, sometimes."

"Excuse me, Connie, but are you absolutely sure about all this? I was in Bill and Zenya's car the night of the Black and White Ball. Bill was screaming about Dave. My goodness, he actually rammed into your car. You and your husband looked appropriately horrified. What was that all about?"

"Bill can be a real asshole when he's drunk," she said flatly. "What we have to put up with from our men, sometimes. If I knew Zenya better, I'd tell her to watch that guy."

"So you forgave him for plowing into your car?"

"We were shocked when he hit our car. But Bill can be a cowboy. Dave says Bill is going through a midlife crisis to end all. I mean, you've seen it yourself. Bill's been drinking too much. He's been loud. He chased us after the party. He's even been seen with . . . Well, that's not important. We realize Bill can get a little unstable at times. He sent us an apology the next morning, along with a case of Dom Pérignon and a large check to fix our car. It's in the shop right now."

I shook my head. "Then why was Bill saying Dave stole the Mark VI?"

"What?" Connie put her hand on my arm, looked in my eyes. Her face drained of color, leaving only dark coral lips and red-stained cheeks. "He said Dave *stole* the sax? He's insane."

I looked at her, not knowing what to think.

"Maddie, who do you think donated that saxophone in the first place?"

Oh ho.

"Dave found it in a bankruptcy auction in Milwaukee. He bought it for under five thousand dollars. We didn't think such a fine instrument should go to a child, or we would have kept it for our Ryan. We were hoping to make this auction the best one ever and we did. The rest of this is all ridiculous."

"I'm sorry. I'm a fool. I should have known. It was such a shock to be in Bill Knight's Hummer and watch him attack you like that. He was just raging."

"Well, Zenya must be used to it," she said, quieting down. "Between you and me, no one would blame her if she took the kids and left him."

"I see."

"But I refuse to get dragged down by the Knights or anyone else, Maddie, and you shouldn't either. The important thing to remember is we raised a good deal of money for the Woodburn last week, and that means many more children will have a chance to study music and develop their art."

"You're right."

"I'm sorry Bill Knight had a tantrum, I'm sorry the saxophone has been misplaced or whatever happened to it, but the insurance covered that and the Woodburn will get its money."

I looked at her, suddenly curious. "Did you insure the Selmer for five thousand dollars?"

"No. As a matter of fact, the policy was written to insure each item for its full auction value, and since we had already held the bidding, we had the current auction value on the Selmer Mark IV established."

"You mean the Woodburn gets a *hundred* thousand for a five-thousand-dollar instrument?"

She nodded.

"Boy, that was lucky," I said.

"Smart," Connie corrected, her natural color coming back once more.

"Jeeps Blues"

few days passed as Holly, Wes, and I got down to work, planning the two parties we had squeezed into our already well-booked lineup. Frankly, it was hard to concentrate on burger trucks and flowerpots. I had begun to believe that someone was watching me. I was convinced that the chain of shootings hadn't ended.

Each night I lay in Wesley's spare bedroom, thinking of the loaded revolver I had put in the nightstand drawer, getting up several times to check on it, eventually leaving the drawer open all night, fearful that someone was out there in the dark, waiting to catch me off guard. Each morning, I closed the drawer again, wondering if any of this effort was necessary or if I was going nuts, wondering if I would ever feel completely safe again.

By Friday, the police were no closer to naming a suspect, as far as we knew, in any of the crimes that had plagued us. There were no breaks on the murder of Sara Jackson. No breaks on the murder of Albert Grasso. After three days of empty dramatic announcements that there were "still no arrests in the linked murders in Whitley Heights," even our local news channels had let the story cool down. And no one but me seemed to give much thought, any longer, to the theft of the vintage tenor saxophone, even though I had dutifully called Detective Baronowski and reported what I had learned from Connie Hutson about the insurance. The policy had been obtained properly, high premiums had been paid, and the Woodburn didn't seem to be out a dime on that one, so perhaps no one was still upset over it. No one except Bill Knight, I thought.

So life went on in that way it always does. After the police allowed us back into my house, it was only a matter of hours before Wes had his crew over there, tearing out the upstairs rooms. I knew I could never sleep in my bedroom again. I didn't even want to climb the stairs. Demolition, Wes had often maintained, was good for the soul. It fulfilled the classic cycle, he said. Death and rebirth. Destruction and rebuilding. He could get pretty Zen over the demo stage of his projects.

Wes had drawn up plans several years ago when I first purchased the property. At the time, we went ahead with construction on the commercial kitchen and office area downstairs but put a hold on spending any more money. Now, however, I was seriously thinking about selling my home. Despite all of Wesley's good intentions, it had been violated in a way no remodel could fix.

I couldn't talk about it. I couldn't even think about it. Wes and Holly didn't know what was going on with me, but the truth was I felt guilty for grieving. My pain was nothing compared with the real suffering around me, of the people who had died and the people who had lost them. Of course I knew that. But this had been my first house. I had thought I'd stay here forever. I had loved this house.

So the demolition stage went on with Wes leading the assault. And the odd thing was, it got a little better after that. Like Wes, I am a fixer and a salvager. It felt like the right thing to do, to repair the house. All this looking over my shoulder and worry was definitely not like me. A redesigned second story, rebuilt from the studs out, might help me to recover my equilibrium. It was possible. And if not, the remodel would make it easier to sell the house quickly and move on.

And then, sometimes, I couldn't even believe the murder of Sara Jackson was real. As I worked with my friends in the large, white-tiled kitchen, the violence that had occurred upstairs six nights before seemed utterly impossible. We had hardly known Sara. How had she come to die in my room?

My mind would wander like that. Off to the unknown and the deadly. And then I snapped back to the present. Holly was laughing about how her hair had turned out. Her straight white-blond hair was gelled back off her forehead with magenta-colored gel. She hadn't intended to get the streaked look, she was saying, but she was philosophical. Holly was always willing to sacrifice herself in the exploration of a new fashion edge.

Wes looked up at me. "You thinking about what happened here?"

"I can't help it," I said. "I'm becoming obsessed. I feel responsible for Sara being here Sunday morning. And yet . . ."

They had that patient look. It wasn't the first time I had made them listen to this.

"And yet, what am I doing now to help? There must be something I can do." I trusted my instincts. I could see connections. I had a great track record for spotting liars and understanding motives. None of these alleged gifts had helped me this time.

"Did the police ever find her boyfriend?" Holly asked as we unpacked the vases we had selected for the Woodburn luncheon. They were fluted cement urns, heavy, classically designed, with a ten-inch diameter.

"I am not getting regular updates," I answered. "The detectives on the case don't return my calls. And Honnett may know something, but he and I are in a transitional period."

Wes looked up at me across the center island where we were working. "Transitioning in or out?"

"I can't tell," I said, opening several large boxes with my box cutter. "It's a mess. His wife is going through a rough time. He's had to help her more than he was expecting, I have been told."

Holly looked up at me. She was on her knees, pulling planters out of the boxes and lining them up on the floor. "A rough time?"

"Mastectomy. Chemo."

"Oh," Wes said.

"I mean, if she really needs him, how can he abandon her?"

No one, it seemed, could argue with cancer. My friends looked worried but said nothing and I began to open boxes of oasis foam and other floral supplies.

"So you never found Sara's boyfriend," Holly prompted again. "Did she just make that up? I can't believe she was lying to me on Saturday night about having to get home to him. She had this whole story down, you know? How he was at home waiting for her. How he was freaking over his Ph. bloody D. What was up with that?"

"I'm not sure," I said. But I had learned that if one is not expecting to be lied to, one often misses a whopper.

"Oh, Mad. I picked up your Wagoneer," Wes said, suddenly remembering. "You know they were bugging us to come and get it." He sounded apologetic.

"Thanks, Wes. I couldn't face it. The bedroom. The Jeep. All my things have been ruined."

Holly quickly sprang up and gave me a hug, a jumble of long arms surrounding me in friendship. She was wearing very short shorts and flip-flops.

"I want to get rid of the Jeep," I told Wes. I waited for him to try to talk me out of it. Wes is sensible. He didn't give in to fear. He was still talking to me every day about giving Honnett back the damned gun.

"That's probably not a bad idea," he said slowly.

I met his eyes. "Why? Did they find something?"

"They had to cut out some of the rear-seat upholstery fabric," he said.

"What?" I stood there, with Holly's arm still draped lightly on my shoulder.

"They found some stains and they had to check them out," he said.

"Ew." Holly got grossed out easily.

"What kind of stains? Blood?" My head raced to the most horrible things these days.

"They wouldn't tell me," Wes answered. "I called that guy at the forensics lab who likes you. Sanchez. Remember? I got nada."

I picked up the phone and dialed the number for Detective Baronowski. To my surprise, he answered his own phone on the first ring.

"Detective, this is Madeline Bean."

"Hello."

"I have just been hearing from my partner that you found stains in my truck."

He didn't answer at once. After a long pause he said, "And?"

"What kind of stains? What's going on?"

"I was planning to call you, Ms. Bean. I've got paperwork stacked up like you can't believe. My partner came down with the flu, by the way. Great timing."

"About my truck . . ."

"I'm getting to that. Give me a second to find my notes."

I waited.

"Okay," he said, and I waited a few more seconds. "Several samples were taken from the rear seat. You understand, when we find anything in your truck, we're going to have to be pretty clear on what was there before you loaned the Jeep to the victim and what may have been brought to the vehicle by Sara or possibly someone who was accompanying Sara. That's where we need your help. We've got to determine if any of the forensics evidence that has been removed from your vehicle belongs to you and your friends. You understand?"

"Sure," I said.

"Right. And this may strike you as a delicate question, Ms. Bean, but I'm going to ask if you can think of anyone who might have left a semen stain in the backseat of your Jeep."

He had to be joking.

When I didn't answer, he spoke up. "I don't make this stuff up. We found fresh —"

"Listen, Lieutenant, it's not that I'm squeamish. I'm not the shockable type. But this is a conversation I never expected to have, in my entire life, with the police or anyone else."

"I don't doubt that."

"Let me just say, for the record, that I have done nothing more horrible than lend my truck to an employee who told me she needed to get home fast."

"We know that."

"As my reward, my home was broken into, a young woman was shot to death in my bed, my Jeep was confiscated, a neighbor was killed, and now you're asking me which of my friends might have left his semen on the upholstery. Is that right?"

"Yes."

Could it, I wondered, get any more freaking odd than this? I had to smile. What gives with this crazy world?

Baronowski couldn't keep the chuckle in now. "If you don't mind," he said. "You know, for the record."

"I know of no one who would fit that description."

"No boyfriend, perhaps. Think back."

"I hate you," I said, beginning to laugh. "No. No one. Not my style, Detective."

"I realize this may seem strange, but we need to rule out any possible, uh, legitimate stains."

The absurdity. The complete absurdity of my life began to crash in on me. I think he was waiting for me to confirm I had no knowledge of a backseat stain.

"I'm twenty-nine years old, Lieutenant. My friends are old enough to ride in my car without spilling anything."

"Okay, good," he said. I had passed some test, apparently, because his voice sounded more inclusive than it ever had. I took the opportunity to ask a question of my own.

"Look, did you ever track down Sara Jackson's boyfriend?"

"Why?"

"If you stop laughing at me, and start sharing some information, I might do the same. I've learned a few more things about Sara myself."

"Such as?"

"You first. Did you find her boyfriend, the grad student?"

"We did."

"What? Who is he? Does he live in her apartment downtown?" I was shocked. I had decided Sara was a nutcase, and dismissed her as a terrific liar. But if she really had a boyfriend, perhaps I had misjudged her again.

"His name is Brett Hurley. Lives in Silverlake. They shared an older cottage there. I can't tell you any more."

"Is he a suspect?"

I received silence for my answer. "So do you have anything to tell me, Ms. Bean?"

"I tried to find Sara's boyfriend myself, but struck out. Last Monday. I wanted to offer him my help, if he needed it. I felt terrible and was trying to do the right thing."

"And?"

"I went to the address Sara had given us on her employee application. It was an apartment downtown."

"We checked it out. Didn't look like she stayed there a lot. Maybe she rented it, but she seemed to live out in Silverlake with Hurley the last six months at least."

"I see. Well, I got to talking to one of her neighbors."

"We canvassed her floor, Ms. Bean. No one knew her very well. Lot of folks move in and out of those kinds of buildings. Lot of foreign students, that kind of thing."

"I met a guy who lives on another floor. He had the impression Sara was a call girl."

"A hooker? How'd he get that idea?"

Wesley and Holly were watching me, listening to my side of the conversation. They were stunned.

"This guy tried to come on to Sara, but she shined him on."

"So that makes her a hooker?" Baronowski seemed skeptical.

"He saw Sara going into the elevator with a lot of different guys."

Detective Baronowski asked for the name of the man I talked with and I gave it to him, along with his apartment location.

"Thanks," he said. "I'll check into it."

"And I'd like to talk to Brett Hurley. Come on, Detective. Can't you give me his phone number?"

I received silence.

"Then would you call him and give him mine?" I gave Baronowski my cell number as well.

"I'll see what I can do," he said.

"Good. You know, 'cause I'm thinking about those traces of semen that were found in my truck."

"They don't belong to the boyfriend. We checked. But you're thinking Sara had a 'date' in the backseat? Anything is possible."

I looked from Holly to Wesley as I hung up the phone.

"From what we just overheard," Wes said sagely, "you are definitely selling that Jeep."

"Frisky"

It was the rare Friday night when I didn't have to work an event. Weekends get booked up early, but not this Friday. Wes and I had been careful to keep our schedule clear in the aftermath of the big Black & White Ball. We had figured we might need downtime. It was with true relief I found I only had to do minimal prep for Saturday's birthday party for Ryan Swinden and then I could actually go out on a Friday night date.

Dexter Wyatt had tried to see me every day that week. He had left charming messages on my answering machine. He had called my cell phone a few times, too. He stopped by the office on Thursday afternoon, unannounced, and when it appeared I wouldn't be back anytime soon, he took Holly out to a late lunch and pumped her for insider information about me. She claims it only took a ride in his BMW Z4 with the top down, two mimosas, and a grilled-shrimp Caesar to get her to divulge all my darkest secrets. Those included the fact that I was free on Friday night.

I liked Dex. I liked him all too well. But he interfered with my thought processes. I needed to keep my brain focused. I had to sort out our problems. Things were still terribly wrong. I could feel it but I still couldn't figure it out in my head. Sara had been in trouble. Grasso had been in trouble. And now maybe I was in trouble.

I could hardly get to sleep at night, thinking about all that had happened in the last week. I had a hard enough time giving myself a break on the best of weeks. On the worst, such as this one, it was unthinkable. In the meantime, I busied myself with my work while my brain took on tangents of its own, spinning away, trying to solve all the world's problems and my own nasty ones in particular.

After cleaning up the kitchen, I was ready to put the last flourishes on Ryan's birthday cake. Wes had baked the cake that morning and frosted it that afternoon. It turned out great. The enormous, three-layer masterpiece in the shape of a tenor saxophone now rested on the kitchen counter. It had been a challenge for Wesley, the swoop of the bell, the detail of every valve, the fine edge of the narrow, graceful neck and mouthpiece, but he has exquisite pattern-cutting skills. Wes is an artist. Holly looked at it earlier and exclaimed, as she does after every cake he produces, "This is your finest work, man."

Both Holly and Wes had been at the house all day, but left to run additional errands. Soon after they departed, the upstairs construction crew stopped by to tell me they were knocking off for the weekend. I checked the clock: 5:25. I said thanks and good-bye. It wasn't until after they took off that I realized I was now all alone. Alone in my house for the very first time since the break-in. I went about my tasks, self-conscious and alert. Overall, I was surprised at how fine I was. I would work another fifteen minutes and then drive back to Wesley's place and get ready for my date.

I looked down at the cake, set out on the counter, and concentrated. It had been smoothly frosted in cream frosting tinted the color of pale brass. Using my most steady hand, I laid down the final frosting details, applying gentle even pressure on the pastry bag. Before me, a thin and perfect trail of black piping outlined each perfectly shaped brass saxophone key. I finished up in a tour de force of outlining technique, edging the entire instrument in one perfect unbroken line of icing. It was complete.

Wes had constructed the cake on a huge cardboard platter covered in black foil. The platter rested inside a flat, unfolded bakery box. I quickly folded the thin pink cardboard to construct the box's sides and top and closed the lid, carefully moving the box to the walk-in refrigerator to keep it cool until the next day.

I then roamed through my house, turning off lights, feeling remarkably good. Perhaps the prospect of seeing Dex again was keeping my mind off other troubles. Perhaps I'm just sickeningly upbeat. Either way, I was pretty happy.

I turned to lock my front door and descended the flight of stairs to the street. I was still driving the rental SUV, and as I turned the ignition, I thought about what sort of car I should buy to replace my old Jeep Grand Wagoneer. Car shopping would be fun. Maybe Dexter would have some suggestions on what I should test-drive.

The traffic was what one expects here, considering it was a Friday during rush hour, which only added to the usual summer crowds of Hollywood tourists. I made my way south and west, looking for side streets that would help me avoid the worst intersections. I turned right on red on Franklin and noticed a black sedan on my tail. I had remembered seeing the same sort of car when I had pulled out of Whitley onto Cahuenga, but I was determined not to give in to my low-simmering, weeklong hysteria. I checked the mirror again. The sedan continued to follow my path as I zigzagged right and left around Highland, staying on Franklin. Nothing unusual about that, but I kept my eyes on my rearview mirror.

Sometimes I get nervous like that. I'll become aware of a certain car. I'll become alarmed if it seems to be taking all the same turns as I do. You live in the city, you should notice these things. I am not going to drive straight to my house, when I'm driving alone, if I'm suspicious. Most of the time, before I can really get spooked, the car that's making me nervous will turn off and be gone. I'm not the best at identifying cars in my rearview mirror, but I was pretty sure the dark sedan was a Honda Accord. I tried to check the license plate but none was displayed in front.

Normally, I'd take Franklin west to La Brea, where almost everyone makes a sort of swing left onto the major southbound street. But I decided to test my nerves. I got in the left-turn lane, just like I always do, and put on my signal. The dark Accord was two cars behind me, also waiting for the left-turn arrow. This is a popular place to turn, as going straight onto Franklin Place leads nowhere. Besides, it gets dark and quiet on Franklin just past this intersection. As the green arrow lit up, permitting left turns,

I pulled forward and then veered sharply to the right, changing lanes at the last second to go straight through the intersection. The woman who was driving the Volkswagen Jetta to my right looked scared out of her wits as she careened out of my way.

In my rearview, I saw the car that had been behind me complete his left turn. However, just as the light was changing to red, the dark Accord behind him jutted over to the right, pulling the same boneheaded traffic stunt as I had just done, coming right up behind me on dark and quiet Franklin Place.

Bad driving was a given in L.A. But my senses were now on hyper-alert. I was looking into my mirror more than I was looking where I was going. I tried to see into the windshield of the car behind me, but I was driving directly into the setting sun and the combination of the glare the sun produced and the dark tint on the Accord's windshield kept me from seeing much. It looked like there wasn't a passenger, just the driver. But I couldn't see more.

I turned left on the first small street I could, Fuller, and gunned my engine. The Trailblazer took off, so I had to get on the brakes fast or risk smashing into the Camry ahead of me. I glanced at my rearview mirror. There was no car at all behind me. The dark Accord hadn't turned. It wasn't following me.

Oh, man. It can give me a knot in my stomach every time. But the relief to find it had only been my stupid imagination was immense.

I zigged and zagged across Hollywood, keeping an occasional eye on my mirror. I had one brief scare, one missed heartbeat, when I thought I saw the same Accord. Dark color. Tinted windshield. No front plates. But I was mistaken. It's a popular model and not everyone has his or her front plates on. This black Accord suddenly came into view as it turned the corner from Larchmont, going east onto Beverly, but it was heading in the opposite direction I was. When it passed me, I admit I was startled. But I got a pretty good look at the driver. It was just a woman in her midforties. Thick red hair, cut in layers. Pretty. She didn't even look my way. I relaxed a bit more after that.

By the time I pulled into the driveway of Wesley's house on Hudson, I was sure no one was paying attention to me. I loved feeling anonymous in the big city. And there was Wesley's new Jaguar, parked in the garage, so I was safe. More or less.

"You going out?" Wes asked, an hour later, sitting on the sofa in the small living room. He looked up and watched me as I stepped into my high heels, freshly showered, changed and made up like I cared how I looked.

I hadn't been sure Wesley would approve of my date with Dexter. Normally, the idea of Wes passing judgment was not an issue between us. But it felt different now that I was living in his house.

"I told Dex I would come over to his place and cook him dinner."

Wes looked impressed. In our line of work, that was shorthand for seduction.

"Are you sure about this?"

"Wes."

"Hey, I'm just asking," he said conversationally. His eyes took in my tight little white linen skirt and low-cut black shirt. "This is the guy you said lacks a little life direction, right? The guy who is too cool for prep school. The one who got mixed up in some art theft you were telling me about?"

I finished putting gold hoops onto my ears and gave Wesley a pained look. "I have enough 'life direction' for ten people. I might like to play with cool prep school boys. And I am going there tonight to find out more about the art theft. This is purely investigational."

"Uh-huh." Wes looked at me thoughtfully. "What are you cooking?"

Now, that was a leading question and Wes knew it. I got a little defensive. "I've made a lot of the dishes in advance," I said, waving nonchalantly to the packed bags I had waiting on the kitchen counter.

"Menu," Wes requested.

"Chilled avocado soup with lime cream, pork carnitas tacos, blackbean-and-corn salad, cilantro-lime rice, Mexican chocolate cake."

"So you're going to bed with him?" Wes knew I meant business when I took the time to bake a flourless chocolate cake.

"I'm not making any comment on that," I said. "If he turns out not to be a con artist or a thief or a murderer, why not?"

"Will you at least do me one favor?" Wes asked, looking more concerned than I would have thought.

"What? Call you at midnight? Let you know I'm safe?"

"No, I was going to say when you make the lime cream, would you *please* thin the sour cream down with some heavy cream first?"

Cooks! It's amazing the two of us could live under the same roof for this long. I threw my little beaded bag over my shoulder and picked up my satchels of groceries and precooked items.

Wes watched me, but couldn't leave well enough alone. "And did you make up fresh salsa?"

"Wes. Of course. Now make up your mind. Do you want to save me from the clutches of a tomcat or do you want to advise me on how much jalapeño I should have used?"

"Both," he said, smiling. "And I'll leave the light on for you tonight."

"Thanks, Dad." That would get him. I smiled as I closed the door behind me.

It took me about twenty minutes to drive to Dexter's house, which was located up on Stone Canyon Road in the hills of Bel Air north of Sunset. He had given me clear directions because it's easy to get lost up on those winding streets. I parked in his driveway, up off the street, and checked out his home.

Some folks really hate the kind of boxy-room, low-ceiling, ranch-style homes that were built by the thousands around Los Angeles in the fifties. Others now call it "Midcentury" design and boast about it in their real estate listings. I wasn't sure where I stood on the debate, but I found I really liked Dexter's relaxed, uncluttered environment.

He met me at the door and smiled his laid-back smile. "Hey, you made it," he said. "Here, let me take those bags. Want a tour?"

He had bought the place a little less than three years ago, he said. His house had four bedrooms, two fireplaces, and the requisite white cabinet/black granite kitchen. As he pointed out this and that, I noticed that he was neat or had a very well-trained housekeeper. His furniture was authentic fifties stuff, with a lot of white upholstered pieces and those cool black leather chairs.

In one hallway, I was struck by a series of black-and-white photos along the wall. Dirty faces of very poor children. Groups of boys playing soccer in a Mexican village square. A heartbreakingly beautiful close-up of a mother holding a small girl.

"Did you take these?" I asked.

He looked embarrassed. "I forgot I told you I liked to take pictures."

"They are amazing, Dex."

"You can't take a bad shot of those kids."

He slid open a large glass door, and I walked outside onto the cross-hatched used brick of his rear deck. A top realtor would call the scene from his pool patio "all-around endless views" and I was impressed.

"I'm actually out here most of the time," he said.

"I can understand why."

The sun was just setting and the sky was tangerine and orange and deeper rust. "Pretty," I said, admiring the peaceful dusk.

"I agree," he said.

I looked over at him, a little surprised. "Most people feel compelled to tell me it's really smog."

"Those who choose to be so freaking literal often miss the beauty of life entirely," Dex said.

"That's true."

"We should pity them." He looked at me, expressing equanimity.

"I do." The in-the-treetops perch of his patio made me feel like I was on top of the world. I reluctantly turned back to the house. "I'd better get our dinner started."

"Can I help?" he asked.

"Can you cook?"

"Nope."

"Then, sure, if you don't mind a few helpful hints."

Dex had dropped the bags off earlier on the granite counter of his open kitchen. He followed me back into the kitchen.

"I can open a bottle of wine," he said, acting a little more like a host than I had expected.

"How about I mix something fresh for us to drink?" I offered. "You have a blender?"

"I knew there was a reason I bought one of those." He smiled and led me to a shelf of appliances stored neatly in his pantry. I found a brand-new blender and plugged it into a socket next to the sink.

"This is cool," he said, walking back to the pantry and returning with a new black chef's apron. He held it up and I smiled, so he looped it over my head and then slowly smoothed it over my body. He let his hands linger there just a few moments longer than were absolutely necessary, then efficiently pulled the string tight in the back and, circling his arms around front, tied it neatly at my waist.

"You're good at that," I said, turning to look at him. His hands on my body had felt great and he could tell I had liked it, the bastard. He let me go slowly and then leaned back against the counter, standing close to me, watching as I washed my hands thoroughly. He was about six feet tall, maybe a little taller, and had clearly spent some time working out. He was dressed casually, wearing jeans with a tan shirt.

I pulled some of the ingredients out of the bags I'd brought and set them up on the counter, including a small, perfectly ripe watermelon,

"What's this for?" he asked, grinning.

"Summertime drink, I thought." I opened the drawer most likely to contain utensils and found the knife drawer on my first try. I pulled out a long serrated knife and, using his cutting board, began rapidly chopping the fresh fruit into about one-inch dice, removing the seeds. Then I asked him to puree it up in the blender.

"This is so cool," he said, showing no fear with an unfamiliar tool.

I found a crystal pitcher in one of his upper cabinets and measured in two cups each of bottled water and Grey Goose vodka.

Dex picked up the Grey Goose bottle and read the label. "You can get just about any man you want with this routine of yours, isn't that right?"

"Any man who drinks too much," I agreed. "So that's something I've got going for me."

I had brought a container filled with fresh-squeezed lemon juice and poured in two cups of that along with a cup of sugar. Then I asked Dex to measure out four cups of the fresh-pureed watermelon, and when he had, I stirred it well.

"What do you call this?" Dex asked, awe in his voice.

"Spiked watermelon lemonade à la Dex." I filled two tall glasses with ice from his icemaker and poured us each a glass, which I garnished with lemon wheels and sprigs of mint. It's in my DNA. Can't help it.

Dex held up his glass and clinked it to mine. The corners of his warm hazel eyes wrinkled when he smiled. "To you, Madeline."

"Aw." I tried the drink. Sweet, sour, and lots of punch. I took another sip. It went down easily, very easily.

"And now that we have our liquid refreshments," he said, taking a sip and smiling, "why don't you ask me what you are dying to ask me?"

"What?"

"Think about it."

"Why the world is round?" I joked, sipping my drink. "Why chickens cross the road?" I'd have to pace myself on the old spiked lemonade if I didn't want to be too dizzy to cook dinner.

He put down his glass and looked at me thoughtfully. "I'm not worried about your ex-boyfriends, Madeline. And I'm giving this thing my best shot. But I think you want to know what really happened that night three years ago when the three best pieces in my brother-in-law's art collection were stolen."

I stopped midsip. Zenya must tell her brother every little thing.

"Or am I wrong about that?" Dex had a very direct gaze.

So, pow! There went my little idea of tiptoeing up to the subject ever so gingerly. A perfect time to take another tiny sip of spiked watermelon lemonade à la Dex.

"LOOK OF LOVE"

old that thought," Dex said, toying with me.

So sly. He knew I was interested in the art theft. Though he might play for laughs most of the time, there was no doubt in my mind the man was extremely smart.

So I went along with the flow, allowing the question of crime to sink below the surface, biding my time, and I set about prepping our little Mexican meal. Dex placed oversize aqua plates on the glass-and-chrome table in the open dining room while I whipped up some fresh tomatillo salsa and served the chilled avocado soup.

We talked all through dinner. He had many questions, and I ended up telling Dexter about my childhood in the suburbs of Chicago. How tame it had been growing up in middle-class Lincolnwood, but how equal parts exhilarating and devastating my childhood had been, even there. It's funny, those getting-acquainted stories we tell to a new person in our life. We reveal ourselves in shades, depending on our mood. The mood moved me to share the story of how I shocked the nay-saying Mrs. Applebaum and won the fifth-grade spelling bee by spelling the word *culinary*, thus foretelling my future career, as well as the horrible time my best

friend Debra and I were escorted into the manager's office at Walgreen's.
I had been sobbing, totally shocked, until Debra, with a pout, pulled several bottles of frosted nail polish out of her Levi's pocket.

"What happened?" Dex asked.

"My mom told me, 'Be careful the friends you pick.' "

"A story with a moral." Dex had an easy smile. "So did you dump
Debra?"

"Of course not. She was my best friend." I ignored good sense and
poured each of us another drink. "That episode did answer one burning
question, though."

Dex looked interested. "You mean about integrity?"

"I mean how Debra, with the same exact allowance as I had, managed
to have the coolest nails in Lincoln Hall Junior High."

Dexter told me more about his life, too. He and Zenya had grown up
in L.A. in the well-off west side of town, the "good" side. Their parents
sent them to the right private schools and belonged to the right country
club. But after his mother had died, Dex was mostly left to raise himself.

"Did your father ever remarry?"

He cocked an eyebrow. "I was twelve and Zenya was fifteen," he said,
serving himself seconds of every dish I'd made from the colorful platters
and bowls I'd brought to the table, pausing his story to comment, "This
corn salad is amazing."

"Thanks."

"Anyway, Georgia—that was our new stepmother—was twenty-one."

"Oh. That can be tricky. Was it bad?"

"I didn't *hate* her."

"Okay."

"I didn't love her, obviously. Hey, I was in like seventh grade. I maybe
had a crush on her. She was definitely hot."

"Boys," I said.

"But in any case, Georgia was sent packing after a few years. My dad
kept busy, though. He managed to marry two other women after that. I
think. I didn't actually go to the last wedding."

"Really?"

"I'm not even sure what their names were," he said pleasantly.

"Not too bitter, though," I commented. "Which is healthy."

He gave me his best smile.

"Then one thing and another," he continued, putting his fork down, "and my dad made the usual bad business decisions and bye-bye fortune."

"Had it been your mother's money?" I asked.

"Of course it had," he said. "And all we were left with, Zenya and me, was the trust fund our mom's mother had set up. Oh, Dad worked with the lawyers for years to get his hands on that. But it was pretty well set up."

"And that's what you live on," I said, wondering how different my life would have been if I'd had such an inheritance.

"Well, I would if I could," he said. "The market is down. I have needs. Let's just say it's going to be gone soon."

"But you still have this house?" I was in the man's three-million-dollar pad, the twinkling lights from the hillside homes beneath us glowing beyond the walls of glass.

"Sure. As long as I can keep it. But I might have to sell. Need the cash."

Rich folks have different problems from the rest of us. I couldn't imagine anything better than the life he was letting slip away. Or perhaps I had it better than I realized. I needed to work. I loved to work. I had achieved a great deal. Dex hadn't been raised to know the joy in such things. No wonder he seemed adrift.

"Oh, you poor little rich boy."

"I like sympathy," he said. "More, please."

"And Zenya?"

"Zenya got a rotten deal. My grandmother left her much less money than she left me. I guess she was expecting Zenya to make a rich marriage and thought she wouldn't need it. I don't know. And Zen is so sweet she did what was expected. She married Bill. What a deal, huh? I only hope she's happy with it."

"Isn't she?"

He spoke quietly. "I don't think so. No."

So all this time, Dex had had to watch his sister wrestle with a difficult marriage and he'd felt guilty because he'd inherited more than she had. I thought it was sad and noble that he wanted to protect her. To Dex, his sister's rich life had too steep a price and he would rather sacrifice his own safety net to get her out of there. He looked at me across the glass table and reached for my hand. "I never talk about this stuff. Not to anyone. My last girlfriend didn't even know I *had* a sister, and here I am,

telling you . . . everything. I don't open up to people. But there's something going on here, Madeline. You're killing me."

The one thing you never expect from a self-confident guy is an ad-
mission of weakness.

"I was only trying to maim you. My aim must be off."

"It's like I'm fourteen again and I like this girl too much." He held on
to my hand and laughed at himself.

My breathing became shallower and I could feel myself get jittery.
You know, like when you want a certain guy to like you and you get the
signal that maybe he really does.

"I don't know anyone like you," he went on. "You're so calm when
things are going crazy. You have this goofy smartness. I never know what
you're going to say. I'm scared I'm not worthy of you. You are something
else."

"Ah, that's just the spiked watermelon talking," I said, smiling a little.

"I have fallen for you. So watch out what you do with my heart, okay?"

I burst out laughing.

"I'm not joking." But then he smiled, unable to maintain such a serious tone for too long. "Ah, crap. I am suddenly thinking of all the girls
I've left along the way. Karma. What a horrible thought. So, are you going
to pay me back for those women I was a bastard to?"

I looked at him. His eyes were teasing, but I thought I saw something
more there. He was clearly a man who had spent a lot of his life avoiding
any dependence on a woman. Since he was a kid. Since his mother had
left him so young. I'm no Sigmund Freud, but anyone watching a
month's worth of Lifetime movies could make such a simple connection.
For all of that, I was so attracted to him.

"Anyway," he said, after a significant pause in which I did not tell him
to get lost but on the other hand did not confess I was falling for him, too,
"anyway, that's why I'm going to have to sell this place. I want to offer the
money to my sister. So she can leave that asshole. She deserves so much
better than that."

"Has she told you she wants to leave?"

"No. She doesn't get it all yet. But she will."

"Does this have anything to do with the art that was stolen?"

"So." Dexter played with his napkin, a linen weave in oatmeal colors.
"We're back to that already."

Without my realizing it, something had shifted, so that solving a puzzle and sorting out a crime seemed so much less important than getting to the heart of this man. But I was not ready to let this topic alone. I had to remember my mother's sensible advice and make a good choice here. I had to consider what he was capable of.

Dexter rose and began clearing dishes and I joined him, picking up two empty serving bowls. His tone was light but resolute. "You want to know anything, Madeline, I will tell you the truth. It will always be that way with us, okay? Let's make it a rule."

"Like you enjoy following the rules," I joked.

"I'll start now. Zenya's husband, Bill," Dexter said, walking around the glass-topped table, but stopping to make eye contact. "What a bastard. He knew I needed money."

Oh no. My stomach sank.

"Anyway, he and Zen and the kid were going to Maui and they asked me to stay at their house." We walked together to the kitchen as he talked. "Bill said they'd pay me for my time. That was before I had this place, so I was like Uncle House-sitter for a few weeks." Dexter began rinsing the dishes. I opened the dishwasher.

"And then what?"

"And then I came home from a concert with a date and the front door was standing wide open. The alarm company was already there and so were the cops. It had been a simple heist. The only things missing were the three most precious etchings from Bill's coveted collection."

"They didn't take anything else? His guitars? Any other art? Zenya's jewelry?"

He shook his head.

"Didn't the cops think that was sort of odd?"

"Look, the artwork had been displayed a few months earlier at the friggin' art museum. Any good crook could read Bill's name on the donor plaque and wait until the exhibit had ended. They must have found out where Bill and Zenya lived and waited until the house was empty. That was that."

I looked at him. For once, the easygoing manner was gone.

"What?" he asked, looking more closed down than I'd seen him before. "You wondering if I had something to do with the theft?"

"Well, did you?"

"Of course not."

"Okay. Whew. That's good." I smiled up at him.

He grabbed me and looked at me for a minute. I felt the rush of too many spiked watermelon lemonades à la Dex. After the strength of his grasp I was unprepared for the softness of his mouth on mine. We stood in the kitchen kissing for so long my knees really did go weak. I had missed being with a man, missed being held. I wanted him to go on kissing me.

He ripped my shirt open, popping the tiny buttons, which I heard hit the polished hardwood floor.

"Dexter," I said, breathless. "Dex, you have no curtains in this entire house."

"I know," he whispered. "Too much money." He began to nibble my ear.

"And the whole place is made of glass. All windows," I pleaded as he slipped my blouse off and cupped my breasts in his hands.

"Are you worried about the neighbors?" he asked, touching me in a way that made me want to pull him down on the floor right there, beg him to stop talking.

"I am feeling," I said as he pulled my skirt to the floor, "a little exposed."

I stood in my tiny white silk thong panties and high heels and nothing else. His hands brushed over me, caressing my skin, touching me all over.

"Do you want me to?" he asked, nuzzling my neck, his hands slipping into my panties and twisting them, touching me, making me gasp.

"The lights," I said, looking to see where the switch was, hoping it was close by because I was so turned on I couldn't have left him for even a moment.

"Leave them on, Madeline," he said, playfully pulling off my last garment. He was now fully clothed and I was fully not.

"Dex, I can't," I protested. But he knew I could. I wanted him. He could feel it between my legs.

"Does it turn you on more thinking I'm a villain?" he whispered as he kissed my hair, my ears, my throat.

"I . . . don't know." I was shocking myself. "Right this minute, I don't care about that at—" He pulled my hand and I followed him, naked, to the nearby living room. On the floor was a bright yellow shag rug.

"Oh no," I said, giggling. "Not on the shag."

"Come on," he said, teasing. "I'll treat you so well, Madeline."

I realized I couldn't stop myself. I wanted him. Even suspecting that he might very well be involved in a crime didn't seem to matter to me. He'd admitted he needed money three years ago. He admitted the "burglars" only took a few very specific items. He bought this amazing house right after the theft. I was beyond wanting to add it all up.

"Look," I said, my breath coming fast, almost losing my nerve as I realized we were standing, entwined, in front of an inch-thick wall of glass. The canyons of Bel Air were just beyond.

He kissed me again. "What? L.A. is at our feet." But then he pulled back and looked at me with such sweetness. "Just tell me you want me, Madeline. It's up to you. We don't have to do this."

While I tried to think it over, I leaned in to kiss him one more time, and the warmth of his mouth on mine made my brain go fuzzy again. It had been such a long time since I had managed to let myself go, to turn off my mind. His hands were experienced and knew exactly the right places to caress and to stroke.

That was the moment I realized I wouldn't stop him. I opened my eyes just as he began to slowly take off his shirt, his broad shoulders backed against the wall of windows. He was gorgeous, so cool and tanned. I don't know what it was that drew my eye away from him and outside. Perhaps some tiny flicker of movement.

In the dim patio light I could just make out a silhouette on the other side of the glass. A woman. Oh my God! A woman was standing right there on his deck. She was watching us through the glass from just a few feet away.

And then I recognized her. The light picked up the red color of her hair. It was the woman I had seen in the Honda Accord. The woman who had been following me.

I screamed.

Dex whipped around, beyond stunned. Then he saw her, too, before she was gone. He bolted for the sliding-glass door, fiddled with the lock, and then tore it open. The cold night air rushed in on me.

"Stay here," he said, his voice sharp with anger at what was happening. An intruder was ruining our night, he must have thought.

"Dex!"

He ran out into the dark yard and I scrambled to get back into my clothes, which I found scattered around here and there. I was shaking, and tears were streaking down my face.

I was thinking a hundred crazy things. Jumbled among the thoughts were my fears of the past week, my sense that I had been a target all along. And then my anxieties mushroomed. Perhaps there was a greater power at work here. How had I so easily become attached to a man about whom I knew so little? Was there anything rational about Ping-Ponging from the cop who lied to me to a crook who swore he'd always tell me the truth? Tonight's bizarre events suddenly seemed to be my punishment for giving in to pleasure, for wanting to start fresh with a new man who might love me. Things have a purpose. Everything was connected. Damn it, I didn't believe in random. I didn't believe in accidents. I always needed to know *why*.

I was sitting in a heap on one of the black leather chairs when Dex came back in the house. He was breathing hard.

"She's gone. I lost her. I heard the sound of a car engine."

I continued crying, not able to talk.

"Look, Madeline. I'm so sorry. I have no idea who she was. You have to believe that. I've never seen that woman before in my life."

"That's okay. It's not your fault," I finally managed to say between sobs. "I've seen her before. Earlier today. I think she's been following me."

Dex's whole manner changed. "Who is she?" He looked at me seriously now. Perhaps he had thought it was some outraged neighbor lady coming to complain about our indecent show. But he suddenly realized something more sinister was happening to me.

"I don't know." I stopped crying and tried hard to think it through. "At first, because of her age, I thought maybe she could be one of the women who worked on the Woodburn gala. Maybe I should recognize her. But I just don't."

And while I was still coming down from this enormous shock, racking my sorry brain for answers, Dex suddenly smiled at me. "Man."

"What?"

He shook his head, still smiling. That smile made all the difference.

He had an interesting effect on me. He didn't let pathos boil over very long, which was a great relief. I looked at his grin and made the obvious guess. "You can't believe how much trouble I can get myself into, right?"

"No. I can easily believe that."

I might have been on the ragged side of drunk and lovelorn and completely freaked out, but I could still take a joke. I grinned.

"It's just that until that lady came along," Dex continued, holding his thumb about an inch away from his forefinger, "I was about this close to having the best sex in my entire sorry life."

"Of that," I answered, "you should have no damn doubt."

"Blues in the Night"

Dexter insisted on following me back to Wesley's house. I complained it was too much trouble; it was late; I was fine. He just stared at me. His car stayed right behind mine all the way home.

My eyes swept across the midnight streets, some residential and dark, some Friday-night raucous, scouring each lane, looking for the Honda Accord. Naturally, I didn't see it.

"You okay?" Dex asked, talking to me by cell phone as we drove down a jamming Sunset Strip.

"Stop calling me," I said, laughing. "I'm fine." I disconnected and waved in my rearview mirror as we inched past the giant billboards.

But I had to think about how fine I really was. Who was that woman? Why had she followed me? And more disturbing, if she meant to harm me, she knew where to find me. I was sure of it. She must have been tailing me better than I realized. I had to assume she'd followed me from Wesley's place in Hancock Park up to Dexter's house earlier that evening, so I had no doubt she knew where I was staying.

On Hudson, Wesley's street, I slowed down and examined every parked car. No Accord with a missing front plate. With Dexter following behind in his Z4, I drove right past Wesley's house and then proceeded slowly up and down the quiet streets in all directions, scouting the curbs for dark Hondas. This is a neighborhood that doesn't encourage street parking for its residents. The few scattered cars parked in the area were more than likely partygoers'. I strained to keep vigilant and yet I spied no Hondas that matched my stalker anywhere within a one-mile radius of Wes's place.

Dexter's and my two-car convoy slowly cruised by the Canadian consulate general's English-style mansion, then past the official, but uninhabited mayoral mansion, the Getty House, on South Irving. By then I was blocks away from Wesley's house, but I wanted to be sure.

My cell phone, thrown on the passenger seat of the Trailblazer, chirped.

I fumbled for it and hit the on button. "Okay," I said, looking in my rearview mirror. "I'm fine. I'm heading to Wesley's right now."

"Just checking." Dex's voice sounded calm over the phone.

I drove back to Third Street and over to Hudson. Then I pulled into the long driveway and Dex pulled his car in right behind me. Before I could unfasten my seat belt and gather my bag and phone, he had walked up to my door and opened it. We didn't talk as we walked together back to the guest house behind the empty main house. The porch light was on outside the door of the cottage. Thanks, Wes.

I turned to say good night.

"You sure you don't want me to come in for a little while?" Dex tilted his head, watching my face in the porch light. He seemed concerned with what he saw. "You know, check that everything's all right." He reached out and softly stroked my arm in a friendly gesture, but I didn't move closer to him and he let his hand drop.

"No. Thanks. I've got to be up early tomorrow morning."

"Right." He looked like he was about to say something more, but then thought better of it.

"I had better go in. Don't want to disturb Wes."

"So Wesley's home," Dex said, sounding reassured. "Good."

With an evening that had wound up resembling some new X-rated extreme sport more than a good, old-fashioned date, there seemed no correct way to end it. "Sorry about tonight," I said. Lame but true.

"Say, don't be. It was an incredible meal. You are amazingly beautiful. I am swooning for you." I laughed as he gently brushed my long, curly hair back with both hands, resting them on my shoulders. "Things could be worse, you know?"

"Sure."

Dex gave me a short, tentative kiss. I kept my eyes open this time.

"You are completely freaked," he assessed sadly.

"Yeah. I know. Let's talk later."

"Tomorrow?"

"I'm working during the day, but maybe later in the afternoon."

"Where are you working?"

"At a kid's party in Pasadena. Say, you want to hear Wynton Marsalis play live?"

I gave Dexter the address and we said good night.

Wesley was still up, reading the latest Harry Potter. He put the heavy book down the moment I entered the living room. That's when I noticed Honnett was sitting in one of the club chairs, ankle resting on knee, foot tapping.

"I called Honnett," Wes said. It was an unnecessary explanation. I had phoned Wes to tell him about the stalker woman turning up at Dexter's house. Now I was sure she'd been following me earlier in the day. It had taken Wes maybe four seconds after I hung up to get Honnett over to the guest house. It was sickening. I was relieved.

"Maddie, sorry to intrude here," he said, looking uncomfortable. How much could he have heard through the front door when I was kissing Dexter good-bye? "Wes was worried about you."

"I'm worried, too," I said.

"Yeah? Well, add me to the list. I wanted to go pick you up, drive you back here, but Wes wouldn't give me the address of your . . . friend. I guess you got back okay." Honnett was doing an impressive job of holding on to some serious rage, keeping his expressions in check, but his voice showed the strain. I couldn't tell what was at play here, the idea that I was in danger or the fact that I was dating someone new, and he wasn't allowed to come rescue me.

"But she's fine now," Wesley said, doing his best to settle us all down.

"Look, you need to call Baronowski and bring him up to speed on what's going on here. Give him a description. It was a woman, right?"

I nodded.

He thought it over—a woman—and appeared to be as stumped as I was. "Did she have a weapon?"

I shook my head no.

"You sure? Because the only crime we have here is maybe trespassing. And if there was no weapon in sight and she left immediately after you spotted her, it's kind of hard to make anything of it. That is assuming we can find her. Do you think your friend wants to press charges?"

"I don't know. She didn't really do anything to us. She just sort of watched us for a while, through the window."

"What were you doing?" he asked, following the trail of the story.

"We . . ." I simply could not think of an appropriate response.

Wesley coughed, and then asked brightly, "Would anyone care for a cup of coffee?" And without waiting for a response, he took himself off to the tiny guest-house kitchen and gave us some room to fight in privacy. I love Wes.

Honnett smiled a little and shook his head. There were clearly secrets separating us now. Things I wouldn't go into. Things about me and another man. Maybe he got the irony of our situation. I don't know. But he looked ill, that was for sure. I considered it. Maybe even as ill as I had felt when I discovered he wasn't all mine.

"You trying to hurt me, Maddie?" he asked softly, still smiling at me.

I thought about it. I can't talk about my unconscious or subconscious or id or whatever, but I didn't *think* I had gotten myself involved with Dexter on purpose to hurt Honnett. On the other hand, I could see the power of his reaction. And it did feel awfully good, I'm ashamed to admit, to see he still cared about me this way. I could see why a woman would do something like that, to provoke a man who dumped her, to make him jealous, just to get a little of her own back. I looked up at him. Any momentary pained expression I might have observed was now replaced by the trusty Honnett mask of calm.

I recovered and picked up my point. "But I'm sure this person has been following me. I've had the creepiest feeling all week that I'm a target. First Sara, then Grasso, and now me."

"Look, Maddie," he said gently, "you've been under a lot of strain. Your house is ripped apart. You're living over here. You told me you're not sleeping much. Your nerves must be shot."

"I'm not mistaken, Chuck. I'm not."

"Well, I'm just saying it's easy to get jumpy. It was dark out. A woman startled you and she may have looked like someone else you barely got a glimpse of."

"I'm not seeing things," I said, my teeth clenched.

"Okay, but I'm going to talk to you like a cop now, okay? I have to say this. What do you know about this guy you were just seeing? You've known him how long? How do you know this woman wasn't an old friend of his, maybe even an ex?"

I stared at Honnett hard. "You mean," I said quietly, "maybe he has another girl he's not telling me about?"

Even Honnett got the real point I was trying to make.

"I just hope," he said, looking at his hands, "this guy of yours is good enough for you. I hope he's a right guy. At least I could live with that. I could be happy for you. I don't want to think about you getting mixed up with some creep. And don't yell at me. I know it's none of my damn business who you go out with now. I'm just saying."

"And that's just you talking like a 'cop'?" I smiled at him. For a bastard with a wife still attached, he did care about me. He did.

"Anyway, the point I'm making is, you are tired. And we have to face it. There isn't any hard evidence anyone is after you."

I tilted my chin down and gave him the eye. "Yeah, right. You know I don't believe in coincidences, Honnett." I waved my hand in front of my face, dismissing the topic. "This is not making me feel better. What I want to know is what the hell is going on? Why would someone want to follow me? How does this connect to the murders?"

Wes returned and put a tray on the coffee table. There were fresh-baked round chocolate wafers, which had been half dipped into white chocolate, along with a carafe of coffee and a pot of tea.

"Thanks, Wes," Honnett said, and then he looked back at me. "Okay. Tell us what you think is happening."

What I wanted was Honnett's cop head, not his ex-boyfriend head, and he was finally getting there. I moved to the sofa across from him and crossed my legs.

"I keep thinking that this must have something to do with Albert Grasso's papers."

"But how?" Honnett asked.

"We looked through them," Wes said, doubtful like Honnett. "There was nothing there."

"But let's say someone thought there was something to worry about in those papers," I persisted. "Grasso knew I had seen them. Maybe others did, too. Maybe they want me dead."

"So, you figure they came to your house on Whitley to kill you last Saturday night?" Honnett seemed detached now and ready to lay it all out. And it's funny. It had annoyed me when he kept insisting I was wrong, but now it spooked me just as bad to realize he might think I was right. "And the shooter made a mistake."

"Right. Let's say that was Grasso. And he mixed up Sara Jackson for me. That doesn't make a lot of sense, I know. Sara and I don't . . . *didn't* really look that much alike."

"But wait, Mad . . ." Wes picked up a teacup, reconsidering this scenario. "Albert Grasso didn't know you very well. Maybe in the dark. She's alone in your house late at night. She has long red hair. Maybe he got confused."

"We're both about the same size . . ." I looked at Honnett to see if he was buying any of it.

"Okay. Keep on telling your story. For now, let's say Grasso killed her."

"Right. Then the people he was scared about, the ones his files may have incriminated in some way, they came by his place and killed *him*."

"Okay," Honnett said, sounding neutral.

I spun out the rest. "Those people who killed Grasso had more cleaning up to do. They see the news and realize Grasso killed the wrong girl. I'm still a threat. So they are sending some hit woman out after me."

"Maddie. Honey. You think anyone outside of the movies uses hit women?" Honnett had gone about as far as he could go.

"I don't know! Okay, not a professional killer." We all laughed. "But this woman . . . She was *attractive*, regular-looking. Hey, what about this? Maybe she was a friend of Caroline Rochette's. She looked about Caroline's age."

"And what would that be?" Wes asked. "Somewhere north of forty and south of death?" He looked pleased to see me smile, and continued: "I suppose there could be some wacked-out posse of killer real estate ladies after your property . . ."

"It doesn't fit," Honnett observed, looking at me. I followed his eyes down. My blouse was held together by paper clips. Dex didn't have a sewing kit. Figures.

"Why not?" I asked, ignoring his gaze. "Leaving aside the killer-realtor theory, what's wrong with the first part of my story?"

Honnett sighed, and poured himself a cup of coffee. "You're talking like 'the Mob,' right? This is not their style, Madeline. But putting that aside . . ." He stirred in a spoon of sugar and looked back at me, getting serious. "First, if Albert Grasso and/or whoever else was part of some scheme was willing to kill to make sure no one read those files, they'd have to kill a hell of a lot more people than you. They would have to kill his gal pal, Caroline Rochette, not to mention Wes and Holly." He waited for my reaction.

"True."

"And now it gets even more complicated. The police detectives in the case have copies of the papers, which was a very smart move on your part. So assuming those papers of Albert Grasso's really do contain something very hot, we all missed it. The people who care about it gotta realize by now we're too frigging dense to find it."

I listened to his logic as it tumbled my theories like the proverbial dominoes.

"So, if there *was* something explosive among Grasso's box of junk and none of us geniuses have discovered it, they'd be fools not to leave it all the hell alone now, wouldn't they? At this point, coming after a little caterer makes no sense."

He was right. Why would they?

Honnett spoke kindly, but he didn't let up until he got me to see it his way. "Honey, killing you is the opposite of what they would want right now. It would only direct suspicion to those papers, which right now no one is really focused on, don't you see? If I were them, assuming there *is* a 'them,' I'd lie low now or get out of town. You know, fly to Belize. I wouldn't keep kicking up dust, Maddie."

"Right," I said slowly.

"And then let's face another fact. There's a good chance there was nothing important among those papers in the first place." Honnett was not averse to rubbing in a little salt.

It stung, but he was right. I had become completely insane, fearing the world was trying to kill me. He made sense. Hell, I had used the same arguments to talk myself down from the ledge of my paranoia all week. Each night, as I rechecked the chambers of the Lady Smith .38, just to reassure myself that she was ready, I thought about how ridiculous it was for anyone to still be after me.

"Thanks for coming out here tonight, Honnett."

He met my eyes, held the contact. I was startled by the emotion I saw there.

"Look," I said, "I'm . . . Well, I'm tired. I need sleep. Obviously. Wesley is here. You should go home."

"I'll stay," he said, looking surprised I'd kick him out.

"That's okay. I'm fine now."

Honnett looked over at Wesley, waiting for support, but Wes didn't insist he stay either.

"If you're sure," Honnett said, sounding tired of fighting me. "Walk me to the door, then?"

The room was small, and Wes took the hint, excusing himself and disappearing into the back bedroom.

"You'll be okay?" he asked.

I looked at Honnett. He seemed older somehow. He still had the great rugged face, the strong cheekbones and jawline of a cowboy. But his clear blue eyes looked a little vague, like he had a lot on his mind.

"How's everything with you?" I asked, standing with him near the door.

"It goes on. The usual. Sherrie has been doing a little better. She's getting out a little more."

"Good."

"So, Maddie. You like this other guy a lot, huh?"

"This is not a good time to go into this, Chuck," I said. I had had enough drama for one evening. I wanted a bath and bed. My own.

"Okay. Sorry. Look, I have to ask for the thirty-eight back, if you don't mind."

The what? I looked at him like he had suddenly slapped me. Now, I could stand a lot of things. I could stand to watch my romantic evening destroyed in an instant. I could stand to find my old boyfriend waiting up for me at home. And I could probably get through a teenager's birthday party in a few hours. But I simply could not part with the gun.

"No."

"I'm sorry?"

"You can't have it back now. You can't. I haven't had time to buy one of my own. And—"

"Maddie—"

"NO! Look, if you're worried I don't know anything about guns, you don't have to worry. I found an instructor. She's really kick-ass. And I've been out on the range, shooting real bullets. I can shoot, too. That is not a worry. But the whole idea," I rattled on quickly, "is to provide me with a little goddamned sense of security in the crazy world, Honnett. And if you take that revolver away from me now, while who knows what freakin' forces of evil are gathering to get me, I'll completely, *completely* wig out. I will. So this isn't even a question, okay? You can't have it back right now. Understand?"

"Bad timing, I get it," he said, taking me and my paranoid outburst with measured calm.

"Okay. So good night. And thanks for coming by."

"Good night," he said, searching my eyes for something. I think he wanted to kiss me. It wasn't going to happen. Access to my lips was closed to all, perhaps forever. Didn't these guys realize that despite the logic and the scenarios, despite their theories and all the cops in the world working on the case, I knew without reason that someone was maybe trying to kill me?

"I'm going to drive around awhile," Honnett said, opening the door to leave. "What sort of car should I be looking for?"

"Honda Accord. Black. No front plate."

He stopped in the doorway, and looked back at me, thinking it all through, I guess. How we had gone from where we were a few months ago to where we were now was a hard journey to map. I was sure he was going to say something more about the time we had been together. But instead, he simply asked again, "An Accord, you say?"

I stood there, exhausted, nodding. And then he left.

"Look Beyond"

Jacked up on Double-Double Animal-Style burgers and third helpings of Chocolate Madness Saxophone cake, three dozen twelve- and thirteen-year-old boys raced through the Hutson backyard, whooping at one another that they could beat anyone at Starcraft.

I was happy to see the party had come off so well. Sometimes "impromptu" works. Wes was pouring Holly and me glasses of champagne to celebrate the fact that our crew had cleaned up and was ready to move on.

Wynton Marsalis had been brilliant, charmed the audience, and cut out about an hour earlier. Even in this wealthy crowd, guests were whispering about how much money Mr. Hutson had spent for this treat. The much-touted battle of the bands, or more specifically, young musicians, was yet to come. But it wasn't our responsibility to get all those carbo-crazed boys and their instruments up onstage. Thank God.

We had leased the tables, risers, and audience chairs, as well as the sound equipment and soundboard. The truck would come to collect it all tomorrow. I raised a flute of sparkling, straw-colored wine and clinked glasses with Holly.

"To more easy gigs," she said, taking a sip of the tiny bubbles that gave joy to this particular vintage of Louis Roederer Brut Premier.

"Amen," I said.

"And no shocking surprises after," Wes said, taking a drink.

"Hey," Holly said, looking over my shoulder. "Someone here for you."

I turned. Dex Wyatt had appeared. He was coming down the path in the Hutson's huge backyard. When he missed the Marsalis concert, I had briefly wondered what was up, but then I got busy as I always do and sort of lost track of time. Suddenly a commotion broke out not ten feet away from where Dex was walking.

"Hey, Uncle Dex!" A fully clothed young man had decided it would be hilarious to sit in the Jacuzzi. He held his alto sax above the bubbling hot water and began playing. Several other young party guests and their instruments followed his lead. You had to love kids.

"Hey, Kirby," Dex called to the boy, saluting him back, and then he walked over to us. "Wes. Madeline." Dex stopped by my side and I could swear the sun got brighter. I'm not making this up. "You okay?" he asked me.

"Fine. You missed the concert."

"Stuff came up I couldn't get out of."

"That's okay."

"Hey, I didn't realize my nephew, Kirby, would be at this thing. How wild."

"You know Holly Nichols, Dex."

"Holly," he said, with a devilish grin. "I've been dying to see you again. And you look stunning."

Holly, standing in full daylight in a proper Pasadena garden, was currently wearing a tiny red Paul Frank muscle tee with the famous image of Julius, the puzzled monkey, on her chest. The shirt ended way above her navel, and it was only after many inches of bare, tanned stomach that her pink hip huggers began. I won't even go into the belly-button ring, or the sprinkle of glitter in her blond hair.

"Thanks," said Holly, dimpling.

"So what has Madeline told you two about me, then?" Dex asked.

"Everything," Holly said.

"Everything?" Dex looked at me, voice squeaking in mock shock.

"I cook with these guys all day long," I confessed to him. "The hot stoves. The bright lights. They get every detail out of me. I should have warned you."

"I'm cool with that," Dex said.

"Great attitude," Holly commented, admiring my new man and giving me a nod. "Mad is like some supernaturally gifted pitcher. When you're at the plate, you never know what she's going to throw at you. So, my advice would be, stay alert."

"You a baseball fan, Holly?" Dex was a sports guy, so he sounded intrigued.

"Well, not really," she admitted.

"She just likes the metaphors," Wesley explained.

Connie Hutson walked up to our group and I turned on my party-planner personality. "Connie, we're just ready to leave. Is there anything else you need?"

"I was coming over to congratulate your group. It's a terrific party. Ryan has had the best time. Despite himself."

"I noticed some of the guests are in the whirlpool," Wes said helpfully.

"Oh, these boys! We've brought out towels and they will just have to play in the contest in soggy clothes. We're about to get started. Anyway, thanks so much for taking us on at the very last minute."

"You're welcome," Wesley said, smiling.

We all began to depart. When we got to the front of the house, I hugged Wes and Holly good-bye and we separated to go to our own cars. Dex had walked out with me and asked if I had time for a private word. I wanted to talk with him, too. We stopped in front of my parked Trailblazer.

"Dex," I said, "I've got to ask you something and I need you to be completely honest with me. Okay? This is serious."

"Sure. What?"

"The woman. Are you telling me you never saw her before? Or is she someone you dated or something. It's important. I need the truth."

"What are you talking about?" Dex sounded genuinely insulted. "I told you the truth last night. I don't know who she was or what she was doing there. What is this, Madeline?"

"I think I'm in some serious trouble, Dex. I need to know what is going on now. A cop warned me I might be being naive. He thought it was likely that woman was connected to you. I just had to make sure."

Dexter stared at me, putting it together. "So your boyfriend, the cop, is getting you all worked up over me, right?"

"I'm not usually like this," I said.

"Madeline, you think I'd lie to you?"

My eyes stung with sudden tears, which I fought to hold back. "Men lie," I said, with more force than I had intended. "I'm not saying you are, right now, but it happens."

"That's a great attitude you've got. What the hell did I do? We are just getting started. Why are you suddenly so suspicious?"

"Don't sound so self-righteous," I said, snapping back. Fearing for my life for the past week had done a number on my legendary self-control. And the last person in the world I wanted to take it out on was Dexter. He stood there in the dappled sunlight of the lush trees, looking angered by my attack. Like he wasn't going to take on the burden of all the men who had done me wrong. But before I could begin to trust him, I had to know what was real to him. In the daylight, I doubted everything about everyone.

"You are hard work, Maddie," he said with a half smile, defusing my anger with the sudden shift of tone.

"Oh, hell."

"That's part of the attraction for me, no doubt. I've had it pretty easy my whole damn life, as I'm sure you have figured out. But I want to work this out, you and me. Did you hear what I said? I said the word *work*. Several times."

I smiled. "Only twice."

"And I know deep down you can't entirely approve of me, can you? But I feel like we have a connection. And if I get my act together, we could be awesome. I've never felt that before."

"Really?"

"Really. And if you want honest, I'll be honest. The girls in my life . . . Well, the girls have been kind of easy to get. You know, I'm lucky like that. But they never last with me. I can't get that attached. I'm like a Velcro guy, but all the girls don't have the right loops or whatever it is that makes Velcro stick together."

I nodded, smiling more.

"No one reaches me. We've talked about this before. But it's different with you. You've got the right kind of loops for me, Madeline."

"Oh, Dex."

"You are completely odd." He touched my cheek.

"Odd." I smiled.

"Odd, but I like it."

"I like you, too, Dex. I do. But there's something very wrong. I know there is. I just feel it."

His smile faded a tiny bit and he finally nodded.

"And until I can figure all of this out, we can't work as a couple."

"Do you have to make some big decision about us today? Why can't we just keep on? Get to know each other a little better."

I shook my head, working hard to resist him. It made my words come out hotter than I intended. "You haven't been completely honest with me. You know it. There's something more going on between you and the art collection that was ripped off than you are willing to tell me. I felt it last night when you were avoiding the questions. Tell me if I'm wrong about that."

We stood near my red rent-a-car, our voices suddenly heated.

"What do you want from me?" He didn't look away from my eyes. "If you wanted a saint, you wouldn't have been hanging out with me this long, Madeline."

"You're not a saint. What exactly does that mean?" I was unable to hold back all my frustration and anger. How dare he make me fall for him! I was no longer content to wait for answers. I had to know where we really stood. "Did you have something to do with the art theft, Dex? Is that it?"

He stared at me, hurt and surprised.

"And what about the tenor saxophone at the Woodburn auction? Did you have something to do with that theft as well? You showed up downtown that night and everything around me started falling apart. And that woman in your yard. Did she really follow me to your place, or did you set me up, Dex? Did you have something to do with these murders that have haunted me?"

"Sweetie . . ." He sounded honestly shocked. "Maddie, this is too much. Are you accusing me of murdering someone? We have to talk. You can't be for real."

"I need the truth, Dex."

"The truth . . ." Dex shook his head. "The truth is tricky, Madeline.

The truth can hurt people. I'm not always sure the truth is such a good idea."

It wasn't the answer I was looking for, but it worked. Here I'd been ranting about how I was afraid to trust him, and I suddenly saw clear as day that all along he had been afraid to trust me. Somehow, the sadness of his voice and honesty of his concern woke me up out of my anxious spell.

I loved his face, even now, showing some strain. He may have perfected his charming facade and fooled everyone with the happy-playboy act, but I saw another man. Dex seemed so lonely to me despite his great humor and easy smiles. So much more real. Maybe I was one of the very few who saw the real Dexter Wyatt. And then my anger seemed to dissolve. I knew he wouldn't lie to me. I couldn't believe he would hurt me. His character may have many flaws, but I believed he wanted to play straight with me. And I realized I was willing to risk being a fool rather than give up on this man.

"Tell me," I said softly.

From behind the large Arts-and-Crafts-style home we heard faint sounds of many instruments tuning up. The battle of the young jazz musicians was about to begin.

"Okay," he said. "We'll do it your way."

I took his hand and we leaned against the car and he began to tell me his story.

"Three years ago, Zenya's husband, Bill, asked me to house-sit. Four weeks. I said no problem, plus he offered to pay me. So you know what happened. There was a break-in and three etchings were stolen. The cops always thought it might be me behind it, but they never recovered the artwork and that was that."

"And?"

"And I didn't do it. I didn't. But I think I know who did."

I looked at him and stroked his arm, waiting for more.

"Zenya called me from Maui the day before the theft. She never calls when she's away, so it was kind of unusual. Anyway, she told me that months before they'd planned the Maui trip, she bought tickets to a Stones concert in L.A. They were for the next night. She'd forgotten about them until just then, she said. She told me where I could find them in her desk and told me to use them. She hated to think they'd go to waste."

"And that's the night you went out and that's when the etchings were taken."

He nodded.

"But that could have easily been a coincidence," I said.

He looked at me. "It was funny. Odd. She never bought tickets to concerts. And Zenya doesn't really go for the Rolling Stones. And she actually called me the day of the concert to make sure I was going. I thought it was all very strange even before the break-in."

That did sound suspicious.

"And that's not all. About a month after the theft, Zenya called to tell me she had gotten lucky with some investment and she was buying me a house."

"What? I thought you said Zenya didn't have a lot of her own money."

His eyes looked pained. "She doesn't. And she told me a big story about how Bill had given her a little money to invest. Anyway, she had a friend who was a real estate agent find a great place for me. Zenya always hated that I lived in an apartment. So she told me she found me a place and she put the down payment into escrow. It was up to me to pay the rest of it."

"And you did?"

"I needed some permanence. I thought it was the only way I'd grow up and settle, you know? I wanted to pay her back, but she wouldn't let me."

"And you think Zenya was involved with the art being stolen? She needed money and kind of paid you your share for not telling the police about the circumstances that got you out of the house that night?"

"I try not to think about the whole thing very much. Pretty weak of me, isn't it? Well, you knew there was some outside thing about me, Madeline. You have always known I don't have the highest moral fiber. I think it's what attracts you to me and pulls you away. Even your mother warned you about hanging out with the wrong crowd."

"My mother was proud of me for forgiving my friends their mistakes," I said. "And Debra turned out great. She outgrew her bad-girl phase and overcompensated. She's an attorney in Chicago now."

"Is that so?"

"But explain more. What happened after those etchings were stolen? What's the bottom line?"

"Just ask Mid-Pacific and North American Insurance. They were insured for twenty million dollars."

Oh my God.

"Sisters"

fter Dexter departed, I sat in my rented SUV, engine idling, thinking too hard about everything. My usual bad habit. The In-N-Out Burger truck backed slowly out of the driveway of the Hutsons' beautiful Craftsman-style home. I watched the guy navigate the turn into the street when I noticed Zenya Knight's Range Rover coming into view. She pulled up across the street and found a parking space. That's right. She was coming to pick up her son, Kirby, from Ryan Hutson's party. I cut my engine and thought hard about what to do.

I'd confront her. I'd find out what I needed to know about Dexter. I flipped my rearview mirror down and looked at myself, taking stock. I was reduced to living by impulses lately. I said aloud, "Get a grip, Bean."

If only I had been able to go back to my own home and take a shower, like I was used to doing after a long event, I'd cool down, rethink, take it slow. But going home had lost its power to comfort. In just one night's time, that sanctuary was lost to me.

I watched Zenya through my windshield as she stepped down from her Range Rover, oblivious to me sitting in my parked car, and crossed the road to the Hutson house. She was beautiful as always, dressed this af-

ternoon in tight tan cropped jeans and a pink top. I detected some slight
family resemblance between Dex and her that I hadn't noticed before—
the same big hazel eyes, the same fair coloring.

I needed to figure out what was going on between her brother and me.
I could prolong my anxiety or I could talk to Zenya Knight. That meant
I'd be stepping right over the line of good family-of the-boyfriend relations
and on into hell. I took a breath and reached for the door handle.

My cell phone rang and I wrestled it out from the depths of my bag.
"Hello."

"Is this Madeline Bean?" The male voice mispronounced my name
slightly. He said the last syllable like "lin" while I pronounce it "line." I
never correct people, though. Let them call me what they like.

"Who's this?"

"My name is Brett Hurley. You don't know me."

I'd heard the name Brett recently. Where?

"Anyway, I got your cell-phone number from a police detective. I
hope that's okay."

Brett Hurley. Sara Jackson's troubled boyfriend. I remembered it all
now.

"I'm glad you called," I said. "I'm sorry about your loss. Do you think
you're up to talking about Sara?"

"Kind of. Yes. Do you think we could meet somewhere?"

On a normal day, I'd ask him to meet me at my office. But I wasn't
keen on being there at the house alone on a Saturday. My house had become the enemy. Besides, how could I ask Sara Jackson's boyfriend to go
to the site of her murder?

"I'm not sure. Where are you?"

"I'm just driving," he said. "I can meet you anywhere."

I thought it over as I watched Zenya walk to the front door of the Hutson home and then correct herself and follow the walkway to the side and
around to the back, where the party was just ending. The muted sounds
of several jazz solos had ceased, as had the applause that had followed.
Now all seemed quiet and guests began departing.

"I'm parked in Pasadena," I said. I was out of ideas for meeting spots.
"Why don't you drive over here and we can talk."

He hesitated a second or two, but then agreed and asked for the street
address. He said he could be there in less than twenty minutes. It was as

good a spot as anyplace for me. I was homeless. I couldn't keep bringing folks over to Wesley's little house. We both needed our space, and Wes had given up too much of his privacy out of friendship for me. I felt horrible about putting him out. If it meant I would take up working out of the trunk of a rental car, so be it.

By the time I had disconnected with Brett Hurley, Zenya was coming back out through the gate, accompanied by her twelve-year-old son, Kirby. He was a sturdy-looking boy who had not yet hit his growth phase, still about six inches shorter than his mom. Kirby's cargo shorts were damp from his lark in the Jacuzzi, and he carried a large instrument case, his gait awkward as he swung the heavy case across the front lawn.

I stepped out of my SUV and called Zenya's name. She shaded her eyes in the afternoon sunlight and saw me.

"Madeline? Hi! I was looking for you inside. Connie told me you left already. And Kirby just told me Dex was here, too. I'm sorry I missed him." She walked across the grass and joined me on the wide sidewalk that edged the huge homes in this leafy neighborhood. Kirby trudged behind.

"Zenya. I wonder if I could talk to you for a minute."

"Sure. Of course." She turned to her son and gave him permission to go back into the party. She said to leave his saxophone case with her. Kirby looked put out in that way teens have when their parents continue to make boneheaded decisions that end up ruining a kid's perfectly good life. But he was happy enough to go back and join his friends. Other parents were arriving and departing with their boys as Zenya turned back to me.

"What's up?"

"I wanted to talk to you about your brother."

"Dex?" She looked so happy. "You two falling in love?"

When I didn't light up in that expected girlfriend way, she quickly apologized. "Oh, wow. Did I say the wrong thing? Madeline, I was just kidding. I'm sorry."

"Dex is a great guy," I said carefully. "It's me. I'm having 'issues.'" Then I laughed at myself, so absurd was this conversation.

"What sort of issues?" Zenya asked, concerned.

"Trust, mainly. I was recently involved with a man I thought I could trust. But then it turned out I couldn't. Or I shouldn't have. Anyway, I'm just telling you this so you understand. I need a lot of real, pure, uncomplicated honesty right now."

"And Dex isn't someone you can rely on for that," she finished, thinking about it.

"There have been a lot of very strange things going on in my life," I explained, trying not to sound like a witch who was condemning this woman's brother's integrity to her face. But of course, that was exactly what I was doing.

"I know. The girl who was killed at your house. I have been worried about that."

"You have?"

"I want Dexter to find someone to care about, Maddie. He needs the right sort of woman to set his life back on track. He's been lost, I think. For a long time, really. And I was so happy to hear he liked you. I thought the two of you could be so good together. But when I heard about what happened the other night at your house, that girl who worked for you, I began to think again. Maybe Dex needs someone who is a little less . . ."

So it goes. Here was me, worried that Dex was less than reputable. Here was Zenya, worried the same thing about me. There was Dex, scared his sister had done something horrible. Go figure.

"I had nothing to do with that poor girl," I said, "except that she did work for me. And she had borrowed my car and was returning it. The police haven't discovered why she died. But I am trying to find out myself."

"What can you do?"

"I don't know, Zenya. But I am worried about Dex, too. I can't help but think he might be mixed up in some funny things."

"Dex? Oh, no."

"Okay. Here I go." I took a breath and rushed on with it all. "You mentioned there had been an art theft at your house."

She looked up at me, a hardness settling in around her hazel eyes. "What are you talking about?"

"I'm worried Dex was involved in it in some way." At last, I'd spoken the truth out loud to another person. I had heard Dexter's story. Now I had to know Zenya's. "Look, I'm sure you don't want to dredge that mess back up, but I have this very bad feeling. After all, Dex was taking care of your house at the time. I keep asking myself, Why wasn't there an alarm? Why didn't it go off?"

"Oh, Madeline. You have to believe me. None of that was Dex's fault at all."

"I need to be reassured here, Zenya. Please tell me about it."

"It was a combination of things that just got fouled up. The alarm had been acting up a lot. For a month, it just kept triggering by itself and we'd had several false alarms. The police hate that, of course. They had sent us a warning notice saying they wouldn't respond to our address any longer if we didn't take care of our false-alarm problem. One more and we'd be shut off.

"Bill tried to troubleshoot it, but the alarm company did nothing to help. We couldn't risk another crossed wire setting the alarm off. That's why Bill insisted we have Dex stay at the house."

"I see."

"We were leaving for Maui, but Bill wasn't comfortable relying on that faulty alarm system. We told Dex not to even set it, in case another rash of false alarms were to occur. Listening to this now with hindsight, knowing we had a theft, the whole thing seems stupid, I know. But we told all this to the police at the time and they checked the records of those past false alarms with the Westec people, and they checked our notice from the local police station warning us against any further false alarms—"

"Oh."

"Maddie." She looked hurt. "How can you be suspicious of Dexter? Why are you digging up all this garbage?"

"I think it was the down payment for his house. Dex told me."

Zenya looked exasperated. "What's wrong with that? He would never have settled down. I was helping him."

I shook my head. "But what if Dexter arranged to have those etchings stolen. He loves you, Zenya. What if he was doing it for you? When the insurance money came, you might have given him a little gift back."

"Maddie, what's going on here? This doesn't sound like you at all. Is it all the stress about that young lady who died? I can understand how her death must have upset you."

I shook my head, yet wondered if she was right.

"You have no need to worry about this," Zenya said, her soft voice back to its normal reassuring tone. "We lost our art. We can't get it back. And that's what insurance is for. As for the money we received from the insurance company, we could have sold our art pieces and received the same amount of money or more! There was just no reason for any of us, including Dex, to steal anything."

I couldn't think of an answer to that. How freaking obsessed must I have sounded? I simply said, "I'm beginning to fall for Dex, Zenya."

She finally smiled. "Look, I love my brother. And I think he has very strong feelings for you. I know I'm the last person on earth to give romantic advice, but if this thing is going to work out between the two of you, you can't let yourself get so worked up over things that are ancient history. Dex isn't squeaky-clean. I'm sure he has enough things in his glorious past to concern any new girlfriend. *But our etchings?* Come on now." She smiled again. "There is nothing there. Leave it alone. That's my advice."

I probably should have. But I had one more question. "Connie Hutson told me her husband never really wanted to bid on the Selmer sax at the Woodburn auction. She said Bill had arranged that little charade with Dave in advance. Were you aware of that?"

"That's not possible." Zenya, always the most agreeable person on any committee, flushed. I don't think she'd ever raised her voice in her life, but she looked like she was getting closer to it every second. I had the most amazing effect on people. "Maddie, what on earth is going on with you?"

"With me? I am asking myself every day what's going on with your family. I want to believe you. I want to believe Dex. But there is too much here that doesn't make sense."

"Well, good luck to you, then," she said, in a tone that could only be described as curt. Maybe this was the first time she'd been pushed to it, but she did "curt" pretty damn well for a beginner. "I hope you make it all work out, no matter what other people might get hurt."

"I can't help that," I said softly.

Zenya, her lovely golden hair pulled back in a clip, folded her arms under her chest and looked at me with disappointment. "I had a different impression of you, Maddie. You, with your super career and your great sense of style and your friends. You seemed to have everything. You're so independent. So strong. So in control. Bill always warns me not to meddle in matchmaking, but even he saw how cool it could be to get you and Dex together. He's the one who suggested I send Dex out to find you last Saturday night."

"You're kidding."

"Please don't be mad at us because we tried to set the two of you up. I thought you could be good for Dex the way Bill is good for me. Sure, Bill kind of runs things in our household, but you know what? There needs to be a leader and a follower. And what's wrong with that?"

"I'm sorry," I said. "I don't agree. I think both people have to do both those things for a real relationship to work."

"Maybe you should leave things alone, Maddie. All those questions you feel you need answers to. Will any of this make a difference? Really?"

"It's a question of trust, Zenya."

"Yes. I get it. But in love, doesn't trust always call on us to make a leap of faith?"

Kirby appeared again, rejoining us at the sidewalk under the huge California live-oak trees, having grabbed another slice of birthday cake. Despite the crumbs on the corner of his mouth, you could tell by his expression he was so ready to leave now.

"Sorry, I've got to go," Zenya said, smiling at me tentatively. "I want us to be friends, Madeline. Dexter means that much to me. I hope you can find it in your heart to give him a chance."

Kirby picked up his heavy sax case and walked across the street to his mom's car. As he was loading it into the backseat of the Range Rover, I noticed a young man was standing a few feet away from me on the sidewalk. Probably one of the departing party guests.

I was suddenly overwhelmed by what Zenya had said. Was it ever possible to get enough proof that a man was trustworthy? Had my past relationship problems pushed me so far I had begun terrorizing admirers, looking for skeletons in every closet like a crazy woman?

"Are you Madeline?" He said it like Mad-a-lin.

It was Brett Hurley. I turned and looked at him more carefully. He was so thin and pale he was either seriously ill or in a rock band. His long black hair was swept straight back and he wore a pointy little beard.

"I'm so sorry about what happened to Sara," I said, feeling awkward. "Say, do you want to sit in my car?"

"That's okay. Let's walk."

It was a beautiful late afternoon. We started off down the pavement, under a bower of shady trees, walking side by side.

"The police detective told me you were looking for me," Hurley said.

"It's true. I was so upset about everything."

Hurley kept his head down, not reacting at all.

"I must admit . . ." I looked over at him. "I hardly knew Sara. She had worked several of the large parties over about six months' time. I wish I had known her better."

"She wasn't easy to get to know. Don't feel bad."

Was it my imagination, or was this guy not too broken up about the death of his girlfriend? "Well, Sara had been trying to get home to you that night and I thought the two of you were close. I worried that you might need some help. That's all."

"What are you talking about?" Brett Hurley stopped at the corner and looked confused.

"That last night after the Woodburn ball. Sara was very upset. She said she had to get back to you. You were on her mind. I thought you would want to know that."

"*I* was on her mind?" he asked, surprised.

"Yes. Didn't you have some disappointing news that day? Something about your dissertation, she said."

"Look, I didn't tell this to the cops, for obvious reasons, but Sara wasn't all she appeared to be. She looked sweet, but looks can fool ya."

"What do you mean?"

"Sara had a lot of schemes going on. She was always working an angle. She didn't look like it, but she was a real operator. Like how she put herself through school. She hooked. Did you know that?"

I shook my head, feigning surprise. Well, I hadn't had a clue before I did a little checking around after her death.

"I'm sorry to tell you this," Brett said, rubbing his little goatee, "but the reason she worked for you was to line up dates. She was sort of free-lance. She wasn't a streetwalker, you know? But if a guy had money, she was willing."

"And you knew about this?"

He nodded. "I told her she was crazy to do it. It wasn't safe. And she just laughed at me and asked if I knew of a better way to lay my hands on five hundred dollars for an hour's work."

Certainly more than the two hundred a night I paid my waitstaff, I mused. How was it I had no idea this sort of thing was going on at my own events? Damn it. Wes and I needed to review our files of temp workers and figure out if we had any other parasites.

"So do you think that's why she wanted my Jeep? To hook up with some guy from the Woodburn party?"

"I don't think so," he said, and began walking again, turning the corner and starting up the block.

"Then why?"

"Look, I'll deny any of this. So don't think you can tell anyone, right?"

I nodded, shocked.

"Sara was running a scam. I'm sure of it. She had found out some rich old geezer was a con man and she figured he'd pay her some money to keep the information from the police."

"Wait. You think Sara was blackmailing some man at the Woodburn?"

"Yeah. She wouldn't tell me about it. But I knew."

"Who?"

"She wouldn't tell me who it was, but the guy was loaded, she said. She was going to meet him after the party that night, that's all I know. Maybe when her car broke down, she thought she'd blow her meeting. So she put on some sad story about having to get home quick to me. She was a great little actress. You know that was her major—theater arts?"

"No, I didn't."

Brett Hurley grunted.

It was taking a moment for me to get my head around this news. "So you're saying Sara wasn't in a rush to get home to you?"

"Sara? Worried to death about me? Like that isn't a laugh. She and I were not doing all that well. I'd tried to leave her a few times, but with Sara, she'd show up at my house and have all this money on her and . . . Hey, I'm an artist. I'm broke. She knew how to reach me. I kept breaking it off with her, but it wasn't sticking. She said she'd have a really big score that night. She told me to wait up."

"You didn't tell the police all this?"

"Are you crazy? That my nasty hooker ex-girlfriend was shaking down some fat cat at the Woodburn ball? Get real. But that's why, when I heard what happened that night, I wasn't so shocked that she wound up dead. I mean, she was kind of asking for it. She didn't think of the consequences. I told her, but she never listened."

"Don't you want to see some justice for Sara?" I couldn't believe he would let the scum who had killed his girlfriend get away with it.

"Justice is funny," he said, looking over at me as we walked together around the block. "It's not black and white, like your fancy ball. Maybe Sara was just one of those girls who was going down the wrong side of the street. Sooner or later she was going to get creamed, know what I mean?"

I shook my head. No one should be written off. I didn't care if this woman was a scam artist or a prostitute or whatever. "No one had a right to take her life."

"So that's your opinion. I don't feel like getting into the middle of this mess, okay? What if the guy who got to Sara decides to come after me?"

"Right." I couldn't believe this guy. "But in the meantime, other people might be in danger."

We had come around a full block. Party guests were still leaving the Hutsons' house, pulling out of parking spaces along the street.

"Like I said, everyone has to look out for himself, Madeline. When this detective told me you were poking around, looking for me, I figured you were maybe getting yourself in over your head. You don't want to go near Sara's trouble, miss. You just don't."

"I'll think that over," I said, trying to sound less judgmental than I felt. "But can't you tell me anything about who Sara was trying to blackmail?"

"Nope. Don't know and don't want to know. But I can tell you this. She said a guy worth twenty million dollars should be willing to pay big."

"Twenty million?" I turned my head and focused on Brett Hurley.

"Yeah. And I think she came onto his scam when I told her some old stories about the time I worked part-time for the County Art Museum."

"What did you say?"

"I was a clerk there three years ago, just part-time while I went to school. You know, low-level typing and filing."

"Did you work with their donated collections and special exhibitions?"

"Say, how did you know that?"

"It's a Sin
to Tell a Lie"

Twenty million dollars had a tragically familiar sound to it. Just when I was working myself up to giving the whole Knight/Wyatt clan a break, the news just kept getting weirder.

"Baronowski here." I had dialed the detective as I drove across town.

"Did you ever find out who left that semen stain on the backseat of my old Jeep?"

"Not yet. We're DNA testing the boyfriend."

"You might want to widen your search to anyone with five hundred dollars handy."

"Yeah, we followed the lead at her apartment complex with that guy, Creski. Maybe Sara was doing a little part-time hooking. If so, and if she picked up a john last Saturday night, we may finally get a handle on this case. Problem is, we have no witnesses yet that saw Sara in that car that night, alone or with a man. But we might get lucky."

"What did her boyfriend tell you?"

"Hurley? Nothing. Pain in the ass. He's an artist with a capital A. Maybe a druggie. He's the type who hates anyone in authority, so naturally we got along great. Still, he seemed pretty harmless, the little twerp. We fingerprinted the guy, by the way, and we didn't match him to any prints found at your house, in case you're wondering."

"Good."

"I gave him your number, like you asked, and figured he'd be hitting you up for money."

"Men," I lamented gently.

"We're adorable. Call me if you learn anything meaningful, Ms. Bean."

Next I dialed Holly.

"Say, don't you have a friend who works at the L.A. County Museum of Art?"

"Megan Grossbard?"

"Right. Doesn't she work in the costume department?"

"Yep."

"Think she knows anyone in security over there? In the area of art fraud?" I gave Holly a quick rundown of what I had learned.

She promised to track down Megan and then called back five minutes later. We could meet Megan at the museum in an hour. The museum didn't close to the public until eight on Saturday night, and Megan and her friend were both going to come in and talk to us.

I called for messages and found one from Honnett. He stressed how important it was for me to phone him back immediately.

"Honnett. It's me, Mad."

"Where are you?" he asked.

"I'm driving home from my gig in Pasadena. And I'm cutting across town to stop and meet Holly first. What's up?"

"I've got to see you."

"Can you tell me on the phone?"

"No. Where are you meeting Holly?"

"LACMA. I'll be there a little early. Look for me outside, in front of the main entrance."

"Right. I'll be there in ten minutes."

All this urgency. What couldn't he tell me over the phone?

The main buildings at LACMA are located in the Miracle Mile area of the city between Fairfax and La Brea, on Wilshire Boulevard. I had made good time, so I drove around the block searching for the ever-elusive street parking. After all, it was nearly five in the afternoon. But it was Saturday and it was Los Angeles and who was I kidding? I paid the steep rate and pulled into the parking lot, and then waited forever while an Astrovan loaded with kids finally pulled out of a spot.

Honnett was already there, waiting, when I walked up to the entrance of the museum.

"Can we sit somewhere?" he asked me.

"What's the matter? You seem nervous."

"Let me buy you a Diet Coke," he offered, avoiding my comment.

I didn't want to sit, so I ended up steering him past the Plaza Café near the courtyard. I checked my watch and warned him I'd have to meet Holly in thirty minutes.

"No problem. I can say this in ten."

"Come with me," I said, and led him down to the art rental and sales gallery, located on the lower level of the Leo S. Bing Center.

"Go ahead and talk," I said, leading him through the exhibit rooms filled with artwork by contemporary young Angelino artists. This was not part of the official museum exhibition space. Each of these works was available for sale or rental. We walked among the paintings.

"I have some difficult things to tell you, Maddie. About this guy Wyatt you've been seeing."

I looked at him, caught off guard. Honnett had been a busy investigator. "So. You know his name."

"The guy hasn't been straight with you. I ran a check on him. And I've had a friend of mine, an ex-cop, do some digging around."

"You did *what*? I can't believe this! Do you realize how completely *jealous* you are behaving, Honnett?"

"I knew you'd react like this. Just hear me out."

I glared at him and he stopped. Okay. I probably deserved some of this. It's true. I had felt some satisfaction over Honnett's jealousy for a little while there. I knew it was immature of me, of course. It is unforgivable that I felt any empowerment from the pain of another, even if that person had hurt me really bad first. How could I? And now here was that jealousy, running amok, ultimately causing us all more pain. Honnett had come to see me this afternoon to share some horrible news about Dexter. How fitting was this retribution. Fate really had that irony thing down.

Honnett saw my face.

"Never mind," he said. "If you don't want to hear it, I'm not going to go on. I can see this was a mistake. I apologize."

So here it was. I was being offered the information I had really wanted all along: evidence that would prove if I should dare to trust Dexter Wyatt. And here was Honnett, the least impartial investigator on the planet, offering it up.

"Tell me what you know," I said, weariness setting in my throat. "Just don't make this about you and me, Honnett. Please. If you have something, I'll listen. But first know this. I really care about Dexter Wyatt. I like him. I am hoping to have a relationship with him. And even if you found out something completely sickening, like he was a criminal in the past, I'm not sure it would matter to me."

Honnett met my eyes, looking like I'd kicked him, which I guess I had. He didn't know what to say.

"So, there it is," I said, a little more gently. "Knowing how I feel about Dexter, do you still want to tell me what you found?"

"Can I help you?" A tall, thin Asian-American woman materialized out of nowhere. "Have you chosen that one?"

She referred to a small abstract acrylic painting nearby, a challenging piece with thick blue streaks and black.

"How much to rent it?" I asked, not having noticed it before.

"Only twenty-seven dollars every two months. Very reasonable. And the rental payments go toward purchase."

"The artist gets seventy-five percent of the money," I told Honnett, who couldn't have cared less about art.

"I'll take it," Honnett told the woman, and handed her his credit card. She praised his great aesthetic taste and hurried off to ring up the rental and work on the rental-agreement papers. He would have to become a member of the museum, she informed him as she glided off. But she would take care to include that amount in his total.

"You didn't have to do that," I said, surprised at him.

"I do what I want, Maddie. Don't worry about me."

"So tell me what you found out about Dex," I said, calmer now. "What can it be? Fraud? Theft? What?"

His eyes told me what he thought about any man about whom I could so casually ask such extraordinary questions. "No, he doesn't have that kind of record. A drunk-and-disorderly. A bar fight back when he was younger. But it's his personal life that worries me."

"Because . . . ?"

"This guy used to date Sara Jackson, Maddie."

The art on the walls swam and then settled down.

"Here's your painting, Mr. Honnett," the salesclerk said cheerfully, bringing a large bag over along with Honnett's charge slip and the rental agreement. He signed them all and took his copies. As she explained again how the art rental program worked, I thought about this shocking new development. Could it be possible? Had Dexter known Sara? And why hadn't he mentioned that fact to me after all this time?

The clerk smiled at the two of us and left.

"How do you know this, Honnett?"

"One of Wyatt's friends told my pal. And then there is Sara Jackson's cell-phone log. She had called Wyatt earlier on the night she died."

"My God, Honnett. Is Dex a suspect in the murder?"

"You know the department doesn't announce their suspects. But off the record, I can tell you he's being looked at. Among others, so that's something."

I hadn't thought I could feel anything like friendship for Honnett, so wrapped in anger had I been over the past few months, but when I heard him try to make the news about Dex sound a little less threatening, I began to unravel some.

"You'll be okay, Maddie. I just wanted you to have all the facts. If that means you have to go on hating me, I know I deserve it."

"I can't hate you."

"So what do you think of it?" Honnett asked, pulling the small painting out for me to view once again.

"At least it's not *Dog Living in Luxury with Cigar*, I said and then, suddenly, I remembered something from the inventory of Grasso's paperwork.

"I'm late," I said, with a start. "I've got to meet Holly and her friend."

Honnett looked up at me as I rushed off to find the elevators.

———

"Three years ago, Bill and Zenya Knight lent some of their etchings to the museum for a temporary show. Would there be any paperwork on it?"

"Of course." The young woman sitting before us was tapping on the keyboard of her computer. "Only three years ago, it should be here."

Holly's friend Megan had introduced us to Divinia Denove, one of the museum's investigators. Both Megan and Divinia had come in on their day off to answer our questions.

"I should have realized it when Caroline Rochette fell into the pool," I told Holly quietly so as not to disturb Divinia, who was searching her computer files.

"Why?" Holly whispered.

"She said something about getting insurance."

"I wasn't there," Holly reminded me. "What exactly did she say?"

I thought back to that day in Wesley's backyard. "She said she must get insurance."

"Like accident insurance?"

"I thought she was making a joke. It didn't make a lot of sense at the time, but then the woman had just tripped into the pool, for heaven's sake, wearing at least sixty dollars' worth of makeup. But now I think she must have meant something else entirely. I think she had come there that day to get her hands on some insurance paperwork that was among that junk from Albert Grasso. There were policies there from Mid-Pacific Insurance and North American Home Insurance."

"Here it is," Divinia said. She had found the file she had been searching for. "We had an exhibit a little over three years ago. 'Black and White: The Genius of the Etchings of the Sixteenth and Seventh Centuries.' The Knights lent us thirteen works." She read over the file, clicking through multiple pages. "It looks fairly routine. Was there a problem?"

I was sitting with Holly and Megan in chairs in front of Divinia's desk.

"They were insured?"

"Of course. We have a blanket policy that covers all the art in the museum. But according to our notes, these pieces were undamaged and returned to the Knights," she said. She scrolled down the screen and looked back at us. "The museum's receipt was scanned into the file. The date of delivery to an address in Beverly Hills is marked and Mr. Knight himself signed upon receiving the works back in good condition."

"Do your records list the appraisal value of the etchings?"

"Well, it's not really our appraisal," Divinia said, smiling. "It's sort of a formality. When the owners fill out the paperwork, they mark down what value they want placed on the works."

That sounded odd.

Divinia noticed my expression. "It's never been taken advantage of. But, as I said, the museum carries insurance against all the artwork we own or borrow. In the case of works on loan, the actual dollar amount is filled in for each individual piece by the lending party. We pay extraordinary insurance premiums, as you might imagine, so we have taken pains to make sure no owner feels their work is undervalued."

"Oh, I just had an amazing idea," I said, wheels turning ever so quickly now. "Would you mind taking a look at the values placed on the Knight etchings?"

"Well," she said, "it is pretty typical for our patrons to undervalue their artworks a little. Most aren't up on the current market value since the pieces were often acquired so long ago. Then we have others who fudge a little on the upside. Let's see." She read through several electronic documents. "Wait now. This is strange."

We looked at her.

"One etching from the Knight collection is a true masterpiece. A Dürer of exceptional quality. Nothing like it has been at auction in years. Who can say what its value might be today? Maybe three million. Maybe six. On this form, Mr. Knight listed it at ten million."

"Wow." Holly looked impressed.

"The Dürer is an extraordinary piece, and in the art world, one can never tell what a truly great work might bring," Divinia said. "So that valuation, in and of itself, is not terribly out of line. But here's the amazing thing. Look at the other etchings in their collection! The other twelve pieces were nowhere near that value. There's a Madonna listed by Raffaello Schiaminossi and Luca Ciamberlano. It is valued by the Knights at five million."

"And its real value?"

"About five hundred."

We stared at Divinia.

"Only five hundred thousand? That's one tenth what they claimed."

"Actually, Madeline, this Schiaminossi is only worth about five hundred *dollars*."

"And they claimed it was worth ten thousand times more?" Holly asked. "Holy schnitzel."

"I can see that the five-million-dollar value they claimed was absurd." Holly's friend Megan spoke up for the first time. "But what harm could it do?"

"I have an idea about that," I told Megan. "And the other works?" I asked Divinia. "The same overinflation of value?" I finally figured out what had happened.

"Yes," Divinia said, laughing. "It's much the same. The greatest real value is two thousand dollars, but all of them are self-appraised in the millions. What does this mean, Madeline?"

"These forms the owner fills out, do they get signed by an official here at the museum?"

"Of course. Several of our people, from the show's curator to the director of the exhibition, in fact. We must be very careful with the artwork that is lent to us."

"And then the forms are used as riders to the museum's own insurance policy?"

"Exactly. But no claim was ever made to our insurer, so what can this mean?"

"I think that Bill Knight had a much cleverer scheme. He used those official documents, the riders from LACMA's insurance carrier with their insanely inflated valuations, to scam his own insurance company. Your paperwork established the worth of his collection, complete with a prestigious museum's curator's signature on the bottom. Knight must have gone out and increased his own art-insurance coverage with his private insurance company to these massively inflated prices after the LACMA show."

"I suppose that's possible. Although I would think any insurance underwriter would look a little closer at something like that."

"I'm not sure about that," I said. "They aren't art experts themselves. They rely on documentation. And the L.A. County Museum of Art documents clearly substantiate these numbers."

She nodded. "And as long as the customer is willing to pay the high premiums, I can see why an insurance salesman would be happy for the business."

I nodded.

"Incredible," Megan said.

"This is fascinating speculation, ladies," Divinia said. "And if it were actually true, it's insurance fraud."

"With the museum as an unwitting collaborator," I pointed out.

"So what do you know?" she asked me, looking worried.

"Three of those art etchings were stolen from the house in Beverly Hills about three years ago, the Dürer and two others. Mr. Knight collected twenty million dollars from his own insurance carriers for their loss. If the Dürer was really worth three million and the other two were only worth a few thousand, I'm beginning to believe he scammed his insurance company out of nearly seventeen million, thanks to some clever paperwork."

And that's why Bill Knight couldn't just sell the etchings to get all the money, as Zenya had suggested. Those pieces were worth seven times more to him vanished than they'd ever be on some gallery wall for sale.

"Come on-a My House"

Sunday morning. Wesley went out to hang with an old college buddy who was down from Palo Alto for the weekend, but not before fretting for an hour over leaving me alone. He urged me to join them, but all I wanted was a little private time, and I was grateful, finally, that he understood and didn't cancel his plans because of me.

I did all the normal things I had been meaning to get to. I went back to bed and grabbed a few more hours of missed sleep. I did laundry. I had fun in the kitchen. From Wesley's well-stocked pantry, I mixed together rolled oats, peanuts, and sunflower seeds, sweetened the mix with plenty of brown sugar, and then enriched the flavor with natural vanilla, tasting and adjusting until I got the blend just right. My eyes roved Wesley's counters and cabinets until I had that "aha!" moment, and chuckled. A few seconds of grinding and soon chopped espresso beans joined the party. Voilà! I'm calling it cappuccino granola. A batch of this private blend was now displayed in a pretty stoppered jar, waiting as a treat for Wes.

I poured milk over a small bowl of cappuccino granola, and stood at the counter reading the Target ads in the Sunday *Los Angeles Times*. It was criminal to have back-to-school sales in July. I checked the book-review section, hoping to find a review written by Dick Lochte. I flipped through the car ads. Would I look good in a Porsche Boxter? I read the real estate listings, wondering if I was in the market for a new house or if I would be able to salvage my wonderful Mediterranean on Whitley. As a potential seller, it rocked to see the real estate market was way up. As a potential buyer, it sucked.

I thought about visiting a few open houses. Wes would love to go with me, but I expected his day with the Stanford buddy would stretch out. I reviewed the hundreds of listings, spanning so many neighborhoods. The euphemisms used to describe any house I might barely be able to afford were heavy with double meanings. *Loads of potential* (tear down). *Maintenance-free backyard* (there was none). I sighed over descriptions of wondrous homes that were way beyond my reach. And then a house listed for almost five million dollars caught my eye. Not simply because the house was located just blocks away from Dexter's, although the proximity did cross my mind.

I reread the no-euphemism-necessary description. *Magnificent Italian-style villa by Bob Ray Offenhauser on a prestigious cul-de-sac in Bel Air. Gated motor courtyard. 2-story entry, large open rooms with high ceilings. Screening room and gym. Magical gardens, sun-drenched pool with indoor/outdoor flow. Ideal for lavish or intimate entertaining. Very private.* Well, that privacy angle certainly had a new appeal.

This was so out of my league, it wasn't even funny, and certainly not the sort of property I was looking for, but I was extremely interested in talking with the broker. The house was a Caroline Rochette listing. Albert Grasso's ladyfriend. She would be sitting in the house all afternoon waiting for potential buyers, like a spider ready to spring on some tasty flies. However, she was now also a ridiculously easy target for me to trap. I wondered how a natural predator such as Caroline would react to finding the tables turned. I showered, daydreaming about past episodes of *Wild Kingdom*, and then dressed, deciding to wear boots in case any metaphorical bug stomping might become necessary.

Outside, I looked at the clear, cloudless sky. It was another hot and sunny day, which does a lot to perk many of us locals up. In case you are wondering why anyone is crazy enough to live in Southern California: the weather. Obvious as this is, it cannot be repeated too many times. It's addictive. And with a little extra rest and some time puttering in the kitchen, I was feeling pretty good again.

I jumped in the SUV and made use of one of the Trailblazer's zillion cup holders. Ah, the simple pleasures. Like the giddy freedom of driving a honking-big Chevy while swigging from a can of Diet Coke, combined with the virtuous certainty one is minimizing the chance of spillage. This was the life, I thought as I drove past the UCLA campus in Westwood and turned north into the Bel Air gates, eyeing real estate that is considered as good as it gets in Southern California.

The Trailblazer easily took me up Bel Air's winding, hilly streets. It was rare to find one of these high-end properties held open at all. It spoke of either desperate sellers or a broker who used every house on her list as bait to catch newbie buyers, most often to sell them some other property. As the road wound upward into the foothills of the Santa Monica Mountains, there were occasional roadside signs bearing balloons, markers that pointed the way to the open house ahead. I steered up to the 10500 block of Mocca Road and pulled into the cul-de-sac, admiring what five million bucks can buy you.

The doorbell played a classical melody. Charming. While waiting, I tried the elaborate brass handles on the double front doors. They were, of course, locked. In a few minutes, one of the heavy doors swung open and Caroline Rochette, appearing much drier than the last time I'd seen her, greeted me, her blond bob sprayed stiff, her pointy chin well powdered, her welcoming expression instantly falling.

"You!"

"Nice 'gated motor courtyard,' " I said, quoting from her house ad as I walked past her into the "2-story formal entry."

"Are you looking for a house?" Caroline was thrown. Should she have on the *salesman* face? Or the *bitch.*

I smiled. "I might be. But I'm actually here to talk to you."

She looked unhappy. "Well, sign in."

I realized she meant for me to sign the guest register displayed on the large entry table in the center of the rounded foyer. No matter that I was bringing all sorts of unpleasant memories to Caroline Rochette's doorstep, she would make sure to show her homeowner clients that she had at least one interested buyer come through the house today. My name was the only one on the register.

"What do you want?" she asked, uncertain.

"Would you show me around the property?" I smiled at her again.

"Oh, all right. Come this way. We'll start with the kitchen. It's in the east wing."

Caroline's sling-back high heels clicked on the limestone floor as she led the way.

She went into her spiel, but didn't give it any oomph. "Wolf restaurant range, Sub-Zero refrigerators, Miele dishwashers, Grohe . . . faucets, custom-built cabinets in maple, granite countertops." Caroline stopped when she reached the far end of the enormous gourmet kitchen.

"Navaho white," I added.

"What's that?"

"This is the lightest-color granite commercially available." The stone used for the counters was a pointillist mix of small white, gray, and black flecks.

"Really?"

"Sure, the white mineral grains are feldspar. It's the most abundant mineral found in granite. The light gray, glasslike grains are quartz, and the black, flakelike grains are biotite or black mica."

Caroline stared at me, trying to figure me out. I silently wished her luck.

"I know about kitchens," I explained. She was definitely not sure what to make of me.

"Did you come here to upset me about Albert?" she asked, pointblank. I had weirded her into submission. I have that talent.

"Upset? That's not the word I would have chosen, no."

"Look, dear, you and I have had our problems. But I want to clear the air, here. You found Albert's . . . body," she said, "and for that I must be grateful to you. Oh, dear Jesus in heaven! What if it had been me? I was coming over to Albert's house that very afternoon. What if I had let myself in with my key . . . and gone back to his studio . . ." She didn't finish that thought, but moved on. "So you saved me from that, anyway, Madeline. I could never have stood seeing that. I am so utterly and completely devastated by Albert's death, I cannot begin to describe it."

"I'm sorry for your loss," I said quietly. "But then I'm glad to see it hasn't interfered with your work."

She gave me an evil look.

"So," I continued, "you're carrying on." I noticed Caroline had the Capresso coffeemaker brewing and a plate of bakery cookies set out on a silver tray. She did not offer me any refreshments.

"Why are you really here?" she asked, vexed.

"You told me there was a problem with Mr. Grasso's insurance papers. How much did you know about it?"

She gasped.

I waited.

"I didn't tell you a thing!"

"Yes, you did. That afternoon when I helped scoop you out of the pool. Look, Caroline, Albert is gone now. Tell me what he was up to."

"I don't know. I really don't know."

"But it was the insurance papers he was frantic about. Wasn't it?"

"I think so. I mean, he was livid about having mislaid them. I told him not to worry. I would get them back. But, of course, I didn't. You prevented that. But then I told him you had no idea there was any reason to look closely at those documents. And even if you did, they wouldn't tell you much."

"There was a rider to his regular policy to cover his coin collection," I said, recalling what I could about the pages I'd skimmed through last week. I mean, who even reads their *own* insurance policy—let alone someone else's boring paperwork?

"He had overvalued the collection," she said. "That was all. I couldn't imagine that it was really the end of the world. He stated a far greater appraised value, and the insurer accepted some receipts as the true value."

"What kind of receipts?"

"Albert bought a little extra insurance for his coins when he traveled to London for a big coin show. For travel insurance, you just mark in the values and pay the premium. Because it's only in case his luggage was lost or stolen, the insurer doesn't care much about the actual value. Whatever you pay to cover is covered. Anyway, it turns out Al used that temporary insurance policy as documentation of value for his collection. Then he bought a new rider to his homeowner's policy for his coins using this inflated amount."

This scam was becoming familiar. "How do you know about it?"

"Al told me. He was screaming at me. He couldn't believe I had been so stupid as to take his private papers out of his house and, on top of that, to lose them."

"So what happened? Were his collectible coins stolen? Did he get paid off by the insurance company?"

"Oh my, no! He wasn't trying to do anything funny. He was just a proud old man. He liked to show people the 'value' of his coin collection. He liked people believing he was worth serious money. What's wrong with that? It was a quirk."

I could imagine Albert Grasso, living in that outdated house, needing to boost his ego by showing off his "worth" to his multimillionaire buddies. He could have told fellow Woodburn board member Bill Knight about his priceless coins. After all, Knight was a collector of precious objects, too. And perhaps they shared insurance concerns. Perhaps Albert even let Bill in on a few little secrets.

"Do you know who sold him the insurance?"

"Oh, of course. It was Al's half brother."

"It was?"

"Yes. He's some wealthy Oklahoma businessman who never understood what Al was doing out here in Hollywood, coaching singers. That was the reason Al embellished the coin collection's value in the first place. To show off to his brother, to impress him. Aren't men so predictable?"

My mind raced with this new knowledge.

"And Mr. Grasso's brother worked for Mid-Pacific Insurance? Or for North American?"

"He was a broker for both those companies, I believe. They both specialize in covering fine art and other treasures."

"I've got to go," I said, thinking a mile a minute. I turned abruptly and headed for the front door.

"Wait!" Caroline followed me through the large house, straining to catch up. "What is going on?"

I got to the door and turned on her. "Tell me the truth, Caroline. It could help both of us. Who was the man who suggested you buy Albert Grasso a new briefcase?"

"What?"

"There is no way to keep this a secret anymore. You've got someone on the side. He'd probably seen Albert pull those insurance papers out of his old briefcase—you said Grasso liked to show them off. This friend of yours said he'd help you shop for the new briefcase; just bring Albert's old one to the luggage store. A handy time for him to grab the documents he was after."

"But I was going to be there, too!"

"Your friend was counting on you to keep your mouth shut. Of course, what he hadn't counted on was your ability to drop the case and lose all the files before you made it across town."

"This is ridiculous."

"I think what's really ridiculous is why any woman would get herself mixed up with Bill Knight." I supposed when a financially needy woman's sole criterion for landing a fellow was that he have multiple millions, she pretty much had to accept whatever damaged goods presented himself.

Her blue eyes were glassy. Her voice was desperately low. "How do you know about Bill?"

"Secret Love"

Caroline Rochette's eyes widened in what could have been a horrified expression, that is, if her Botox injections had left her with any discernible facial expressions left to give. Instead, I received a blank, if wrinkle-free, stare as she groaned, "How could you know? Have you been following Bill and me?"

Ah! Freaking! Ha! So it *was* Bill Knight at the center of this scam, cheating on his wife, Zenya, cheating the insurance company, and trying to manipulate Caroline Rochette.

Caroline seemed ever more alarmed when I didn't respond. "Damn it to blazes. I need a cigarette." Her mouth twisted in anxiety, finding an expression at last, undoing all the smoothing that careful plastic surgery had done.

In this whole wacked-out scenario, Bill Knight was the only name that made sense. Sara Jackson's boyfriend had said she was blackmailing some rich guy. It had to have been Bill Knight.

Spending those days typing up the boring insurance valuations at LACMA three years back, an art student like Brett Hurley must have understood just how bizarrely high Knight had hiked up the values on his pieces—it was the sort of thing he might recall again years later and jeer at. While Hurley laughed at the deception, Sara probably saw its criminal potential. Clever Sara. She took an idle comment by her boyfriend and found a way to squeeze money out of it. But to find out if Bill Knight had cashed in on his lies, she had to do research. She would have needed to make sure there was a big illegal score, or what good was her hunch?

Honnett had told me that Dex had dated Sara. Maybe Sara made a play for Dexter, scouting for info. That's the way I wanted to think about it right now. Sara Jackson using Dex. If she put her knowledge of the inflated art prices together with stories she'd coaxed from Dexter about the theft and insurance score made by his brother-in-law, she knew that Knight had twenty million reasons to pay her to keep quiet.

Maybe that's what happened the evening of the Black & White Ball. Bill paid Sara. That could have happened right before we left the building. Then Sara found her car had stalled and begged Holly for a ride. It could explain why Bill Knight was really raging as he drove like a mad bombardier out on the streets of downtown—maybe he was letting off steam after paying blackmail money to Sara Jackson. That's a hell of a better reason to go nuts than freaking out over an old saxophone.

And with a large roll of cash in her bag, it also explained why Sara didn't want to stand around some parking garage waiting for AAA to come start her car. She made up the story about her boyfriend needing her, but her worry that night had seemed pretty genuine.

And maybe there was another stage to Sara's plan. If she double-crossed Bill Knight, she stood to make even more money. Insurance companies pay big rewards to informants.

But while I stood in the elegant foyer, unraveling this puzzle of art and fraud and blackmail, Caroline Rochette had major worries of her own. Among other things, her secret affair with Knight had now slipped out.

"I know you're close with Zenya," Caroline said, her body language all squirmy, like a rat that had been cornered. Well, a petite rat wearing Manolo Blahniks, batting thick eyelashes that curled aggressively.

"Caroline, you're in trouble. Bill Knight was using you. You better look out or you're going down, too. So if you are thinking about calling and warning him—"

"I won't." Right. Like I believed her.

"Pay attention, Caroline. If things get ugly, you'll be losing a lot. Your friends. Your position at the Woodburn. Your job. You'll be lucky to get off with a humungous attorney's bill, a trillion hours of community service, and a record. And that means you lose your real estate license and folks who own houses like this one won't even let you wipe your shoes on their doormat."

She sobbed, but no tears fell from those heavily lashed blue eyes.

"The police are already on to Bill Knight, so be smart. You don't want them coming after you next."

"I didn't do anything," she wailed.

Divinia Denove had phoned the LAPD the previous night, as well as the insurance carriers who had paid off on the twenty-million-dollar claims. Even without evidence pinning the art heist on Knight, they had a clear case of insurance fraud since the etchings had been grossly overvalued.

"Clear the air here, Caroline. It's not just about the insurance anymore. It's about murder."

"Oh my God." Caroline looked ill. "This doesn't have to do with that girl who was killed in your house, does it?"

I felt like dipping Caroline into the swimming pool, one more time, just to jar her awake. "Sara was blackmailing Knight," I explained patiently. "She may have planned to double-cross him on top of that. Knight could have decided to end all his problems."

"I had nothing to do with any of this," she said, shifting into defensive overdrive.

"Here's some advice. Barter. If you know anything else about these crimes, you had better get yourself over to the police and tell them immediately. While it can still do you some good."

Caroline Rochette's eyes darted to the window, but there was not a looky-loo in sight; no one coming up the drive to look at the five-million-dollar home this sunny Sunday.

"Did you know," she whispered, "Sara Jackson had been taking voice lessons from Al?"

"What?"

"She had only been to the studio a few times. She paid cash. She wasn't on his books, so we didn't tell the police about it. Al didn't want us dragged into that murder at your place."

"Let me get this straight. Sara Jackson knew Albert Grasso?"

"She started coming to the house about two weeks before the Wood-burn gala. I didn't like her. She was common."

"You mean she was coming on to him."

Caroline Rochette nodded.

"And he responded?"

Caroline made a face. "Men like young girls."

I had to think all of this through. Sara Jackson was using her body to get closer to Albert Grasso. Caroline Rochette was having an affair with Bill Knight. Who knew such things went on in my quiet little neighborhood?

What had Sara been up to with Albert Grasso? Perhaps she was tying up loose ends, digging around for more details behind the fraud, somehow connecting Grasso's insurance-selling brother into the mix, scouting out a couple more potential blackmail victims. She might have hinted about Grasso and his brother to Bill Knight, like she was getting more proof, so he better pay up.

I'd bet money that was what spooked Knight into sending Caroline after Grasso's briefcase, to remove those insurance documents. The papers would have given Sara the name of the insurance carriers, and Knight probably feared that a besotted Albert might admit to fudging with his coin-collection values if Sara pressed the right buttons.

Bill Knight's crime had gone so flawlessly for so long. He'd have no choice now but to plug up these disastrous leaks. When the scheme to grab Grasso's briefcase and papers began to unspool, Knight must have completely flipped out. Did that lust for self-preservation change the man? He'd been content to do a little diddling with paper numbers before, but had he now been pushed over the edge? Did Bill Knight kill both Sara and Grasso?

I looked back at Caroline, who by now had dropped several real tears over her predicament. Her heavy mascara had left two smoky tracks down either side of her tight little face, and one eyelash was coming loose at the corner of her eye. I reached for the doorknob.

"Please! *Please!* DON'T LEAVE YET!" she yelled after me, desperate, as I opened the massive front doors, only to find an elderly African-American man with a thin young blonde standing on the front step.

"Very devoted realtor," I said to them as I walked swiftly down the drive.

Outside the house, I turned on my cell phone to make a quick call to Detective Baronowski. I told him what I had learned and was reassured to hear that all the wheels had been turning properly. They were working on Bill Knight's arrest warrant and would soon have the man in custody on suspicion of insurance fraud.

I disconnected, and then instantly received an incoming call. From the number displayed on my cell phone, the caller was Dex. My heart skipped in a completely annoying manner.

"Dexter?"

"Madeline. Where are you?"

"I'm running around solving shit. It's exhausting—you've got to believe me. I am trying *very hard* to find a way to trust you, Dexter."

"I know, honey. You're like making this your life's work."

"I'm dogged. And I'm right in your neighborhood."

"Come over."

And in five minutes I was at his house.

He wanted to kiss me. I wanted to talk. This pretty much sums up my view of male/female needs.

"What's up?" he asked, his arms around my waist.

"Here's the thing. I need to hear about you and an old girlfriend of yours."

"Now?"

"Yes. Tell me about Sara Jackson."

He turned so I couldn't see his face. He didn't answer.

"Dex?"

He turned back and took my hand. "You know about me. You know I've had a lousy track record with women. I'm not a model of virtue. But, Madeline, do we have to go *there*?"

"Where?"

He smiled. "To a place where you drag up every horrible mistake I've ever made with a woman and throw it at me? Because I just want to say, if we're going *there*—we will be there awhile."

"Dexter." I looked deeply into his eyes, seeing only affection and some chagrin amid the mysterious multicolor of his shade of hazel. I could detect no trace of deception. I sighed. It was official. I couldn't read this man at all. "Dexter, you don't have to tell me about any other woman from your past, ever. But I have to know about Sara."

He looked at me. "You can't leave this one alone?"

"Dex, it's things like this here that break down the trust. You know?"

"I know," he said.

"Why didn't you tell me you had been dating the girl who was killed at my house?"

"At first, I didn't know. Really. That first night I drove you home, no one ever mentioned who was dead there. You never said her name. The next day, when I watched the news, I pretty much freaked out. Sara had been a psycho, but no one deserves what happened to her. I was stunned that this girl I used to know could have died at your house. Then I took Holly out to lunch, remember? Holly told me that Sara worked for your company. One of those insane coincidences. What are the chances of that? I started thinking this city *really* isn't big enough. When the girls with whom I've had flings start working for the ones I'm just getting to know, I may have used up a town. That sort of thing."

"And then . . . ?"

"And then you and I were having such a rocky time of it, Madeline. The more I wanted you the more I could tell you were scared of me. So when was the right time to tell you I had spent a lousy month going to bed with a chick that I ended up finding out was a *hooker*, for Christ's sake, and one who was no doubt using me? If I told you that, how likely was it that you would have jumped into my arms?"

If he was lying to me, he was just too good. "Using you?" Did Dex know that Sara was blackmailing his brother-in-law? "In what way?"

"That girl liked to smoke dope."

"Dexter Wyatt, do you sell drugs?"

"No! No. But she thought I was rich or something and that I'd have druggie pals . . ."

So this was the answer. Dexter Wyatt was afraid to tell me he had once slept with the dead hooker in my bedroom because he thought I'd be bugged to learn my new boyfriend hung out with prostitutes and potheads.

And you know what, he was right.

"So we're over now?" Dex asked, his voice low.

"I'm not sure how we ever got started," I said, rubbing the sting out of my eyes.

"Aw, Madeline." He looked so sad. "But tell me this at least. Do you trust me, sweetie? Do you know I'm telling you the truth?"

"I think I do."

"But it doesn't help much, does it?"

"The idea of dating a bad boy had a lot of appeal . . ." A tear escaped, damn it.

"But the reality bites," Dex finished for me, and, putting a gentle arm around me, added, "I know."

"Consequences"

What the hell are we doing here?" I whispered to Wesley as he let me into the kitchen entrance at Zenya and Bill Knight's luxurious home in Beverly Hills on Monday morning. All the previous day and night, I had expected to get a late call canceling today's flower luncheon. After all, hadn't Zenya's husband been arrested? Wouldn't she call off this gathering of Woodburn ladies on a morning like this? "Is it still on?"

"Apparently." Wes shrugged, looking mystified. "Zenya just left to take the little girl to a friend's house for the day. The boy, Kirby, is around. And the husband . . ."

I stared at Wes, not believing this.

"He's in his study," Wes finished, keeping his voice low.

"Oh my God, Wes." It wasn't every day I turned a guy in to the police while I puttered around in his kitchen and threw a party for his wife. I was on the edge of freaking.

Meanwhile, Wes filled me in on where we were with the event: "Holly is out on the covered patio with Annie and Kara, finishing decorating and setting up."

We had planned to do our flower-arranging lesson outdoors. Three rows had been made of rented tables, which Holly and our other helpers were draping in dark green canvas and presetting with the vases and flowers and greens. The floral foam was being presoaked and placed in each vase, to make everything easy, and a pair of good florist scissors was placed at each setting so that each of our twenty ladies would have her own workstation from which to trim stems and weave vines and play with the flowers.

"Any word from Detective B?" Wes asked.

"Nothing. He never called me back yesterday and I've left two messages this morning." I'd left long overanxious recitals of all my fears, all the way up to the speculation that Knight may have been behind the murders of Sara Jackson and Albert Grasso. Even though I had no evidence, I was sure I was on the right track. The logic of it. The motivation of all the players. It just gelled. But still Bill Knight was free! And what was worse, he was right here. And what was worse than that, so was I. I felt flushed with concern.

"What do you want to do?" Wes asked.

"Let's just keep going," I said. "What else can we do?"

The Woodburn Ladies Flower Lunch, donated by our firm in the auction and hosted by Dilly Swinden and her cochair Zenya Knight at the Knight home, went down in the short history of Mad Bean Events as the most surreal event we had ever produced. Every time the doorbell rang with the arrival of a new guest, I was sure it would be the police coming to drag away the man of the house.

The Woodburn women, in blissful ignorance of the drama behind the scenes, displayed the completely opposite attitude on this day. They were relaxed, cheerful, and beautiful as always. They wore their version of casual clothes, summer-weight pants and capris in bright colors, little backless sandals with high heels, expensive ankle chains and earrings. Their adorable tiny designer bags rested on a table we'd set out for that purpose. The collection of these ladies' purses alone must have been worth over fifteen grand, and that wasn't counting the contents of their Louis Vuitton wallets.

Everyone was having a grand time. All the committee women I had met over the months while planning the Woodburn fund-raiser were there. Connie Hutson, Dilly and Zenya, even Caroline Rochette had the nerve to show up, soaking up the shock and sympathy of her many friends over the death of Albert Grasso. It was almost too much social facade for me to bear. As they laughed and complimented one another on a new pair of shoes or a belt, I was overburdened with knowing too much of what was going on beneath the surface. Behind the smiles, many of these women were anything but carefree. They were women desperate to hang on to their youth, women worried about money, women who had affairs with other women's husbands they must hide. I found it difficult to put on a friendly face and be as shallow as the situation demanded—which was really a disability for a party planner.

While I got lost in my thoughts, Wes and Holly stood in front of the flower tables and passed out six stems each of alstromeria and snapdragons and demonstrated how to use the number three to design a simple and elegant formal flower arrangement. By making a triangular pattern in the deep floral foam with your three most important flowers, like the large white casa blanca lilies we'd provided in this case, you next fill in with two each of the other flowers around that triangle and form a symmetrical and appealing shape. All the while, as they quickly learned to remove the pollen sticks from the lilies, or artistically arranged their ferns, or daintily sipped on tall glasses of iced tea, or playfully commented on others' flowers, the Woodburn ladies looked relaxed and pleased. The only ones in the entire house who were tense appeared to be Wes, Holly, and me.

Zenya pulled me aside as the group was about to start on their second flower arrangement, a simple design with roses and hydrangea that Wesley would show them how to place into tall, square-shaped vases.

"We're still friends, right?" she asked me, smiling sweetly.

What could I say? Yes, right. I have managed to break your brother's heart while at the same time working to put your no-good husband in prison, but of course we are buds.

I worked on my faux-happy skills a little harder and tried to smile back at her. "Why would you ask that?" It sounded lame, even to my own ears. "Are you having a good time?"

Zenya squeezed my hand and went back to her guests. They were all having a ball. Clearly, they'd all aced the honors course in keeping their secret worries hidden, while I'd forgotten to sign up for that class at all.

After the two very different flower arrangements had been completed and excessively admired, the beautifully filled vases were set in a cool spot where they'd stay until it was time for the ladies to take them home. The party moved on to the pavilion on the far side of the swimming pool, where we had set up lunch. Dilly Swinden made a little speech before the lunch of lobster salad, thanking her committee for all their hard work. She asked Zenya to take a bow and say a few words. As I walked back into the house to find the extra corkscrew, I heard the faint tinkling of the front doorbell.

I walked quietly into the dark hallway and listened.

"What is this?" Bill Knight asked, his voice loud and surly. He had answered the doorbell himself, his wife and everyone else seeming to be in the backyard.

"Bill Knight. You are under arrest for suspicion of—"

Knight tried to slam the front door, but one of the uniformed officers in the group pushed it open, hard, and then another grabbed Bill. While Bill was a big man, he would never have been able to shake them all off. I saw four officers and Detectives Baronowski and Hilts.

More scuffling and swearing ensued as the officers struggled to get a pair of handcuffs on Bill. Handcuffs! In his own home in Beverly Hills. I had expected this. I had. But I was shocked, anyway, to be right there and see the end of this drama unfolding. The officer read Bill his rights, but Bill was cursing through most of it and threatening so many horrible repercussions on these policemen that I doubt he heard a word they were saying.

"Dad!" Kirby Knight darted out of a bedroom and into the fray.

"Kirby," Knight yelled out to his son. "Go get your mother. Get her to call our attorney. Tell her to get those idiot women out of this house right now."

"But, Dad!" Kirby's eyes showed the kind of raw pain a twelve-year-old's face can still show, before life teaches him how to bury it away completely and the man he becomes grows accomplished at never revealing it again.

No one saw me standing with my back flat against the dark hall wall, thank goodness, and I ducked quickly into the kitchen before Kirby ran past me and out into the garden party.

Wesley was coming toward the house as I emerged.

"Kirby just made the announcement," he said, but I could tell that by the reaction among the party guests.

There had been a sudden hush followed by furious movement around the lunch tables. In a few seconds, the casual luncheon had turned into an emergency military retreat. Many of the Woodburn ladies must have suddenly discovered immediate engagements that had to be tended. The flower arrangements were collected and departures were rapid.

Zenya saw me coming out on the lawn and separated from the friend or two who had stayed behind to soothe her. Two other women were on their cell phones, speaking to their attorney husbands, lining up representation for Bill Knight before he even had a chance to make it to the police station.

"Madeline," she said, her face as beautiful as ever, but shocked and disbelieving. "Did you hear? It's awful. Everyone is leaving. I don't know what to do."

"We'll clean up here," I said, feeling so sorry for this woman. For this family. But I wasn't responsible for the crimes her husband had committed. I looked away, as more guests made speedy exits. Even so, I felt a sort of tangential guilt at having tracked the insurance plot down to her husband and delivering his head on a platter to the cops. Could she really care about Bill Knight? Dex might not know anything about her feelings at all.

"What am I going to do, Maddie?"

"You'll do fine," I said. "I think your husband may have been capable of some very unpleasant things, Zenya. You may not know him as well as you thought."

"Bad things? Like what? You think he stole the etchings?"

I nodded.

Zenya thought it over. "I had a long talk with Dexter last night and he agrees with you. I told him I couldn't believe it, but now . . . But now even if it's true, Maddie, what can I do? He's still my husband. The father of my children. He may have gotten some things mixed up with our insurance and found some loopholes, like Dexter explained, but I have benefited from it, too, haven't I? I live in this house. I spend our money. I may not have known about what happened to those etchings, but I guess I share the blame. I have to stand by him, don't I?"

"It's worse than simply insurance fraud, Zenya," I said, catching sight of Caroline Rochette as she got ready to leave. "Please tell me something.

That night after the Woodburn ball, when Bill was driving like a crazy man, did you go straight home? Did he stay with you all night?"

Zenya looked like it was hard for her to focus on anything but the past ten minutes, but she tried. "He went out again."

"Please, Zenya. Please tell me what happened that night. Just how you remember it."

"He left you in the middle of the street downtown, which was so horrible. Then he told me to call Dexter to find you and round you up. He was very specific that I had to get Dex to go. He thought the two of you might make a cute couple. Fancy that. Then he cooled down a bit and decided he wouldn't go chasing over to Pasadena for a showdown with the Hutsons. So we came home."

"About what time?"

"I don't know. Maybe one."

"And after you came home?"

"He was restless. He went to his study and was on the phone, I think. Pretty late, but that's not unusual for Bill. I went to bed at one-thirty and Bill said he thought he'd go take a drive. I don't know what time he got back home. He was out late, though. I awoke around three-ten A.M. and he still hadn't returned. What is this, Madeline?"

It was exactly as I had feared. Bill Knight did not have an alibi for the time Sara Jackson was getting shot at my house. I tried to work out the timetable in my head. Perhaps Zenya had mentioned to Bill the reason I had needed a ride home that night—that I had lent my own wheels to one of my waitresses, Sara Jackson. She probably told Bill how Sara was going to return my car that night. Bill could have seized the opportunity to get rid of Sara Jackson as a threat for good.

"What is going on?" Zenya was as anxious as I'd ever seen her. She had just witnessed her lovely party be turned to shambles by the arrest of her husband. And I was standing there on her grass telling her it was much worse than simple insurance scams.

"That woman who was shot at my house," I said, my throat dry. "She knew your husband."

"Don't tell me this," Zenya whispered, shaking her head. "Were they having an affair?"

"I don't think so," I said. "But . . . your husband wasn't being faithful to you, Zenya. I can't believe I'm the one who is telling you this, but I just found out yesterday."

"What are you talking about?" She looked completely perplexed, her hazel eyes wide.

Caroline Rochette walked by us and stopped. Oh no.

"I took your advice, Madeline," Caroline said to me. "Just in time. I am through with all the lies."

"Good," I barely whispered. Zenya and Caroline were standing together. I was seriously concerned about spontaneous combustion.

Caroline turned to Zenya. "I'm sorry, Zenya. I had no desire to hurt anyone. You simply have got to believe that. I'm afraid it all spun out of control so fast, I got a little lost."

"What are you talking about?" Zenya asked her. And then her eyes focused and she knew. "You were sleeping with my husband."

"I was worried about Albert. He seemed to be growing a little tired of us. I couldn't lose him . . . I know it makes no sense."

Zenya Knight, the sweet flower child of the fund-raising crowd, spun and slapped Caroline Rochette's face so hard the crack of it silenced the few remaining departing guests.

Caroline Rochette, after a lifetime of delusion, denial, and dermabrasion, had finally resolved to confess her sins. She needed to, once and for all, get the whole story out, and a dizzying right hand to her cheek wasn't going to keep her quiet.

"Please understand," she begged Zenya, "Bill came to me and said he was leaving you anyway. I believed him, Zenya. How was I to know he was such a liar? He came to me at a vulnerable time in my life. I'm just telling you all of this so you know the real man those police just arrested. I didn't want you ruining your life supporting him without knowing this."

Zenya raised her right hand again and Caroline, her cheek blazing red, didn't flinch. But Zenya lowered it, her anger directed in too many other directions to take it all out on poor Caroline Rochette.

Wesley signaled to me that our truck had been loaded and we needed to split. I had never been so grateful to leave one of my own parties in my life. I told the women I had to go.

Caroline Rochette did not stick around an instant longer. Zenya stood in the middle of her empty backyard, almost alone. Her son, Kirby, walked up to his mom, hanging his head as he hugged her.

"Things always work out, Kirby my boy," I heard her saying to him as I walked away. Whether from a natural talent for bouncing back up, or a lifelong habit of putting a sunny spin on every bad turn in life, Zenya had her soft smile back in place, ready to cheer up her son.

"I called Uncle Dex," Kirby said. "He's coming right over."

"Good boy," she said, rubbing his hair.

"Mom. What are we going to do?" Kirby's strained voice could be heard even as I walked across the lawn.

"We'll improvise, sweetheart," I heard Zenya say to her jazz-playing son. "You're so good at that. You'll teach your mom."

When I reached Wesley at the front of the house, he looked grim. It had been an unprecedented party. We'd never had a hostess lose her husband in the middle of the meal before. First time for everything.

"It's okay," I said to Wes. "I think Zenya is ready to hear the truth about Bill now. She has some big shocks ahead. But I think she'll be able to roll with them."

"Mad," Wes said, ignoring my words. "I just got off the cell. They're letting Bill Knight go."

"*What?*"

"Rich men get a different kind of justice, right? Bill Knight's lawyers have already raised the roof. Since this is just a suspicion-of-insurance-fraud arrest, with no priors, they're letting him go on his own recognizance."

"But, Wes! The murders of Sara Jackson and—"

"I know, Mad. The cops don't have any evidence to make that sort of charge right now. I just talked to Honnett, who was calling for you, by the way. They didn't find Knight's fingerprints in your house or in Grasso's house. They have no witnesses that place him at the scene. He said he was home with his wife on the night of Sara Jackson's murder."

"But he *wasn't!*"

"I'm just telling you what Honnett told me. The police don't have any real evidence."

"Shit. This is all taking too long. I can't stand it. Zenya said Bill went out early Sunday morning, after the Woodburn ball. And now the cops are going to need more time to pin down everything that asshole has done."

"You're right," Wes said. "Look, I need to return the rental tables. What are you doing?"

That was an extremely good question. I felt that too-familiar clawing of fear in the pit of my stomach. What was I going to do now? A murderer was very likely going to be out on the street in a few hours and I was pretty sure who he would come after.

Me.

"SURPRISE"

I was in serious trouble. I ran all the way up the path to Wesley's guest house and used my key to enter. Bill Knight was about to be released. My name would have been mentioned a lot. Tracking down the valuations from LACMA and talking to the cops. Telling his mistress, Caroline, about his ulterior motives. Letting his wife know about his affair with Caroline. Sticking my nose into every horrid secret the jerk had tried to get away with. Bill Knight might figure that if he eliminated me, he would be home free. Or he might just want payback.

It was maddening. There wasn't much evidence tying him to the murders of Sara Jackson and Grasso and they wouldn't lock him up for good until they had some. I had to find more proof fast. If I waited for the cops to do it, I might be dead first. It was only a few strides to get to the guest bedroom.

Inside, I stepped out of my shoes and changed into a clean pair of shorts. Then I pulled open the nightstand drawer and touched the Lady Smith .38. I had no holster or other method of carrying it safely, but I didn't care. I grabbed the loaded gun, shoved it into my big Hawaiian-print bag, and slung it over my shoulder, trying to calm myself down. Trying to chill.

When I got back out into the main section of the guest house, I noticed something odd. I must have missed it earlier when I raced to my room. Holly's shoes were kicked off in the corner of the kitchen. The silver open-toe wedgies she'd been wearing at today's party. It wasn't unusual for Holly to stop by Wesley's after a gig. It was a tradition, really. But where had she gone?

"Holly?" I walked through the little cottage. The bathroom door was open. It was empty. The other rooms were silent.

I opened the front door of the guest house and looked across the pool to the main house. The chandelier light was on in the empty living room, but I hadn't seen Rolando's truck outside today. Holly must have gone over. While I knew Wes could be delayed returning the rentals, I would feel much safer hanging with Holly.

Outside, I barefooted it across the warm grass. The French door that led to the sunroom was unlocked. Wes had told the crew to lock up when they left the site for the day, but maybe Holly let herself in with the key and forgot to relock it.

I had the sudden high-school-girl urge to surprise Holly and scare the heck out of her. I crept along the sunroom and into the main hall. The house was a shambles of dust and drop cloths. A ladder leaned against one wall. I edged along the hall to the front foyer. I was about to yell, "Surprise," when I heard a voice. Holly was talking. Maybe I shouldn't give her a heart attack while she was talking on the cell phone. Maybe it was Donald. She'd been missing him a lot since he'd been out of town. The good angel won out over the bad. I would eavesdrop before I pounced, hiding in the entry closet. Inside the tiny space, I couldn't hear a thing.

So I gave it up. I came out of the closet and headed for the arched doorway that led into the step-down living room. The large empty space was covered in hideous cranberry-colored deep-pile carpet. Wes planned to tear it out and refinish the hardwood floor underneath. With my bare feet, I noiselessly entered the room.

When I turned the corner, I froze.

Standing in front of the gigantic fireplace in the middle of the room, facing me, was Holly. Standing with her back to me was the woman with the red shag haircut. The one who had followed me in her Honda Accord through Hollywood, and shown up to spy on me on Dexter's deck. She was now pointing a hand at Holly, a hand holding a 9mm semiautomatic handgun. I remembered it from the charts.

I ducked back out of sight, my heart pounding out of my chest. Holly had seen me. I was certain she must have. But she hadn't reacted at all. Oh my God. What did that woman want with Holly?

I tried to move silently as I rushed out to the back sunroom. Who was that woman, anyway? *Who was she?* I had to do something to rescue Holly. I opened my shoulder bag and saw the .38, heavy at the bottom. I blanched, frozen for a moment, unable to think clearly. I reached past it and grabbed my cell phone, quickly dialing Honnett's number, resenting the sounds of the little beep tones as I hit each number. Several rings, and then his machine. I despaired. I left him voice mail. I called 911 and waited for the second ring. They would pick up. They would—

"*Drop it!*" a woman's voice said.

I jerked around. The red-haired woman stood in the doorway of the sunroom, her gun pointed at me.

"Drop it right now or you are dead."

I let the cell phone hit the tile floor.

"Kick it over here. Now!" she yelled.

I had a frantic panic that she had killed Holly, but I tried hard to control the fear. I hadn't heard a gunshot and her weapon didn't seem to have noise-suppression equipment. I prayed Hol was all right. The woman snapped off the power button on my cell phone and dropped it back onto the floor.

"What did you do to Holly? Who are you?" I stared at her. She had fair skin and faded looks, like she had been pretty at one time. Close up, I could see that despite her good bone structure, her skin looked worn, covered with many fine lines. She would have looked a lot better if she had been wearing some makeup. With her sparkless looks, it was hard to see a resemblance, but her coloring was similar to Sara Jackson's—the same dark red hair and freckles.

"You really have no idea who I am," she said, amazed.

"Are you related to Sara Jackson?"

She shook her head, amused.

I couldn't help staring at the gun in her hand. She held it firmly and capably, two-handed for support. I had the fleeting thought that Andi, my gun trainer, would be impressed.

"Why have you been following me?" I asked, trying to stay calm. "Do you know Dexter Wyatt?"

"I have the gun, so I'll lead this conversation, okay?"

She acted like a pissed-off cop.

"Which reminds me," she continued, "I want my thirty-eight back."

Her .38? The gun Honnett had lent to me, the engraving had included an initial. *S* perhaps. And a former cop. Sherrie? Sherrie Honnett. Oh my God.

"This can't be happening," I said, my brain swimming. Honnett's wife. The age was right. As a cop, she'd be familiar with firearms. But what the hell was she doing pointing a Beretta 9mm at my heart? "Sherrie, put the gun away."

"Finally," she yelled at me. "I've known about you for a long time, and now you finally know me. Perfect."

"What are you doing here?" We stood in the empty sunroom and I was becoming more alarmed by the minute. "What did you do to Holly? Did you hurt her?"

"Your girlfriend is sleeping in the other room."

Sleeping! My stomach jumped. I steadied myself and tried to follow what she was saying.

"I let myself into that little cottage where you live, looking for my revolver, and I found your friend instead. She began yelling and getting hysterical, so I brought her to this house, where I could leave her for a while. My plan was to come back and wait for you. But I took too long, didn't I? And here you are."

"I don't know why you've been following me, Sherrie. Or why on earth you think you're entitled to break into my house or hurt my friends. But you have got to wake up now. You can't get away with this behavior."

"I don't intend to," she said, in disgust. "I'll take responsibility for it all. You don't know me very well, but you'll see."

The woman was completely irrational. I kept the anger out of my voice this time. "You must be very upset, Sherrie," I said, making eye contact with her. "You've been sick. You need your husband by your side. I know that now. I'm aware of everything now."

"You, little girl, know nothing. You have no idea what you are talking about." Sherrie Honnett looked like she would like to spit on me. Or shoot me. "Sit down on the floor," she ordered. "Over in the corner. Now. Move."

I sat down where she told me to, and she followed my actions with the gun, carefully settling herself on the floor ten feet away from me, resting the Beretta on her knee, pointing it right at my chest.

"I know you must love your husband," I said, trying again.

"You have no idea what I feel," she said, still gravely annoyed. "He is the most honorable, exceptional man you have ever met, Madeline Bean. You don't appreciate that, of course, because you are a class-one bitch. But that man is the best there is."

Her eyes were gleaming. Her voice was harsh.

I kept quiet, trying not to obsess over the opening of the unblinking gun barrel as it stared at me.

"I met him ten years ago when I was working at the Hollenbeck Division," she said. "Chuck served his probationary period there, but he wanted more excitement, so he moved to the Seventy-seventh Street Division in South Central. Did you know any of this?"

I shook my head.

"Figures. You take up with a man and know absolutely nothing about him. What do you care, right?" Her eyes challenged me.

"I do care," I said, wondering if this was what she wanted to hear, trying not to piss her off any further.

"Then you'll be delighted to learn that Chuck was a favorite out there. He tried new things. I was so damned proud of him in those days. They would always pick Chuck first to work the dangerous undercover assignments. He did good work."

I had no idea how I was going to get out of the corner of this dusty sunroom alive. I had no choice but to keep Sherrie talking, and she clearly had a lot more she wanted to tell me.

"Is this cop stuff boring you, honey?"

I shook my head no. "What happened next?"

"He worked the South Bureau Narcotics Task Force and was part of some amazing busts. In time, the department knew how much trust they could place in Chuck. He was given the 'problem probationers' ready to be fired for various things in their performance as cops. Chuck would turn these cops around and keep them from being fired. Do you have any idea what sort of man this is, Madeline, this man you have treated like crap?"

Wait. Was Sherrie angry with me for getting involved with her husband or for treating him like crap? Hold on. "What about your career?" I asked, trying to get it just right. "You were a great cop."

"My own career with the PD was minor league. I always worked hard, but Chuck was the star in the family. He was on the gang task force until June 1998, when he was handpicked to be the senior officer in the Robbery Homicide Division. Do you understand what sort of man he is?"

The level of hero worship combined with the intensity of her feelings were enough to frighten anyone. The unwavering gun barrel scared me even more. "Sherrie. Please, let me talk. When I first met Honnett, I had no idea he was still married."

She actually laughed at me. And why shouldn't she? "You saying he lied to you, like some common scumbag? You're talking about Lieutenant Charles W. Honnett of the Los Angeles Police Department," she said. "This man doesn't lie, kid. Do you actually think you're going to sell that story? He doesn't lie."

She was right. Technically, he hadn't lied to me. He just never went into the details. And to be 100 percent fair, I had never asked for a detailed review of his previous relationships. I thought men hated to be quizzed. I had been trying to be a free spirit. For all the good it did me.

"Sherrie, he said he had been married before. That was all. Married before. And this was a long time ago, at a time when the two of you were separated. How could I know? Then, later, when he told me more about you, about how he was getting back together with you, of course he and I split up. That was it. I know he loves you, Sherrie."

A tear fell from her eye. I was shocked I had gotten through. I kept talking. "There is no need for you to get into bigger trouble over a . . . a misunderstanding, really. No need for guns or any of this. Men sometimes make mistakes with women, no matter how good the guy might be. The important thing is that Honnett loves you and he went back to you when you needed him."

"Shut up," she said. The gun never wavered in her hands. She had years of training on pistols, I realized. And this was, after all, her service gun.

I thought of her other gun, the expensive .38 Honnett brought to me after I'd begged him for his help. He never told Sherrie, of course. Probably hoped she wouldn't notice it missing. That was Honnett's style of honesty. Never say too much. Never explain. Right.

"He came back to you, Sherrie," I said, trying to convince her she had nothing to fear from me.

"Chuck never would have come back to me if I hadn't told him about being sick. He said . . ." Her calm monotone became ragged and she sobbed once, then pulled it together. "He told me he'd met someone. He said you weren't like us. You were different. Some sort of cook. Young and liberal and all of that. Kind of like some arty bohemian. I asked him if this new girl had any idea what kind of hero he was. And do you know what he told me? He said you didn't pay much attention to what he did on the job." She shook her head, remembering. "This great cop, but what do you care about any of that? It was all wrong. I worshiped that man, but he wanted you. I didn't know what else to do. I had to get him to pay attention to me again, so I told him about the cancer."

"I heard you've been sick."

She shook her head. "You heard wrong."

"You don't have cancer?"

With one hand she pulled off the red wig she had been wearing, keeping the other hand, the one holding the Beretta 9mm, steady on me. Beneath the thick shag wig, her own brown hair was pinned up under a net.

"We'd been living apart for over a year. He kept drifting farther away. I had to tell Chuck something. So I bought a wig and told him I'd been going through chemo."

This woman was so seriously nuts.

"That's when he paid attention. He realized we needed to work out our troubles," she said. " 'Cause he thought I was dying. Not because he wanted me."

I stared at her.

"It was no good, you see? You had ruined him by then. He wasn't mine anymore. Nothing I tried made any difference. He asked the therapist we were seeing how long she felt I would need his support. She told me that one night after a session. I knew he would be leaving me any day to go back to you."

"I'm sorry. I swear I never knew."

"So you can see why I'd want to check you out."

"You started following me."

"Chuck told me you were a party girl and came home late at night. I knew about your Grand Wagoneer and I got your address on Whitley off of your driver's license. I went to your house one night. I watched you come home. That first time I saw you I had such pain. Like fire. You were so young. You were so young and thin and vibrant—that's the right word. I hadn't expected that. And I watched you go into the house and turn on some lights."

"When was this?" Some creepy strange woman had been stalking me. I had felt it. I had known it. But I had always managed to push it out of my thoughts. It was creepier by far to hear about it from the point of view of the stalker.

"A week ago Saturday night. Or I should really say early Sunday morning."

And it all clicked into place. This jealous/crazy woman had been staking out my house on the night Sara Jackson had returned my Jeep Grand Wagoneer. Sherrie Honnett had not known what I looked like then. She mistook Sara for me.

"You'll Never
Go to Heaven"

t was Sara," I said, my voice dead.

"I thought it was *you*. So young. So pretty. She let herself into the house by the kitchen door. She left the door ajar and I entered behind her. She was already walking up the stairs when I entered the kitchen."

I was shocked. Why had Sara Jackson gone up to my room? I had never figured that out.

"She was standing in your bedroom, opening drawers, playing with your jewelry box."

I was astonished. "My what?"

"She was holding up a pair of emerald earrings. Now, why would I imagine that that young woman fooling with your earrings was anyone else but you?"

"Sara was ripping me off?" Of course she was. Alone in my house, she had to investigate to see if there was anything around worth stealing. From what I knew now about Sara Jackson's character, I should never have given her the combination to my back-door lock. But at that time I was careless, trusting. A fool.

"When I realized I'd killed the wrong person, I had to think it over," Sherrie said. "The girl was going through your pathetic little jewelry box. When you think about it, you owe me some thanks. I shot a burglar in the middle of the act. If only I had known, I might have spun the story correctly at the time. I'd be wearing a medal today."

"You shot her."

"With the Lady Smith, as a matter of fact." I remembered the revolver that was currently loaded and resting at the bottom of my shoulder bag. Sherrie was smiling, recalling that night with a chillingly inappropriate, matter-of-fact calmness. "It was an odd scene now that I recall it. I told her to leave my husband alone. I told her I had cancer. I told her she could fall in love with any man in the world and he would fall in love with her back."

Oh my God. What had Sara Jackson, the sometime prostitute, made of this bizarre woman begging her to leave her man alone?

"She laughed at me, Miss Madeline Bean," Sherrie said calmly. "The little bitch told me that it was cold old women like *me* who made her work easy. She said I deserved to lose my man. She showed not one single ounce of remorse, do you understand?"

I nodded, getting the picture.

"And to shut the smug bitch up, I told her to sit on the bed. She ignored me and turned back to the jewelry case. So I had to take my gun out and tell her again."

I was about to be sick.

"And that wasn't smart, I know," Sherrie said, sounding almost apologetic. "Chuck would be angry. And I didn't want him to be angry, even though he had just that very day broken my heart into a million pieces. He said he loved you. In our therapy session on Saturday afternoon. He said he needed to be honest with me."

My head couldn't take in everything she said. Like this last bit. Honnett had never used the word *love* with me. Ever. So there I was, for months holding a grudge against this man for his betrayal. I had convinced myself that I had read him wrong, that he had never really cared about me. While for months, Honnett was painfully extricating himself from his entanglement with a sad and sick wife, telling her he loved me before he would ever say those words to me.

"So I had to make a decision." Sherrie picked up the story, enjoying my captive attention. "Chuck would never understand why I had gone over to your house to meet you, Madeline Bean. He'd be angry with me for going inside. I had to think very quickly, but there was no way I could get out of it. And all the time, this girl that I thought was you kept berating me. She had a filthy gutter mouth. No God in her at all. She kept swearing at me. I was holding the gun on her and she didn't care. She kept calling me disgusting names."

I shook my head, unable to imagine Sara's foolish toughness.

"I was horrified," Sherrie whispered, "horrified to see whom my Chuck had given his heart to. Madeline Bean was a stupid, foulmouthed whore," Sherrie said, still in that eerie casual tone of voice like she was talking about a recipe. "And I had to shoot her to shut her up."

I swallowed down my sudden feeling of nausea.

"And it gets better," Sherrie said. "The irony. You'll like this part. When I was leaving your house, I realized I had been observed. I almost peed in my pants when I spotted him out there in the dark. At one-thirty in the morning, when no one should have been anywhere near your house. Some nasty old man was hiding in the bushes. Probably some Peeping Tom, but that pervert picked the wrong night to peep. When I came out of the house, he ran away like a scared squirrel."

"Who was it?"

"Some man who lived up on the next street. I had to track him to his house," she said, remembering back. "I'm sure he heard the gunshots. It was dark, but he may have seen me. I couldn't take the chance."

Albert Grasso must have come down to my house early Sunday A.M., perhaps looking for a way to get his briefcase papers back. And during his late-night prowling, he'd had the bad fortune to witness Sherrie's spur-of-the-moment burst of terrorism. Grasso fled, but not before Sherrie was able to discover where to find him. She must have come after him later and killed him, just to cover her tracks.

"You are the one to blame for all of this," Sherrie said adamantly. "You backed me into a corner, and when you wouldn't listen to reason, I had to kill you."

"Sherrie. That wasn't me, remember? I *would* have listened to you. But you were talking to some twisted hooker who was in my room to steal my things. It was Sara Jackson who taunted you, not me."

"Shut up! That's not what this is all about. I don't care about myself.

Not at all. I am just a vessel for justice, which is exactly as it should be. I prayed to God for years over my marriage. I asked God for babies, but He didn't have that blessing for me. I was confused about that, I'll admit it. I was lost for a little while. But I prayed and I found God again. God didn't see fit to give me children, but he does have a job for me, Madeline Bean, and I'm doing it the best I know how."

This was not going to end well. She had a job to do. I wanted to scream.

How had Honnett managed to put up with her for so long? Or did her mind unravel so slowly that her quirks and moods might go unrecognized as they shrank further from the bounds of sane behavior? Perhaps Sherrie had the gift of hiding her inner turmoil from her husband, her mental illness progressing to a state where she had nothing left but vengeance and fury, without Honnett seeing into the depths of her despair.

"I know what I have to do," she continued. "I have to leave this earth. I have taken two lives, and although they were hateful lives, I can't stay. I know I have broken the law. So I'm not crazy. But then there's Chuck. Do you think he could forgive me?"

"You're still his wife, Sherrie," I answered carefully. "There's always hope."

She shook her head sadly. "No. He's too good. He'd have to send me away. But I had one more task to perform before I go to God. I had to look after my dear husband. I had to find the real Madeline Bean and decide if you were honorable enough for this man."

"But, Sherrie, Chuck and I broke it off months ago. We haven't even kept in touch."

Sherrie ignored me. Her voice held utter contempt. "And I discovered your true moral character."

I thought about the night she was standing out on Dexter Wyatt's deck in the moonlight, looking in. "But, Sherrie," I said, worried. "Chuck and I were not even seeing each other then. We were over."

"Didn't take you long, did it? You were already catting around with another man. No better than that insulting hooker I killed in your bed. You never loved Chuck like he deserves. And he loves you, don't you see?"

I stared at the barrel of the Beretta. "You're going to kill me because I'm . . ." How could I say it so she'd wake up? "Because I'm not a good-enough person. Why don't you just tell Honnett. Tell him."

"I noticed my favorite gun was missing the other day, and I can tell you, it worried me. It worried me greatly. Did you know that pistol had been a gift to me from Chuck on our first wedding anniversary? I love that gun."

Oh God.

"And as it happens, that thirty-eight can be tied to those two shootings, can't it? I couldn't very well have this weapon traced to the killings. I just came here to retrieve my own property. So where is it?"

"It's in the trunk of my car." I wanted to get out of this empty house. I wanted to be outdoors.

"You're lying."

Something else occurred to me. The other night I told Honnett the stalker woman drove a Honda Accord with a missing front plate. He had to have known right then it was Sherrie who had been following me. He'd gone kind of quiet and I'd put it off to his mooning over the wreck of our relationship. But no. He had more to worry him that night. He had to have noticed Sherrie's ever-more-disturbing behavior, realized she was unstable, and then discovered she had been acting out against me, but he never mentioned a word of it to me.

"Where's the gun?" Sherrie shouted at me.

"In my car. If I was lying, I'd have said I don't have your gun any-more."

"Well, we'll see. Get up now, missy," Sherrie said, gesturing with the barrel of the black 9mm semiautomatic. "Up with you. I want you to sit over on this bed here." There was an old paint-splattered daybed over in the corner of the sunroom that the guys used as a platform to paint the high moldings.

She was going to shoot me here in Wesley's empty estate, just as she had shot Sara. Just the same, on the bed.

"Stand up!" she yelled.

There was a tap at the front door. We both heard it.

"Don't make a sound," she said, walking up to me and putting the bar-rel of the gun up to my neck as I got to my feet.

The tapping at the door continued. We heard a heavily accented man's voice call, "Miss Maddie?"

"Who is that?" Sherrie whispered in my ear. She held me by the back of my waistband, still keeping the gun on my neck.

"I think it's Rolando," I answered. "He works here on the property."

"Miss Maddie, I need the garage opener."

"Rolando has the key to this house," I lied to Sherrie. "If I don't answer the door, he's going to let himself in."

Her breathing became more rapid. "Don't screw this up," she said to me, holding me by the waistband of my khaki shorts and pushing toward the door. "Just tell him through the door that he should go home. No work today."

"He won't believe me," I said. "He works for—"

Sherrie struck me on the side of my head with the gun. I almost dropped from the sudden crash of black light and pain. "Tell him to go or I'll kill two people today."

"Rolando," I said through the door.

"Miss Maddie? I need to put some things in the garage."

"Not today, Rolando."

"¿Que?"

"He doesn't understand a lot of English," I explained to Sherrie, worried she was going to shoot both of us for my freaking inability to remember one word I learned in high school Spanish.

"Tell him to go," she insisted.

"Go, Rolando. Go home."

"What, miss?"

"Damn it," Sherrie said. "Open the door slowly and tell the idiot to get out now. You have ten seconds or I'm shooting you both."

Sherrie slowly opened the door inward and pushed me forward, two feet away from the barrel of the 9mm and a step closer to fresh open air.

The man standing at the door grabbed my arm. He yanked me so hard I lost my balance. Before I could tell what was happening, I was falling, tumbling to the ground, pulled out of the line of fire.

Some villains are all punk talk; they intimidate their victims by making grandiose threats. When put to the ultimate test, they can't pull the trigger. But that couldn't be said for Sherrie. Sherrie had never been bluffing. She had been a police officer too long. She was calm in the face of sudden danger. She had been trained to shoot in situations that were going down wrong, and ask questions later. And now, here, in the bright Hancock Park afternoon, something was seriously going wrong.

As I began falling away, she pulled the trigger of her semiautomatic, squeezing off two shots in rapid succession. Stunned by my sudden fall, Sherrie hadn't fully adjusted her aim as I barreled downward. The slugs whizzed by, much too close to my head. I watched in slow motion as her bullets did, however, find a home. They struck down the man standing on the front step, my savior. Only it wasn't some innocent, startled Mexican-American construction worker who went down. It had never been Rolando at the door. It was Sherrie's beloved husband.

Chuck Honnett fell backward, his face expressing shock, pain, clutching at his chest.

What the hell had he been thinking, just walking up to the front door and pulling me out like that? *My God!* I saw his face for a second after he was hit. He never figured Sherrie would hurt him. But he hadn't counted on what kind of a wreck she had become, how the sudden confusion of the moment and her cop instincts and her tortured brain might propel her to make a deadly mistake. Or maybe he hadn't cared about his own safety at all. This wild and rash action was the way he'd chosen to clean up after his disaster of a wife. That's what men like Honnett did.

I pulled myself to my feet and tripped my way across the front of the house, then dropped again and rolled into the thicket of overgrown bushes, thankful that Wesley had not yet relandscaped. I'd have been shot before I ever made my way to this cover, no question, had not the horror of recognition as Sherrie saw her own man fall to the ground stunned her into a momentary trance. Her husband lay unconscious not six feet in front of her, having taken what I figured were both shots at extremely close range to the chest. I had not chanced another look back to check on him as I clawed my way to shelter, propelled by some force of survival instinct I'd never felt before. When I was deep into the shrubbery, I tried to get into a position where I could see what was going on.

"Chuck?" Sherrie could hardly focus her eyes on Honnett's fallen body. "Chuck, honey? What did you make me do?"

I had no idea if Honnett lay dead or dying, but I crawled up against the house, pulling myself back through the shrubbery, leaving bloody

scratch marks on my face and down both arms as I scraped through the
brambles to find shelter.

I was alive. Chuck was dead. Sherrie was armed. My brain could only
think in sentences of three short words as I tried to get a grip. I almost
laughed, so strung out was I into shock. I owed my life to voice mail,
whose inventor I now owed the best dinner of his life.

I tried hard to focus. Think slowly. And the giddiness subsided. My
message. It must have jolted Honnett out of his denial. Sherrie, his disturbed wife, had been tracking me. And now she had Holly and me
trapped in a big empty house.

Honnett knew that Sherrie had been tailing me and maybe he had
hoped that would be as far as it went. A small, sad matter—his sick wife
pathetically watching his girlfriend—something he could make right
somehow before it escalated out of control. But my message had been
short and clear. Sherrie had a gun. At last, Honnett had to face the truth.
And so he came to my rescue.

Sirens were faintly perceptible in the far distance now. Maybe Honnett had called for backup before he approached the house. Maybe the
neighbors were cowering in their mansions, hearing gunshots on their
quiet streets, frantically dialing 911.

Sherrie fell to the stone-paved sidewalk to get closer to the man she
had just shot down. She was talking to him softly, telling him he would
be all right. Not to worry.

It was unnerving to hear her coo at his unconscious form, gun still in
her hand, while he bled to death on the front walk. The tension as Sherrie dithered on about love and God and the pain she endured, as she
threatened the peace in leafy Hancock Park, was unbearable. But as long
as Sherrie held a loaded weapon, she could rant about whatever she
wanted. That was her power now.

I prayed the police would show up in time. I prayed hard. Sherrie had
momentarily forgotten to track where I had gone. But upon hearing the
faint sounds of sirens, she snapped back to the here and now.

She stood up and yelled, "Where did you go, bitch? Come out here
and see what you did to Chuck! You whore!"

I don't think she saw me, but she guessed the general direction in
which I'd fled. I was sitting, masked by a thicket of camellia bushes and
other greenery, up against the exterior wall right below the bay window of

the living room, trying not to move, not to make a sound, as the explosive crack of two shots rang out. The bullets had been fired in my direction. One hit the stucco not three feet from where I sat cowering against the house, hugging my knees. The other struck slightly higher and shattered a pane in the multipaned bay window. Shards of glass blew out, a few falling on me.

The last time I saw her, Holly had been in that room, I thought, desperate. Please, God, I begged. Let Holly be all right. Let her be all right.

Sherrie screamed in rage. The sirens grew louder, maybe now only three blocks away.

They'd never make it in time. Sherrie had a semiautomatic weapon with a clip. She was not limited to six bullets. She could keep sniping away and pretty soon I'd be dead.

She crouched down again, just outside the front door, stooping over Honnett's motionless body. I could hear her crying as she called to me and begged me to come out so she could finish her job.

I slowly pulled my Hawaiian-print bag off my shoulder with as few movements as was possible so as not to set the bushes shivering, and I pulled out the Lady Smith .38 revolver with the custom-engraved S.

Two more shots spat out in my direction. The cops had not arrived yet, maybe never would. Holly and I were going to die. I peeked between the foliage and could see Sherrie pretty clearly. The front entry of the house was only about thirty feet from where I was hiding. She was bending low and leaning close to Honnett.

It was impossible. Even if I was an excellent markswoman, I would never be able to hit her with only six shots. I was using a short-barreled revolver and was in a horrible position. And I wasn't a sharpshooter. I'd miss her. I'd give away my position. And I'd probably end up shooting Honnett.

Two more shots hit the windows above me, raining down a hailstorm of glass, as the police sirens blasted much more loudly, hiccupping as they turned onto Hudson.

Sherrie was frantic now. She stood up and planted her feet shoulder-width apart, just the stance Andi had instructed me for best positioning during a firefight.

Sherrie's 9mm pistol shot out again, and this time the lead came within inches of finding me on the ground. She was aiming lower now. Two more bullets bit into the dirt near my hand. I was pinned, afraid to scramble away, fearing the movement in the shrubs would give away my position, knowing I was about to die.

I looked up through the branches as Sherrie peered in my direction. She didn't want to leave Honnett, or she could easily have walked over and finished the job. Then behind Sherrie, inside the house in the open doorway, I saw Holly Nichols, swaying slightly. Blood dripped down the side of her face. Holly was a tall woman, an athlete in high school. I knew with sick certainty she would try to save me. She looked determined to grab Sherrie from behind.

The two police cars were screeching to a stop in the middle of Hudson, distracting Sherrie from noticing Holly coming at her from behind. But then she must have realized something was wrong. She swung 180 degrees, facing Holly, gun ready.

"Holly!" I screamed, standing up in front of the blown-out bay window and planting my feet shoulder-width apart. "Get away!"

What happened next went by in a blur. Holly fell back into the house, slamming the heavy door. Sherrie snapped her head toward the sound of my voice. She didn't even waste a shot in Holly's direction. Sherrie turned and pointed her Beretta directly at my chest. At about the same time the cops were jumping out of their cars, drawing their guns, screaming for everyone to put down their weapons, I was pointing my gun at the center of Sherrie Honnett's body, steadying myself to fire. It was odd—in the middle of that escalating melee, I felt no fear. I heard a dozen lead bees whiz by my head as I pulled the trigger on the Smith & Wesson .38 six times.

Sherrie crumpled on the front steps of the house as three more patrol cars tore up Hudson and screeched to a halt.

The four officers who were already in position in the street, barricaded behind their cars, were joined by six others. All of them immediately turned their service guns on me. One screamed, "*Drop your weapon right now or we will fire. DO IT!*"

I threw my gun out on Wesley's front lawn.

"Put your hands on your head," a voice yelled.

I did it. "That man," I yelled back as they swarmed forward with guns still out. "That man is Lieutenant Chuck Honnett. Sherrie shot him. She shot him. I was trapped."

I was pushed facedown on the front lawn. A uniformed female officer stepped on my shoulders and put all her weight on me, holding me hard with my face in the grass, her gun pointed at my back.

"Maddie," Holly shrieked, opening the front door. Then she yelled at the cops, pointing at me, "Don't hurt that woman!" More sirens screamed up the quiet upscale street as Holly pleaded, "She's the good guy."

"Lotta Sax Appeal"

Two days passed. I hadn't been sleeping well. Nightmares. Which was pretty understandable, I suppose.

I was still living out of suitcases in Hancock Park while my own house remained ripped open, under construction. Between Wesley and me, neither of us had a residence that hadn't been the recent scene of some terrible, violent, bloody action. We desperately, giddily contemplated an escape, maybe to Holly's one-bedroom apartment in West Hollywood, but then Donald was coming home any day. The pair had big plans for a climactic reunion. Neither Wes nor I needed to witness that.

So Wesley supervised the cleanup of the blood and damaged stucco and blown-out glass, and each time I walked past the main house, I tried not to stare at that spot near the bay window where I had almost been killed. It was enough to make taking a Xanax or two sound almost interesting.

Former police officer Sherrie Honnett survived the firefight in the front yard on Hudson, barely. But despite the efforts of the paramedics as her ambulance screamed up to the emergency entrance of Queen of

Angels–Hollywood Presbyterian Medical Center, she was pronounced dead on arrival. I learned later that one of the three bullets that hit her was a .38. I had been the only one there carrying that caliber.

It was kind of a miracle that I came through the ordeal unharmed, save in the most trivial way—several dozen deep scratches down my arms and legs from the bushes—and the more profound—the shudder in my soul from the unrelenting horror that I had shot someone. I realize my pain is nothing compared to the shocking finality of death, but it stung almost unbearably hard just the same. I knew I would have to learn to live with my wounds, and as for Sherrie, I would hope that she had found some peace.

Chuck Honnett had been relatively lucky, if the word *luck* can even be used when describing a gunshot wound to the chest. It turned out one bullet grazed his arm. He had only been hit seriously by one of Sherrie's shots. But at point-blank range, even one blast of a 9mm bullet can do a severe amount of damage. Sirens wailing, Honnett also had been transported to Queen of Angels and then rushed into surgery. One lung had been damaged and he lost a lot of blood. I'd been told by his doctor that Honnett's wounds were relatively minor considering just how close he'd come to death. Sherrie had missed Honnett's heart by an inch. Ironic, no?

On Wednesday morning, I awoke from a vivid dream, another nightmare. A man very much like Honnett was sitting with me at an old-fashioned saloon and he was forcing me to drink shot glasses of whiskey. I had a horrible pain in my chest, which I somehow figured was from drinking too much, but he kept smiling and making me take another shot.

Since dreams often use puns, this was not the most ambiguous image on the planet. Me and Honnett. Heartache. Shots. You can see why I don't need a shrink just yet to analyze my dreams.

It was only six-ten but I woke myself up fully to shake the fear of my dream away. What had I been trying to tell myself? Was my subconscious still in turmoil because I took those "shots" at Sherrie? Undoubtedly. Or maybe it was more than that. I wanted to blame Honnett for getting me into this mess. He had put me in a position where I had to take shots at his wife. But in the light of day I knew it hadn't been his fault. From the first day we met, Honnett had tried to avoid getting too involved with me. I had been the impulsive one, the one who insisted we get together, so innocent of any consequences or danger.

No matter my nightmares and their true meanings, I could always find a way to blame myself. Here I was again, back to that. And I knew what Wes would say and what Holly would say. All this self-pity wasn't doing me much good. I sat up in bed. I needed something to distract me from my own emotional devils. And just at that moment, a new idea popped into my head. It was so irresistible, I immediately grabbed for the phone.

Maybe I should have been more mindful of who I telephoned at six twenty-three on a Wednesday morning, but I dialed the number of Connie Hutson anyway.

"Hello?" It was Connie's voice. She'd picked up on the second ring.

"This is Madeline Bean. Sorry, Connie. Did I wake you?"

"No, of course not. I'm just going to the gym to work out. I've been meaning to call you," she said. Many of the Woodburn ladies had avoided me since Bill Knight was arrested in the middle of the flower party, followed by the latest round of shoot-outs, which all made screaming headlines. It was one thing to have a caterer with a colorful past, but it seemed I'd stepped over the line from colorful to notorious. These were all sensible, conservative women. It was human nature to be wary of associating with anyone who seemed to attract gunfire as much as I had lately.

"I understand," I said. "Listen, I have a quick question. Do you have just one minute?"

There was a slight hesitation and then Connie said, "Just one."

"Do you remember back on the night of the Woodburn gala, exactly what all did Bill Knight buy at the auction?"

"You mean the Selmer Mark VI? He had the winning bid on that."

"I know. But did he or Zenya get anything else? Anything from the silent-auction tables, maybe?"

"Yes," Connie said, sounding surer of it now. "Everyone lines up after the affair to find out what bids they won and pay for their items. We had different lines, set up alphabetically by last names, so letters A to F lined up in one line and so on. I was supervising that process and it's terribly hard. Everyone is in a hurry to pay and go home. No one has any patience at that time of night. And our volunteers were also tired. They had just been processing the silent auction bid sheets for an hour and also wanted to go home. Anyway, I remember Bill insisting he check out his items before he paid."

"Was that unusual?"

"Well, yes. You understand, all the money raised at the silent auction goes to a good cause. Most bidders are aware that they get no real guarantees with anything they purchase. Besides, they can look everything over carefully before they bid. No one has ever tried to return anything in all my years working on these auctions."

"But Bill wanted to check out his items?"

"Yes. But then he did spend a lot of money to get that saxophone. I didn't think that much of it at the time."

"So what did he do?'

"The Knights also had the highest bid on the Baby Bundle Basket in the silent auction. Bill took that and the Selmer case back to the little office and checked them over, I suppose. It was a good thing he did, since he discovered that the saxophone was not in the case. Now, Maddie, I really have to run."

"I know and I really appreciate this, Connie. Just one more question: What exactly was in that Baby Bundle Basket?"

"It was a lovely item donated by Haute Baby on Beverly. Know them? They sent in a huge Moses basket filled with their designer baby bedding and clothes. If I were ever crazy enough to have another baby, I'd have wanted to bid on that myself."

"Isn't it odd that the Knights would buy baby clothes?"

"Maybe they planned to give it as a gift."

"Perhaps. Do you remember how much they paid for it?"

"Nineteen hundred dollars, which was well over the retail value. Very generous of them, especially—since now that we're talking about it—I remember one of the gals mentioned that she found the baby clothes left out in the office."

"What?"

"Apparently, when Liz Reed was closing up the little office, she noticed a stack of baby clothes left on the desk chair. We figured Bill had looked through his basket and then forgot to repack it in all the fuss about the saxophone."

"But he took the basket," I asked, "and the baby blanket?"

"Yes."

And the Selmer Mark VI! I had figured it out. Bill Knight had stolen his own freaking saxophone.

"Thanks, Connie. Sorry to keep you so long."

Bill Knight had gone into the little office and was alone with the sax. That had to be how he pulled it off. He tossed the baby clothes aside, put the Mark VI into the basket, and covered it all up with the baby blanket, leaving it behind for the moment in the office. Then he brought the empty sax case out and made a huge fuss. While all the auction volunteer women were in shock about this unprecedented theft and also trying to handle the huge lines of party guests impatient to check out and get their auction items, he must have swooped back into the office, grabbed his baby basket, and stormed out of the Tager Auditorium.

I remembered it now. I was standing at the bottom of the steps with Zenya. Bill had roared down the stairs holding a large something, which he threw into the back of the Hummer H1 while he yelled at us to jump into the vehicle.

Bill Knight stole his own bloody vintage saxophone. Damn. It had to be. It fit his freaking MO. Why not pull the stunt again? The Woodburn wouldn't lose a cent. In fact, they'd get a lot more than they would if the sax had been sold to a reasonable bidder for a reasonable price. He'd known that the tenor was insured. He was on the Woodburn board, so he knew Albert Grasso was taking care of insurance on all the big items. He figured he could bid up high and look like a very big man indeed. And then, he simply stole his own sax. That way, he got the collectible instrument he coveted, wiggled out of paying for it, and helped the Woodburn get a whopping $100,000. He must have figured himself to be some modern-day Robin Hood. I was startled to realize it all made sense. In fact, I was surprised Bill Knight hadn't bid $200,000 for the sax. Or a million.

And then I had another brilliant zing of recognition. What had Zenya said? Bill left her at home that night of the ball and went out to take a drive. More loose threads were beginning to tie up.

Bill must have been surprised, that stressful night, to find his wife had invited an unexpected guest along for the ride home. As I imagined it, Bill had paid off his blackmailer, Sara Jackson, and then gone through the charade of discovering that his precious saxophone had been stolen. When he finally emerged out of the Tager Auditorium, with his baby-blanket-wrapped Selmer resting in a designer baby basket, he must have made a few last-minute alterations to his plan.

Bill's fake rampage through the streets, up on curbs, ramming cars, must have been to impress this impartial witness with the authenticity of his anger. He put on a good rousing reaction scene. He'd been "ripped off." Then he ditched me. What was that about?

I thought about what he did next and realized he told his wife to call her brother, Dex, to come to my rescue. For a last-second plan, it hadn't been bad. Bill Knight had deflected suspicion from his own involvement in the missing Selmer and drawn Dexter out of his house. Now why would Bill Knight want to involve Dexter in this late-night farce? Of course, to make sure Dex wasn't at home late that night. As I recalled, at about the time Dex and I were just sitting down to breakfast at the Original Pantry Café, Bill Knight had gone out again. Taking a drive, Zenya said. I suspected he drove directly to Dexter's house in Bel Air and—oh my God!—found a way to ditch the Selmer *there*.

And if that was true, Bill Knight was going to use his brother-in-law as his patsy. He must have always had a backup plan, just in case any investigators got a little too close for comfort. He intended to blame his brother-in-law for the Mark VI heist if the shit hit the fan. And I had a horrible hunch that just such an unsavory object was about to do just such a messy thing. I jumped up out of bed and got dressed fast.

An hour later I was standing at Dexter's front door.

"The Bean Stalks Again"

The morning sunlight picked at the golden highlights in his hair as Dex stood there, looking down at me. His expression was friendly, if a little subdued. "You've caught me off guard, Madeline. I didn't think I'd get to see you again. I've been leaving you messages, but when you didn't call me back, I pretty much knew where we stood."

"Dex . . ."

"You don't need to explain. You didn't want me bothering you anymore. I knew."

"That's not it," I said, feeling incredibly awkward. I had been so attracted to Dexter Wyatt that I don't think the analytical centers of my brain had registered just how physically handsome he was. No wonder I had fallen under his spell. So much beauty is kind of dangerous. "Look, I haven't been fair to you, Dex. I've had a lot of things going on that have nothing to do with us. But still, they kind of took over my life. You know how that can happen."

"I know."

"I'm really sorry."

"No. You don't have to be sorry. Look, I watch the news. I get it. Anyway, I've been worried about you. Say, come in." He suddenly remembered we were just standing in his open doorway. I followed him to his living room, the glass walls presenting their magnificent canyon views.

Dex waited for me to begin talking, but when I couldn't get started, he took the lead like an accomplished host. "That woman who interrupted us the other night. She's the one who was killed at Wesley's house, wasn't she? Shit, Madeline. A cop."

"I know." We both shook our heads.

"The police were out here twice with questions. I tried to remember all I could about that night she was trespassing. They seemed pretty pissed off I never filed any sort of report about it, but who the hell knew she was so off her rocker?"

"You couldn't have known."

Dex shook his head, still working it through. "You were totally wigged out that night, which was completely understandable, but even when you thought you recognized her, I wasn't sure. I'm sorry I doubted you."

"That's okay. The whole thing was too weird, wasn't it?"

Dex grinned. "It seemed more likely she was some old lady here in the hills who got a little cranked up over my love life, such as it is."

Dex had a way of defusing my tension like no one else. "On the contrary. By now I'll bet all your neighbors have bought themselves binoculars and telescopes. Bet they can't wait until Dex Wyatt brings home a date." I meant to laugh at myself and lighten up the mood. But he was serious now.

"I'm so sorry for everything, Madeline. That's all I can say. I'm sorry."

"I know. So am I."

"And that woman was your cop boyfriend's *wife*, it turns out. I can't get over it. Usually *I'm* the one with the messed-up lovers. Kind of a relief for me that it was all about you, this time."

I smiled in a rueful way, acknowledging his efforts to joke me out of my mood. He could be very sweet, could Dexter Wyatt.

"The reason I'm here," I said, "is I'm suddenly positive your brother-in-law, Bill, is planning to damage you. I'm afraid he's planning to trade secrets with the cops to save his own skin. Maybe he can deal down the indictment on insurance fraud if he gives them evidence for a robbery conviction, I don't know, but I'm sure it is bad bad news for you, Dex."

"What are you talking about, Madeline? What robbery? The etchings three years ago?"

"Maybe. But I'm also worried about the Woodburn's Mark VI."

"The sax Bill bought at the auction," Dex said, just catching on.

"Well, he never paid for it. But I do think he stole it."

I spent five minutes reviewing all my suspicions with Dexter and he followed it all. He was surprised to learn that Bill had been behind the call he got from Zenya, begging Dex to drop everything and find this poor, lost party planner in big, bad downtown L.A. He was angered to hear that Bill had gone out later that night, leaving Zenya alone to, according to my theory, hide the stolen saxophone.

"We have to search your house," I told him. "Then we can call the police. Bill has made you his fall guy, Dex. If Bill gets to them first with a clever story, and leads them to where 'you' hid the stolen goods, you could wind up in jail doing your brother-in-law's time."

"Well, it was no big trick getting into my house," Dex said, furious. "Zenya has a copy of my front-door key. If Bill took it, she'd never have known." He stood up with the kind of energy a man has when he'd like to punch someone. "Where do you think we should look?"

"You know your house," I said. "Is there any storage area that you don't use very often? A location you might be expected to ignore?"

"No. I can't . . ." As he spoke, Dexter's expression changed. "Wait a minute. I have a wine cellar. Down a flight of stairs, built into the rock foundation. I've never used it and one day last winter I realized the key doesn't even work in the lock anymore. I was meaning to get the lock replaced, but since I don't collect wine, it wasn't much of a priority."

"Where is it?" I was sure he must be right. Bill had Dexter's house key. Perhaps Bill had the locks replaced sometime when Dex was out of town. If the wine room was in a location that was out of the way, Dex might never have noticed.

Dex led me through his kitchen. At the far end was the pantry, and inside of the pantry was a small door. Dex opened it and showed me a short flight of cement steps that led down.

"This is it. There's a small room at the bottom of the steps. But the key that used to work when I first bought this house doesn't unlock the door anymore. It's kind of a shame, because the previous owner told me he had the room specially climate-controlled to preserve fine wine."

"Dex. We have to get in there. Do you have an ax?"

"An ax?" He looked at me, startled. "Well, I've got a small ax out in the garage. I use it for firewood."

One of Dexter's self-admitted best qualities, I recalled, was his ability to start a wood fire. I smiled at the unlikely Boy Scout and encouraged him to go get his ax.

In a few minutes, he came back and descended the staircase to the wine-cellar room below. He swung the ax at the wooden door and splinters began to fly. It was only a few minutes before he'd hacked the frame and door to something that looked like it had been attacked by a grizzly, but the metal lock still held. I waited as he continued his assault. Five minutes more and the job was complete.

Dexter brushed away the shredded door frame and pushed open the door. I rushed down the steps to join him.

The small room was lined with shelves. It was cool and dry, which I suspected was due to the separate climate system and air conditioner, which we could hear humming away. On the floor in front of us sat a lovely basket covered in pink toile fabric, white satin, and rose-colored grosgrain ribbons. In it was a long bulky bundle wrapped up and completely covered in a pink-and-white velvet baby blanket. I stepped into the small room, careful to avoid all the wood splinters, and lifted the corner of the blanket.

"Now that's a beautiful baby," Dex said.

We stared at the world's most perfect silver tenor saxophone.

But that was not all we found in the wine cellar. On the shelves were three large works of art. The missing etchings. The three pieces that had been stolen from the Knights' home three years back.

"That bastard was going to turn me in to the cops," Dex said, his voice hoarse. "He was planning this all along. He set me up. I'll bet he was behind the rash of 'false' alarms three years ago, setting the stage so he could arrange to have me stay at his house that night. I'm sure he told Zenya to call me and insist I take those concert tickets, too. And he probably encouraged her to help me buy this house, just to make me look good and guilty. And to seal the deal, he planted the stolen art in my cellar."

"He was only after the insurance money," I said. "He didn't care about the art at all. It was more useful for him to use it to frame you. Just in case he needed it."

Dexter grabbed me and for a moment I thought he was going to kiss me. He looked deeply into my eyes and then recovered himself and let me go. "I've got to call the police."

"That's good."

"But what if they don't believe me?" he asked.

"They can find out who changed the lock on this door. Maybe the locksmith can identify Bill."

Dex knelt down and found the door lock amid the pile of wood shavings on the floor. "This is a common lock, Maddie. Something he could have bought at Home Depot. Bill may have changed it himself."

"We'll think of something," I said. And then I did actually think of something. "Come on," I told him, grabbing him by the hand. "Come with me."

Dexter drove as I used my cell phone to get the right location. We pulled up to a small parking lot on Sunset. Jon David Realtors. They were one of the most successful brokers in Los Angeles. This office mostly served the Hollywood Hills and West Hollywood.

"You!" Caroline Rochette sat in her work cubicle. Her voice carried the edge of such honest alarm that several other agents sitting nearby looked up to see what could possibly have caused one of their own to express a true feeling.

"I want to list my house for sale," I said loudly, causing the other workers to settle down and mind their own business. I noticed them turn back to their phones and their PC monitors.

"Is this some sort of joke?" she asked me, but her eyes were now on Dexter. "I'm sorry," she said, batting heavy lashes, her mood and tone of voice changing. "We haven't met. I'm Caroline Rochette." She had a business card in Dex's hand before he had a chance to know what had hit him. "Can I help you?"

"I'm serious," I said to Caroline. "If you want my home's listing, there's a price."

She dragged her eyes back to me for an instant. A new listing or a gorgeous young man. It was really the acid test for Caroline. Her eyes came back to rest on me.

"What do I have to do?"

"Tell me about the theft of the etchings from Bill Knight's house."

"I have no idea what you are talking about!" Caroline stood up and picked up her purse, a cunning little black lizard bag. "Come outside, won't you?" she asked in an overly pleasant tone, more for the cube farm, I imagined, than just Dex and me. We followed her out a side exit and stood in the parking lot.

"Look," she hissed at me. "I am telling you this because I don't want to have any part of any of this ever again."

"Good," I said.

"But you were telling the truth? You want me to sell your house?"

"Yes."

"Good, then this is what you are waiting to hear."

Dexter looked at me and then back at the little blonde who was pulling a cigarette out of her purse and lighting it.

"Albert needed a favor. His daughter, Gracie, wanted to work at the White House as an intern before that was a dirty word. But Al just didn't have contacts high enough up. I think Bill Knight knew someone. Anyway, Gracie got her job. So when Bill asked Albert to do him a favor back, of course Al wanted to show his gratitude."

She took a long puff of the cigarette and exhaled smoke as she talked.

"Bill told Albert to go to his house in Beverly Hills and pick up a few art pieces, then hold on to them until Bill got back with his family from Maui. You know what happened. It made the papers that there had been a theft. Albert got nervous, naturally. He wasn't sure what was going on. Bill had sent him the door key. He'd assured Al there wouldn't be an alarm set, so Al would have no trouble doing the favor. Al was set to go to the police and explain the mistake, but Bill called him from Hawaii. He told Al not to worry, Bill would take care of the cops. When he got back to town, Bill came and picked up the pieces. That's all Al ever knew about it."

"So Albert never called the police and told them?"

"No. As time went on, Al figured out what must have happened. But by then, he was afraid he might be arrested for the theft himself, if Bill didn't back up his story. And the police were more likely to believe Bill. He could be a charming bastard when he wanted to be. Just ask me."

"So Grasso said *nothing*?" Dex was pissed.

I was, too. "Even though it was Albert's half brother who was taking the fall with the insurance company?" I asked. After all, Grasso had to know his brother would lose a lot of clout if one of the policies he had sold ended up costing the insurance companies millions and millions in settlement money.

"I think that was the part that Albert actually liked," Caroline said, taking another deep drag on her cigarette. "Anyway, no one ever came around to Al to ask about it. It all just died down. And now that he's dead, poor man, I don't ever want any of this to be dragged up again."

"Think again, lady," Dexter said. "We're all going to the police right now."

"What? No," Caroline said, shaking her head. "No, I won't go."

Dexter caught the look I was throwing him and changed his approach. "Caroline," he said, pulling her a step away from me. "How did an attractive woman like you ever get mixed up with difficult men like them, anyway?"

"Rotten, rotten luck," Caroline said with feeling.

"You deserve better than that," he said, looking deeply into her thickly fringed eyes. "I know you want to do the right thing."

When Dexter Wyatt fixes a woman with his undivided attention, she feels it down to her designer T-straps. Take my word for it. I could see Ms. Rochette melting right before my eyes.

"Hell!" Caroline said. "I want to do the right thing."

She threw down her cigarette, and before she could make a move, I put my own boot down and stomped it out.

"JUST ONE MORE CHANCE"

joined the rest of the audience in the Tager Auditorium in applause. All around me people were coming to their feet, giving a standing ovation to the seventeen young musicians of the Woodburn Jazz Band after their hard-swinging version of Freddie Hubbard's "Little Sunflower."

Each soloist got a chance to take a separate bow. Ryan Hutson, newly promoted to the rank of tenor sax player, stepped forward, beaming. Hanging from a thick strap around his neck was his shiny silver horn, the exquisite Selmer Mark VI, which had been returned to the Hutson family in due course. This boy had done a fine job on his solos, improvising like a champ. Ryan bowed to the cheering audience and then stepped back.

Another boy took his turn in the spotlight, and soon Kirby Knight stepped forward. Met by applause, he smiled shyly out to the crowd. I admired this young man, the night's star performer, for carrying on despite his family's turmoil. Dark and raw emotions seemed to shine through his music. Artists are lucky that way. They have an outlet for their feelings, even the painful ones.

My eyes searched the audience for the hot spot from which the loudest burst of applause could be heard. There, across the aisle and several rows closer to the stage, I saw Zenya Knight and her little girl. And right beside them was Dexter, clapping away for Kirby.

I was thankful that Kirby's father wasn't present. Bill Knight was awaiting trial on several new and serious charges. He wouldn't be able to avoid jail time on all they had against him, or so I'd been told. Zenya had already taken steps to get her life back. She'd filed for divorce and put their Beverly Hills house on the market. With just a little prompting from her brother, Zenya had decided to use Caroline Rochette to handle the sale. I'd heard they had already received a purchase offer. So it goes.

"You ready to go?" my date for the evening asked.

I looked up at Honnett and nodded.

"This was great, Maddie."

"Talented kids amaze me," I said. "Where does musical genius come from?"

"I wonder if they realize how lucky they are," Honnett said, "to have this school and parents that support them."

"Are you kidding? They're teenagers."

Many of those in the audience had ties to the young folks in the band, and so they milled about the lobby, talking excitedly, waiting for their sons, siblings, nieces, or other loved ones to be allowed to leave after the concert. Honnett and I walked toward the parking garage alone.

Honnett smiled. "You know, I want to thank you for inviting me tonight. This was inspiring."

"I'm glad you could come," I said. "I was afraid you might not be comfortable sitting for so long."

"I'm doing fine." He'd stayed in the hospital for only a week and then had spent several more on pain meds resting at home. Honnett had proven remarkably resilient. He'd taken to punishing workouts, pushing his physical therapist to a frazzle, seeing improvement every week.

At the elevator to the parking structure under the Woodburn, Honnett turned to me. "Please, Maddie. Can we stop and talk? I've got something I'd like to say to you."

"Wait until we're downstairs," I said. I was so lame.

In all the weeks that had passed since I had been attacked and he had been shot and his wife had been killed, Chuck and I had not been able to talk about what had happened. When I first visited him in the hospital, with his tubes and IV lines dangling, I didn't want to worry him any more than he obviously was. Then later, after he'd been released from the hospital, I kept in the background. I cooked him a dozen gourmet dinners but always managed to get Holly or Wes to deliver them. Honnett called me, of course, but I let the phone machine collect his thank yous. The few times we talked, I cut the conversations very short. Eventually he stopped bringing it up, this painful event we had between us.

Over the past few weeks, instead of dealing with Honnett, I kept busy working out, catching up with friends, straightening up my disordered life. I put a lot of time into the business, throwing myself into a dozen parties. We got an official wedding date from Holly and Donald, on top of everything else, so we were hip-deep in planning-a-wedding details. This spoke volumes about the success of Donald and Holly weathering their long time apart and even more about the restorative powers of a climactic reunion. We were so relieved to have some good news upon which to focus, we let the wedding discussions take up a lot of our free time. In addition, the construction on the upstairs of my house was almost complete and the remodel looked fabulous. Soon I would have to decide whether I could bear to move back in or whether Caroline Rochette would earn another commission.

And then last week, Honnett began leaving messages asking if we could get together. I was as confused as ever, but I knew he couldn't be put off much longer. It was so hard to separate what I felt about the man from the disaster that had been brought into our lives by Sherrie.

I looked over at Honnett as we rode down the elevator in the parking garage in silence. He had driven to the Tager Auditorium in his own car and I'd met him there, having borrowed Wesley's Jag. Our cars were parked side by side on the lowest level. Down there, the air had the acrid odor of gas fumes, so I tried not to breathe in too much of it as we made our way to our cars.

"Maddie . . ." Honnett began, sounding very serious.

"Did you hear that I'm getting a reward?" I asked him, keeping the conversation anything but personal. "The companies that insured the Knights' etchings pay a ten percent finder's fee to anyone who recovers stolen objects. So anyway, they estimate that the true value of the Dürer and the other etchings are close to four million dollars, can you believe that? So they are offering Dexter Wyatt and me four hundred thousand.

Of course, they will only pay us if they can recover the money they paid out to Bill Knight, and that means Zenya will lose any chance of getting a decent settlement in her divorce, so it's not all roses and chips. But I thought it was kind of hilarious, you know, in a sick sort of way—"

"Maddie," Honnett said, interrupting, "are you going to let me tell you that I love you?"

I stopped talking, of course.

"It isn't going to change your mind about me. I know that. I just needed to say it to you. I needed for you to hear it. Think of this as your way of relieving a guy of a terrible burden, okay? No need to answer. There."

You'd have thought it would melt my heart to hear those sweet words from this man about whom I cared so much. But I couldn't let myself melt. Maybe the reason for all my nightmares and sleepless nights and avoiding his calls was this: I suspected, deep down, Honnett and I were relieved his wife was finally out of the picture now. How vile was that? To be relieved a woman was dead.

I turned to Honnett. "You really can't know how you feel. Neither can I. There has been such a lot of extreme stress and anxiety. We need time to let things settle down."

"I don't."

"But Sherrie—"

"This isn't about Sherrie," he said. "I've loved you for almost as long as I've known you. But I didn't have any right. I knew that."

"Oh, Honnett."

"When I told you at the beginning that I was too old for you, you laughed at me. Remember that? You thought I was putting you off. Like I thought you were too young for me to take seriously."

"I'm not that young. You're not that old." His age had never mattered to me.

"I just meant I was old enough to know better. I'd lived enough life to know I had screwed mine up. I had problems at home. How could I abandon my own mess and start with someone as bright and new as you were? Life doesn't work like that. You just don't get a free pass to start over that easily."

"I didn't understand."

Honnett nodded. "Before I met you, Sherrie was getting out of control, more and more. The department asked her to take a medical leave, but they were more concerned about her state of mind than any other health issues. Her behavior . . . I was worried about her, but I was angry, too. We'd never been the greatest match, Sherrie and I, but now nothing she did or said made any sense. We split up, which was the direction we were heading in all along, and she just got worse."

I put my hand on Chuck's arm and he paused, his eyes meeting mine. "When she came to me after I'd been moved out for a year and told me she had cancer, I didn't know what to think anymore. Maybe her suicidal moods were due to the chemotherapy or maybe just the cancer itself, working on her nerves, making her act crazy. I saw her moods were getting worse. When she told me she needed me back, that she wanted us to start seeing a therapist together, I knew it was the right thing to do. It was the only way to get Sherrie to see someone who could help her. Of course, I should have known better than to believe anything she told me. Hell, she never listened to the shrink. She didn't have cancer. The chemo was just a made-up story. More of her lies and games."

"I know."

"That's why I had to leave you, Maddie. I had to go back and try. I wanted to do things right, to see if I could help her get squared away. I couldn't move forward with you and me until I had."

"But you never told me," I said. "How could I understand what you were going through if you were keeping all these secrets? We had this relationship going, but you didn't trust me. You didn't want me to know the truth. Or to really know you."

He thought it over and I could tell he didn't like what he was thinking. "Maybe you're right." He shook his head. "At the time, I wanted to protect you."

I sighed.

"It really worked well, didn't it?" he asked, his voice almost light. "Instead of keeping you safe, I brought unholy hell down on top of you. I put you in danger. I caused you unbelievable pain, Maddie. That's what damned good my love is to you."

We had been standing by our cars, and I asked if Honnett wanted to sit down in Wesley's S-Type so we could get out of the musty air. He shook his head and said he should be going, anyway.

"Then just give me one more minute and hear this," I said. "I don't hold you responsible for anything that happened. I don't even blame Sherrie, really. Maybe it's natural to hate the people who try to hurt us, but that's not how it works with me. After all these weeks and all this thinking, I don't have any anger left in me. I just feel very sorry about how much pain Sherrie was in. And very sorry for what she must have put you through. So really, Honnett, you may as well give up this guilt you are carrying around. I don't blame you at all."

"Maddie." Honnett looked at me for another long moment, and then said, "I better get going."

I met his clear blue eyes, not sure there was any more we could say, and nodded.

"I guess I should I leave you alone for a while," he said.

"Or not," I said softly.

"Sure. Then I'll call you." He smiled then, a regular Honnett-style smile. "And thanks for bringing me here tonight. It was the perfect evening out for a man feeling his age while he's recovering from surgery, all those kids blowing their horns, full of talent and life. I love jazz. It's cool you remembered that."

Standing in the parking garage, watching Honnett climb into his Mustang and lower the convertible top, I realized I had become a different person since the day the two of us met. I don't know if the changes are good or bad, but given enough time and bumps, I suppose growth is inevitable. Can't stay in Neverland forever. Damn it.

Honnett waved at me as he pulled away. I stared after him as more families now entered the parking structure. He was a different man in my eyes as well. Maybe a little less the iconic hero, a little more human. Sherrie had been right. He was an honorable man.

I drove off and thought again about Honnett and me and the difficult subject of how his life with Sherrie had hurt us. Can we ever escape the past lives of the person we get involved with? I sped over to my old house and parked the Jag S-Type on Whitley, stopping to pick up my mail before heading back to Hancock Park. As I stepped out of the car, I saw two familiar friends out walking in the evening.

"Hi, Teuksbury," I said, bending to scratch the weimaraner on the head. "Hi, Nelson."

"Well, hello, Maddie. We see the construction crew is gone. So is your house finally done?"

"Just about. There's some finish work needed inside, but they have done an incredible job. And how are you and Miss Teuks?"

"We're doing pretty well," the old man said, bending to pat her on the side.

"I just came by to pick up my mail."

"Oh, Maddie," Nelson Piffer said diffidently. "I have a little confession to make. I've been meaning to tell you but . . ."

"But what?" I looked at my elderly neighbor and wondered whatever could he be talking about.

"It's about your old car. You know, the old Jeep. This is a very indelicate subject to bring up, so I hate to be the one to tell you this."

I was more than intrigued. "Tell me."

"Teuksbury and I were taking a walk a couple of months ago. It was a dark night, but right here in the middle of Whitley, we could see a bitch was getting it on with a stray, a Dobie mix, looked like."

"Dogs? Dogs *making love*?" I covered my smile, as I could tell Nelson took such subjects a little more seriously than I ever could.

"Yes. It was the little lurcher from two houses down. Trixie. God only knows what she was doing running out in the street, but when those bitches are in season, it's a good job keeping them in."

"I would imagine," I answered, a little too circumspectly considering my own intemperate past.

"The point is, it is also a good job trying to separate a breeding pair once they're in the act."

Poor Trixie. I could relate.

"And I knew Ms. Fellows would go mental if she found her little Trixie knocked up by some rogue stray. Well, this is a long way around, Maddie, but the point is I did finally detach the rascals. Of course, then the male was quite aggressive."

I could well imagine.

"I had to think fast. Your car was unlocked, so I put my Teuksbury and Trixie in the backseat of your Jeep, just to keep them out of harm's way until I could chase off the Dobie mix."

That semen stain on my backseat. I laughed out loud. Good luck to the LAPD crime lab on matching that sample.

And then it all suddenly struck me. Standing out in the cul-de-sac at night with Nelson Piffer and his sweet Teuksbury, I got a glimpse of the impossible challenge of my need to problem-solve, made simple and clear and hopeful for a brief second. Like a pile of a thousand spiky pieces that might make up several finished jigsaw puzzles, it's anyone's guess most of the time which pieces in life fit into any given puzzle. The key to order was proper sorting.

And over the past few months I'd watched so many jigsaw pieces pile up: the trash left on my doorstep, the disappearance of a priceless saxophone, the theft of three etchings, the death of a waitress, the murder of a music teacher, and add another piece named Dexter Wyatt, and then another named Chuck Honnett—all needing proper sorting before any puzzles could be solved.

It was my nature to tackle that pile, impossible though it might seem, but what made it worthwhile was an instant like this: this rare and sudden joy—this one sharp, simple moment of seeing the puzzles truly sorted out. The deaths, the thefts, the men . . . and even the mysterious stain on the backseat of my old car.

An hour later, I was back at Wesley's place. What had followed that gleeful moment of clarity—the belief I finally *got* it—was the natural onset of gloom over all the things I, in fact, *didn't* get. I had come no closer, for instance, to understanding my own heart. I couldn't even sort out what feelings I still had for Chuck Honnett. Even though I was over my anger and my hurt. Even after he said he loved me. Still, we could never erase what had happened. He hadn't trusted me. I hadn't trusted him. I had shot his wife. How could we move forward? It was too damned complicated.

At the guest house, I found a large manila envelope leaning up against the door. It said TO MADELINE on the front. It must have been hand-delivered because there was no postage attached or even a full address.

As I let myself in, I began to rip open the envelope.

"What's that?" Wes asked, looking up as I entered the door.

I pulled out the contents and showed them to Wesley. In my hands were a dozen black-and-white photographs, size eight-by-ten. They were amazingly well focused and beautifully composed. The subject of one of the photos was Serena Williams as she accepted a special award at the U.S. Open in New York. Other photos were candids of the tennis star and others on the court swinging rackets, and backstage at the awards, and at the after party. A note slipped out, attached by paper clip to a ticket.

Wesley looked even more curious.

"It's from Dexter," I said, reading the note. "He sold two of his pictures to *Sports Illustrated*."

"You have got to be kidding!"

"Isn't that great? He says they are asking him to shoot some stuff in color in Bangkok in a few weeks, an international tennis tournament. He sent me a ticket. Said he'd like me to come."

"Oh, Mad."

"Oh, Wes." We both stood there shaking our heads. "It's a lucky thing that men do not tempt me anymore."

"Well, that *is* a lucky thing," Wes said. "I hadn't heard that news yet."

"Late-breaking update," I said, smiling, "hot off the presses. I have finally learned my lesson about men."

"Impressive," Wes said, offering me support. "I can see you are a changed woman. Mature. Sensible. Strangely calm in the eye of the storm."

I smiled at him.

"And your enlightenment . . . from where did this deep well of wisdom spring?" he asked.

"From a sadder but wiser little lurcher named Trixie."

Wes enjoyed his laugh.

"No. I'm serious here."

"So where are you off to?" Wes asked.

"To go call Dexter."

Wes laughed again.

"Well," I said, "I've got to congratulate him, don't I? *Sports Illustrated*. Wow. That boy takes direction."

✓ FARMER   **MYSTERY**

Farmer, Jerrilyn.
Perfect sax

$ 22.95
2003-55846

**FINKELSTEIN
MEMORIAL LIBRARY
SPRING VALLEY, N.Y.**
Phone: 845-352-5700
http://www.finkelsteinlibrary.org

JAN 16 2004

11c 9/04